# *A*
# LETTER
## from
# ITALY

# BOOKS BY ROSE ALEXANDER

*The Lost Diary*

ROSE ALEXANDER

# *A* LETTER from ITALY

Bookouture

Published by Bookouture in 2024

An imprint of Storyfire Ltd.
Carmelite House
50 Victoria Embankment
London EC4Y 0DZ

www.bookouture.com

ISBN: 978-1-83790-764-9
eBook ISBN: 978-1-83790-763-2

# PROLOGUE

LONDON, 1945

The nights were darkening earlier now that autumn was well and truly here, but the trees were still in leaf and provided cover for the woman slinking past, carrying something clasped close to her chest. Every now and again she looked around her, as if fearful of being followed, observed, watched.

The tiny bundle she held in loving arms barely stirred. The baby was not yet two days old. As the new mother crept through the silent streets, lined with bombed-out buildings, in the front gardens of which tangled weeds erupted between broken paving slabs, her mind was in overdrive, working out a plan. In her feverish, post-natal befuddlement, nothing seemed to make sense.

With every halting step she took, she was getting closer. Closer to the place. But she couldn't bring the infant with her, not now. She needed to see him first, explain, prepare the ground. She glanced skywards, as if hoping for divine guidance, but the star-studded heavens told her nothing. The rope of despair tightened around her heart, making her chest ache. In fact, everything ached: her head, her stomach, her feet. Only her arms, treasuring the new life they held, felt no pain.

As she stumbled onwards, it finally came to her. What she could do. It was a last resort; it was all she had.

She picked a door, one that was smart with fresh paintwork, the step scrubbed clean, free from the stain of war and bomb damage, the letter box polished and shiny. It looked like a door that someone took pride in and looked after. It was the best she would find.

As she rang the bell, she wished with all her throbbing, aching heart that she didn't have to do this. If there had been any other way, she would have taken it. But if she arrived holding the infant, she had no idea how he would react. It was better this way. It would give them time. Give him time.

A woman answered. As the door swung open, a questioning look descended on her face.

'Could you look after my baby for an hour or so?' the new mother asked. 'I'll be back shortly. I'm sorry to ask but...' She left the sentence trailing.

Before the woman could respond, the mother thrust the infant into her arms and was gone. The woman glanced down at the baby, then looked back up again, in the direction the mother had gone, but she could no longer see her. She seemed to have melted into the dusk.

The woman frowned and the baby stirred, making little sucking movements with its tiny mouth.

'Alf!' the woman called, her voice tinged with a note of alarm. 'Alfie? Are you there? Something ever so strange has just happened...' She retreated inside, still calling for her husband, and the door swung shut behind her.

# CHAPTER ONE

BROADSTAIRS, APRIL 1972

The attic was dark and gloomy, lit only by the feeble electric bulb dangling precariously from a rafter. Disturbed by the opening of the access hatch, dust motes danced haphazardly in the thin shaft of light. Sadie, hauling herself off the top of the ladder and into the confined space, paused for a moment to sneeze, and then sneeze again.

Once ensconced uncomfortably under the rafters, she looked around. As she took in her surroundings, her will almost failed her. Boxes were piled in disorderly heaps in every corner, broken chairs lay on their backs as if shot down in battle, an old rug rolled into a long sausage looked as if it could be harbouring any manner of bugs: spiders, flies, woodlice – please God nothing worse than that. Sorting out all this accumulated junk before the house was sold seemed both a gargantuan and an impossible task.

Perhaps she could get the people who were going to take the furniture to also clear out up here? But before she did that, she needed to find out if there was anything important that should be salvaged. It would be so much easier, Sadie thought to herself, if she didn't have to tackle it by herself. But she was an only child and her father had been dead for a decade or more. Now, with her mother's sudden passing from cancer that had gone undiagnosed for some time, Sadie was entirely alone in the world, and, though she was fully an adult at twenty-seven years of age, the sense of abandonment and desolation was intense. She needed to do this, as a form of.closure, the saying of a final goodbye.

Sadie shivered involuntarily. She'd turned the heating on when she'd arrived on the early train from London, where she lived in a flatshare with her best friend Kim in a backstreet near Paddington station. But it had barely taken the edge off the unseasonably cold weather. Outside, she could hear the bitter wind that scythed in off the North Sea rattling the tiles, and of course there were no radiators up here in the attic. She'd delayed clambering up here as long as she could, making tea and lists, scooping the post off the doormat and opening the important-looking letters, tidying the already immaculate sitting room.

But eventually she hadn't been able to procrastinate any longer.

With a sigh, Sadie crept forward, bent double due to the lack of headroom. She pulled a box from the top of the nearest pile, opened the flaps and peered inside. The first thing she saw was a photo album. She took it out and opened its stiff, creaky cover. The pictures were old and faded, sepia-toned images of people Sadie had never met. There was nothing written on any of the pages to indicate who the characters were and Sadie hadn't a clue whether they were her father's or her mother's side of the family. She paused on one page, where a couple of stout and redoubtable-looking ladies stood on a blustery promenade, holding tightly on to their decorous hats. It looked as if it dated from the 1920s, if not earlier. Sadie wished she knew who these women were and what seafront they were visiting. Bognor Regis, perhaps, or Brighton.

As she turned the pages, tableaux of other lives lived in other decades flitted before her eyes, young children who were presumably now old, old people who, like her mother, must surely be dead. A picture of her mother and father on their wedding day, looking so young and hopeful, brought tears to her eyes.

Closing the album, she placed it on the floor beside her. Delving into the box once more, she drew out an old, broken jewellery case, and then a music box, which elicited a sudden stab of memory. It had been hers when she was a small child, but had broken, the tune no longer playing, the dancer in her pink tutu no longer twirling. It had been cast aside when it became useless, and she had forgotten all about it. Opening the lid, she had a faint hope that perhaps, by some miracle, it would work again and she would be transported back to that safe place of childhood where she had a mummy and a daddy and all was well with the world.

Of course, the music box did not play.

Sadie put it back in the box, which she then hefted off to the side. She should have brought some stickers so that she could label what was to be chucked. It would be almost everything. Apart from the pictures of her parents, was there any point in keeping the albums when she didn't know who anyone was? Probably not. But then again, throwing away family history seemed wrong.

She'd make the decision later, she told herself.

Eventually, after an hour or so, she'd worked her way through most of the rest of the stacks and not found anything valuable or important at all. Beginning to feel bored, disheartened and hungry, Sadie decided she'd look through one more box and then take a break. Her hands were filthy and the feel of the ingrained dust on her fingertips was starting to grate like nails down a blackboard. Reaching inside, at first she thought the box was empty. And then, right at the bottom, she encountered another carton, shallow and oblong, the kind you might get from a posh shop to package a gift in. There was no store name or logo on it, though. Just one word, written in felt pen, in the top right-hand corner.

*Baby.*

Immediately, Sadie's curiosity was aroused. There was surely only one baby it could refer to. Herself. What carefully curated mementos of her birth and childhood would it contain? Eager to find out, Sadie decided to take it downstairs and open it somewhere more comfortable than sitting here, cramped up under the sloping roof.

Carefully, she retreated down the ladder, clutching the box tightly. Her hands were grimy, her fingertips black with dust, so she went first to the bathroom to give them a good wash and then into her bedroom, where she sat down on her bed. She lifted off the lid and scrutinised the box's contents.

There was a tiny pair of shoes, blue leather, with groove marks on the straps to show what hole they had been buckled on. Beneath them lay a hand-crocheted hat in a rather sickly shade of salmon pink. It didn't look very well used, but then again, babies grow fast, don't they? Presumably she had outgrown it long before it had become worn out. Next out were a couple of photographs. A tot Sadie presumed was herself in a high-chair, gazing bemusedly at a circle of adults and a birthday cake with one candle in the middle. A picture of a picnic in a sylvan glade, where she seemed to be attempting to crawl off the rug and into the wild undergrowth. Sadie smiled to herself.

Her mother had often told her that, when she was little, she always wanted to make for the place she wasn't supposed to be. Adventurous, her mother said she was as a child. Sadie supposed that leaving home and going to live and work in London might fit this description too, but it suddenly didn't seem very much of an achievement, hardly intrepid. And she'd never been abroad at all.

She pondered this as she pulled out of the box a piece of pale cream paper, folded in half. At first glance, she assumed it was her birth certificate. That was lucky, that she'd found it! She presumed she'd need it if she ever did want to venture overseas and required a passport, or indeed if she ever got married. She ran her eyes over the text: her name, her date of birth, her mother's and her father's names, and her father's occupation.

And then she read something that made her blood run cold in her veins and set her heart palpitating. Underneath the handwritten words, typed in red ink between two red lines, was the following:

CERTIFIED to be a true copy of an entry in the Adopted Children Register maintained at the General Register Office.

At first, Sadie didn't understand, couldn't understand. And then gradually, realisation dawned. It was there, in plain red and white.

She was adopted.

The room spun as giddiness took hold, and Sadie clutched the windowsill to steady herself. She felt panicky and nauseous, barely able to breathe, all the oxygen sucked out of the atmosphere, leaving her gasping for air.

*Adopted.*

*Adopted.*

*Adopted.*

The words swirled and whirled around in her mind, unbelievable and yet undeniably true, surely wrong yet definitely right. None of it made any sense. How come she hadn't known? How come no one had ever told her? How come all her life she'd been left in the dark about this fundamental fact about her own existence?

The questions roared and snapped, and Sadie could not calm them because she did not have the answers. And now that her mother was dead, she couldn't imagine how she would ever get them.

# CHAPTER TWO

Betty was about to clock off for the day when a lamp in the 'Home' section in the panel in front of her lit up. Glancing over her shoulder at the supervisor, she knew even before they made eye contact that she'd have to answer it. It was 3.59 p.m. – still one minute to go until her shift ended.

'Number, please,' she said, in her best telephone voice. The only official qualification to become a telephonist was to have passed the School Certificate at age sixteen, which Betty had achieved with flying colours, earning the top grade of Distinction. But everyone knew that, in reality, only those deemed to have good speaking voices would be considered for the role, plus it was necessary to be over five foot four in order to be able to reach the top sockets of the junction boxes. Betty, whose mother had set great store by correct diction, and who was five foot four and a half, had therefore qualified on all three fronts.

'I'm calling for the district nurse, Betty love,' the voice came over the airways. 'I know it's a bit late but she's supposed to be coming to me tomorrow and I need to tell her my nephew will be here in the morning so she's no need. I don't like to waste her time, not when there's a war on!'

Betty smiled to herself. 'Good afternoon, Mrs Bishop,' she replied. 'Nurse is still out on a visit at the moment – I put the call through to her half an hour or so ago. But I'll ask Mr Aldridge who takes over after me to let her know.'

'Thank you so much, Betty love, and you have a lovely evening.'

Mrs Bishop rang off. In an instant, Betty had her head-phones off and had jumped down from her stool. The best thing about her job was knowing all the telephone subscribers in the area and being able to help them, not just with connecting their calls but also with a cheery word, or the passing on of a message, as with Mrs Bishop just now. But it could also be a disadvan-tage, because it was very easy to get sucked into everyone's prob-lems and difficulties. It was important to try to keep a professional distance, though Betty's kind heart sometimes prevented that. She knew that Mrs Bishop, who lived not far from Betty herself, had become very frail of late, her health having taken a knock since her grandson was killed in action in North Africa. It was good to hear that her nephew was taking care of her.

With a sigh at the thought of all the pain and loss this war was bringing, Betty said good evening to the supervisor and made her way from the telephone exchange to the main post office and out through the heavy oak doors. Outside, it was a beautiful evening, the sun still a few hours from setting, a gentle breeze blowing down from the moors. It always took Betty a bit by surprise to emerge from the building to be greeted by the daylight. In the windowless room she worked in, it was easy to lose all track of time and to forget whether it was night or day.

Turning in to Malton's ancient market square, Betty was so lost in thought that she didn't notice it for a moment. The sound of multiple footsteps coming from round the corner, getting louder every minute. For a sudden, terrible heartbeat, Betty thought it must be German soldiers, that the much-dreaded invasion had happened, quietly and secretly, without any warning, and now they were here, the Nazis, to wreak their awful havoc on the innocent people of Yorkshire...

And then the source of the noise came into view: a long column of men, mostly young or at least under thirty, surrounded by army officers on all sides. A crowd had gathered and a murmur ran through it: who were these people and what were they doing here? And then the whispered response, the rumours, spreading along the ranks of onlookers like a fast-burning fire.

'Prisoners...'

'Prisoners of war...'

'Italian POWs...'

Hearing the latter, Betty, whose heart rate had returned to an almost normal pace after the initial shock, scrutinised the men more closely. They *looked* Italian, at least insofar as Betty had an idea what an Italian should look like, having never seen a person from that country in her life before. They were none of them terribly tall, and many had the olive skin and dark hair Betty associated with Mediterranean climes. Rather than marching, their gait was more of a lope, casual and uncoordinated. Definitely not Germans, who would most likely be goose-stepping and making Nazi salutes, Betty thought.

As the file passed by, one of the men caught Betty's gaze and smiled at her, a lopsided smile, kind and open, that reached his eyes and indicated a simple desire for friendship. Immediately, Betty looked away, hoping no one else had seen, embarrassed even though there had been nothing but amity in the look. She wasn't completely sure how she was supposed to react to the sudden arrival of men who were, after all, the enemy – even if it was a widely held view that the Italians were not the true villains in this war.

The men marched on and gradually the sound of their footsteps receded. As soon as they were out of sight, the whispers of earlier were replaced by a loud hubbub of eager chatter. Everyone was talking about these strange arrivals, speculating about where they had been captured – North Africa, perhaps Egypt or Libya or Tunisia – how many of them there were – two hundred, three hundred, more – and where they were going. Only on the latter was there agreement.

The men were being taken to Eden Camp, just a mile or so from town. Army officers had arrived at the beginning of the year to start work on building the accommodation huts and rumour went around that these first prisoners would be responsible for completing the construction work. That would occupy a number of them, and the rest would be put to work on local farms, smallholdings and market gardens, all of which were crying out for labour.

'They're hard workers, these Eyeties, so I've been told,' said a woman standing close to Betty. She seemed to be addressing her comment to anyone in the general vicinity.

'Farmers themselves, most of them, before they were forced to swap their shovels and rakes for guns,' agreed another.

'There's no doubt we need them,' chipped in a third. 'When harvest comes they'll be working dawn til dusk.'

'But they are the enemy, only here because we beat them.' The second woman sounded suddenly doubtful. 'So I suppose we should be wary.'

Betty watched as woman number one shrugged. 'I don't think they mean us any harm,' she asserted, confidently. 'Nice young lads, they looked. I think they deserve our sympathy, more than anything else. My Aunt Hilda went to Italy once, the Riviera, in the 1930s. Beautiful, she said it was, and the people so friendly. They love children, in particular. A nation that loves its bairns has got to be good at heart, hasn't it?'

This final comment seemed to settle the matter for the

entire group and, shopping baskets tucked under their arms, the women strolled away.

Betty continued on her way home and, once there, bustled around the kitchen preparing tea for herself and her father, Harold. Her older sister Jane had recently got married and moved to Scarborough, and their mother, Ann, had died two years ago. Since her untimely death, and in Jane's absence, keeping house naturally fell to Betty. For all three of them, the grief had been unbearable at times; Harold was still a compass without a needle, adrift without his adored wife, however much he tried to put on a brave face. Betty did her best to care for him and help him through his sorrow.

By the time he burst through the door, everything was ready.

'How was your day then, Betty love?' asked Harold, as he washed his hands vigorously with carbolic soap and water at the kitchen sink. 'Any juicy titbits overheard at the exchange?'

They both laughed as he said this. It was common knowledge that some operators liked to listen in to calls and were not above discreetly disseminating the gossip; a police investigation here, an illicit affair there. But of course Betty never did this; it simply wasn't in her nature to pry or spread tittle-tattle. Today, however, she did have news. She told her father about the Italian POWs.

'Well, that'll stir up the old place, won't it,' chuckled Harold, as Betty set his plate in front of him. 'Thank you, love,' he added.

'It's beef-and-dumpling-stew surprise,' she told him, suppressing a smile. She wondered fleetingly if this was the kind of food the Italians would be getting, over at Eden Camp. What would they make of such ordinary, country fare? Betty didn't know what Italians ate but she was sure it wouldn't be Yorkshire stew. Poor men. They'd have a lot to adjust to, now they were on British soil.

'What's the surprise?' asked Harold, reaching for a piece of bread.

Betty turned to him, utterly straight-faced. 'The surprise is – there's hardly any beef.'

Harold gazed at her, in confusion at first and then, cottoning on as Betty began to giggle, with a broad smile. 'I see. Very clever.' He chortled. 'Well, it's hot and the gravy's thick so I reckon it'll do me.'

Betty sat down beside him with her own, smaller plate. Everyone had lost weight since the start of the war and Betty had found that her appetite had diminished accordingly. She toyed with a piece of carrot and thought about Eden Camp, her mind straying to one particular inhabitant, the man with the kind eyes who had smiled at her. At the memory, a smile played briefly on her own lips.

There was no doubt that the Italians carried with them a hint of exoticism that wasn't often found around these parts. Perhaps Betty's father was right.

Perhaps their arrival would indeed liven things up a bit.

# CHAPTER THREE

BROADSTAIRS, APRIL 1972

An hour later, Sadie still lay slumped on her bed, crushed by the unimaginable secret she had so innocently and unwittingly uncovered. Sapped of all energy and unable to move, she was a rag doll that had lost its stuffing. Everything was so confusing, so bewildering. She couldn't understand why her mother and father had never told her, never given the slightest hint, the smallest clue. The last thing she wanted to do was blame them, hate them; they were her parents, she had loved them both with all her heart. She'd been devastated when her father had died ten years ago, and was again now, at her mother's passing.

But finding out what she now knew had turned the wave of emotions she'd been experiencing into a tsunami.

Mustering the strength to sit up, Sadie flipped on the bedside light. Holding the certificate in trembling hands, she read it over and over again, searching for any piece of information she had missed, anything that would tell her who she really was.

But there was nothing.

A desperate urge to talk to someone seized Sadie. She could phone Kim, tell her everything. Kim would help; she would know what to do. And then Sadie sank despondently back down onto the bed. She couldn't speak to Kim. They didn't have a phone in their flat. They'd decided it was too expensive and they didn't need one as they could make and take calls at work. Now that thrifty decision seemed like the worst one Sadie had ever made. But then, could she even put into words what had happened? At that moment, she wasn't sure she could, or ever would be able to.

Outside her window, dusk had bruised the sky in shades of blue and black and purple. The wind buffeted the conifer trees at the bottom of the garden and the sound of rooks cawing filtered through the tightly shut window. It was a wild spring evening. A fitting day for having one's world turned upside down.

Slowly, Sadie placed the adoption certificate down onto the old-fashioned quilted sateen eiderdown she'd had since childhood. Reaching for the box, she gazed into it. In her shock and disbelief at finding the adoption certificate, she hadn't noticed that there was more paperwork inside. Digging deep into her inner reserves, Sadie steeled herself to read it. After all, surely there could hardly be anything worse than what she had already stumbled upon.

Taking the plunge, she pulled out what seemed to be a leaflet of some kind. Unfolding it, she saw it was from an adoption agency, containing information for prospective adoptive parents. The main heading caught her eye: *What to expect when you adopt.*

What had her parents expected? Had she, Sadie, lived up to those expectations? Had they been too embarrassed to tell her of her origins? Frightened that she'd reject them if she knew the truth? Yet more questions invaded her already saturated mind until her head began to ache. Picking up her pillow, she buried her face in it as if that way she could block out the world and the colossal bombshell she had just been hit by.

After a long time, Sadie finally roused herself. Her stomach was rumbling but she knew she couldn't eat. The house felt like a prison, the air inside it torpid and stifling. She needed to get out, to breathe freely.

Downstairs, she grabbed her coat from the rack in the hall, pulled it on and went outside. She shivered on leaving the house, but the cold no longer seemed to matter. She was numb all over, still unable to fully comprehend what she had learnt.

Down on the beach, the wind whipped up waves that fell in silvery explosions onto the dark shoreline. In the daytime, in the summer, it was blissful here, the golden sand backed by the gaudy colours of the beach huts. Usually, Sadie loved it in winter, too, loved the wild power of the waves, the whistling of the wind, the salt smell of the sea. But today she barely noticed any of the things that usually bewitched and beguiled her. Lost in thought, she trudged along the waterline, not caring that her shoes were soon drenched, her feet freezing. When it began to rain, she didn't even think of turning back, but ploughed on as the downpour lashed her cheeks and ran in rivulets down her hair.

Eventually, soaked through and shivering, Sadie turned for home. In the bathroom, she turned the hot tap on full and contemplated her mother's bottle of Badedas bubble bath that sat on the glass shelf beneath the mirror.

*Things happen after a Badedas bath.* The familiar slogan from the magazine and TV ads reverberated around Sadie's head. Her mother had loved this stuff and Sadie knew that the moment she opened the lid and let the woody, redolent scent escape, she would be transported back in time, to when she had felt safe and secure, not adrift and drowning as she was now.

She had loved her parents so much. It had always felt

curious that she didn't look anything like either of them –
though not so curious that it had ever crossed her mind that she
wasn't their child. But there had been intermittent feelings of
being out of place. Sadie had just assumed everybody felt that
way, and she and her folks had never actually argued, unlike
Kim and her mum, who'd always been having massive barneys
that involved slammed doors and threats to leave home forever –
not just from Kim but from her mother, too! Living in such a
harmonious household had made Sadie feel a bit superior; *she*
didn't drive her mother and father to distraction. But perhaps
the reality was that her parents had always been treading on
eggshells, aware that Sadie was the cuckoo in the nest but not
wanting her to know this.

Sadie regarded the Badedas again. She hesitated for a
moment longer. And then, reasoning that she couldn't feel any
more miserable than she already did, she picked up the bottle,
flipped open the cap and poured a stream of the green liquid
into the rapidly filling bathtub. Immersing herself painfully into
the scaldingly hot water, she sank beneath the bubbles. When
she resurfaced, she was crying, but not the sporadic tears that
had been falling since her mother had told her of her diagnosis.
This was full-on weeping, the shuddering, shaking kind that
makes the weeper feel utterly wrung out.

By the time she had finished sobbing, the skin on her fingertips was wrinkled and shrivelled. Wearily, Sadie pulled herself
out of the bath, grabbed a towel and wrapped herself in it.
Finally thoroughly warm, she wanted to stay that way. In her
bedroom, she pulled on layers of clothing: a vest, blouse, tank
top and woolly jumper, a pair of tights under her jeans, then
thick socks and a hat.

She was hungry, she realised, having not eaten all day. She
should have a look in the kitchen cupboards and the fridge, see
if there was anything to make a meal from. Maybe her mother
would have left stuff in the freezer, it occurred to her, and then

she immediately started crying again as she imagined opening the drawer and finding some shepherd's pie or casserole Evelyn had frozen for a future supper that would now never come.

It would be too much. It was all too much. Far, far too much for one 27-year-old orphan to cope with.

# CHAPTER FOUR

Drawing back the curtains, Betty was met by bright sunshine. It looked set to be a beautiful day, which would be a welcome change to the generally soggy spring they were having. Betty wasn't on shift at the telephone exchange today, so she'd planned to accompany her father on his rounds, something she often did when she wasn't working.

Bowling along the country lanes in Harold's rickety old truck, signs of the season were all around, in the verges billowing with grasses and tall fronds of cow parsley, in the oak trees resplendent in full leaf, in the crystal-clear sparkling brooks that tinkled beneath old stone bridges. The beauty of it all made Betty's heart swell. For a while, after her mother's death, she and her dad had not been able to see the loveliness of God's own country. She was glad that this ability had returned to her now.

Leaning forward slightly, she began a rhythmic tapping on the dashboard. Her father listened carefully and then, when

Betty's tapping stopped, began to do the same. A couple of minutes later, they both burst out laughing.

'You better keep your knowledge of Morse code secret,' joked Harold. 'I reckon you're better and faster than half the army fellas. They'll be wanting you as a new recruit.'

Betty smiled briefly and then fell back to looking out of the window. She'd messaged her father that it was good growing weather for beans, and he'd messaged back did she mean 'Beans' as in their surname, or 'beans' as in the green vegetable?

Harold had taught both Betty and her sister Morse when they were just little girls. He'd learnt it himself as a signaller in the Great War, and enjoyed passing on his knowledge to his daughters. Betty had always shown a great affinity for such knowledge, and had been proficient by the age of ten. Jane, it had to be said, was nowhere near as enthusiastic. Now, in the long hours Betty and Harold spent in the truck, traversing the hills and dales, it was a way of keeping themselves entertained.

Nevertheless, her father's mention of recruitment to the forces jarred a little with Betty. Her best friend Val had joined the Wrens as soon as she was old enough, a year ago, and since then Betty had been champing at the bit, wishing she could follow suit and throw herself into important war work as so many women were doing. But now that her father was a widower, Betty's duty was to him, first and foremost. She couldn't even conceive of joining up herself and leaving him all alone when he was still so grief-stricken and vulnerable.

On their rounds they dropped in to farms and smallholdings dotted across the landscape, before finally arriving at the wholesalers in Pickering, where they ate their sandwich lunch.

'Thank you so much for coming with me,' her father said, settling down onto the bench opposite Betty. 'I don't know what I'd do without my helper! It's so good of you to give up your days off to keep me company. Other young girls would be wanting to spend time with people their own age, not an old codger like me.'

Betty smiled sympathetically and laid a hand over her father's. 'Don't be daft, Dad,' she responded. 'I love coming on the rounds with you, you know that. And anyway,' she added, trying to keep the wistfulness out of her voice, 'there aren't many young people around these days, are there?'

As she spoke, the familiar feeling hit her, of missing out, of not putting herself forward in the nation's hour of need. Her father nodded and smiled sympathetically at her.

'I'm sorry life's a bit dull for you,' he continued. 'So many gone. Your friend. Samuel...'

He left the sentence hanging and Betty didn't finish it for him. Val wrote regularly but what was happening to her childhood sweetheart Samuel, where he was, whether he was even still alive, was a mystery. The pair of them had been brought up alongside each other and the assumption had always been that they would become a couple. As soon as Betty turned sixteen, they had started walking out together. Only a couple of months later, Betty had waved goodbye to Samuel, who had just passed his eighteenth birthday, as he set sail to the Far East. At first, he had written regularly, long letters telling Betty everything about his experiences; the epic voyage that took him, via Freetown, Cape Town, Bombay and Colombo, to Singapore, the hot humidity of the city state, the fabulous orchids and tropical fruits he was seeing and tasting for the first time.

But since the catastrophic fall of Singapore earlier in the year, and the capture of all Allied personnel by the Japanese, she had heard nothing.

Apart from the worries that constantly assailed her for what he might be suffering, there was something else that continually troubled her. With every day that passed, Samuel felt more and more distant, not just geographically but also emotionally, so much so that Betty could hardly picture his face any longer. His prolonged absence had made her realise that, although she had known him for years, she didn't really know him at all. She wasn't sure that they even had anything in common. There was just the weight of expectation that they were made for each other, that they would be together, and all the rest a vacuum.

Lunch break over, father and daughter headed back to the truck and set off again.

'Why don't you have a go behind the wheel,' suggested Harold, throwing Betty the keys. 'It's good to keep your hand in.'

Betty climbed up into the cab with alacrity. She loved driving, sitting high up in the driver's seat, commanding the road, skilfully braking and double-declutching with ease. That was something she could do that most women couldn't: drive a lorry. A shiver of pride ran through her as she turned the vehicle onto the road out of town. They were heading for Castle Howard now, the local stately home. There would be a dinner for local army personnel there tomorrow night, and a big order had been put in.

'I'll keep a couple of bunches of asparagus for us, Betty love,' her father said, as they wound their way through the lanes. 'It won't be quite the same without any butter to smother it with, but it's nice and fresh, only just picked. It'll still taste good.'

'It will,' agreed Betty. 'We're lucky to be able to get all this veg. I've heard from Val that, over the winter, her cousin's family in Leeds could hardly get anything but potatoes, turnips and cabbage.'

'That's a shame,' replied Harold. 'Well, be grateful for small mercies and all that.'

They arrived at the gatehouse for Castle Howard. Harold didn't need to announce who they were; the gatekeeper knew Mr Bean and his daughter well. He waved them through and soon they were trundling along the long driveway. Betty gasped as she always did when the stunning building came into view, the long facade topped with the shining dome and fronted by the statue of Atlas. Always a bit of a dreamer, whenever Betty came here she imagined being a member of the Howard family, dressed like a princess, floating down the cantilevered staircase to take her place at the head of the enormous mahogany dining table, or leading the dancing in the galleried ballroom. She sighed and reached out towards the dashboard with her left hand.

'How the other half live,' she tapped.

Her father chuckled. 'I'm happy with what I've got,' he responded.

And so was Betty, of course she was. But it was only natural to sometimes think of other lives, other futures. Perhaps this was a result of the war. Opportunities had been opened up for women, offering them the chance of a far wider range of jobs than had ever been the case before, allowing them to live away from home, to travel, even, in some cases, to compete on equal terms with the men. There was a longing in Betty's heart for some of this freedom, a hankering after the adventures she saw others enjoying. Before the war began, she had always been happy with her lot in life, but now she couldn't even tell if that was because she really was satisfied with all that she had or if she'd just been too young to know different. It was all so confusing, so hard to work out what were legitimate desires and what were ridiculous aspirations.

Stifling a sigh, Betty focused her attention back on her driving. The archway that led to the tradesman's entrance had been built for a coach and horses, not a large truck, and it was a tricky manoeuvre to pass through it in one piece. Harold clapped as Betty achieved it with ease and swept to a halt on the ancient cobblestones.

A labourer working in the kitchen garden looked up at their approach, regarding the truck with mild curiosity that changed to wide-eyed surprise when Betty climbed down from the driver's side. Her good mood immediately restored, she suppressed a giggle. She enjoyed men's shocked and astonished looks when they saw a woman driving, as if they were amazed the truck had survived such an ordeal.

Her father appeared by her side. He drummed his fingers on the truck's metal side.

'Probably never seen a girl behind the wheel before,' Harold's Morse spelt out, echoing Betty's own thoughts. And then he added, 'Especially as I think he's one of those Eyeties from Eden Camp.'

Betty surveyed the man with more curiosity. He certainly looked Italian. Black hair, dark eyes under heavy brows, average height, lean and muscular. He was nothing like Samuel, who was stocky and blond, blue-eyed. It suddenly occurred to Betty why the man seemed familiar. He was the one who had made eye contact with her as the parade of prisoners passed through Malton.

A shiver ran down her spine. She couldn't help but notice that he was very good-looking. It wasn't just that, though. As she had discerned before, he also looked kind, and intelligent. Catching Betty's scrutiny, the Italian smiled at her, the lopsided grin that Betty remembered and which invited a response.

She smiled back.

'You drive good,' he said, miming the turning of a steering wheel. 'Like man!'

Betty took this as the compliment she knew it was meant to be. 'Thank you,' she replied.

Harold chuckled and then, as if remembering what they were here to do, moved towards the back of the vehicle.

'Come on, love,' he called. 'Better get this lot into the kitchen.'

Betty smiled shyly at the Italian, and made as if to follow

her father. Before she could do so, though, he had stepped towards her.

'My name is Gianni,' he said in heavily accented English, holding out his hand to hers, then hastily withdrawing it and wiping it on his overalls before offering it again. 'Gianni Urso. What you called?'

Some might have viewed it as a little presumptuous of him to ask her name, Betty thought. But she didn't. He seemed so sweet and genuine, wanting only to be friendly, to reach out to the people in whose country he had so unexpectedly found himself.

'I'm Betty,' she replied. 'Betty Bean.' Tentatively she offered her hand to him and, as he took it, a spark of electricity thrilled in her veins. Overcome with confusion, she snatched her hand back. For a moment, neither of them moved, but the static energy remained between them like an invisible force field.

And then her father was back beside the van, hauling out another sack of potatoes.

'I need to go,' Betty murmured. 'Bye,' she called over her shoulder, as she turned her back to retrieve a box of asparagus stems. Walking towards the kitchen door, she was aware of Gianni's eyes upon her. Straightening her shoulders, she tried to push away what had just happened between them. She had never experienced such an immediate attraction to anyone before and hadn't even begun to process the confusion it had engendered in her. Nothing to do now but carry on with the job as normal, hope that all the bewildering emotions that were fizzing inside her would just go away.

Fixing her eyes on the chef, who stood waiting to check off the delivery, she was taken totally by surprise when Gianni appeared beside her and wrested the box out of her hands.

'I bring for you,' he said, insistently. 'I carry.'

Seeing that resistance was futile, Betty let him take it. She watched as he and Harold made quick work of the rest of the load.

Back in the cab, her father driving again now, Betty could not stop her mind straying to the polite, friendly Italian, who was also undeniably handsome. She wandered where in Italy he came from and what it was like living here in Yorkshire, so far from home, a prisoner. There were so many questions she'd ask him if she had the chance, about Italy and being a soldier and his family— Abruptly, she tore her mind back to the present. What was she doing, dreaming about this man? Yes, he seemed nice, kind and so well-mannered. But that was it. He was nothing more to her than a casual acquaintance, met once or twice, and that was it. She'd almost certainly never see him again.

# CHAPTER FIVE

With a heavy heart, but at least no longer freezing cold, Sadie picked up the box and took it downstairs. In the sitting room, with its shabby but clean furniture, she lit the electric fire and sat on the floor in front of it. Then she turned the box upside down, emptying its entire contents onto the multicoloured swirls of the carpet. Piece by piece, she selected each item in turn and inspected it carefully.

The tiny shoes, the crocheted hat, the photos. She tucked them carefully back into the box. Next, the adoption certificate and the leaflet from the agency. And then, one last piece of paper. Her heart in her mouth, Sadie seized it up. She'd been so stunned and shocked that she hadn't noticed it before. Her heart beating at twice its normal rate, she unfolded the paper. It was a letter, dated 1 October 1945, and it began with the unemotional words *To Whom It May Concern.*

An inexplicable fear seized Sadie; sweat moistened her palms and her stomach turned over in apprehension. She was unclear about exactly what it was that she was so frightened about, she just knew that she no longer had any control over her emotions. It was like being on a ship in a storm, tossed to and fro, no chance of finding stability.

Forcing herself to be strong, she let her eyes wander over the words on the white sheet.

*14, Mornington Crescent, London NW*

*TO WHOM IT MAY CONCERN*

*This is to confirm that, on Sunday, 30th September at about seven o'clock in the evening, a woman I'd never seen or met before came to my door and asked me to look after her newborn baby for a short while. I hardly had time to agree before she had thrust the infant into my arms and left. She never came back.*

*In the early hours of Monday, 1st October, frantic with worry for the child's wellbeing, my husband and I called for an ambulance. When it arrived, we handed the baby over to them. I was not able to give any further information about the mother or her whereabouts.*

*Yours faithfully,*

*Mrs Jean Jackson*

Sadie's world had already fallen apart, but now the entire universe seemed to cave in on her, the sky imploding and the ground disappearing from beneath her feet. This was incomprehensible, so much worse even than she had originally believed. Not only was she adopted, and in her twenty-seven years on this planet no one had thought to tell her, but she had been literally handed to a stranger and left to fend for herself. How could this be true?

She had expected clearing her mother's house to be difficult and sad, but never in her worst imaginings had she anticipated the reality of what had happened today in the quiet seaside town of Broadstairs. There was no way she could go back to London, to work, to the flat. She didn't know what to say to anyone. She didn't know who she was any more.

Somehow, the hours passed. Sadie was too dazed to move. She just sat, numbed to the core, for hour upon hour.

On Monday morning, she managed to get up to call in sick to the office. That small act sapped her of all her energy and, for the rest of the day, she lay in her bed, rubbing the sateen cover of the quilt between her fingers, trying to take the same comfort from this action that she had when she was just a little girl.

Events of her childhood ran endlessly through her mind as if she were watching a ciné film; Christmases, birthday parties, holidays by the sea in Cornwall or Norfolk. Her mother and father had loved her beyond measure; she had always felt that, known that. But it had all been a lie. They'd pretended to be what they were not – her real father and mother. Sadie couldn't comprehend how it had been possible for them to maintain this falsehood over so many years, why they had never thought they should tell her, why she herself had never guessed.

But then again, now she came to think about it, maybe she had, or maybe she'd had at least an inkling. All Sadie's friends had siblings and it occurred to her now that her parents had never given her a satisfactory answer to why she was an only child. When she would beg for a baby brother or sister, her mother would reply that 'one was enough', and Sadie, for all her longing, had accepted it. But it didn't ring true, she saw that clearly now. When she got older, teenage Sadie had had feelings of alienation, of not fitting in, but, once this stage had passed, she had rationalised it as being how everyone felt at that age. It was normal.

Or was it?

A sudden rush of utter confusion and bewilderment swept

over her. She didn't know any more, it was all inexplicable, devastating.

The loud, shrilling sound of the telephone cut through her reverie, making her jump out of her skin. She sat motionless, a hand at her heart. She couldn't answer, couldn't speak to anyone, whoever it was. Bracing herself, she squeezed her eyes shut and waited for the call to ring out.

When it had finally done so, she relaxed a little, her shoulders slumping in an unleashing of tension that made her feel weak. She thought about Kim, that she should phone her at work as she might be worried about Sadie, where she was and what she was doing. And then there was Simon, her handsome, charming boyfriend. She'd have to let him know what was going on, but he was abroad at the moment, in the Far East. Telling him the story on a long-distance line was more than she could face, even if there wasn't the time difference and the cost of such a call to take into consideration.

The phone rang again. Its trilling bell echoed around the empty house, filling every corner with noise. When it finally subsided, Sadie had come to her decision. She had read in magazines how hard it could be when adopted children tried to find their birth parents, the danger of rejection, of impossible expectations that could not be fulfilled. But she shoved all these negatives aside.

She determined, then and there, that she would find her real mum and dad, and she wasn't going to let anyone or anything stand in her way.

# CHAPTER SIX

Beneath the sign boldly announcing BOVRIL, Betty and Val were saying goodbye on the station platform, after Val's fleeting visit to celebrate her birthday. Val's mum and dad were there, too, along with several of her younger siblings, who, with their propensity to dash madly around, added to the general atmosphere of mayhem.

'It's been lovely to see you,' said Betty, throwing her arms round her friend and hugging her tight. Tears were pricking behind her eyelids, not just for Val's impending departure but also at the memory of saying farewell to Samuel in this very same spot two years before. They had both been beguiled by the idea of Samuel setting off on his journey to become a war hero, caught up in the romance of it all, too young and innocent to really understand the true implications of what was in store for him.

A long whistle rang out into the soggy air. Both of them looked round to see the train approaching. The crowd stirred, gravitating as one towards the platform edge. Those travelling began to pick up suitcases and travel bags. Val's dad seized hold of hers, ready to escort her to her seat.

'Well, that's it then,' said Val. 'Bye, Betty. Take care. See you soon!'

And with that she was gone, swallowed up by the hordes surging on board.

Betty remained where she was. When the train finally pulled away again, she scoured the passing carriages for Val but could not make her out amidst the crush of waving arms and all the faces with their plastered-on smiles.

As Betty left the station, a sudden onrush of tears temporarily blinded her. It had been such a fleeting visit, but so lovely. Val had regaled her with tales of dragon-like commanding officers, iron discipline and gruelling PT sessions. She'd told Betty how 'biscuit beds' had to be 'barracked' with the sheets and blankets folded just so, shoes polished to such a high sheen that you could see your reflection in them, and uniform kept immaculate at all times. This last was of particular importance to Val; always keen on fashion, she'd chosen the Wrens because it was well known that their outfits were by far the best of all the women's services.

Despite all her lurid stories and colourful descriptions, it was clear that Val was having the time of her life, and the familiar curl of envy stirred in Betty's belly. She was jealous of her friend's lack of family responsibilities; all those numerous younger siblings would remain at home, helping Val's mother out, leaving Val herself free to go out into the world.

As Betty trudged through the rain, a sudden feeling of boredom, a painful ennui, surged through her. Everything in her life was so predictable. The war, on the other hand, though terrible in so many ways, was also exciting, thrilling even. Biscuit beds notwithstanding, Val's new life sounded wonderfully action-packed and exhilarating, whereas here she was, doing the same job at the same place where she'd been since she was sixteen. It was hard to shake the oppressive feeling that, for Betty Bean, nothing had changed, nor ever would.

Lost in thought, Betty did not see the pedestrian coming towards her until she'd bumped right into him.

'Sorry, sorry,' she apologised.

'It's no problem,' the man replied.

The voice seemed familiar. For a fleeting moment, Betty couldn't place it. And then, with a rush of adrenaline that coursed through her body with all the force of a tidal wave, she realised she'd walked slap bang into the kind and handsome Italian called Gianni, whom she'd spoken to briefly in the Castle Howard kitchen garden just a couple of weeks ago. And who had barely left her thoughts since, no matter how hard she had tried to erase him from her memory.

'I'm so sorry,' she repeated, thrown off balance by the surprise encounter. She could feel the colour rising in her cheeks as she spoke. 'I-I wasn't looking.'

'It's all right,' responded Gianni, with a gentle laugh. 'I seen you before, haven't I? Miss Betty Bean.'

Not wanting Gianni to see her red cheeks, Betty barely raised her eyes from the pavement as she nodded in acknowledgement, surprised that he remembered her name. But then again, she'd recalled his, and recognised his voice, so perhaps it wasn't so very strange. Betty's heart leapt at the thought that perhaps he'd taken as much interest in meeting her as she had him. And then she hastily dismissed such a fanciful notion.

There was a pause and a moment in which either one of them could have walked on. But neither did. Betty flicked her eyes up to Gianni's, noticed briefly their gentle brown warmth, and then dropped her gaze again, self-consciousness flooding over her.

'You not driving the truck today?' Gianni asked, in his accented English that gave everything he said an Italian flourish.

Now Betty did manage to look directly up at him. 'Not today,' she replied. 'I've just seen my friend off, back to her barracks. I was heading home to...' She tailed off, not sure what she was going home to do and certain that, whatever it was, it would be of no interest to Gianni.

The rain started to hammer down harder than ever, Yorkshire stair-rods that bounced back up from the already streaming pavement, soaking Betty's legs and dripping into her shoes. Instinctively, Gianni reached out a hand and gently ushered her under the shelter of a shop awning. Just as it had in the kitchen garden, her body tingled to the electricity of his touch.

'We need to get out of the rain,' he exclaimed. 'Shall we go to a café and I'll buy you a cup of tea?' he continued, and then, a broad grin spreading across his handsome face, added, 'I've learnt already how important tea is to you British.'

Betty laughed, finally relaxing a little. 'You're not wrong there,' she agreed. She regarded Gianni doubtfully for a moment, not wanting to say what was going through her mind.

'Don't worry,' Gianni said, 'I see what you are thinking. Why is a prisoner-of-war wandering the streets of the town, bumping into people?'

Awkwardly, Betty shifted her weight from one drenched foot to the other. 'Well, er,' she stuttered, lost for words. 'I just...' Then she gave up trying to be polite, bending over backward to avoid offence. Gianni didn't seem to be the type to get upset about things. 'Yes,' she went on, emboldened, 'I was wondering that. But I didn't mean to be rude.'

Gianni chuckled, his brown eyes crinkling in amusement. 'It's all right, no problem. In fact we are not guarded when we are out. We go to work in the day and we must be back in camp for curfew. But if we finish early, like me today, we can go into town. We get some small pay to spend. It's nice – to see the shops, the people. To feel a little bit free again.'

Taking Betty completely by surprise, tears pricked behind her eyes at the conclusion of Gianni's explanation. When he spoke of freedom, the wistfulness in his voice made Betty realise how tough it must be to be incarcerated – even if the regime was relatively lenient – and to be so far from home and all you know and love. It put her own feelings of constraint, the invisible ties that bound her to her father and meant she couldn't leave him, into perspective.

The rain redoubled its efforts and a housewife tutted as she tried to exit the shop under whose awning Gianni and Betty were sheltering. They needed to move from here and a cuppa in a warm café, just until the downpour was over, was a very appealing idea.

'I'd love some tea,' she said to Gianni. 'The place just over there is nice.' She pointed across the road to where a striped awning hung over a window opaque from the steam and condensation inside.

Once they were settled down at a cosy corner table, a pot of tea brewing in front of them, Betty searched frantically in her mind for a topic of conversation.

'Where are you from in Italy?' she asked.

'Well, really I not from Italy at all,' responded Gianni. 'Sicily is my home. A town called Taormina, close to Mount Etna.'

'Mount Etna!' exclaimed Betty, intrigued and alarmed at the same time, her interest in Gianni's history overriding her bashfulness. She'd learnt about Europe's active volcanoes in geography lessons at school, and of the famous eruption of Vesuvius in Roman times. 'Aren't you terribly afraid?' she questioned. She wanted to reach out and take his hand, hold it tight, protect him from Mother Earth's powerful forces. 'I know I should be. I wouldn't be able to rest easy in my bed at night, knowing a lava flow could come at any time and sweep us all away!'

Gianni laughed, a hearty laugh that set his brown eyes sparkling. 'It's not so terrible. And when Etna erupts, it does so slowly. There is time to get out of the way.'

'Phew,' breathed Betty, relieved to hear this even if not completely convinced. She tried to picture it in her mind, a bubbling volcano constantly releasing a plume of smoke into the soaring Mediterranean sky, the azure sea below and, in between, Gianni's town, Taormina, its inhabitants bravely going forth into each new day, not knowing when the mountain might unleash its full fury. She shuddered involuntarily.

'You are cold!' exclaimed Gianni. 'I give you my jacket...' He made as if to take off his regulation-issue coat and then stopped. Like all of the POWs' uniform items, it was emblazoned with a large yellow diamond on the back. It was clearly inappropriate for a British woman to wear.

Betty, realising the same thing, hurriedly shrugged off the need for an extra layer. 'No, there's no need, really.' She could feel the colour rising up her cheeks again. To distract herself – and hopefully Gianni, too – she pointed at the café's notice-board, where a poster advertised the latest offering at the Palace cinema. 'I love watching films,' she said, 'especially the Hollywood ones.' She let out a long sigh of admiration and longing. 'Everything is so glamorous in America. It always seems so much bigger and brighter than here. Though I'm fascinated by Italy, too, and Sicily,' she added, hastily, lest Gianni should think her uninterested in his homeland. 'I wish I could speak Italian like a *signorina*.' She said the last word with the best approximation she could muster of an Italian accent and then burst out laughing.

Gianni chuckled too, before a frown of concentration settled on his face. He seemed to be trying to summon up the words to respond. It was clear that he was still getting to grips with the English language – though Betty was surprised and impressed by how much he already knew.

'Me, I like the cinema, too,' he said eventually. Betty wondered if that was what he had wanted to say, or whether he'd given up on his original intention. 'And I want to learn English more better. So – I teach you *Italiano*, you teach me English. Yes?'

'Well-I-er,' Betty stuttered, taken aback by Gianni's enthusiastic suggestion. 'I suppose we could. Every now and again. Maybe.' She thought about her father, what she would say to him, and then of Sicily again, the smoking volcano, the herb-scented, sun-baked countryside of her imagination. It was so exotic, so remote, so desirable. Why shouldn't she learn some Italian and bring a little of that wonderful foreignness into her world, which war had made bland and grey? The conflict had taken enough away from all of them; surely it was acceptable to claw back small pieces of joy and happiness where one could?

'In fact,' she went on, as Gianni regarded her expectantly, 'I'd like that. We could meet in the station café.' She suggested this venue as one where people were always coming and going and where they would therefore attract less attention.

'Good!' Gianni seemed genuinely delighted. 'I finish work five in afternoon, am in Malton five thirty. Back to camp by seven thirty, latest. Is perfect for me!'

His enthusiasm was so infectious Betty had to smile. 'Good,' she said. 'Next Tuesday, then? I'm on the eight a.m. to four p.m. shift, so I can meet you at five thirty.'

They finished their tea and Gianni said he'd escort her home. Outside, the rain had stopped, to be replaced by a misty drizzle.

'Does it always rain like this in England?' Gianni asked, somewhat hopelessly, as he looked around him at the drenched streets and sodden shop canopies. 'So much water!' he added, his tone and expression bemused. 'Where it all come from?'

Betty smiled. 'It's not always this bad,' she replied, as Gianni moved to her right-hand side so that he was between her and the road. Betty was impressed at this display of faultless manners. 'But often,' she added, playfully. 'You'll get used to it. And there'll be snow in winter. I hope they'll keep you warm in the camp.'

Gianni frowned and shrugged. 'Will be all right.'

They reached the market square, where Betty halted. She thought it best if Gianni didn't take her all the way to her house.

'You can leave me here,' she said. 'I've... um, I've got some shopping to do.' They stood for a moment, looking at each other, lingering glances that seemed to hold a world of emotion and unvoiced longing. Then Betty turned abruptly on her heel and headed for the grocery store, calling back over her shoulder, 'See you on Tuesday. Don't be late!'

'I won't,' responded Gianni. 'I be there, don't worry.'

*It's just language lessons*, she thought to herself as she perused the paltry goods available on the shelves. The butterflies fluttering in her stomach made it hard to concentrate on bags of flour and boxes of eggs, and, when she held out her ration book to the shop assistant, she was unable to quell the trembling of her hand. *Language lessons, Betty Bean*, her internal voice reiterated. *That's all.*

And there was nothing wrong with that. Nothing at all.

# CHAPTER SEVEN

The morning started out bright and sunny, the energetic, hopeful spring sunshine that is almost always washed out and defeated by midday. Sadie stood for a moment on the doorstep outside her flat, bracing herself. The fleeting thought crossed her mind that she didn't have to do this. No matter what she had vowed to herself, she didn't have to try to find her birth mother.

She'd spilled it all out to Kim the evening before as they'd sat in their tiny living room making toast on the bars of the electric fire. Once Kim had got over the shock, she had cautioned Sadie against what she was going to do.

'Are you sure it's a good idea?' she'd said, frowning. 'I mean, people can get terribly disappointed in these cases. And sometimes – I've heard,' she added, almost apologetically, 'the birth parents aren't that keen on knowing the baby they gave away. It – well, it doesn't always work out, is what I'm trying to say.'

Sadie had jutted her chin forward in a gesture of defiance. 'I know all that. I'm aware of it. But I'm going to do it anyway.'

'Oh Sadie,' sighed Kim, with a resigned smile. 'You're the stubbornest person I know. I just want you to be careful what you wish for. Something like this is never going to be easy.'

'Thanks for the advice,' Sadie had retorted. 'But I've made my mind up and nobody is going to stop me.'

She reminded herself of that fighting spirit now, as she inwardly quailed at the enormity of what she was embarking upon. Perhaps she should take Kim's advice and let sleeping dogs lie. But no. She was not going to give up. She'd prefer 'determined' to Kim's 'stubborn' but, either way, she was not a quitter.

Head held high, Sadie stepped out onto the street and resolutely set off for the bus stop. She could have taken the tube to Mornington Crescent – it would be quicker – but she always felt that she could think better on the bus. And she had a lot of thinking to do.

Ensconced in a seat on the top deck of the number 27, Sadie pulled a battered A–Z out of her bag. Opening it, she studied the layout of the area, one she was not familiar with. Mornington Crescent was exactly as described, a wide arc of a street curving around behind the iconic Carreras cigarette factory. Jean Jackson lived at number 14. She would go straight there, knock on the door, speak with Jean and find out exactly what had happened on that night at the beginning of October 1945.

Thinking this, Sadie pushed aside the worm of doubt that was niggling inside her and refused to allow herself to be cowed. Fixing her gaze outside the window, she focused on the London landscape rumbling past. Rebuilding after the war had been ongoing for years but there was still plenty of evidence of the bombing: gaps in the rows of Victorian terraces, fissures in the walls of houses still standing, cracked and cratered pavements. *Like the gaps and broken bits in my life story,* Sadie thought, a sudden tide of sadness washing over her.

She couldn't imagine who her mother must have been, to have left her here in the middle of this huge city, never to return. Hadn't she been cute enough? Pretty enough? But that was silly; negative thinking that would get her nowhere. Sadie didn't know much about babies, but she knew that mothers invariably loved them to pieces, whatever they looked like. It was stupid to imagine she had been rejected for not coming up to standard. That could not possibly be the case. It must have been something else. It had to have been. But what?

On Hampstead Road, huge new blocks designed by leading architects had been built to replace the John Nash housing destroyed in the Blitz. Sadie read the names as the bus trundled along; Silverdale, Coniston, Cartmel, monikers intended to evoke the cool air, high hills and tranquil waters of the Lake District. Was this what it was all about? An attempt to rebuild herself, to give herself a history, now that the one she had always known had been torn away from her? If it was, she wondered if it would work, if she could ever come to terms with what she had discovered, especially when the key players, her mother and father, were both dead. A bolt of the now-familiar anger, fierce as lightning, shot through her. How could they have done this to her? And then the rage subsided, to be replaced by sorrow. She was sure that they had thought it was for the best that Sadie shouldn't know her origins. Only time would tell if they were right about that.

By now the sun, as expected, had gone in, and a blustery wind that brought with it angry squalls of rain had taken over. It felt a long way from the bucolic idyll projected by the buildings' names and Sadie shivered, even though the bus was warm.

Arriving at the stop outside the tube station, Sadie got off the bus and looked up at the huge white building in front of her. The Carreras factory, with its columns and two huge, black marble cats, dominated one whole side of Harrington Square, which was in fact more of a triangle around which traffic sped in three lanes. On another of the sides stood a council block, built in a distinctive Art Nouveau style. And on the third side were three colossal tower blocks, each with a different primary-coloured top – one red, one yellow, one blue – like crayons in a child's pencil case. Sadie stared across at these skyscrapers. Thank goodness Jean Jackson didn't live there, that this was not where she had been left. But of course she couldn't have been – they were only built in the 1960s, long after Sadie had been born.

Squaring her shoulders, Sadie rounded the factory corner and came to Mornington Crescent. Number 14 was like all the other houses in the street: tall and thin, on five floors. The upper-ground-floor windows were rounded at the top in the Georgian style and along the first floor ran an elegant iron balustrade. Most of the other houses lacked this adornment, which was not surprising. Such accessories had often not been replaced since being melted down and used in the war effort.

Sadie hesitated, almost losing heart again. Could it really be that simple? Could she ring the bell and, straight away, get the answers she craved? There was only one way to find out. On approaching the front door, however, she saw that there were three bells to choose from. Jean Jackson's letter gave no flat number. Perhaps the house had been subdivided since the war? That was common, an attempt to alleviate the housing shortage and also because few people had the money to maintain a whole building themselves.

Sadie rang the middle bell. For a few moments, there was silence. And then she heard a scuffling behind the door, the sound of a metal chain clanking and a key turning. The door swung open the minutest chink. Sadie squinted through the gap, trying to make out who was there. The interior of the house was in darkness and she could see nothing, just hear a voice, thin and wavering, drifting towards her.

'Is it you, Marge? Or Dot? Who is it?'

Sadie tried to peer further inside as she still couldn't see anyone. 'No, it's not Marge or Dot,' she replied. 'You don't know me. I'm – well, I'm looking for someone.'

The door banged shut. Sadie's heart sank. She was about to try another of the bells when, with a squeaking of hinges, the door swung open to reveal a tiny old lady, one hand resting on an elaborately carved walking stick, staring at her.

'Who are you?' the woman demanded, not unreasonably in the circumstances.

Sadie took a step forward. 'I'm Sadie,' she said, holding out her hand to the lady's free one. 'Pleased to meet you. I'm looking for Mrs Jean Jackson? Is that you?' She gazed expectantly at the old lady.

With a dubious look on her face, the old lady ignored Sadie's outstretched hand and turned her back. 'Well, you'd better come in, Sadie whoever-you-are,' she said, over her shoulder.

Sadie became conscious of her pulse quickening as nerves took over. Equal measures of elation and terror filled her body and her hands began to tremble. Had she really found the woman who might hold the key to her past so quickly?

# CHAPTER EIGHT

'*Vorrei un biglietto di andata e ritorno per Roma, per favore,*' said Gianni, the mellifluous words flowing from his tongue.

'*Vorrei un...* Um, what was the next word again?' asked Betty, already unsure of what Gianni had said. Every lesson taxed her brain to the utmost, but, over the year and a bit that she'd been meeting with Gianni to learn Italian, she'd made steady progress, and she loved the mental stimulation.

'*Un biglietto,*' he repeated, enunciating every syllable with exaggerated care. '*Bi-li-et-to.*'

'*Biglietto,*' copied Betty, and then again, '*biglietto,*' attempting to add an Italian cadence to her pronunciation. The idea that she would ever actually be in Italy, trying to buy a train ticket to anywhere, let alone Rome, the Eternal City, was preposterous. But it was fun imagining that she might.

For a moment she let her imagination take a further step, not just to being in Rome, but being there with Gianni— Immediately, she stopped herself indulging in such a ridiculous fantasy, because of course this would never happen. Every lesson, every day, Betty was aware that she and Gianni were on borrowed time. One day the war would end and Gianni would leave Yorkshire and Samuel would return.

Betty's mother, on her deathbed, had asked Betty to look after her father, and had also told her that knowing Betty had Samuel to take care of her enabled her to go in peace. Perhaps if Betty's mother had not died and the war had not started, Betty and Samuel would have drifted apart, despite the family pressure for them to be together. But these two events had cemented them as 'promised' to each other, and everyone, not least Betty's father and Samuel's mother, was relying on it now.

The impossibility of it all was never far from Betty's mind.

'Now try the whole sentence,' urged Gianni.

Summoning her thoughts back to the present, Betty took a deep breath, then paused for a moment, mouthing the words silently before saying them out loud.

'*Vorrei un biglietto di andata e ritorno per Roma, per favore.*'

'*Bravo!*' Gianni congratulated her, bestowing on her one of his trademark lopsided grins that made her insides turn over. 'You are learning so good.'

Betty's cheeks flushed bright red, much to her dismay. She might be improving her Italian but she couldn't seem to make any progress on her propensity to blush at the slightest provocation. She laughed, and put her hands on either side of her face in an attempt to conceal its puce colour.

Composure restored, she had another go at the whole sentence and, once Gianni had given her an A-star and multiple cries of '*perfecto*', decided she'd had enough for one day.

'Your turn now,' she told him. 'Let's talk in English for a bit. How is work going? Busy with harvest time, I expect.'

'Yes, you're right,' responded Gianni, solemnly. He took his job very seriously, always anxious to be seen to be working hard. Betty had sometimes wondered why he was so committed, so dedicated to providing food for a country he'd been battling against not so long ago.

'What do your folks think?' she asked, tentatively. They knew each other well enough by now, she hoped, that she could broach such topics. 'About you being here and labouring for a foreign power?'

'My folks?' cried Gianni in response. 'They are happy for me that I'm out of the fighting, well away from it all, and that I'm well fed, with a roof over my head. You know, Betty, that life is hard in Sicily. Many families are poor. Yes, we have the sunshine and our island is beautiful. But you can't eat beauty.'

Betty grimaced at the thought of hardship in Gianni's homeland. 'And when you were captured,' she went on, 'what happened? It must have been terrifying. Were many... killed?'

Just saying the word 'killed' made it real, that this was war they were talking about. Although it was all around them, in the army uniforms of those waiting on the station platform or drinking tea in the café, in the newsreels and newspapers and on the wireless, the conflict still felt incredibly remote from where they were on the edge of the North York Moors.

Gianni gave a small snort of laughter. 'No one was killed, Betty. We surrendered without a shot being fired.'

'Gosh.' Betty was dumbfounded. She had imagined a fierce gun battle, artillery fire, grenades – though the reality was that she had no real idea how this war was being fought. She knew about the trenches of the Great War from school, but things were more sophisticated now, and so much was being done from the air, on both sides. The Blitz had pulverised cities the length and breadth of the country, from London to Bristol, Glasgow to Liverpool. Betty took a warming gulp of tea as she thought of the terror of being caught up in the relentless aerial bombardment of those bombing raids.

Gianni was stirring his tea, the spoon going round and round the cup, though the sugar must all have dissolved by now.

'None of us wanted to be there, in that North African desert. None of us believed we should be fighting the British – we consider your country our friend. And as for the Americans – there's hardly a family in Sicily that doesn't have a relative who has crossed the Atlantic in the hope of a better life. They are our cousins, not our enemy.'

Betty nodded. 'I didn't know that, but I understand.' Over the year and a half since the Italians had arrived at Eden Camp, the local residents had got used to their presence in their midst. A few of them had sweethearts among the local women and no one seemed unduly concerned about this, either. The guards even lent the inmates their own clothes so that they could go out for the evening dressed in civvies. For Betty, finding out that Gianni had not fired a weapon in all of his time in the military made her feel a lot better about how much time she was spending with him.

And how much she enjoyed that time.

She became aware of Gianni's intense gaze upon her, a lingering look that turned her insides liquid. Goosebumps broke out on her skin and she shivered involuntarily, even though it was warm in the café. For some inexplicable reason, tears began to prick behind Betty's eyes. She wanted this moment to last forever, this time that she and Gianni spent together to be infinite. A scene flashed before her eyes: her and Gianni, walking across a summer meadow, arms entwined...

'Betty?' Gianni's voice cut through her daydream. 'It's time I should go.'

As she nodded her reluctant agreement – she could stay all evening, chatting with Gianni – he jumped up to pull back her chair and help her to her feet. His manners really were impeccable. They strolled back towards the market square, Betty walking as slowly as possible to prolong the moments before parting, past the billboards with the recruitment posters urging men and women to join up.

Betty had spent most of the last couple of years wishing she could follow in Val's footsteps and join the WAAF or the WRNS or the ATS, but all the time knowing that she couldn't abandon her father, couldn't leave him to fend for himself, especially in the light of the vow she'd made to her mother.

Now she had to acknowledge that this wasn't the only thing holding her back. Increasingly, though she could hardly admit it to herself, she didn't want to leave Gianni. Her feelings for him had crept up on her and were getting stronger by the day, and, however hard she pushed them away, she couldn't get rid of them. Gianni was with her all the time, in her daydreams and her night dreams. She would often lie awake in bed thinking of him, picturing his handsome face and his lopsided grin, his warm brown eyes and strong, hard-working hands. With all her heart, Betty wished that she could stop time right where it was, with her and Gianni close together in Malton and nothing to ever wrench them apart.

This thought in mind, Betty pushed open the door to her father's little cottage and stepped inside. There, lying on the doormat, was the day's post. The envelope on top of the pile was unmistakable in its official appearance.

Picking it up, she contemplated it for a few moments, biting her lip, plucking up the necessary courage to open it. Eventually, she took a deep breath and, not even bothering to use the paperknife, tore the flap apart and pulled out the piece of paper nestling inside.

It was just as she thought. She was twenty now and these were her call-up papers. The heading, in block capitals, read:

### NATIONAL SERVICE ACT 1939 TO 1941 MINISTRY OF LABOUR AND NATIONAL SERVICE

*Dear Madam*

*1. I have to inform you that in accordance with the National Service Acts you are required to submit yourself to medical examination by a Medical Board on 6th September 1943...*

The sixth! That was only five days away. Betty read on as if in a trance, right down to the bottom of the page.

*10. Immediately on receipt of this notice you should inform your employer of the date and time at which you are required to attend for medical examination.*

*11. If you are called up you will receive a further notification giving you at least a week's notice. You should accordingly not voluntarily give up your employment because you are required to attend for medical examination.*

Despite the cautionary instruction, Betty didn't have any doubt at all that she would pass the medical examination. She was fighting fit, hardly ever had a day's illness in her life, a picture of health. She'd have to write back, explain to them her situation, her role keeping house for her father, whose work in food distribution meant that he was essential to the war effort.

Distractedly, she slid the paper back inside the envelope and hid it behind the clock that stood on the hall table. She'd deal with it later. There was another letter on the mat, also for her. She picked it up, recognising the handwriting straight away, even though it had been so long since she had heard from him.

Samuel.

There had been no correspondence since his capture eighteen months ago. No letters, no official news – and no way of knowing whether he was getting the letters Betty and his mother Julie sent so assiduously. It seemed almost impossible that one had arrived now, a bolt from the blue, coinciding with her being called up.

With trembling hands, Betty carried the missive into the kitchen and put the kettle on the stove. She needed more tea for this.

Sprinkling the most frugal amount of leaves she could get away with into the pot, she filled it with boiling water and set it on the table to brew. Bracing herself, she finally opened the letter. The top of the paper bore the indecipherable characters of the Japanese language and then, in English, IMPERIAL JAPANESE ARMY. The words below were typed, with only Samuel's signature in handwriting. Betty read with bated breath.

Dearest Betty

Hoping this finds you well. Have not received word from you and am waiting patiently for a letter. We are working hard but thoughts of you make it bearable. Missing you dreadfully. No more for now. Please pass to Mum.

All love,

*Samuel*

That was it. After so long, just these few words. Biting her lip, Betty blinked back tears as she poured a cup of tea, adding a dash of milk and a few grains of sugar. She cast her eyes over Samuel's words again. He was not getting the letters she sent but he was nevertheless still relying on her, depending on her. So was her father, still grieving the loss of his wife. And Samuel's mother, too, to whom Betty must impart this briefest of news about her precious, beloved son.

Sadly, Betty shoved the letter in her pocket. As it so often did these days, the weight of all this expectation on her narrow shoulders felt suddenly overwhelming, insupportable. Day after day she put on a brave face, but, all the time, inside she was breaking. Things she had agreed to in the naivety of youth were constraining and limiting now, not least her commitment to Samuel.

Eventually, Betty got up from the table and slowly washed up the tea things. Her mind flitted to the big event that was happening at Eden Camp the next evening – the summer dance. Val was already on her way back from Leeds and she and Betty had planned to put on their glad rags – such as still existed after years of rationing – and enjoy themselves.

In the light of Samuel's letter, should she cancel the arrangement? Betty considered the dilemma for a bit. She couldn't let down Val, who'd arranged leave and gone to the expense of a train fare. And if she did, she'd have to explain to Val the reasons why, and she wasn't anywhere near being able to put into words her complicated feelings about Samuel, Gianni, her obligations, her desires...

No. Betty would go to the ball. It was just a little dancing, some fun and light-heartedness. Where was the harm in that?

# CHAPTER NINE

The music was already playing loudly in the mess hut that had been turned into a temporary dance hall as Betty and Val arrived. The camp's inhabitants had conjured up a gramophone from somewhere, but that was lying unused for now. Instead, a young man energetically played a jovial tarantella on the accordion. Already, couples were on the floor, coursing backwards and forwards in easy choreography.

'So where's this famous Gianni-bloke, then?' asked Val, with a smirk. Betty had mentioned him in letters but of course had not said anything about her feelings for him. Now she just shook her head dismissively and replied, 'I don't know. Should I?'

Val slapped her arm playfully. 'I'm not daft,' she teased. 'I can tell he's something special, however much you try to hide it.'

Betty realised that she wasn't going to fool Val that easily. 'He's nice,' she said with a shrug. 'He's taught me so much Italian. He says I'm really good now.'

Val winked lewdly. 'I bet he does,' she rejoined with a guttural chuckle.

Betty pulled herself up to her full height of five foot four and a half inches. 'I don't know what you're insinuating,' she said, with faux primness. 'He's a friend.'

'Whatever you say,' responded Val, rolling her eyes skywards and casting Betty an arch look.

A couple of young men came over and asked them to dance. Soon Betty was jigging around the floor to an unfamiliar tune, not quite sure what she was supposed to be doing with her feet but happy to follow the man's lead. Luckily, he didn't seem too bothered when she stepped on his toes. When the music came to an end, Betty thanked him and said she needed a glass of water. Going over to where soft drinks were laid out on a trestle table, she scoured the room for Gianni.

She spotted the groundsman, Bert Lewis, hovering at the edge of the dance floor. Bert knew all the men and was on good terms with most. Betty considered going to ask him if he had any idea where Gianni was but immediately thought better of it; Bert was a terrible gossip and, if he got the faintest whiff of a romance between Betty and Gianni, it would be all round the camp in moments.

Another tune began and ended, and another, and there was still no sign of Gianni. Betty started to wonder if he'd decided not to come. Perhaps he was ill, or too tired after the day's work.

Nevertheless, he had promised he'd be there.

The accordion stopped playing and someone began fiddling with the gramophone. Suddenly a vibrant jive tune was blaring out at top volume. Where was Gianni? For the umpteenth time, Betty looked around the hut, peering into every corner, not that there was anywhere anyone could realistically hide. With a growing sense of disappointment, she realised that he wasn't coming. Suddenly the dance didn't seem fun any more, and she contemplated going home early. Val would be disappointed but she'd understand.

And then, just as the music reached its crescendo, the hut door opened and in through it burst Gianni. Immediately on seeing Betty, he rushed over to her.

'I'm sorry, Betty,' he apologised. 'Very sorry. Farmer's truck – it broke down – had to change wheel. Got back late and then I must wash and—'

Betty shook her head. 'It's fine. Slow down. Did you run all the way here from the other end of the camp?' She knew that Gianni's sleeping quarters were on the furthest-flung edge of the rows of huts.

Gianni nodded and took a few deep breaths. Then suddenly he regained his composure. He held out his arm to Betty. 'Madam, would you care to dance,' he said, in his best English accent. As Betty linked her arm in his, he leant towards her. 'You look so beautiful,' he whispered in her ear. '*Bellissima.*'

Betty blushed as she always did when paid a compliment, and wished as she always did that her body would stop doing that to her. But in moments they were whirling around the dance floor and the red cheeks could be explained away by exertion rather than self-consciousness. Betty's whole body thrilled to Gianni's touch, to their proximity, to the heady smell of him, of soap, clean laundry and shaving foam mixed with manliness, that filled her with longing.

They danced and danced, with just a brief pause when Val came over and Betty introduced her and Gianni, until the camp officers, who'd been ranged around the walls and had joined in on more than one occasion, called time. Gianni led Betty outside, into the cool, crisp night air. The sky was a blanket of blue velvet, star-studded and still.

'I wish I could walk you home,' said Gianni. 'Make sure everything is all right.'

Betty smiled wanly. It was hard to know what to say, when she so badly wanted this too. But it was late now and Gianni would not be allowed to leave the camp at this hour, even if Betty could accept his offer. 'It's fine,' she replied, faintly. 'I've got Val to keep me company. And in fact' – she gestured towards the hut – 'one of the officers said he'd give us a lift in the army jeep.'

A flash of something crossed Gianni's face. Jealousy? Disappointment? Betty couldn't tell. And as soon as it had come, it was gone again, leaving her wondering if she had imagined it.

'I wait until you go,' Gianni said. 'To make sure.'

Betty nodded. They stood for a moment, the air around them pregnant with expectation. And then a crowd of others surged forth from the hut and suddenly there were people milling around all over the place.

'There's the chap,' said Betty, pointing to a tall, thin man with a moustache. 'He's the one who said he'd drive us.'

She began to make her way towards him, but a gentle pressure on her arm held her back. She turned to face Gianni.

'I wish you didn't have to go,' he whispered, his eyes full of longing.

Betty met his gaze. 'I know,' she murmured. A crystal-clear silence descended between them.

'Betty, *ti amo*,' murmured Gianni. 'I love you.'

Betty gasped. Her heart began to beat at double pace. She was overcome by an uncontrollable urge to grab hold of him, hold him tight, let herself be swallowed up by his strong embrace.

'I... I...' she began.

'There you are!' Suddenly Val was beside them, clutching her shoes in her hand, cheerfully interrupting. 'I was looking for you.'

Betty turned towards her. 'I'm right here,' she replied, forcing a carefree laugh.

'That was a wonderful evening,' Val went on, as if unaware of the moment she had disturbed. 'Wasn't it?' She narrowed her eyes and gazed pointedly at Gianni. Betty squirmed with embarrassment, but fortunately the tension was broken by another flurry of people leaving the dance hut. Val hobbled barefoot over the stony path to catch up with an old school friend and say goodbye.

Gianni and Betty were left regarding each other, the air between them taut with expectation.

'And I love you, too,' she replied, quietly. She wanted to throw her arms round him, hug him close, hold him tight, never let him go. But she couldn't do that. Not here, not now, not ever. Instead they stood, inches apart, hovering so close but not quite close enough, surrounded by people but feeling as if it were just them, until the moment was once more broken by Val, limping towards them. Taking Betty's arm and leaning heavily upon it, Val steered her towards the vehicles waiting to speed the party-goers homeward.

Betty looked back over her shoulder. Gianni was standing there, gazing after her.

'I love you,' Betty mouthed again, wondering if he could lip-read, hoping that he could.

Val stumbled, almost throwing Betty off balance. 'Ouch,' she exclaimed, and then, 'bleeding hell. I need someone to carry me. Where's that handsome Italian of yours when he's required,' she continued, her voice full of ribaldry.

Betty managed a weak smile. 'I'm not surprised you can hardly walk,' she said, with forced jollity. 'Why have you taken your shoes off?' She ignored the enquiry into Gianni's whereabouts.

'Too tight, too uncomfortable,' groaned Val. 'I'd rather walk on hot coals the rest of the way home.'

'You are daft sometimes,' Betty responded, her mind only half on Val and her sore feet. 'Lucky for you we've got a lift.'

*Not lucky for me, though*, she thought dejectedly. Gianni's words, his declaration, still hung expectantly in the air, as did her response. If only the two of them could amble back to Malton together, in perfect step with each other, stopping to gaze at the beauty of the night sky, allowing time and opportunity for them both to exchange words of endearment... But this was the stuff of fairy tales, not real life.

Reluctantly, Betty whispered a last soft goodbye to Gianni and climbed into the jeep. As they drove away, she craned her neck to look out of the window and watch until his solitary, waving figure had disappeared from view.

# CHAPTER TEN

At home, the latch on the door clunked loudly as Betty opened it. No matter how quietly she tried to do it, the noise always resounded around the whole house. She stood in the narrow hallway for a moment, listening. No sound from upstairs. Hopefully she hadn't woken her father. She bent down to take off her shoes. Her feet were tired and aching just like Val's, but her mind was buzzing and active, the music – and Gianni's last words to her – ringing in her ears.

Normally after a night out she would have been eager to see her father and tell him everything about the evening. But not today. Because recently Harold had been rather quiet whenever Gianni's name was mentioned. She and her dad were so close, and Betty was so used to being indulged by him in every way, that it came as a shock when the cold shadow of what could only be described as disapproval fell between them.

Holding her shoes by their straps, she tiptoed to the kitchen. She was desperate for a glass of water; all that jitterbugging and jiving had made her thirsty. Imagining herself and Gianni still on the dance floor, she swayed her hips and swished her skirt from side to side as she entered the room – and nearly jumped out of her skin.

Sitting at the table, still as a statue, was her father.

'Dad!' Betty exclaimed, clutching her hand to her heart to slow its erratic beating. 'You scared the life out of me. What are you doing?'

Her father had a strange expression on his face, of concern and tiredness and – what was the other thing? Betty couldn't put a name to it. Suddenly stricken by anxiety, she rushed over to him and knelt down beside him.

'What's the matter?' she asked, urgently. 'What's wrong? Are you ill? Here, let me feel your forehead, see if you have a fever...'

Harold shook his head. 'I'm fine, Betty love,' he said. 'Nothing wrong with me at all.'

Betty stood up again and contemplated her father anew. There was definitely something strange about him.

'What is it then? Has something happened to Jane? To the baby?' Her older sister was pregnant; she had told them recently, a few weeks ago. The thought that something might have gone wrong made bile rise in Betty's throat.

'Jane's fine,' answered Harold. 'There's nothing for you to worry about on her account.'

Suddenly feeling exhausted, Betty sank down into a chair facing her father. She'd never known her father behave so strangely before.

'Then what is it, Dad?' she questioned, more calmly now. 'I know something's up.'

Harold let out a long, heartfelt sigh. 'I don't know how to say this without upsetting you, love,' he said. 'But it's about that Italian chap. Gianni.'

Betty's heart sank. Did Harold know something bad about him? Had he got a reputation among the farmers? Gianni had had several employers since he arrived, moving around as the work dictated. Her father travelled all over the county, he knew everyone Gianni worked for. He would soon find out if Gianni was in trouble of any kind. But even though that seemed the logical explanation for her father's concern, it didn't make any sense to Betty. Subconsciously, she knew it was nothing to do with Gianni's trustworthiness or reliability. She had a sudden feeling of impending doom.

'What about him?' Try as she might, she couldn't keep the defensiveness out of her voice. 'What do you think he's done?'

'He's done nothing wrong, Bets,' Harold assured her. 'It's just that... look, I'm your father, I know you better than anyone, especially since your mother died. We've always got on well together, haven't we?'

Betty wasn't sure why he was asking this question; he knew that they had. She loved him beyond measure. 'Of course we have,' she murmured quietly.

'So I know I can talk frankly to you,' Harold when on. 'And I think... I'm worried... that you and this Gianni chap are getting a bit too friendly. Spending rather too much time together.'

Betty couldn't speak. Dread and embarrassment flooded through her, paralysing her limbs and rendering her mute. She thought of the words Gianni had so recently spoken, his words of love, and of her response, so traitorous to Samuel but no less true for that. Eventually she managed to get up, go to the sink, pour herself the glass of water she'd originally come in here for, drink it. She still hadn't said anything.

She went back to the table, sat back down, the glass on the table in front of her, beads of water sliding slowly down its sides.

'Dad, he's a friend,' Betty protested, though she knew in her heart that he was more than that by now. Much more than that. 'I haven't done anything I shouldn't, I promise you. I just enjoy his company – and you're proud of the way I can speak Italian now!'

Despite himself, Harold chuckled, his familiar guttural laugh that Betty knew so well. 'I am, my love. You're a quick learner, you've shown that over and over again. The Morse you learnt twice as fast as Jane, and then your distinction at School Certificate, not to mention your job at the telephone exchange. You're a clever lass, no doubt about it.' He paused and took a deep breath before resuming, suddenly stern again.

'Clever enough to know.'

Betty was feeling a little cross now, her stubborn side, which didn't often come out, rising up inside her. 'Know what?' she demanded, unable to keep the defensiveness out of her voice.

'Know that whatever's going on between you and the Sicilian lad has to stop. It can't go any further.' Harold leant back in his chair and ran his hand across his eyes as if that would enable him to see – and speak – more clearly. 'You're a young lass and it's only natural that you want to go out and have a good time and there's nothing wrong with that, nothing wrong with having male admirers. There were a few girls I pursued before I met your mother, I can tell you. I know I'm old now but I do remember what it's like to be young. I don't want to stop you having fun, blimey, we all could do with a bit of that with this bleeding war going on and on.'

Betty sat up straighter in her chair, surprised at her father's choice of language. He wasn't usually so coarsely spoken.

'But you have to remember your commitments, love. Not to me, but to Samuel.'

At those words, tears sprang to Betty's eyes and a huge, overwhelming feeling of guilt surged through her.

She stared down at the table, with all its familiar dents and pockmarks. It must be at least seventy years old, this table.

'Yes,' she whispered, barely audible. 'Yes, you're right. And I do remember, I promise you I do.'

'Well that's all right, then,' concluded Harold. 'I'm glad to hear it. And thank you for being so honest.'

He got up then and, after planting a goodnight kiss on the top of Betty's head, made his way slowly up the steep cottage stairs to his bedroom. Eventually Betty, too, left the kitchen. She paused in the hallway and removed her call-up papers from behind the clock. In her bedroom, she stood at the window, gazing out at the moon-drenched landscape, the shadowy outlines of trees and hills beyond the cottage garden. The high of the dance had slammed brutally into the low of her father's warning, leaving her feeling utterly overwhelmed.

She took the War Office letter from the envelope and studied it, the print just visible in the half-light. If she stayed in Yorkshire, close to Gianni, she would fall further and further under his spell. Joining the forces would mean being sent far away, where she'd be able to forget about him and not bring any more worry and anxiety to her father.

It was obvious what Betty had to do. She had to leave.

# CHAPTER ELEVEN

Sadie followed the elderly lady into the dark hallway. It was lined with fuzzy-looking pictures that, in the same way as their owner, seemed so old that their colours had faded. As Sadie walked past them, dandelion-clouds of dust motes filled the air. She felt a bit like the fly that went unwittingly into the spider's parlour, or perhaps Pip entering Miss Havisham's house for the first time. There was something ghostly about the woman and her house, as if both were at death's door.

'Are you Mrs Jackson?' she asked, tentatively. She didn't know what she would do if the answer was no. She was in here now.

The woman did not reply until they arrived in what must once have been a grand drawing room but was now almost empty, just an antique sofa and an armchair in front of a huge, empty fireplace. Turning with a dramatic flourish, the old lady responded, intoning her words as if making a speech.

'I am Olivia de Montfort-Sanderson!' As she spoke, her humped back seemed to straighten and her diminutive height to increase by a few inches. 'I was a famous actress in my day,' she went on. 'I can show you photographs.'

Sadie suppressed a giggle. This was all quite surreal. But if this wasn't Jean, it was also wasting her time.

'I'd love to see your photographs,' Sadie said. 'But I'm looking for someone who used to live at this address. Mrs Jean Jackson. Do you know her? It's quite urgent that I find her.'

Olivia paused for a moment, as if searching her decades of memory.

'Yes!' she expostulated, finally. 'Yes! I know Jean, of course I do. Let me make us some tea and I'll tell you all about her.'

'No, honestly, there's no need,' Sadie protested. Her heart was banging uncomfortably in her chest. Olivia knew Jean! This was promising. But she wanted facts and information, not tea. 'I don't want you to go to any trouble. If you could just tell me what you know about Jean Jackson and where I might find her.'

But Olivia was already on her way to the door, breathing a little quickly and leaning on her stick. 'My dear,' she intoned when she'd caught her breath. 'There is *always* a need for tea. Conversation is not possible without something to grease the wheels.'

'Well, let me at least help you,' insisted Sadie. She couldn't imagine how Olivia was going to manage a tray of tea things, or even two cups, with her stick to contend with. And if she went with her host to the kitchen, she could perhaps prompt her about Mrs Jackson while they waited for the kettle to boil.

'No, I won't hear of it,' replied Olivia firmly, putting paid to Sadie's plan. 'You are my guest. And an honoured one at that.'

Despite her impatience and racing heart, Sadie almost giggled again at Olivia's old-fashioned turn of phrase. 'All right then,' she said, realising when she was defeated. She had waited so long already, twenty-seven years to be precise. Five more minutes wouldn't make any difference. She sank down onto the sofa, and the motion was accompanied by a hail of dust rising into the still air. Sadie sneezed, three times.

'Bless you,' Olivia called back to her, her voice echoing down the corridor.

Sadie sat and waited, gazing around her. The mantelpiece was covered in cardboard invitations propped against the wall and she longed to get up and examine them, but that would be far too nosy. Instead, she studied the many paintings that hung from the picture rail: portraits, countryside scenes, animals. They might be grand masters for all Sadie knew – her knowledge of fine art was non-existent. She wondered about Olivia's past, her life as an actress. Was she all alone now, her family and her contemporaries dead? It seemed to be so.

After what seemed like an age, in which Sadie kept thinking she should go and find Olivia and insist again on helping her, a faint rattling sound reverberated from the end of the hallway. It got gradually louder until eventually it was outside the room. Sadie watched anxiously as Olivia entered, pushing a trolley with one hand while the other tapped along with her stick. The teacups shook violently and a spurt of tea erupted from the spout of the teapot as the trolley bumped over the threshold into the room.

Unable to stop herself, Sadie leapt up and grasped the trolley's handle on the opposite side to Olivia, helping her to steer it to a resting place near to the armchair but almost knocking Olivia off her feet as she did so.

'Sorry,' Sadie said with a gulp, as Olivia got her balance back. 'Sorry, always been a bit clumsy, me. Are you all right?'

Olivia cast her an imperious glance. 'Never better,' she responded, obviously refusing to acknowledge any physical impediment. 'Now, sit down. I must tell you about the time when I was playing Ophelia opposite Olivier himself... I had the audience in my hands.'

Sadie gulped, nonplussed.

'Um, that sounds wonderful,' Sadie uttered, wondering how to tactfully steer the conversation onto the purpose of her visit. She paused for a moment while Olivia, with a shaky hand, poured the tea and passed her a cup. It was weak and, when Sadie lifted it to her lips, it smelt dusty. She took a polite sip and then discreetly looked around for somewhere to put the cup down. There was nowhere, so she resorted to balancing it on her lap while she restarted her enquiry. 'But before we discuss *Hamlet*, I have a question to ask you, actually. About Jean Jackson. You said you knew her?'

'Probably,' answered Olivia, without having seemed to give it a moment's additional thought. 'I knew everyone, darling. Absolutely everyone. When I stood in as understudy for Peggy Ashcroft playing Desdemona at the Savoy Theatre in 1930, I got a standing ovation. *Kill me tomorrow; let me live tonight.*' In her passion, Olivia stood up and flung her arms open wide as if she were on stage, not in a faded time-warp drawing room far from theatreland.

*'But half an hour! But while I say one prayer!'*

At the conclusion of her little speech, a look of indefinable sadness descended on Olivia's crumpled features, which must once, Sadie was sure, have been envied and admired. As she sat back down, it was as if all her thespian past fell off her, buried beneath the weight of advancing years and obsolescence. There were other actresses, now. Olivia's day was done.

'Um, I don't think Jean Jackson was an actress,' Sadie ventured, tentatively, wary of mentioning the word and setting Olivia off again, and also worried about the effect this trip down memory lane was having on the old lady. 'She – well, I don't know whether she had a job at all. I just know she lived at 14 Mornington Crescent in 1945. Did you live here then?'

'In the war I was entertaining the troops,' replied Olivia. 'We went everywhere. Cairo. Alexandria. Casablanca. Now *there's* a city. So romantic. Ahh, I could tell you a thing or two about Casablanca.'

*Please don't,* begged Sadie silently. This was getting her nowhere.

'Look, I'm sorry to rush you,' she said. 'But I don't have long. As I said before, I need to find Jean Jackson urgently. Can you tell me anything you know about her?'

Olivia thought for a moment, her forehead more crumpled than usual.

'Jean Jackson. Jean Jackson?' She shook her head, apparently confounded. 'No, I don't know any Jean Jackson. A very ordinary sort of name. Not my sort of person at all.'

Sadie suppressed a sigh. Olivia was in her own world, lost in the past. Sadie suspected that she had not really taken much notice of what she had asked her on the doorstep and had only invited her in because she was so lonely. Sadie was someone to talk to. It made her feel desperately sad. But she couldn't solve Olivia's loneliness, or give her back her youth and her fame.

'Thank you so much for the tea,' she said, politely, 'and our little chat. I've really enjoyed talking to you. But I have to go now. My, er, my boyfriend is waiting for me.' She crossed her fingers behind her back at the white lie. 'I'll see myself out.'

With a brisk shake of Olivia's hand, Sadie sped off along the dingy hallway. She felt bad for disturbing the old lady. But most of all she felt annoyed that she'd spent all that time with Olivia and got nowhere. She only had the weekends to conduct this search; she couldn't take any more time off work. If she wasn't successful today or tomorrow, she'd have to wait another week, which seemed an intolerable delay. But what if Jean Jackson didn't live there any more? That seemed increasingly likely; surely, however batty Olivia was, she would know her neighbours' names?

Sadie stumbled through the doorway, out onto the street and along the uneven pavement. Once outside, she took huge lungfuls of air as if cleansing herself of the weight of the past that pervaded Olivia's home. As she did so, a dreadful thought descended.

Perhaps having Jean's address wasn't going to be the answer after all. Perhaps it wasn't going to help her quest one little bit.

# CHAPTER TWELVE

IN THE ATS, SEPTEMBER 1943

The days after the summer dance at Eden Camp were a whirlwind of activity, as Betty got ready for a complete change in her life. She attended her medical, received her posting and handed in her notice at the telephone exchange. She packed a small bag of personal items and polished her shoes until they shone.

And then she went to see Gianni.

They met outside the camp gates and went for a walk through the fields. It was a glorious late summer day and the wheat, tall and golden, the last to be harvested, swayed to and fro in the light breeze like the sea ebbing and flowing with the tide. A skylark rose from the ground and up to the blue arch of the sky, singing its glorious melody.

'I'm going away,' Betty blurted out. 'To join the ATS. I have to, now I'm twenty. I'm sorry.' All of the rest of the reasons could be left out. She couldn't have explained them anyway.

Gianni halted, abruptly. He gazed at Betty and then

suddenly tore his eyes away and focused on the sky above, where now a kestrel soared, looking for prey.

'You want to go?' he asked.

Betty shook her head, helplessly. 'I don't know. I do and I don't.' She hugged her arms across her body and then continued, resolutely this time, 'But it's not a matter of wanting or not wanting. I don't have a choice.' It was easier to see it this way. Clearer.

Gianni ran his hand across his forehead and then turned to look at her again. 'I understand.' He took a step towards her and Betty felt the warmth of him, his life and vitality. 'Although maybe, at the same time, I don't,' he murmured into her hair. Time stood still as Betty's heart broke in two.

Lifting his head away from hers and looking straight into her eyes, Gianni spoke. 'I will miss you,' he said, simply.

'Me too.' She couldn't keep the misery out of her voice, however much she tried.

'Oh Betty.' All attempts at restraint, at distance, fell away as Gianni threw his arms round her and drew her close. 'It will be all right.'

She lifted her face up to his and suddenly he was kissing her and it was the most passionate, most meaningful kiss Betty had ever had. She wished it could last forever.

When the kiss eventually ended, they stayed entwined for long moments.

'I should go,' Gianni said in the end. 'I must get back to the camp and you should go home to your father. He deserves all your time until you leave.'

Betty's heart flipped over. Gianni was always so considerate, so thoughtful. To put Harold before himself – that was the sign of a true gentleman. A gentleman who was surely good enough for her, but who she could never have. It all felt so unfair, but so immutable. There was nothing Betty could do to change what had happened in the past, the ties that bound her and Samuel together. Clutching Gianni's hand, she raised it to her lips and kissed it, and then held it between both of hers. Looking up at his face, she saw that his anguish mirrored hers.

But there was nothing to be done.

Slowly, dragging their feet, they made their way back to the gate. There, they stopped again, and kissed. The excitement, the thrill, of being so close to the man she loved coursed through Betty. And then, when the kisses ended, utter despair consumed her. A band of pain tightened round her chest and she thought the sorrow of parting might suffocate her.

'Goodbye, Betty,' whispered Gianni, softly. Deep creases furrowed his handsome forehead and moisture glistened in the corners of his eyes. Betty's heart ached to see his anguish, which so closely mirrored her own. 'I love you. But you know that anyway.'

'I love you too,' she replied simply, her heart shattering into smithereens with every word.

For a few more moments they clung together until, unable to bear the pain any longer, Betty pulled away and turned towards home. 'Goodbye, Gianni,' she murmured, and then she began walking hurriedly away, blinded by tears, stumbling and tripping over stones and tree roots, attempting to stifle her sobs.

'We'll meet again,' she heard Gianni call after her. 'Don't know where, don't know when. But we will.'

Tears streaming down her cheeks, Betty lumbered on, chest heaving, following the well-worn path that led back to Malton, away from Gianni. She knew more certainly than ever that she had never felt for Samuel any of the feelings she had for Gianni. Samuel had been a friend, a companion, a familiar and comforting face – but he had never been her passion. She had never felt, with Samuel, that she could climb any mountain and ford any stream. Samuel had never made her feel that nothing was impossible, that love opened every door in the world and all they had to do was walk across the thresholds together and all would be well.

Samuel had not made her feel this way. Gianni had. But she had to leave him. There was no other way.

If she had been in any doubt about this, when she arrived back at the cottage she found another letter from Julie, Samuel's mother, waiting for her. Julie had gone to live with her sister in the Peak District after Samuel had left, so Betty had not seen her for a long while. In the absence of news from her son, apart from that one sparse letter, Julie wrote often to Betty, telling her how much Samuel loved her and how Julie was sure, knew without a shadow of doubt, he was keeping going for her. How wonderful their wedding would be, when it was all over.

Betty could not let them all down: Julie, her father, her dead mother, her sister, Samuel himself. It was inconceivable. Carefully folding the letter back into the envelope, she bit back tears and went into the kitchen to make the evening meal.

BETTY's initial training took her to Scotland, to the ATS Signal School. She travelled by train all the way to Inverness and then by army transport to Strathpeffer. She and the other recruits were accommodated in a huge hotel called the Ben Wyvis. They spent their days learning Morse code, easy for Betty as she was already proficient in it, able to read and transmit at a speed far in excess of the minimum expectation of fifteen words a minute. They also had lessons on the basics of electricity, magnetism and map-reading, and rehearsed drills on what to do in the event of air raids.

The hardest thing was learning to work the live radio. The expert army signallers running the course taught the new ATS women how to tune out all the unwanted signals and atmospheric noise and just concentrate on the one particular signal they were following. Picking out the Morse of an individual sender amidst all the other code that was coming across the airways was extremely taxing and Betty ended every day exhausted.

Ten days after she'd arrived in Scotland, she was called to a meeting with Lieutenant Osborne, the commanding officer at the Signal School. Quaking with fear, sure that she was going to be told that she hadn't made the grade, Betty traipsed along the long corridor to his office, dragging her feet in her reluctance to hear her fate. The best she could hope for was that she'd be offered another position, a cook maybe, or even a dispatch rider – women were doing that job now, she'd heard. As long as she wasn't told her services were no longer required and sent back home with her tail between her legs, to face all the complications that awaited her there, she'd make every effort to bear whatever she was told with fortitude.

Lieutenant Osborne answered her knock at the door with a barked instruction to enter. Inside, Betty found him sitting behind his desk, reading glasses balanced on his forehead, piles of paperwork all around him.

'Corporal Bean,' he said. 'Welcome. Please take a seat.'

Betty wanted to say there was no need for her to sit down, just tell her the bad news and get it over with. But of course she didn't. Nervously, she sat, perching on the edge of the chair. No point in getting comfortable; she wasn't going to be there long.

'I've had some reports of how you're getting on,' Lieutenant Osborne began.

Betty braced herself for what was coming next.

'And I've heard that you are streets ahead of all the other recruits,' he went on. Betty listened, open-mouthed with astonishment. This was not what she had been expecting at all. 'So you are to be taught not just to listen to enemy transmissions, as you have been doing so far, but also how to encrypt and decode messages sent between British forces.'

Betty was speechless, struggling to work out exactly what this meant.

'You will need to sit an IQ test, which, from what I've been told, you will pass with flying colours.' Lieutenant Osborne paused and fixed Betty with a piercing stare. 'And you will, of course, have to sign the Official Secrets Act and promise not to talk to anyone about this aspect of your work.'

Trembling, Betty tried to form a coherent response. 'That's, I um, it would be a privilege,' she eventually managed to utter. She got up to leave, assuming the interview was over.

'One more thing,' said the lieutenant as he distractedly shuffled through some papers. 'You'll be stationed abroad. Don't know where yet. But I'm assuming that won't be a problem.' He looked up at Betty and smiled at her briefly, before his face resumed its normal austere expression. 'Not married, are you? No children? None on the way I hope?'

Betty blushed. Confound this childish habit. 'N-n-no,' she stammered. 'Neither. Not at all. Absolutely not.'

'Good.'

The tone of the lieutenant's voice indicated that he had called their meeting to an end.

From then on, Betty and one or two other specially selected ATS women had lessons from Lieutenant Osborne in low-grade cipher, which involved using grids to form messages, a little like a crossword puzzle, and book cipher, a system using numbers for words. This latter code was changed and reissued every month so that it remained secure. Though Betty had never thought she was particularly good at maths or puzzles, she didn't find the tasks they were set too taxing. The most difficult part was the concentration required; it was essential to be absolutely focused at all times.

Also difficult, if not impossible, was eradicating Gianni from her mind. She realised that the only option for them both was to cut all contact. So one evening she sat alone in her room

and wrote him a letter. It was the most difficult thing she had
ever had to pen.

*Dear Gianni,*

*I hope you are well and the weather is not too cold yet. It is
quite chilly up here in Scotland, and the hotel where we are
staying is very draughty, but I have plenty of warm clothes and
Jane knitted me a scarf, which I am wearing as I write.*

    *I hope you understand how hard this is for me to say. But I
think it will be better if we don't keep in touch. It's not what I
want, but what I think is necessary. Thank you for teaching
me Italian, making me laugh and being such a good...*

Here Betty's pen faltered, her trembling hands making it
impossible to continue. She couldn't say 'friend', when Gianni
was so much more than that. But if she wrote 'sweetheart' or
'lover' or any such word on the page, it would be the ultimate
betrayal of Samuel.

In the end, she wrote, *companion.*

She ended the letter by hoping that he would one day soon
be able to return to his family in Sicily. As she wrote her signature, a tear dropped onto the paper and smudged the ink into an
indecipherable blob. She had tried so desperately hard not to
cry, but it was not possible.

Reading the letter back to herself, she hated how it
sounded; so stilted, so formal and unlike Betty's true self. But it
was impossible to say what she really felt. That she was hopelessly in love with Gianni, that she pined for him, that she
missed him every moment of every day. And that she had
vowed to herself to put him out of her mind and forget all
about him.

After all, there was no point holding on to hope where there
was none.

# CHAPTER THIRTEEN

AT SEA, OCTOBER 1943

Two months after joining the ATS, Betty travelled to Glasgow to board HMS *Arcadia*. As she stood on deck, gazing out to sea, the ship's horn sounded its imminent departure. Slowly, the vessel began to move down the Clyde and towards the open ocean. They were part of a flotilla of eleven boats with four accompanying frigates. Besides Betty and her fellow ATS recruits, none of whom she had met before, hundreds of male troops were aboard. A thrill of nervous anticipation rippled through Betty as the ship gathered speed. Whatever lay in wait, she could certainly no longer say that her life was boring and mundane. She had wanted adventure, and now here it was.

The ATS senior commander on board, Captain Treacy, called the women in her charge together to address them all.

'You are probably wondering where you are going,' she said, her voice battling against the strong wind. As one, the assembled women pricked up their ears and leant in, desperate to hear what she had to say. They had been given khaki drill uniform, which indicated somewhere hot. South Africa? Egypt? Palestine?

'Your destination,' the officer went on, keeping all her listeners agog as she paused dramatically, 'is Naples.'

A buzz of excited chatter rippled through the ranks of women, rising in volume by the second. None of them could believe it, least of all Betty. Italy! That place of dreams and longings. All those months learning Italian and now she was actually going there. But at the same time as giddy apprehension fizzed in her stomach, her insides felt hollowed out with longing. How could Italy do anything but make her think of Gianni – the person she had sworn to forget?

The women were dismissed and some went below to settle into their cabins, but Betty stayed above deck. She needed time to think and clear her head. She felt in her pocket and her hand closed around an object, smooth and hard. She pulled it out and studied it: a small heart, carved from creamy lime wood, with a hole drilled through the top, through which looped a string attached to a key, also hand-sculpted in intricate detail. Turning the heart over, she read for the millionth time the inscription on the back:

*From GU with love x*
*Eden Camp 1943*

After she'd told him not to write, Gianni had sent her one more letter of farewell, and included within it the handmade keepsake. For a moment Betty contemplated throwing the treasured memento, with all its memories and layers of emotion, overboard, losing it forever in the churning, turbulent waters of the Clyde.

But she couldn't do that.

Instead, she slipped it back into her pocket, tucked safely

away where it would be her secret, her one reminder of a lost but beautiful love.

The *Arcadia* drew level with a troop-carrying ship, packed with men returning on leave.

'Hello, sailor,' called out a loud, raucous voice next to her.

'They're soldiers, darling!' exclaimed another, in a much posher, more refined accent. At which comment all those in the vicinity burst out laughing.

Despite her troubled mind, Betty couldn't help but smile too. She turned to see who had spoken. Along the rails beside her stood three women, all in the same khaki-coloured uniform as Betty herself sported. One was tall and platinum-blond, with an air of breeding about her. Definitely where the posh voice had come from. On the far side of her was a slightly older-looking woman, maybe in her late twenties, with glossy chestnut-brown hair, a wide mouth and heavy eyebrows. She was good-looking in a brassy kind of way and Betty had the distinct impression that she was the kind of woman her father would refer to as 'no better than she should be'. Nevertheless, Betty liked the look of her. She seemed friendly and open, and, as Betty was thinking this, the other woman flashed her a huge, warm, broad smile.

There was one other person standing alongside them, someone small with mousy brown hair, wearing a uniform several sizes too big for her, which gave the impression of a child dressed up in her mother's clothes. She seemed as nervous and unsure as Betty herself. Always a champion of the underdog, this immediately made Betty want to get to know her. She looked like she needed a friend.

'Have fun, work hard, be kind.' That was the advice her mother had always given her and Betty would never forget it.

'Hello,' she said, tentatively, to the three women in general. The reality was that they all needed pals. They were heading for a dangerous country; much of Italy was still under the control of Axis forces. Betty shuddered at the thought of the potential peril that lay ahead.

'I'm Betty,' she went on. 'Betty Bean, from Malton, North Yorkshire. I used to be a telephonist but I'm a cipher now.' She beamed at the three women beside her, trying to make her smile so wide she could draw the trio into it.

'Bravo!' said the glossy-haired one, in a fake public-schoolboy accent. 'Well done you. I'm on supplies, myself. Couldn't hack the Morse code. It was just like when they tried to teach us Latin at school, after they decided working-class children should have the chance to learn like the posh people. Hah!' The exclamation exploded out of her. 'Fat lot of good that did. Never understood a word of it. But we're all here now, aren't we, heading for bleeding Italy!'

Betty burst out laughing. 'I know,' she agreed. 'Exciting, isn't it? What's your name?'

'I'm Deborah Castle,' replied the woman. 'Never Debs or Debbie, if you please. I'm the full Deborah, every time.'

Betty was still chuckling. She was immediately drawn to this cheerful, plain-spoken colleague and had warmed to her already.

'And you are?' She addressed her next comment directly to the timid woman, wanting to make her feel welcome. She seemed so ill at ease, as awkward as her poorly fitting clothes.

'I'm Susan Davies.' Her voice was so tiny that Betty could hardly hear her above the noise of the wind and the rumbling engines. 'I was no good at learning Morse either. I'll be on teleprinters.'

'Nice to meet you Susan, and Deborah.' Betty held out her hand and shook both of theirs.

'And I'm Lily French,' said the blonde, in her lazy, upper-class drawl. 'French by name and through-and-through English by nature. I'm a cipher, too, though goodness knows how I'm going to get on with it, out in the real world. I've never worked a day in my life.'

There was a small, stunned silence. Betty wasn't sure if she was joking. She stared at Lily. Everything about her exuded entitlement and wealth: her height, her hair, her perfect teeth and svelte figure. Even the dull regulation khaki looked amazing on Lily; she could be modelling it for the magazines. Betty could well imagine that she had led a life of easy luxury; that was obvious in her every pore.

'Well,' Betty said, encouragingly, 'we're all going to be learning on the job, so to speak, so we'll have to work it out together, support each other. We'll be fine.' She spoke with a confidence she didn't feel. But all she could do was pretend to be self-assured until she actually became so.

'Shall we get in the queue for the cabins?' Lily suggested. 'I'm dying to see where we'll be cooped up for the next week or so. As in, I'm literally dying. I get the feeling I won't have my own bedroom with bathroom and dressing room.'

Betty smiled as she saw the looks of amazement on Deborah and Susan's faces. She could tell that Lily was being a little irreverent, exaggerating for effect. Betty guessed it was her way of dealing with the uncertainty. She was probably as nervous as the rest of them, just putting on an act to deflect it.

'Let's do that,' she suggested. 'We four should stick together, don't you think? I'd like that.'

'Topping,' replied Lily, as Deborah also nodded vigorously in agreement. Susan said nothing but followed the three of them as they made their way to where an officer was organising the sleeping quarters. Luckily, there was no problem getting a four-berth cabin between them and, as soon as this was sorted, they went to collect their kitbags – not nearly such an easy task.

The bags, in the shape of huge sausages, were heavy and utterly unwieldy to carry, and the women were also wearing their army greatcoats and carrying gas masks and steel helmets. None of this made for easy lifting.

'Lordy, Lordy!' exclaimed Deborah as she attempted to pick hers up.

'Let me help,' interjected Betty. 'I think it's easiest on the shoulders...' Her words tailed off as she used all her breath to heft the bag's weight upwards. Somehow she managed to load Deborah up, but then she had her own bag to contend with.

'This is when I wish I were a man,' panted Betty, 'then it would be easy.'

'All you need is to be a foot taller, have a short back and sides, facial hair and certain other equipment,' quipped Deborah, grinning lewdly beneath her ungainly burden, 'and you'll be there.'

Betty laughed and then stopped abruptly, gasping for air. 'Don't make me laugh when I can hardly breathe as it is,' she puffed. 'Come on, let's go, before we drop down dead like poor overloaded mules.'

She looked around her to see where the other two were. Susan had not bothered to pick her bag up, but instead was dragging it along behind her like a reluctant and overweight dog. Lily, on the other hand, was standing looking helplessly about her. Within moments, a dashing soldier had come rushing over.

'Need any help, darling?' he asked her, with a cheeky grin.

With an imperious wave of her hand, she indicated towards her sausage bag. 'Cabin 454, level 2,' she instructed, 'if you would be so kind.'

Marvelling at Lily's ability to effortlessly command subservience, Betty and Deborah followed on, Susan trailing behind.

'So much for not fraternising with the men,' muttered Deborah under her breath as she, Betty and Susan laboured with their burdens.

Betty suppressed a giggle.

After a torturous ten minutes or so they finally got to their cabin, where, once they'd got the door unlocked, they sank down onto the bottom bunks. Or at least, Betty, Deborah and Susan did. Lily regally instructed her hapless helper where she would like him to deposit the bag. Not that there were many options. The cabin was tiny, with barely room to move between the bunks. There was a small cupboard each for personal items but most of their stuff would need to be stowed beneath the beds. Thank goodness they wouldn't be on the ship for too long, thought Betty. They'd certainly get cabin fever if they were cooped up in here for weeks on end.

When they had the room to themselves, they started to unpack. Each recruit received a 'housewife' – a set of sewing materials – and a shoe-shine kit, in addition to the standard issue of clothing: two skirts, two jackets, three shirts, four collars, three pairs of stockings, two pairs of pyjamas and two pairs of brown lace-up shoes.

And then there was the underwear.

Lily began to pull hers out of her kitbag, laying it out elaborately on the bottom bunk.

'So, ladies,' she declared, in the manner of an auctioneer assessing a prized collection of priceless antiques. 'I have for your delectation and delight today a number of items the like of which you have never seen before.'

Deborah chuckled, a guttural, throaty sound that was thoroughly infectious. 'You're not wrong there,' she interjected, with an exaggerated wink.

'Madams, take note of these three pink bras, carefully manufactured to cover the modesty of any young ATS or Wren. We have in addition three pink suspender belts, brass clips, no lace.'

'No lace!' cried Deborah, her voice full of faux indignation. 'But I can't wear no plain suspender belt. I demand lace.'

Deborah, Susan and Betty fell about laughing.

'If I could please continue,' commanded Lily.

The three members of her audience fell silent, apart from intermittent sniggers. 'Next exhibit, three white vests and three pairs of silk knickers.'

'What, real silk!' Susan's eyes were wide with astonishment.

'No, you daft banana,' replied Deborah, digging her in the sides with an elbow. 'It's artificial, innit?'

Lily frowned. 'Young lady, artificial silk is all the rage on the Continent.'

'Right,' responded Deborah, sarkily. 'And I'm the Queen of Sheba.'

Betty started laughing again, uncontrollably this time. She just couldn't stop. Perhaps it was the release, after all the tension and heartache of the last few years, losing her mother, saying farewell to Samuel, leaving her dad, parting from Gianni... It all came out in an unstoppable wave of hysteria.

'And finally,' Lily exclaimed, picking up a huge garment made of voluminous quantities of white cotton, 'these wonderful, extraordinary, superlative BLOOMERS!' She flicked the item so that it snapped in the air, and then held it against herself. Even with her height, they reached down to her knees, and were quite the most unflattering piece of underwear ever invented. The women had all been given strict instructions, at training camp, that bloomers must be worn over knickers, every day.

Betty, still doubled over with hilarity, was joined, nervously and timidly, by Susan, who, once she had started, was also soon holding her sides. Following Lily's lead, Deborah grabbed a pair of the offending bloomers and held them in the air. Lily began to sing the bawdy music hall song 'Don't Put Your Daughter on the Stage, Mrs Worthington', while both she and Deborah played out a vaudeville act, insofar as the cramped space permitted, complete with facial expressions and provocative gestures. When she got to the lines, 'But don't you think her bust is too/developed for her age?' Lily thrust her bosom forward and pulled her mouth into a suggestive pout.

By this point Betty was so helpless with laughter that she could hardly breathe. Tears streamed down her face and for the first time in ages they were happy ones, not sad.

When the little gang had finally regained the power of speech, Lily sat upright again, her shoulders hunched and head bowed due to the limited headroom offered by the bunk above.

'Well honestly, girls,' she declared, still chuckling intermittently, 'none of our parents needed to worry about our virtue when we have these to preserve it!' She whirled the bloomers around on the end of her index finger in a final flourish. 'Chastity protectors. What better name can we give them?'

That set them all off into gales of mirth again. They were still giggling when a bell sounded, calling them to lunch. As they set off through the narrow corridors and up the stairs to the canteen, Betty's spirits were higher than they had been for days.

She was embarking on a great new adventure, a future she could never have imagined, and she had three new friends to share it with. Life had never been so uncertain – or so exhilarating. As well as the fun and camaraderie, she had a crucial role to fulfil as a cipher operator, releasing men to go into the field of battle to shore up the frontline. She had to put this commitment first, above all others. Scary as it was, men's lives might depend on it. The future of the war was in all of their hands. This was enormous; bigger than any love, more important than any personal dilemmas or problems.

Betty was nothing if not a grafter. Whatever she did, she did to the best of her ability. If others worked hard, Betty worked harder. She would not let her country down at the hour of its greatest need.

Passing over the deck on her way back from the dining room, Betty clenched her fists and bit her lip. A fierce wind blew now, as they made their way down the coast and across the Irish Sea. She was on her way, no time for looking back, for regrets. She must live in the moment, make the most of every opportunity. The past must not hold her back; she would not let it.

She was a cipher operator now and, as such, had one goal: to do her job and help to win this war.

# CHAPTER FOURTEEN

After the disappointment of her first attempt to find Jean Jackson, Sadie took refuge in a café, where she bought a sandwich and a cup of coffee. By the time she left its warm and steamy interior, the day had settled into a sulky dullness, as if spring was a concept it refused to entertain. Back in Mornington Crescent, the only colour came from a window box full of jaunty primroses in gaudy shades of yellow, purple and orange, which seemed to smile at Sadie as she passed.

As she retraced her steps to number 14, a black cat emerged from the basement steps and slunk across the pavement in front of her. Sadie bent to stroke its glossy head and it regarded her incuriously, narrowing its eyes, before jumping up onto a wall, out of her reach.

'Have a nice day, cat,' Sadie murmured, and then started as she looked up and came face to face with a man almost blocking her path. He must have come out of a side entrance while her attention was on the cat. He was staring at her as if she was deranged, which, given that he clearly thought she'd been talking to herself, was perfectly understandable, if a little regrettable.

Sadie hoped and assumed he'd walk straight past her, but instead he smiled kindly. 'Are you all right?' he asked, speaking very slowly, as if to someone who seemed to have lost their mind.

'Oh, yes, fine,' Sadie assured him. 'Just the cat – you know – I always talk to cats!' She laughed but it came out too loud and too shrill and must have made her seem even more unhinged. Totally embarrassed by now, she stepped around the man, acting as if she had every right to be there and knew exactly what she was doing and where she was going, even though she really didn't have a clue.

At number 14, this time she pressed the bottom bell. After a few moments, she heard footsteps ascending from the lower ground floor, and soon a head appeared. It belonged to a woman, who looked to be in her forties. *Fingers crossed*, thought Sadie as, behind her back, she did just that.

'You all right?' the woman asked, a touch of hostility in her voice. 'I don't know you, do I?'

'No,' answered Sadie. 'I'm – er, I'm looking for someone called Jean Jackson. She used to live here.'

'Jean Jackson?' the woman responded. 'Mrs Jackson who used to live upstairs?'

Sadie's heart turned over. Could she really have found someone who could provide her with the information she craved?

'Why do you want her?' asked the woman.

For some reason, Sadie hadn't thought through her answer to this one at all. 'Um, er, it's a bit complicated,' she stuttered. 'I mean, it's hard to explain.' She saw the expression on the woman's face change. 'It's nothing bad,' she said, hastily.

'Right.' The woman eyed her suspiciously up and down.

'It's just that I believe she may be able to help me with

something. Give me some information I need.' Sadie was getting desperate now. How much to give away, on a doorstep, to a total stranger?

'I'm Mrs Orchard,' the woman said. 'And what's your name?' she asked, continuing to regard Sadie with a certain scepticism.

'It's Sadie,' said Sadie.

'And this information you want is...?' Mrs Orchard left the question hanging, enormous in the sunshine.

'I recently found out that I'm adopted,' Sadie blurted out. 'And I think Mrs Jackson might be able to help me find my parents. Or my mother at least.'

Mrs Orchard's gaze was unwavering. 'And why do you think that?' she questioned.

'Well, I, it's...' Sadie floundered. 'My mother gave me to Mrs Jackson to look after. That's all I know.' She finished, holding up her arms in a helpless gesture.

Suddenly, Mrs Orchard smiled and her whole demeanour changed. 'Right,' she said, after a short pause. 'I know you're genuine, because I remember that night you were left – or at least, I remember Jean and my mum talking about it. She was right shocked by what happened. Between you and me, it turned into—' Mrs Orchard stopped abruptly, as if conscious of what she was about to reveal, and ran her hands down the floral apron she was wearing. Her confidence of earlier had gone and she appeared flustered. Sadie watched and waited, spellbound, afraid that if she made the slightest sound the woman might clam up.

'I wasn't Mrs Orchard then,' she continued, once she'd regained her composure. 'I was only ten or eleven. Diamond was my maiden name – Bridget Diamond. I knew Jean because she was a good friend of my mum's, like I said. They used to go to the laundrette together, have a right laugh there. I remember the story – Jean told my mum the very next day. She couldn't understand why the mother never came back.' Bridget paused again, as if suddenly struck by the weight of the past. Sadie almost intervened to say that she, too, could not understand this, but again she didn't want to interrupt Bridget's flow.

'Jean was rehoused by the council, as was my mum. She went to Somers Town and I took over this place. I don't like those new flats. Apart from anything else, I'm terrified of heights—'

'Do you know where she went?' Sadie asked, cutting across Bridget's explanation, trying to keep the desperate urgency out of her voice. 'Where she lives now?'

Bridget frowned, her forehead scrunching up in concentration. 'It's one of the new blocks,' she said, gesturing vaguely in the direction of the three tall towers that Sadie had seen from the bus.

'Which one?' asked Sadie, hurriedly, as if Jean might escape if she didn't get to her soon. 'Which block and what flat number?'

To her dismay, Bridget shook her head. 'That I couldn't tell you,' she said.

Sadie wanted to cry. She'd assumed there was no way Jean Jackson lived in one of those blocks, had hoped this must be the case, because to ask at every flat in each of the three towers would take her months.

'But my mum will know,' Bridget added, cheerily.

Sadie almost collapsed with relief. 'Can you ask her?' she responded, urgently. 'Can you ask her now?'

Bridget smiled. 'She's supposed to be resting after the flu,' she said. 'But I can see how important this is to you, and it would be to me, if I were in your situation. I'm going round to visit her this afternoon. I'll find out and I'll let you know. Just give me your number.'

Sadie wanted to scream. Her and Kim's decision not to have a telephone installed in their flat suddenly seemed utterly stupid. She'd have to wait until Monday at work to find out Jean Jackson's address.

'Can I come back later today?' she asked, frantic with pent-up anxiety and stress. 'When you've got back from your visit? Or I could meet you at your mum's place. I just need to know as soon as possible, that's all.' Her voice faded off towards the end of this statement, but Bridget seemed to understand her plight.

'All right,' she agreed, 'Why don't you come back round here at six p.m. and I'll tell you what I've found out. But give me your phone number anyway just in case something crops up and we miss each other.'

Sadie fervently knew there was no chance of that. She'd be waiting outside Bridget's door from five, if not earlier. As calmly as she could when her fingers were sweating and her hand shaking, she managed to write down the number of the office where she worked. 'It's only Monday to Friday, nine to five thirty,' she explained. 'It's where I work. I don't have a home phone.'

Bridget chuckled. 'Me neither. Would be nice though, wouldn't it? If my Peter gets his promotion at work, I'm going to get one fitted. It'll just have to have a lock on it, stop the kids using it!'

Sadie laughed faintly. Bridget's plans for a telephone were of no interest to her at all but she had to pretend to care. She needed Bridget on side. 'Can I give you some money for the phone box?' she suggested. 'In case you need to call.' She was hoping against hope that this wouldn't be the case, but she wanted to cover all eventualities.

'Oh no, you're all right,' replied Bridget. 'It's only a local call, isn't it. What's two pence between friends?'

Sadie smiled. 'Thank you so much,' she gushed, falling over herself to express her gratitude. 'I can't thank you enough.'

'It's no problem. It'll be good if you – well, if you find out who your mum and dad were.' Bridget gestured back indoors.

'I'd better be getting on now,' she concluded. 'I'll see you later. Six o'clock.'

And with that, Bridget disappeared back down the stairs to the lower ground. Overcome with emotion, Sadie's knees went weak and her head spun. She leant against the house wall to steady herself, still scarcely able to believe that she'd actually made progress. By this evening, she would know a bit more about what had happened twenty-seven years ago when her mother had handed her over to a stranger.

Even if her mum had never been traced up to now, surely there'd be something, some tiny snippet Jean Jackson could tell her that would help Sadie uncover the mystery.

# CHAPTER FIFTEEN

AT SEA, OCTOBER 1943

Each day on board brought Betty and her new friends closer. Mornings were spent on gruelling PT and drill sessions under the authoritative command of Captain Treacy, who made no allowances whatsoever for the difficulty of performing the routines while the ship rocked and pitched on the swell of the Bay of Biscay. Susan spent twenty-four hours confined to the cabin, laid low with seasickness, with each of the other three checking on her regularly. Deborah was caught smoking behind the lifeboats with some of the men and put on a charge, which meant paying a fine and doing extra cleaning duty.

Once they reached the Strait of Gibraltar, the four frigates that had been their escort since Scotland departed. The Mediterranean was considered safe now, so there was no further need of protection. They sailed along the coast of North Africa, which slowly developed from a purple smudge on the horizon to a clearly visible shoreline dotted with sand-coloured, low-built houses around which tall palm trees swayed in the breeze. Betty shivered involuntarily at the sight, so exotic, so otherworldly, something that in all her wildest dreams she had never imagined seeing.

One morning, Captain Treacy kept the women in rank after drill, telling them she had an important announcement to make. Betty had a sudden feeling of dread. Don't say they were all going to be sent back home, surplus to requirements after all.

But the announcement was something completely different. 'I must inform you that, yesterday, Italy declared war on Germany,' she said. Murmurs of surprise, astonishment and anticipation came from all sides. Nobody had expected this. 'So you are now heading for a country that is officially on the side of the Allies. I must warn you that Axis forces still control the north, but you will be well protected when we land in Naples, by both the American and British troops. Your roles in Italy are crucial to the success of our cause.'

Suddenly, the war and everything they would be facing when they arrived in Italy seemed terribly, frighteningly close. Betty was gripped by the recurrent fear that she would not be able to do it, that she would fail as a cipher operator and let everyone down, not just her immediate colleagues but the whole British war effort, all of the troops and pilots and sailors—

'Penny for them?' Lily's voice interrupted her fervid imaginings.

'Oh!' Betty blushed and dropped her gaze, embarrassed for Lily to witness her panic. 'It's nothing.'

Lily regarded her with an appraising look. Betty had the sudden feeling that she could confide in her, that despite the other woman's vastly different background and aristocratic family, the solid gold cigarette case she passed around with aplomb and her plummy accent, she would understand.

'Just feeling a bit apprehensive, I suppose,' Betty admitted. 'What if I don't measure up?'

Lily rolled her eyes and reached out to pat Betty's shoulder sympathetically. 'You are a silly thing,' she said, laughing kindly.

'You've no idea how clever you are, have you? Don't you realise that we're the top one per cent, us ciphers? The brightest and the best. They wouldn't have sent you all the way out here if they didn't know that you are more than capable.'

Betty bit her lip. She couldn't tell Lily about the additional training she had done in code writing and decoding; she was sworn to secrecy. And even though, in her heart of hearts, she knew that what Lily said must be true, it was still hard to believe it.

Lily leant towards her, interrupting her thoughts. 'Look at me, Corporal Betty Bean,' she demanded. 'And repeat after me, "I am as good as any man, if not better".'

Betty burst out laughing. 'I can't say that,' she said.

'Yes you can,' insisted Lily. 'You will say it, *and* you will believe it.'

Betty pursed her lips, ran the words through in her head. It was too hard. But judging from the look on Lily's face, she wasn't going to take no for an answer.

'I'm...' Betty started, hesitated, tried again. 'I'm as good as any man.' The words hung for a moment before the breeze tore them away. 'There,' Betty concluded. 'I've said it now. And I'll do my best to believe it.'

'Good.' Lily tapped a cigarette out of the gold case, stuck it in her mouth and held her hand around it to shield the flame as she lit it. Knowing Betty didn't smoke, she didn't offer one to her.

'Think how lucky we are,' she said, once she'd taken a long draw. 'Well, I am, anyway. I'd never have been allowed to do anything like this if it wasn't for the war. I'd be stuck at home filing my nails and being a debutante. This is my chance' – she grabbed Betty by the arm to emphasise her point – '*our* chance to have a real adventure before we die.'

Early the next morning, they reached Sicily. Betty and her new friends, up at dawn, gasped in amazement at the sight of

Mount Etna, its towering summit suspended in clouds tinged pink by the dawn. Everyone on board was utterly awestruck, transfixed by the sight, none more so than Betty, who'd never seen a mountain before, let alone a live volcano. But nevertheless, after only a few minutes she slipped away back to the cabin, leaving the others staring and pointing and chattering excitedly.

To think of Sicily meant to think of Gianni. It seemed to Betty that there was no way to escape being constantly reminded of the man she had left behind and who, no matter how she loved him, could never be hers.

The ship docked briefly at Catania and, as well as all the personnel and supplies they offloaded, they took fresh food aboard. Crates of glimmering oranges and bright, fresh lemons began to pile up on the foredeck.

'Cor blimey,' Deborah cried out to the other three as they marvelled at all the mounds of delicious fruit. 'What I wouldn't give to get my hands on some of that!'

Lily shrugged insouciantly. 'Well, let's ask, shall we?' Stepping forward with her usual bravado, she picked up a large, shiny orange and began miming peeling and eating it, gesticulating towards the deckhand who was in charge of the unloading. Betty nearly died at her nerve! But on the other hand, the promise of the fruit would make anyone bold; citrus had been more or less unavailable back home since the start of the war. Betty was salivating just imagining how good it would taste.

The man nodded his assent and uttered something that Betty couldn't hear. Immediately, Lily was calling the others forward. 'Come on,' she urged. 'He says we can take as many as we want. Look at these lemons, too. The smell is divine!'

Tentatively, Betty followed Susan and Deborah towards the piles of crates. An intense citrusy scent hung in the air, mingling with the smell of ozone and sunshine. Lily had a lemon in her hand now and was holding it to her nose, inhaling deeply in and out, in raptures of delight. 'Gorgeous!' she enthused, and reached out to pass it to Betty. 'Have a whiff of that. When was the last time you smelt fresh lemon?'

Betty reached out to take the fruit but, just as her hand closed around it, she caught sight of something out of the corner of her eye. On the side of the crates was printed, PRODOTTI DI TAORMINA. Betty's heart lurched as it had when she'd caught sight of Etna that morning. The lemon was heavy in her grasp, its aroma intoxicating, the feelings it evoked so strong that Betty had to lean against the tower of boxes to steady herself.

How could she see the name of Gianni's hometown, that idyllic place he had described so vividly to her, nestling between the mountain and the sea, and not long for him anew?

# CHAPTER SIXTEEN

AT SEA, OCTOBER 1943

By midday, the flotilla was ready to leave. But the *Arcadia* had developed engine trouble. The other ships pressed on, full steam ahead. There was safety in numbers but they couldn't wait, as the goods and troops they were carrying were urgently required essential reinforcements to those already in Naples.

When the *Arcadia* did finally set sail, it was already dusk. They passed Messina, a cluster of houses with red-tiled roofs, and then, just as night was falling, Betty spotted in the far distance the volcanic island of Stromboli.

'I never thought I'd see a live volcano,' she said to Deborah, who was at the railings beside her, 'and now I've seen two in two days.'

Deborah chuckled. 'It's funny what life throws at you, isn't it? Things none of us could ever have imagined.' Then her expression darkened. 'I wish I could tell my ma and pa all about it.'

Betty frowned and looked quizzically at her friend. 'Are they... no longer around?' she asked, hesitantly.

Deborah looked down at the water far below them, churning as the ship cut its course. 'No. They died in an air raid, one of the first ones. That's the main reason I joined up. Nothing to stay home for.' She didn't look at Betty as she said this but at the distant shoreline, as if seeking something there. 'No reason to go back, either, when all of this is over. Perhaps I'll stay. Signorina Castle has a much nicer ring to it than Miss, doesn't it?'

'Signorina Castello,' corrected Betty, translating Deborah's surname.

Deborah chuckled sadly and Betty laid a hand on her arm. 'I'm sorry you lost your folks,' she said. 'That's really tough.'

Deborah stood back from the railings and smiled brightly. 'Yes. But I've got you three now, haven't I? That's all I need.'

Deborah left to go down below and Betty stayed on deck, pondering on what she had told her. The dark bulk of Italy was now on their right-hand side. A few lights sparkled through the darkness but the landmass was mostly shrouded in shadow. For the millionth time, Betty wondered what they would find there when they finally landed. Settling down into bed at nine o'clock, she hoped for a good night's sleep before they disembarked into the unknown.

But that night a storm blew up and the ship was tossed from side to side. Even those who didn't feel seasick hardly got a wink of sleep. Betty was in the middle of a hectic dream in which both her father and her sister were on board with them when an enormous, booming noise violently broke through her slumber.

All four women were wide awake in seconds, sitting on their bunks in their regulation blue-and-white striped pyjamas, bedclothes clutched around them, terrified eyes staring out into the pitch darkness. This was surely no ordinary tempest.

At the same moment, the entire ship seemed to shake, as if someone had picked it up and rattled it vigorously. Regaining some presence of mind, Lily reached out to turn the light on. Nothing happened. The electricity had gone off.

'It's the weather,' said Deborah, definitively. 'We just have to wait for it to blow itself out.'

But as soon as she'd finished speaking there came the klaxon call of sirens, blaring out into the ominous stillness that had settled after the initial noise, loud and insistent, summoning all aboard to the lifeboat muster stations.

'Oh my God, oh my God, what's happening?' pleaded Susan, as she fumbled in the dark for her clothes.

'I don't know but I think it's bad,' replied Betty through gritted teeth. 'We need to get on deck as soon as possible. Forget about getting dressed, just grab your coat and let's get out of here.'

Somehow her decisive instruction seemed to pull the others to their senses. In the corridor, the emergency lighting glowed feebly, giving only just enough illumination to see by. But they knew their way blindfold by now. Moving as quickly as they could without running and risking a trip, they emerged into the murky night. Rain was hammering down and the moon was obscured by cloud, so it was hard to see exactly what was happening, but as soon as they got to the deck the steep incline indicated that the ship was listing badly. Betty checked that her friends were still with her. She could just make out their stricken faces, white with fear and already pinched with cold.

'Come on, girls,' she urged them. 'We'll be fine. Look' – she pointed towards the lifeboats – 'they're already getting people off. It will be all right.'

Susan looked sick with dread. Betty reached out, grabbed her hand and pulled her alongside her. The wooden deck was slick with water, deeper than could be caused by the rain alone. Betty knew enough to understand that, if the boat was shipping water, it was a very bad sign.

All around, shouts and cries rang out, mostly incomprehensible, snatched away by the wind and drowned by the rumbling of the lifeboat winch, but every now and again Betty caught a snatch of something audible.

'We've been torpedoed...'

'... hit a landmine...'

'... sabotage...'

The rumours whirled and swirled around them and none of them were helpful just then. The only fact that mattered was that the ship was sinking, and quickly, and this was exacerbated by the rough seas. In the distance, a few twinkling lights indicated that they were not too far from land. But in such conditions, could they really get there? And if a German submarine had launched this attack, would it really allow safe passage to shore?

There was no time to ponder this. The ATS women were being loaded into the lifeboats first but it was a race against time as the ship lurched and sank even deeper. The blaring sirens, the clanking of the winch, the shrieking wind, the frightened yells, combined to create a cacophony of sound that was overwhelming. All around, men and women were vomiting, either from fear, seasickness or a combination of both.

As Betty and Susan fought to progress along the steeply tilting deck, a great wash of water flooded over the side, sweeping before it deck furniture, unsecured life-jackets, items of clothing, anything, in fact, that wasn't tied down.

'Watch out,' shouted Betty, holding on to Susan even more tightly. She braced herself for the onslaught of the wave reaching them, and somehow they both managed to stay upright. But, glancing fearfully behind her, Betty saw that Lily had fallen and was struggling to get up. Thrusting Susan forward to the crew member who was helping people aboard the lifeboats, she let go of her hand. Out of the corner of her eye she saw Deborah scrambling to her feet and staggering towards the muster station.

Immediately, she turned round and waded through the flood back to Lily. Grasping hold of her arms, battling to get a grip, Betty put all of her strength into hauling Lily upright. Lily's eyes were empty, staring into space, and she seemed dazed, unable to focus. She must have hit her head, thought Betty, frantically.

'Come on, Lily,' she urged, 'you've got to walk. I can't carry you.'

Tugging on Lily's arms, Betty managed to get her moving. But then another great whooshing wave came barrelling towards them, this time knocking them both flying. Betty's eyes, nose, mouth were full of water, she couldn't find the surface, didn't know which way was up. Her legs were caught on something and no matter how she kicked she couldn't seem to get them free. Flapping and floundering, lungs bursting, she was desperate to breathe, desperate for fresh air.

As she fought and struggled in vain, Betty found herself thinking, *It can't end like this. I haven't even got there yet.*

# CHAPTER SEVENTEEN

Suddenly, just as she thought it was all over, Betty's head burst free of the flood and she was breathing, swallowing great slugs of air, feeding her lungs with every drop of oxygen she could get. The swell of water receded a little and she saw that she'd tripped over one of the benches that ringed the main deck and had got her feet caught in its iron supports. Hauling herself upright, she wrested her legs out of their trap, then pulled off her greatcoat and dumped it. It was so sodden it was weighing her down and becoming an impediment. Rid of the unwieldy garment, she gazed around, desperately trying to locate Lily. Where was she? Betty felt a terrible responsibility for her friend. She needed to find her, to help her, to make sure she was safe.

Behind her, something caught her eye. Two of the male soldiers, somehow still wearing full uniform including caps, were beside her.

'It's all right, miss,' said one, with a broad Brummie accent. 'Hold on to us. We'll have you in a lifeboat in no time.'

'No, I can't,' pleaded Betty. 'My friend, I don't know where she is. I can't leave without her.'

'Sorry, miss,' responded the other man, who sounded Scottish. 'Orders are to abandon ship immediately. You have to go. Now.'

'No!' shouted Betty. 'I'm not leaving without Lily. She fell, right here. You have to help me find her.'

A look shot between the two men. And then they relented.

'She's got blond hair,' yelled Betty, battling to make her voice heard above the wind, as if anyone would be able to spot someone's hair colour in the darkness and chaos.

'The swell and the listing would have washed her to port, if she's fallen,' asserted one of the men. 'That way.' He pointed in the general direction he thought they should look in and the three of them began to wade across the deck.

But however hard they searched, there was no sign of Lily.

'We can't stay here any longer,' said one of the men, eventually. His tone was gentle but firm. 'You must look after yourself now.'

With a shuddering, gut-wrenching howl, Betty allowed herself to be escorted onto the last lifeboat. She hadn't saved Lily, posh, funny, forthright, kind, generous Lily.

And she'd never forgive herself for that.

Frozen to the bone, Betty huddled on the bench seat, teeth chattering, numb with cold and sorrow. It was impossible to comprehend what had happened. As far as Betty knew, Susan and Deborah were safe. But Lily had disappeared, swallowed up by the storm and the raging seawater that engulfed the stricken HMS *Arcadia*.

Someone handed Betty a life-jacket and, with fumbling fingers, she pulled it on over her sodden pyjamas, which clung to her skin like a too-tight glove. There was only one other ATS woman on the boat; all the rest of the passengers were men who had stayed to the last to make sure that no one was left on the

*Arcadia*. Everyone was shell-shocked and freezing. For a moment it seemed as if the storm was abating but then a sudden wave lifted up the tiny craft and, a few seconds later, slammed it down again. Betty clung on to the side, shutting her eyes as the sea rose up to engulf her, feeling it tug at her grip, wanting to drag her away and drown her. She held on, willing her tired, cold muscles to action, forcing herself not to let go.

Just as she thought she could not carry on, the lifeboat righted itself. But the ordeal was by no means over. More waves followed, each of them flooding the boat with water, soaking all the occupants anew, over and over again.

Betty had never been so miserable in all her life. Shivering uncontrollably, she didn't even care what happened to her any more, didn't care if the German submarine came and finished off what it had started by torpedoing them again. All she could think was that, if she were saved and Lily were not, she'd never forgive herself. In her pyjama pocket was the keepsake Gianni had carved for her. She had managed to grab it as they had fled from the cabin and, though she could barely feel her fingers, she clutched them around it now, hoping it would act as a talisman to give her succour and bring Lily safely back.

Two of the soldiers were rowing, struggling to keep the lifeboat headed for the shore, where all they had to guide them were a few dim lights shining out amidst the black curtain of the night. The gale lessened a little but the sea was still turbulent and, though the waves had subsided, the swell intensified, throwing all on board relentlessly from side to side. Those who hadn't already vomited up the contents of their stomachs did so now, including Betty.

By now there were several inches of water in the bottom of the boat, further adding to the misery. One of the men passed Betty a bailer and instructed her to bail for all she was worth. At least it gave her something to do and to focus her mind on. She bailed and bailed, even though her frozen hands could hardly keep hold of the container and, every time she held it over the sea to empty it, she thought she'd drop it and lose it.

Gradually, as the men bent their backs into the oars and Betty and the others bailed out water, the sky began to almost imperceptibly lighten. Dawn was breaking, covering everything in a silvery light. Betty baulked at the sight of the expanse of sea that lay all around them, the distance they still had to cover to reach land – and the vast area where Lily could be floating, desperately waiting for someone to find her.

Eventually, the boat came ashore on a stony beach, alongside a pier with railings painted white and blue. On the road above the beach, a small crowd had gathered, watching as the lifeboat disgorged its passengers. Betty suddenly felt hideously self-conscious, dressed only in sodden pyjamas that clung to her every curve, hair dishevelled, barefoot. Slowly, she squelched over the shingly sand, dragging her weary limbs like a ninety-year-old rather than a twenty-year-old.

As she neared the gathering of locals, their excitable clamour grew louder and louder, until she was almost among them and someone rushed forward with a blanket to throw around her shoulders and a helping hand to get her to a nearby bench where she could sit down. Betty understood individual words she heard but, in her state of exhaustion and desperate worry about Lily, none of it made much sense. A hand thrust a tiny glass of something towards her and she drank it, feeling it burn its way down her throat and into her stomach. Brandy, she realised. Almost instantaneously her head started to throb, but she did feel a little warmer. Trying to orientate herself, and take in her surroundings, Betty gazed around her, to see steep cliffs rising up from the water, upon which multicoloured houses seemed to be pasted as if in a child's collage.

Not far from where they had landed was a small harbour, where a multitude of wooden fishing boats swayed lazily on the swell. Beyond it all rose the spectacular, jagged peak of yet another volcano – the world-famous Vesuvius. Three volcanoes in as many days. It was hardly believable. The scene was so beautiful and so awe-inspiring that she almost began to cry again. It struck home more forcefully than ever that she was here, alive, that she'd survived the torpedoing of the transporter ship.

But Lily had not.

The next few hours passed in a blur. As the sun came up, Betty's saturated clothes began to steam and the salt made her skin itch dreadfully. Just as she was getting to the point where she thought she was going to have to tear her pyjamas off, army jeeps arrived carrying clean uniform, which Betty quickly dressed in. Of course the men had not brought a hairbrush, so she was sure her hair resembled a bird's nest, but that couldn't be helped. Eventually all the survivors were taken to the jeeps, and Betty climbed into the back, sat down on one of the benches and promptly fell fast asleep, her head lolling on her neighbour's shoulder. When the jeep jerked to a halt Betty jolted awake. The driver came round to let down the flap.

'Here we are,' he carolled, in a cheery, sing-song voice. 'Your lodgings and your workplace while you're in Naples.'

They had pulled up outside an enormous villa, rendered in pale burnt sienna, complete with huge windows and baroque flourishes. Flamboyant palms and ferns grew abundantly in the forecourt, and two majestic parasol pines cast their welcome shade over the huge front door.

'Gosh,' whispered Betty. 'It's very... grand.' In her state of emotional exhaustion, she couldn't think of any better word.

'Villa Teresa, requisitioned from a noblewoman, so I've heard,' responded the army driver. 'The Duchessa di Taormina, no less.'

'Right,' said Betty, still monosyllabic. The word 'Taormina' rang in her ears, reminding her again of Gianni. It seemed a lifetime, not just twenty-four hours, since she had gazed in awe at

the majestic Etna, and smelt the Sicilian oranges and lemons –
and even longer since she had last seen Gianni. She hadn't even
really started her army career yet and already she'd had a brush
with death and an experience she hoped would never be
repeated. She had been so frightened – terrified. Still was. Had
Gianni felt like this, when he was fighting in North Africa? He
had brushed it off so lightly whenever they had spoken about it,
but, now she had had her own experiences of the horror of war,
Betty began to doubt that things had really been as calm and
easy as he made out. The only conclusion she could draw right
now was that war was always horrific. Especially when it took
the life of a dear friend.

A man dressed in a major's uniform emerged from the
villa's enormous wooden doors and down the steps to where
Betty was waiting.

'You're one of the last women to have arrived,' he said. He
had a brisk, no-nonsense air and Betty quailed a little in his
presence. He didn't seem overly sympathetic to her ordeal.
'Come on in. I've arranged hot water for washing and lunch is
already being served.'

A wash would be marvellous, but though she was starving
Betty could hardly think about eating when Lily's whereabouts
was unknown.

'But how many are missing?' she asked, urgently. 'Has Li—
Corporal French arrived? She... I don't know if she managed to
get on a lifeboat. I'm really worried about her.' She added the
last sentence when she realised that the officer was already
consulting his watch, and looked as if he was about to disappear
off somewhere.

'The vast majority of the ship's manifest has been
accounted for,' the major answered. 'Boats are out searching the
area as we speak for any other... survivors. Now...' He paused
for a moment, seeming to suddenly register Betty's stricken
expression and frightful appearance. 'I'm sure we'll find your

friend,' he said in a considerably softer tone. 'But you must look after yourself. We've got a huge operation on our hands here and we need all you ATS women on top form and fighting fit. Every man's job you do frees up one of us for the frontline.'

Betty nodded weakly. She knew this. She would do her best. 'I won't let you down,' she murmured, with the little strength she had left. 'Just please try to find Corporal French as soon as you can.

'Of course.' The major consulted his watch again. 'Now I really must be going. The washrooms are to the right and the mess is in the basement.' He turned to go, then stopped and held out his arm to help Betty up the stone steps. 'You've had a tough twelve hours,' he said, briskly but not unkindly, 'but work begins tomorrow.'

With a huge amount of willpower, Betty dragged herself to the bathroom and then to the mess hall. She was aware of being in a palatial building adorned with richly painted frescoes and lit by huge crystal chandeliers, but other than that she hardly noticed her surroundings. She was dead beat, barely able to keep her eyes open.

As she entered the room where the meal was taking place, she halted for a moment on the threshold. Long tables stretched from wall to wall and all were crowded with uniformed men and women. A cacophony of noise rose up, chatter and laughter. Betty stared at the massed ranks, summoning the energy to go to join them. Suddenly a voice, louder than all the rest, rang out.

'Betty! Betty, over here!'

Gazing in the direction it had come from, Betty saw Deborah, standing up and bawling across at her. Gratefully, Betty hobbled over to where she and Susan were sitting and sank down into the empty chair next to them.

'What happened? What took you so long?' asked Deborah, hiding her anxiety beneath a veneer of humour. 'We've been here ages. We saved a bunk bed for you and Lily in one of the dorm rooms; we found a nice little corner where we can all four be together.'

At this, Betty almost burst into tears. 'But we don't know where Lily is,' she wailed. 'She's lost. She could be... she could be dead.'

There, the word was out. Betty's worst fear. Deborah and Susan stared at her in alarm, wide-eyed and open-mouthed as they absorbed what Betty had told them.

'We thought she was with you,' said Deborah eventually, her voice low and fearful. 'They told us there were two women on the last boat, that you'd come ashore at Sorrento and would be here soon.'

'There was another woman,' replied Betty. 'I don't know who she was and I don't know where she went. I fell asleep in the jeep. I think maybe she has another billet. In any case, she wasn't Lily.'

A stunned silence greeted this remark. Everyone around the three women was still laughing and joking and talking and arguing, but they were quiet, absorbing the terrible news. Betty picked at the meal, which was pretty unappetising. Susan saw her pushing a potato around on her plate.

'Supplies are still coming in to feed us all,' she commented. 'That's what I heard. When the men first got here from the landings at Salerno, they had nothing. No food, no water. They lived on their rations and fruit they bought from the local people, and had to drag water from any well they came across. They say it will get better soon. But then again, lots of stuff sank with the *Arcadia*...'

She let the sentence hang. Betty wasn't overly enamoured with the idea of eating plain boiled potatoes and mutton tough as an old boot for the foreseeable future. But it didn't really matter at all when Lily was gone. She'd eat nothing but spuds for the rest of her life, if that could bring Lily back.

# CHAPTER EIGHTEEN

LONDON, MAY 1972

Sadie was almost breathless with pent-up excitement as she stood outside Bridget Orchard's house later that day. She'd been too buoyed up to go home and had instead spent the intervening hours roaming around the nearby Regent's Park. In the Italianate garden, the borders behind the neat box hedges were bright with spring flowers. Of course Sadie had never been anywhere near Italy, and she had no idea if this was what Italian gardens actually looked like, but for some indefinable reason she always felt at home here. It made her think of grand old palaces in sunnier climes, all weathered stone draped in fragrant climbers, fronted by formal lawns, water features and cypress trees.

It didn't take Sadie long to retrace her steps to Bridget's house. Once she got there, she brushed some dirt off the boundary wall and perched upon it, prepared to wait for any length of time. She remembered the black cat that had crossed her path that morning; perhaps it was that which had brought her this amazing good luck.

In the end, it was nearly 7 p.m. before Bridget arrived, strolling down the street as if she had all the time in the world. As soon as Sadie saw her she wanted to rush up to her, grab her by the shoulders and shake the information out of her. Why was she walking so slowly? Didn't she know how urgent this was?

Clenching her fists, she felt her nails cutting into her palms and it was a welcome distraction from her torment.

'Hello,' said Bridget, once she was outside the garden gate. 'I hope you haven't been waiting long.'

Sadie shook her head. 'No, not at all,' she lied. 'Um, how was your mother? I hope she's getting better.' It was unbearable to spend time on pleasantries and small talk when there was so much at stake, but Sadie hadn't completely forgotten her manners.

'She's as well as can be expected, thank you,' replied Bridget. 'But you don't want to talk about her, do you? You want to find out about Jean.'

Sadie gulped and managed to stop herself shouting out, 'Of course I do!' Instead, she muttered a suitably subdued, 'Yes, please.'

Bridget cast her a triumphant smile. 'Well, I've got Jean's address,' she said. 'And Mum says she'd probably be more than happy to talk to you.'

It was all Sadie could do not to scream out loud.

'But the only thing is, she's off to Brighton for a couple of weeks or so to visit her son who lives down there. So you'll have to wait until she gets back.'

The agony this statement wrought upon Sadie almost split her heart in two. 'Oh, right, I see,' she mumbled eventually, feeling that Bridget, who was still smiling brightly, expected her to say something. Bridget was being so helpful, but this was the last thing Sadie had wanted to hear.

As she struggled to recompose herself, Bridget fumbled in her handbag for something. Pulling out a piece of paper, she handed it to Sadie with a flourish. 'Here you are,' she said. 'The fifteenth she'll be back, and this is where you can find her. She's no phone, either, but Mum says try in the afternoon because Saturday mornings she does her shopping and Sunday morning she's at church.' Bridget cast Sadie a conspiratorial smile. 'And between you and me, she likes a tipple in the Queen Vic after she's done with her praying, but she's always home by two.'

Sadie almost snatched the paper out of Bridget's hand. 'Thank you,' she gushed, for the second time that day. 'Thank you so much, I'm so grateful, you don't know what this means to me.'

Bridget shrugged. 'You'd do the same for me, I'm sure.' She paused. Sadie sensed her wondering whether to say anything more. 'I hope it goes well for you,' she added, eventually.

Sadie felt there was so much left unsaid beneath this statement. Perhaps, despite her willingness to help, Bridget thought trying to trace her birth parents was a bad idea, just as Kim did. But stuff it, Sadie thought defiantly, as she thanked Bridget again and waved goodbye.

Though having to wait two weeks for Jean's return felt intolerable, at least she was on her way to her final goal. It was far too late to turn back now. Come what may, Sadie would pursue this to the end.

# CHAPTER NINETEEN

NAPLES, OCTOBER 1943

At six in the morning the next day, Betty, Susan and Deborah were in the internal courtyard of the palatial Villa Teresa, doing drill under the command of Captain Treacy. The rudimentary uniform items that Betty had been given yesterday had been augmented by extra pieces, so she now had a jacket and a cap. Deborah and Susan had also been issued with replacements for what they had lost when the *Arcadia* went down. Betty noted that Susan's new clothes fitted a lot better than the previous ones, which hopefully would mean she was more comfortable when going about her business.

However, the reissued uniform did not seem to be helping Susan on the parade ground. She constantly fell out of time with the others, her turns were always a little behind those in front and behind her, she marched with an uneven gait that had the commanding officer barking angrily at her and her salutes were never sharp enough. Betty could sense that the other ATS women were losing patience with Susan. Every time she made a mistake, they all had to start again, which hadn't been so bad on board ship as they didn't have a day's work to do once drill had ended. But now they were here in Naples, Betty feared that Susan would become very unpopular indeed.

That morning, however, Betty felt that she, too, was letting everyone down. She had slept badly, despite her exhaustion, plagued by desperate worry about Lily and fears for what fate might have befallen her. Now her feet dragged and she was always a couple of seconds behind everyone else. Mustering all her resolve, she forced herself through the hour, and was enormously relieved when the officer called 'fall out' and then 'dismissed'.

Wearily, she made her way to the second floor of the palatial Villa Teresa, where the cipher and teleprinter rooms were situated. It felt odd to be going there with Susan but without Lily. Supplies were based on the ground floor, so Deborah had already headed off in that direction. Betty had not even begun to get her bearings in the building and, though she was conscious of its magnificence, opulence and huge size, the fascination she would usually have felt being in a place like this was entirely absent. Nothing interested her while she was still so full of trepidation about Lily.

Lieutenant Corder of the British Eighth Army was in charge. He showed Betty, Susan and the dozen or so other women also assigned to Y-Signals to their workstations. On some of the desks sat radio receiving equipment, headsets and piles of paper strips on which to record the Morse code transmissions. On others stood machines that resembled large, ungainly typewriters, equipped with electrical cables, rotors, wheels and coils of wire connecting everything together; these were the Typex devices. The teleprinters were even larger; each one had a keyboard and printer powered by an electric motor.

Due to the extensive training they'd received before leaving the UK, each ATS woman knew exactly what her role entailed. Everyone else looked as if they were raring to go. Only Betty and Susan, devastated by Lily's absence, were hesitant and unconfident that October morning.

If Lieutenant Corder picked up on their distress, he didn't acknowledge as much. Once each woman had taken up their place, he commanded them to get to work. There were three shift patterns in each twenty-four hours: 8 a.m. to 4 p.m., 4 p.m. to midnight, and midnight to 8 a.m. This was the first shift of the day and they would hand over to the next team in eight hours' time. Picking up her headset, Betty settled into her chair, trying to take up a comfortable position. She knew that, by the end of the session, her shoulders would be tense, her neck stiff and her head aching from the effort of tuning out everything she could hear but her own allocated signal.

All the cipher operators were tasked with listening in to encrypted enemy transmissions conveyed in Morse code. They translated the code into letters and noted them down in blocks of five. Most of what they recorded was sent by the teleprinter operators to a mysterious location back home, known only as BP, to be decoded and unencrypted. But some of what they did was purely to provide a record that would identify the 'fist' of an individual radio operator, that was a person's particular rhythm and pattern of transmission.

In each role, accuracy was vital. One mistake, one letter skipped, could spell disaster. If the code that arrived at BP had been incorrectly transcribed, the messages would be misleading or incomprehensible, and this might mean that an attack was not intercepted or that a vital plan being hatched by the enemy went unnoticed.

Wishing with all her heart that Lily was here beside her, Betty adjusted the headset, switched on her radio, turned the knob to her assigned frequency and began to listen, tuning out all else. And though she concentrated hard and was confident that she didn't miss anything, her eyes were constantly flicking around the room towards the door, half-expecting that, at any moment, Lily would walk in with her familiar confident stride and, with a flick of her blond hair, take up her place beside Betty.

But by the time the eight hours was up, the seat next to Betty was still empty.

Released from duty, Betty didn't have the heart to do anything. She went back to their dorm room and stood for a moment in front of the full-length windows that looked out on the Bay of Naples, the azure sea glinting in the still-strong October sunlight. It was a stunning vista and normally one that would have cheered Betty up whatever her mood. But now all she could think was that the sea was cruel and merciless and that, somewhere in its depths, Lily had been held and captured, never to return.

Climbing into her bunk, Betty lay down and pulled her sheet over her head, blocking out the light. She was still so tired that she fell asleep almost instantly and dreamt of the yellow cornfields of home, where she could make out two people walking away from her. They morphed into the figures of Lily and Gianni and, wanting to be with them, Betty chased after them, but, try as she might, she couldn't catch up; they remained close but forever out of reach. Desperate, she shouted after them, calling them back to her, begging them to return.

In her dream, she was still shouting when she became aware of Deborah leaning over her, her hand on her shoulder, shaking her and saying, 'Betty, wake up, wake up. Look who's here!'

Slowly, Betty came to full consciousness, opening her eyes and gazing around her. Deborah stepped to the side. And then Betty saw her. An angel, standing between the bunk beds, dressed in a long, trailing white skirt and blouse, her hair wrapped in a towel as if she had just washed it. Which was strange, thought Betty, as she'd never considered that angels had to perform the same ablutions as human beings.

'Betty,' the angel said, in Lily's voice.

For a second, Betty was more confused than ever. And then, with a flood of joy, she realised that the angel sounded and looked like Lily because it was Lily.

Sitting bolt upright, Betty banged her head on the bunk above. 'Ouch,' she groaned, and then immediately after, 'Lily. You made it. Or is this a dream?' She turned to Deborah, grabbing her arm and begging her, 'Pinch me so that I know it's true!'

But then Lily's guttural laugh rang out and she stepped forward and flung her arms round Betty in a huge, enveloping hug.

'Yes, Betty, it's me. I'm really here. I'm alive, hale and hearty as ever.'

Betty had never been a fainter but in that moment she almost collapsed in relief. 'Oh my goodness,' she breathed, 'I can't believe it. But where have you been? We were so worried about you, we thought you'd...' Her words tailed off, too awful to voice.

Lily grinned. 'Well, I've had quite the adventure, I can tell you.' Her voice was a little hoarse, as if she'd been doing a lot of shouting. 'Let me sit down next to you, Betty, and I'll tell you everything.'

Lily settled herself down onto Betty's bunk and Deborah and Susan sat on the one opposite, leaning in to make sure they didn't miss anything, although the distance between the two sets of beds was less than three feet.

'It's all quite surreal really,' began Lily, once she'd lit a cigarette and taken a drag on it. 'I can't remember exactly how I got there, but one moment I was on the *Arcadia* and the next I was in the sea, clinging onto a life ring and wondering where the hell everyone else was.' She spoke with a lightness of tone, and punctuated each sentence with a laugh, but Betty knew she must be putting on an act. Lily must have been terrified, ship-wrecked and all alone, even if she wouldn't admit to it.

'It was bally freezing, the rain was lashing down and I must admit I thought my number was up. But after some time, I really don't know how long, I saw a light in the distance. It was moving, so I guessed it was a boat of some sort. I waved and shouted and hollered and I tried to kick myself towards it, but I was so tired by that point that I barely moved. Fortunately, though, they saw me. The boat came and picked me up, pulling me on board like I was a particularly ungainly fish.'

'Gosh,' breathed Susan, eyes wide as saucers. 'That was a lucky stroke.'

Lily nodded. 'They didn't know quite what to make of me,' she went on. 'At first I think they thought I was some kind of mermaid, and it took a lot of sign language to convince them I was a member of the British forces.'

She paused for dramatic effect as the others laughed, longer than the joke probably warranted but they were all so relieved that Lily was alive that everything suddenly seemed hilarious.

'I'm trying to think what the sign language for mermaid is, or armed forces for that matter,' teased Deborah.

Lily chuckled. 'It's quite complex, I can tell you that much,' she replied. 'But anyway, we got there in the end. It was quite a nice boat, it had a cabin and everything. They gave me some dry things to put on and I thought – I hoped – they would head straight to shore to deliver me to salvation. But no!'

Betty, Susan and Deborah all had their eyes fixed on Lily, waiting with bated breath for what happened next.

'They had to catch a tuna before they went back and that was that. So for twenty-four hours, I sat in the cabin while they chased down their prey. I knew you'd all be worried about me, but what could I do?' Lily raised her eyebrows and grimaced. 'I was at their mercy.'

'Gosh,' exhaled Susan, again. 'You're so brave. I'm sure I would have cried and annoyed them so much that they wanted rid of me as soon as possible.'

'They were pretty hard-bitten men,' responded Lily. 'I don't think any amount of tears would have changed their minds. But anyway, eventually they caught their fish and we landed at this darling little place called Amalfi, but then they had to bless the boat and sell the catch and – well, eventually I managed to persuade them that I needed to get to Naples pronto and so they got the brother-in-law of someone's cousin or something, who had a beaten-up old truck, to drive me to the outskirts of the city, where they dropped me off at a checkpoint. And here I am!'

For a moment there was silence, and then Betty, Deborah and Susan erupted into whoops and cries of delight and they all fell upon Lily and hugged her until she begged for mercy.

'Right,' said Lily, when they'd all recovered. 'I'm going to get dressed and then I vote we all go to the NAAFI for tea. I might have only just arrived but I've heard that the mess food isn't up to much. I vote for ham and chips all round, and a decent cup of tea.'

She turned round and rummaged among the pile of new uniform she'd been issued. A moment later, she stood up straight, flamboyantly holding up a pair of enormous bloomers.

'Look what they gave me,' she exclaimed, 'we can be torpedoed and shipwrecked and left with nothing but the clothes we stand up in, but the British Army will still provide the stuff that's really important. Chastity protectors! Wear them with pride!'

Betty, Susan and Lily simultaneously burst out in gales of laughter. Already the ordeal they had been through had begun to fade. They were there to do a job and that was where their focus must be. For the first time, Betty started to actually believe the words that Lily had made her repeat. That she – and the other women – were as good as any man. That without their vital contribution, the war and its outcome might be in jeopardy.

'*Forza*,' she whispered to herself. 'Come on, Betty Bean. You can do this. Now Lily's back, anything is possible.'

# CHAPTER TWENTY

NAPLES, OCTOBER 1943

With Lily safe and sound, life returned to normal – or at least the new normal of living and working in a foreign country still partially occupied by enemy forces. The four women had less opportunity to get together now, as they all worked shifts and their free time didn't always coincide. Drill was performed in much smaller groups, though, whenever Betty ended up in the same one as Susan, she noticed that Susan's performance hadn't improved at all. Lily, on the other hand, who always arrived with seconds to spare, just managing to slot into place in time, was a dab hand, her turns and salutes so sharp she was always receiving commendations.

One day, about a week after their arrival in Naples, Betty and Lily found themselves both on the same shift to start at 4 p.m.

'Right, Betty,' said Lily, after drill and breakfast. 'We've got ages until we start work. Let's go exploring! Aren't you just dying to look around this fabulous palace we've ended up in?'

Betty nodded. 'I suppose so,' she replied. 'I mean – yes, definitely. I think I was in such shock when I arrived, and then so scared about what had happened to you, the building just sort of washed over me.' She paused for a moment before adding, 'What'll we say if someone catches us somewhere we're not supposed to be? We should have our story ready.'

Lily burst out laughing. 'Oh, Betty Bean,' she exclaimed, 'you are such a good girl. You're not a natural rule-breaker, are you? Whereas I, on the other hand, most definitely am.' She stretched out a long, languid arm in Betty's direction. 'Come on, take my hand. It will be fine. If anyone asks us what we're doing – which they won't – we'll say we got lost. Simple as that.'

Giggling at the illicit excitement of their exploration, the two women set off. They headed in the opposite direction from that which led to the offices, footsteps echoing along the marble-floored corridor. They found a second staircase, not grand and sweeping with stone balustrades like the main one, but hidden behind a curtained entrance, cold, dark and narrow. It was obviously meant for servants but, venturing up it, the women discovered it was a short cut to the floors above and the part of the villa where their workrooms lay. They quickly retreated once they'd realised where their first foray had taken them, not wanting to catch the attention of the officer in charge.

Back in the main portion of the villa, they wandered along wide passageways, opening doors that led to room upon room of equal magnificence. The ceilings of what must once have been the state rooms, where important guests and foreign dignitaries were entertained, were so high you could have fitted two British houses on top of each other inside them. Not one was unadorned, but instead all were painted with elaborate, finely detailed frescoes, depicting voluptuous Renaissance women lounging on daybeds, being fed grapes by nymphs and cherubs, or scenes of hunting among sylvan glades, or the gods and goddesses of ancient times ruling over Mount Olympus. As if the ceiling art didn't provide enough decoration, the walls were hung with paintings in gold-leafed frames, portraits of austere-looking men dressed in their finery or astride their horses with glossy manes, family groupings of dark-eyed women and children with olive skins and piercing gazes.

As they made their way back to their dorm room to collect their caps ready for duty, Betty's imagination ran away with her, just as it used to do whenever she and her father had delivered to Castle Howard, back home in Yorkshire. She pictured herself as a grand Neapolitan lady, sweeping along the passages of her magnificent home, master of all she surveyed.

'I'd love to meet the duchessa who owns this amazing place,' she breathed. 'I wonder what she makes of us lot invading her home.'

'Me too,' agreed Lily. 'But I suppose she's living in some other gorgeous house somewhere, while the war rages.' She halted, spinning round to take in the full splendour of their surroundings.

'I have to say that I've been to some grand places in my time,' she mused, 'but this is really something else.'

'Gosh, you did live the high life, didn't you?' teased Betty.

Lily paused to examine a marble statue that stood on an elegant pedestal. 'Oh yes,' she said. 'We often visited Blenheim, Chatsworth, Chartwell...'

'Winston Churchill's house?' questioned Betty, incredulously.

'That's right.' Lily ran her hand over the marble lady's smooth, pale cheek and the folds of her gown, and then offered by way of explanation, 'Daddy knows people. You know how it is.'

Betty didn't at all, but Lily's life sounded so intriguing she wished she did. It was all a far cry from her father's little cottage in Malton and arriving at stately homes through the tradesman's entrance. Not that she was jealous – merely curious. The war was throwing people from all different walks of life together.

Betty would never have met someone like Lily in normal circumstances.

They got back to their room, where Lily went to stand before one of the three full-length windows overlooking the Bay of Naples. Betty joined her, feasting her eyes on the breath-taking view.

'It'll be so strange to go back, when all of this is over, won't it?' said Betty.

'Oh, Lord,' exclaimed Lily. 'Let's not even think about it. I know what's in store for me. Getting hitched to a rich heir and making an entire career out of hosting dinner parties and hiring nannies to look after the children.'

Listening to this, Betty thought how strange it was that, despite her wealth and privilege, Lily still had unfulfilled hopes and ambitions. 'But if that's not what you want—' Betty began.

'Of course it isn't,' interrupted Lily. 'But I don't think I've got the imagination to hark after anything different. I'm wondering, though, if perhaps I might find an American while we're here. I quite fancy living in New York.' She gave the city's name a transatlantic twang as she said it. 'But then again, I can't see myself settling down with one man for the rest of my life. Far too dull and predictable.' She sighed and twiddled with the loops of the tieback that secured the heavy damask curtains.

'What about you, Betty Bean?' she asked, focusing her gaze away from the tassel-tie and onto Betty. 'What's going on in your love life?'

Betty blushed.

'I can see there's something,' demanded Lily, teasingly. 'Who's your sweetheart and are you really planning to be faithful to him, here in romantic Italy with so many gorgeous officers all around?'

Betty's stomach lurched. Lily was so forthright, her ability to disarm so unerring.

'I, er, well,' she stumbled, 'my um, my – the man who

everyone expects me to marry was captured after the fall of Singapore. Samuel, his name is. I've only received one letter in all this time, so I don't really know how he's doing or where he is, or even if he's still alive.' She didn't add, *And the problem is that I don't think I've ever been in love with him because I met someone else and the feelings I have for that man are completely different, he has stolen my heart and I don't know what to do about it...* Of course she didn't say this. No one could know about her emotional betrayal of Samuel.

'That's too bad,' sympathised Lily, suddenly serious, the joking over. She hesitated for a moment, as if digesting Betty's words. 'I'm sure he'll come back safe and sound,' she concluded. Betty could tell by her tone of voice that Lily was not nearly as certain of this fact as she made out. Neither was Betty, and that created dilemmas and problems of its own.

'Well, we better get going, back to work.' Lily turned away from the beautiful view with a groan. 'You know,' she went on, 'sometimes I hear Morse code in the way a tap is dripping, or someone's footsteps over the tiles. The other day Sergeant Foster kept coughing and I started transcribing the coughs into letters...'

Betty laughed, glad Lily's interrogation was over, her attention diverted. 'I know what you mean.'

Lily glanced down at her watch. 'Cripes,' she declared. 'It's three minutes to four! Where did the time go? I thought we had oodles of it.' She looked at Betty with a challenging air. 'We're going to have to make use of that secret staircase we've discovered if we're to get to our desks on time. I don't know about you, but I don't want to be put on a charge for tardiness.'

Betty, torn between the fear of being late and that of being caught straying into an unauthorised part of the villa, opted in the end for the former being the worst option.

'All right,' she said. 'But we better be quick! And quiet.'

Forgetting all plans she had had to comb her hair, Betty

rammed her cap further down onto her head, and she and Lily scarpered out of their dorm and towards the back stairs.

Fumbling along in the half-light, Betty had a moment to think whether it would actually have been quicker to take the main staircase after all. But Lily was forging on ahead and Betty didn't want to be left alone in this gloomy, somewhat spooky place, so she had to hurry after her. Nevertheless, Lily arrived at the top some paces ahead of Betty, and did not notice when Betty stumbled and tripped. Doubled over, Betty paused for a moment as she waited for the pain in her knee to subside. The folds of the black curtain that shrouded the entrance to the staircase had fallen in front of her, obscuring her view, but she heard Lily opening the office door and then the surge of footsteps and voices as those on the shift that had just ended trooped out.

A charge for lateness was now inevitable; Betty was resigned to that fact. But she didn't want those leaving to see her disgrace. She'd wait until they'd all gone on their way. But, just as she was about to emerge, a sound caught her ears. Someone was still there. Betty stayed put, hoping this stray person would be gone in a moment.

But instead of the footsteps fading into the distance, they came closer.

Shifting the edge of the curtain a tiny fraction, Betty saw Susan sidling out of the office doorway, shooting furtive glances in all directions. Once she had established that the coast was clear, Susan began to walk fast, almost running, towards the back stairway where Betty was hiding.

Betty was about to call out to her, say hello, but something stopped her. She stood stock-still, the curtain draped in front of her, allowing Betty only the smallest gap to observe what Susan was doing. Why she was spying on her friend, Betty couldn't have explained. She just hoped against hope that Susan wouldn't find her and question her about what she was up to. As Susan approached, Betty held her breath and remained motionless, straining to see through the gloom. Susan had something in her hands, but what was it? She got nearer and nearer, but it was not until she was right next to where Betty was hiding that Betty could make out the distinctive shape of what the other woman was carrying. It was a stash of paper, dozens of the narrow strips upon which the cipher operators transcribed Morse code in blocks of five letters.

Betty's heart missed a beat. It was absolutely forbidden to remove paperwork of any sort from the cipher room. But even more than that, Betty couldn't understand why on earth Susan would want them. They were indecipherable German code that had to be sent off to the mysterious BP to be broken. They surely couldn't mean anything to Susan, or anyone else for that matter.

So what on earth was she planning to do with them?

# CHAPTER TWENTY-ONE

The puzzle of Susan's possession of the cipher strips niggled at Betty over the following few days. She pondered discussing it with Lily but decided not to. There was probably a perfectly innocent explanation, although admittedly Betty couldn't actually think what that might be. In any case, Betty was working too hard to allow herself to be distracted by anything, least of all odd behaviour from Susan, who was the meekest and mildest person Betty had ever met. She couldn't possibly be up to no good; and, with that thought, and caught up in the constant flurry of activity that was life in the forces overseas, Betty dismissed the whole business from her mind.

The months flew by and soon it was November, and then December. Depending on the requirements of the day, Betty would spend her shift either on one of the listening stations or working on encryption of messages to be transmitted by the teleprinter or Typex machine operators. However tired she was, and however great the stresses and strains of the job, Betty always performed every duty to perfection and with deadly seriousness. It was stressful at times because getting it wrong, mixing up the signals coming from almost identical frequencies, making a mistake in the encryption of a message, could have such dreadful consequences for those battling it out on the frontline. But Betty loved the work, the intellectual stimulation that was so much greater than that demanded by the telephone exchange. Even on long shifts when concentrating so hard made her brain ache, she still regarded it as an honour to be trusted with such important tasks.

Before long, Betty, Lily and Susan were rewarded for their hard work by being promoted to the rank of sergeant. Betty's slight lateness that day she'd tripped on the staircase had gone unpunished, but poor Deborah was always getting into trouble. She was currently working off a charge for turning up to the supplies department without her hat after swapping it for a soldier's cap in the NAAFI one evening. So she remained a corporal, for the time being at least.

In the dorm the evening of their promotion, the friends got out their housewives in order to sew on their new stripes. Betty had hers done in no time, her stitching neat and deft, the three coveted stripes perfectly level on the arm of her jacket. Lily, however, was not good at sewing. She kept breaking her thread and unthreading her needle. After half an hour of suppressed curses and grunts of frustration, she threw the jacket down onto her bunk.

'Grrr,' she growled, angrily. 'I'm literally all thumbs.'

Betty picked up the jacket and inspected the stitching. She couldn't help but laugh. It looked as though an elephant had done it, using something the size of an oar for a needle. And the stripes were completely crooked, sloping drunkenly down the sleeve in a manner that was definitely not going to pass muster with Captain Treacy on parade.

'I'll do it for you,' she told Lily. 'It'll only take me five minutes.'

Lily flung herself flat on her back on her bunk and shut her eyes. 'You are an angel, Sergeant Betty Bean. Thank you.'

Swiftly, Betty unpicked Lily's stitches, which didn't take long as they were so huge and badly secured, and re-sewed the stripes.

'There, done,' she said, a few minutes later. 'All fixed.' She turned to Susan, who was still quietly labouring over hers. 'Would you like me to help you, too, Susan? I don't mind,' she said, kindly.

Susan barely looked up from her work. 'No, it's fine,' she snapped. 'I can do it, thank you. I'm not that incompetent.'

Betty frowned. She hadn't meant to be disparaging. She recalled Susan's reaction when, a few weeks earlier, Betty had offered to help her to practise drill. Betty's intention had only been to save Susan from being the butt of resentment from others because of the delays she kept causing by getting it wrong. But Susan had seemed to take offence then, just as she had now. She obviously wasn't someone who liked to be helped, Betty realised, perhaps seeing it as a form of criticism. Well, if that was the case, Betty would make sure not to make the same mistake again.

AT WORK A COUPLE of days later, Betty went straight to her desk and picked up her headset. The overnight shift had only a couple of people on it, and Betty's equipment shouldn't have been used or even touched since she'd left it at midnight the night before. So when she noticed that one of the wires had become detached from the earpiece, at first she couldn't believe it. She fiddled around with it a little to see if she could reattach it, but her efforts were in vain. It probably could be fixed – but not by Betty herself.

Glancing around her, she saw that Lily had settled down and turned her radio on, but that a couple of the other women were also staring at their headsets, looking distraught by what they had found. Betty asked them if their sets were also damaged and, when they replied that they were, she went to find Lieutenant Corder.

'Something's happened to the equipment,' she told him. 'It looks like it's been vandalised.'

The lieutenant gave an exaggerated sigh of aggravation. He clearly wasn't having a good day and Betty hated that she'd made it worse. But he had to know.

'I'll come and have a look,' he replied, irritatedly. Betty wasn't sure if he was cross with her for disturbing him or with whoever had tampered with the headsets. She hoped it was the latter.

After his inspection, Lieutenant Corder became even more disgruntled. He called for Signor Conti, the Italian civilian who was responsible for maintenance in the department, and gave him the headsets to take away and fix. Then he produced two spare headsets so that at least some of the women could get to work.

'I'm going to split the shift,' he announced, looking around the room. 'Sergeants French, Bean, you have four hours off, come back at midday please. Sergeants Marshall and Robinson, you can use the new sets. Corporal Hatchard, take over from French, please.'

Dismissed when they had least expected to be, Betty and Lily scurried out before Lieutenant Corder could change his mind.

'I feel a bit guilty,' said Betty, as the pair reached the majestic staircase that was now so familiar. 'You know, that feeling like when you were a child, if you were out of school during the day at a doctor's appointment or something and you'd always think everyone was looking at you and wondering why you weren't in your classroom!'

Lily chuckled. 'I know what you mean. But neither of us are

shirkers, so I suppose there's nothing wrong with enjoying ourselves during time off we've legitimately been given.' She paused halfway down the stairs. 'So what do you say to a trip into the city? We could go to the Spanish Quarter, grab some lunch at a café. I get so tired of the mess food.'

Betty hardly had to consider the suggestion before she had thrust away any lingering feelings of skiving and agreed. On their way out of the Villa Teresa, they checked the mailboxes in the entrance hall. Lily handed Betty a slim envelope from amidst the pile she leafed through. Immediately, Betty recognised the handwriting; it belonged to Samuel's mother, Julie. She still wrote often, not just because she was so fond of Betty but also, Betty was sure, because Betty was Julie's only connection to her son, a surrogate daughter in place of the child of her own who was so far away, fate unknown. The lack of correspondence from prisoners held by the Japanese was something everyone in Britain was aware of by now, nearly two years after the fall of Singapore. Families had campaigned for more information, putting advertisements in the newspapers asking anyone who knew anything to respond, and begging the British authorities to do more to help them find out what was happening to their loved ones. But very little mail made its way from the Far East to Europe, and people had no way of knowing if their own letters were getting through.

While Lily nipped back to use the bathroom, Betty ripped the letter open. As her eyes scanned the words, she felt a strange sensation tighten round her heart. Julie was clearly desperate for news of her son, and begged Betty to let her know if she had any correspondence with him at all. Of course Betty would do that; no doubt about it – if she ever did.

'I have heard that they eat nothing but rice over there,' Betty read. 'And you will recall Samuel's dislike of rice. I worry dreadfully about how he is coping with the food.'

The problem was that Betty did not recall Samuel's aver-

sion to rice. Increasingly, the longer they spent apart, the more
she found herself struggling to remember much about her childhood sweetheart at all. Perhaps they had never been as close as
everyone – including herself – had always thought.

Julie went on:

*It is his dreams of you and your future together that will be
keeping Samuel going, I know. He loves you so much and was
so looking forward to your wedding day. I'm sure that, as well
as working hard in Italy, you are living a very exciting life. In
the thrill of it all, please don't forget Samuel, just as he will
certainly not have forgotten you.*

Betty closed her eyes as if she could block out not only the
words themselves but the pain they caused. It would be impossible to explain to Julie, or Samuel, or anyone back home in
Malton, that her feelings had changed, that she was no longer
the same girl she had been when she and Samuel had said
goodbye.

Her thoughts drifted to Gianni, her mind's eye conjuring up
their parting, that field of shimmering wheat, the skylark's song,
the arching blue sky. Their kiss. At the memory, her stomach
turned over and her heart twisted in two. She loved Gianni. She
was promised to Samuel.

But should she really be held to a promise she had made so
young?

# CHAPTER TWENTY-TWO

LONDON, MAY 1972

If someone had asked Sadie to put into words her feelings as she rang Jean Jackson's doorbell two weeks later, she wouldn't have been able to. A heady mix of excitement, trepidation, anxiety and exhilaration was swirling through her veins. She had thought obsessively about her birth mother and father in the intervening period since Bridget had given her Jean's address. One fact kept resurfacing: if her parents had told her about her adoption when they had still been alive, she probably wouldn't be conducting this search. It would have felt like a rejection of them, as if Sadie was saying they had not been good enough.

Since they'd been gone, Sadie had been grief-stricken, and part of that was the loss of connection. She'd thought she didn't have any living relatives. And then suddenly she'd discovered that maybe she did, maybe she had a mum and a dad, siblings perhaps, all alive, people she could connect with. *Because everyone wants that, don't they*, she thought, *everyone wants and needs bonds and attachments.*

The thought that that yearning might be satisfied, here today, was overwhelming.

And as well as her own feelings, she also had Mrs Jackson's to consider. As far as Sadie knew, her visit was going to come as a complete surprise to Jean, unless Bridget's mum had seen her or somehow got the message to her. What would her reaction be when faced with the baby she'd once held as she waited in vain for the infant's mother to reappear?

Sadie couldn't imagine what it would be like to be in such a situation, and nor could she really work out how she herself would react if it happened to her. It was so hard to think of what circumstances had caused her mother to do what she did. Her first emotion on finding the box had been gut-wrenching horror, but now she mostly felt confused about it. Whether this visit to Mrs Jean Jackson would increase the confusion, or lessen it, was anybody's guess right then.

The buzzer sounded and the huge metal door at the base of the tower block clicked. Taking a deep breath, Sadie pulled it open and entered the building. The lifts were right ahead. Jean lived on the thirteenth floor. Unlucky? Sadie pushed such stupid superstition out of her mind.

The elevator was spacious and modern but still had that urine smell that Sadie always associated with the stairwells and lifts of multi-storey car parks. She wrinkled her nose as it made its laborious way upwards. It was the first time she had ever been inside a tower block and she wondered what it was like to live in one. *Cities in the sky*, the town planners and developers had called them. But many local people had mourned the loss of their communities, the gossiping on the front steps, the chatting over the garden fence.

When the lift ground to a halt, Sadie realised that she'd purposely let her thoughts wander to inconsequential trivialities to prevent herself from exploding with the tension of it all. Stepping into the hallway, she braced herself for the most peculiar and potentially consequential moment of her life.

Arrows on the wall pointed her to the left, to flat 133. Thrusting her shaking hands into her pockets to try to still them, Sadie followed the directions, along the corridor and round a corner. And there, standing in the open doorway, stood the woman who must be Jean Jackson.

She was around Sadie's own height, and had her dark blond hair arranged in an elaborate beehive. Instinctively, Sadie smiled. She'd suggested to her mother that she try this style once and Evelyn had been horrified at the thought.

'Fashion is for the young,' she'd sniffed, disparagingly. 'If I went to the greengrocers looking like I think I'm twenty-one, they'd laugh me out of town.'

Jean Jackson had clearly said goodbye to her twenties a long time ago, but apparently didn't have the same inhibitions.

'Are you the girl?' Jean's voice was clear and direct, with the accent of a true Londoner, 'girl' sounding more like 'gel'. 'Is it really you? Sadie, isn't it?'

Sadie stopped in her tracks. So Bridget's mum *had* told Mrs Jackson about her. She tried to read Jean's expression. Was it friendly and welcoming? Or hostile and annoyed? After all, she might not want to be reminded of a time that must have been difficult for her, if not traumatic. To have someone else's baby foisted upon you, and then to have to work out what to do with that child, couldn't have been easy.

But as Sadie scrutinised Jean's face, the woman's mouth broke into a huge smile. Jean stepped out of her doorway and towards Sadie, arms open wide. Somewhat taken aback, Sadie found herself enveloped in a massive hug that smelt of perfume, mothballs and the lingering vestiges of tobacco smoke.

When Jean finally released her, all Sadie's worries and fears had miraculously melted away, to be replaced by a deep sense of belonging. Perhaps something innate in her had recognised her protector of twenty-seven years previously, the woman who had looked after her and made sure she was safe.

'Come in, my dear, come in.' Jean ushered her into her flat and along a hallway that opened out into a large sitting room with windows on two sides. Sadie gasped at the expansive view of London that lay beyond the glass; the multitude of houses and, among them, the gleaming Post Office Tower with its revolving circular dome, and Centrepoint, a 1960s skyscraper even taller than this one.

'First time you've been up in one of these, I expect,' said Jean, watching Sadie's reaction to the vista before her. 'Nice, isn't it? But it's not like the old days, up here. I miss that big old Victorian wreck, despite the cold and the damp in wintertime.' For a moment Jean looked wistful, but then she seemed to shake herself, and turned back to Sadie with another of her huge smiles. 'But mustn't grumble. No use hanging onto the past, is there.' She paused. Her smile faded and she glanced anxiously at Sadie. 'But what am I blethering on about, silly old woman that I am. Of course you want to talk about the past, that's what you're here for, isn't it?'

Sadie stared at Jean, lost for words. She felt suddenly rather faint.

'Do you, er, would you mind if I sat down?' she stuttered, and then plopped down onto a G Plan sofa that was conveniently close by. Blood was pounding between her ears and she dropped her head into her hands in an attempt to stem the rising nausea.

It was a few moments before Sadie had recovered from her near faint. She looked up to see Jean walking into the room with a tall glass in her hand.

'I was going to offer you tea or coffee,' she said. 'But then I thought you needed something sweet, so here's a glass of pop for you. I buy it for the grandkids, don't tell their mother.' She winked at Sadie and then gave a little laugh, and her laugh was infectious and beguiling, like fast-flowing water in a brook.

'I like pop,' Sadie said, weakly. 'And my mother never let me have it, either. She said it was bad for the teeth.' She took the drink gratefully and had a sip. It was cool and refreshing.

'I, er, I,' she stumbled. How much did she need to explain? How to start the conversation, after so long considering it, deliberating over every word? 'I think you know already. I'm Sadie. You... my...' She gave up, unable to continue.

Jean sat down on the sofa beside her. 'I know, love. Don't get yourself all het up. Bridget's mum told me soon as I was back from Brighton. I came home a little sooner than planned on account of a hospital appointment – I got the letter the day I left and I couldn't reschedule, so—' She broke off and smiled at Sadie again. 'But I'm rambling on again, aren't I? Enough to say Mrs Orchard put a note under my door telling me to get in touch as soon as I could, so of course I did and she spilled the beans. I could hardly believe it. That little mite, that tiny one I held and cuddled, all grown up and so pretty, too.' Jean reached out her hands to Sadie's shoulders and sat back a little, putting her head to one side and then the other as she appraised her. 'No, more than pretty. Beautiful, I should say.'

Sadie attempted a smile. She felt absolutely overwhelmed. The moment, imagined for so long, was too big to deal with.

'So – tell me everything about yourself,' Jean said. 'I want to hear it all.'

# CHAPTER TWENTY-THREE

NAPLES, DECEMBER 1943

Lily returned, looking and smelling divine. She was the proud possessor of a bottle of perfume she'd managed to find in one of the local shops, and lipstick in a colour almost the same as Yardley Parade Ground Red, which was all the rage, and had obviously celebrated the unplanned outing by liberally applying both.

'What's up?' she questioned, on seeing Betty's pallid demeanour.

Betty shook her head and slipped Julie's letter into her pocket. 'Oh nothing,' she replied, breezily. 'A letter from my... well, I suppose she's my future mother-in-law. She misses Samuel so much. And I feel bad sometimes, for living in relative safety here while he's suffering so far away.'

Lily shrugged and grimaced sympathetically. 'That's tough, I agree. But you making yourself miserable won't change anything for him, will it?'

There was no denying Lily's logic. But, like so many things, following her advice was easier said than done.

It didn't take long to walk to the Spanish Quarter, along streets that bore the scars of the city's suffering. The few houses still standing were overcrowded, with no electricity or running water, and most looked as if a breath of wind would bring them tumbling down to join all the other ruined and destroyed buildings. Tiny children ran around barefoot and dressed in clothing not nearly adequate for the cold; women, bent double with age, searched in the rubble for anything salvageable to use or sell, and groups of youths prowled the streets, ready to steal food or equipment from any army vehicle left unguarded for more than a few seconds.

But despite all of this, Betty loved the chaotic city and its tough inhabitants. During the Four Days of Naples, the local population, including a phalanx of boys as young as seven or eight, had risen up against the Nazi occupiers and driven them out of the city. And what the Neapolitans lacked in material goods they made up for with their indefinable *joie de vivre*.

Picking their way through the rubble-strewn streets, a voluble crowd gathered in a tight narrow alleyway caught Betty and Lily's attention. As they got nearer, they saw at its centre a young woman, dressed in a simple dress patterned with small roses. In her arms she held a tiny newborn infant, still scrunched and red from birth, wrapped in a beautiful hand-embroidered shawl. The baby gazed up at the many pairs of eyes fixed upon it, oblivious to all the fuss. Everyone's demeanour was reverential, as if the arrival of this minute scrap was akin to the second coming. The mother, in particular, had a look of pure joy and pride on her tired, worn face. Next to her stood a man with a toddler perched on one shoulder; father and sister, Betty assumed. Other children were also crowding around, looking on. A girl, around eight maybe, hair neatly tied in pigtails, reached out to the baby and lovingly stroked its face. Betty had never seen such adoration of an infant by a whole community before, but then again she'd never seen such a newborn baby. In England, women stayed at home for days, if not weeks, after giving birth. Betty's sister's child was due in March next year and Betty felt a twinge of homesickness, that she would not be there to welcome him or her to the world.

'*Congratulazioni*,' Betty said, simply, as she caught the mother's eye. 'Your baby is beautiful.'

'*Grazie*,' replied the mother. '*A Dio piacendo crescerà forte.*' God willing he will grow strong.

Betty smiled. 'I wish you all the best.'

She and Lily lingered for a few moments longer, as yet more friends and neighbours arrived to give the baby their blessing.

'Come on, let's go,' said Lily, eventually. 'I'm getting hungry and we haven't got that long until we need to be back at work.'

'Sure,' replied Betty. 'I don't want to be falling up the back staircase again. That bruise on my knee didn't fade for weeks!'

Lily nudged her teasingly with her elbow. 'Shouldn't be so clumsy,' she laughed, with an exaggerated eye-roll.

The pair strolled on, eventually reaching a square where there were many cafés frequented by forces personnel. Selecting the most popular one, Betty and Lily sat down and ordered tea and buns. They had enough food at base but it was a fairly monotonous diet, though there was plentiful delicious fresh fruit. The women supplemented their fare with treats that the American servicemen could provide. Deborah, who seemed to have a different boyfriend every week – sometimes more than one – would often return from a date with types of chocolate or candy none of them had ever seen before, Hershey and Life Savers, Charms and Peanut Blocks.

A couple of American sailors came to sit at the table next to Betty and Lily, resplendent in their smart uniforms and caps. A girl Betty thought could not be more than four years old imme-diately appeared beside them, her hands held out, begging. The waitress brought plates of egg and chips to the men and shooed her away, but she just ducked beneath the table, only to pop back up again as soon as the waitress had gone. One of the sailors folded a piece of his newspaper into a cone and filled it up with chips. He gave it to the little girl, who scampered away, delighted to be so richly rewarded for her bravery and audacity.

Once the child had disappeared, the sailors noticed Betty and Lily.

'Afternoon, girls,' one of them said. 'How's your day going?'

Lily fixed the men with a sharp stare. 'It's Sergeant Bean and Sergeant French, actually,' she retorted. 'The girls are all at home in their nurseries with their nannies.'

Betty sniggered, hiding her mouth behind her hand and trying to turn it into a cough. She loved Lily's absolute forthrightness.

'We're very well, thank you,' she answered politely, once she'd managed to straighten her face.

Lily took out her cigarettes. No gold case now, since it had been lost at sea. She proffered the packet around.

'I'm Bill,' said the first man, striking a match to light his cigarette. Not wanting to be left out, Betty had taken one, though she hardly ever smoked, and Bill lit it and Lily's, too.

'And I'm Bert,' said the other. 'And that's not a joke.' At which they both laughed heartily, somewhat belying this statement.

'And what are you two lovely ladies doing out here?' asked Bert.

Betty cast a glance at Lily, and not just in anticipation of how she might react to being called a 'lovely lady'. They had been told not to speak of their work to anyone. She wasn't even sure if they were allowed to say they were cipher operators.

Bill kicked Bert under the table. 'I think you meant to say "sergeant",' he said. 'What are you two lovely *sergeants* doing out here?'

At this, even Lily couldn't help but laugh. Betty giggled, but she was still regarding Lily anxiously, wondering what to reply. Fortunately, Lily took control.

'Oh, we're in Y-Signals,' she said airily, taking a long drag on her cigarette. In awe at Lily's nonchalant sophistication, Betty took a puff of her own, hoping it might imbue her with some of Lily's flawless composure, but all it did was make her choke and splutter.

'But if we told you what we do we'd have to shoot you,' Lily continued with unabated insouciance. 'So we won't.'

Betty giggled again. Lily really was priceless. 'What about you?' she interjected once she'd recovered. 'Er, what ship are you on?'

The men told them they were Merchant Mariners, plying back and forth across the Atlantic on boats carrying essential cargo, military equipment, office supplies, food – everything needed to run a war.

'We took part in the landings on Sicily,' Bill said. 'That was a blast. Harder than we expected, but we routed them in the end. I don't think most of these Italians ever had much of a stomach for the fight, but the Germans are another matter.' He balanced his cigarette on the ashtray and tucked into a mouthful of his meal.

'How the hell did you two get to Naples?' asked Bert. 'It was only men for the first month or two, out here.'

Lily waved her hand expansively. 'We were on the *Arcadia*, so we were quite literally washed ashore. But stiff upper lip and all that. We just get on with the job.'

'No way!' exclaimed Bill. 'Well, that is some story you'll have to tell the grandchildren. I reckon that was the last torpedo to be fired in the Med in this war – the other subs all left a while ago. The last one, and you copped it!'

'We're all right,' said Betty, discreetly stubbing out her cigarette. She wouldn't try that again; far from making her look elegant and sophisticated, the coughing had turned her face red as a lobster.

'Hey, you want to come to a dance next Saturday night?' asked Bert. 'At the naval HQ, down in the port. It's going to be really somethin', the band will be playing and everything. A pre-Christmas bash, you know. Got to celebrate the holidays, even overseas.'

'Yes,' said Lily and 'No,' said Betty, at the same time.

Lily looked at her with raised eyebrows.

'I'm on shift then,' explained Betty, hastily. 'But I'm sure Deborah will go with you.' It was unlikely Susan would. She never seemed to want to go out in the evenings.

Lily shrugged. 'That's a shame.' She turned to Bert and Bill and began making arrangements.

Betty's heart twisted and turned as she thought of the fun she was missing and why. She could have swapped her shift with someone if she really wanted to. The thing was that her friends knew about Samuel, but she hadn't told them about Gianni. The secret weighed on her, as secrets do, getting heavier every day. Being in Italy, hearing Italian spoken every day, served as a constant, and painful, reminder of him. In reality, both Samuel and Gianni were far away and there was nothing to stop Betty innocently going out and having fun. Except for the fact that she had no inclination to.

Betty was still feeling despondent by the time she and Lily arrived back in the cipher room at midday, and even Lily's buoyant mood faded as they encountered Lieutenant Corder looking thunderous. Calling everyone together, he told them he had an announcement to make. A heavy weight of expectancy hung in the room. It was clear it was something important.

'You will know about the damage to the equipment,' he intoned, his tone grave. 'Signor Conti confirmed that it could only have been caused by deliberate sabotage.'

At this, a gasp of amazement went up around the room. No

one could believe it. Betty's head reeled at the idea that there was a saboteur in their midst. Susan's purloining of the transcription strips flitted across her mind. Betty flicked her eyes around the assembled company. Every single one of them, Susan included, appeared shocked and horrified to the core.

'Everyone must be on their guard, eyes and ears open,' concluded the lieutenant, 'until we have caught the culprit.'

Throughout the rest of the shift, Betty could not rid her head of the mystery of the vandalism. It couldn't possibly be Susan. Susan, sweet and self-effacing as she was, didn't have the gumption to do something criminal, and anyway, obviously she wouldn't do anything to put men's lives at risk or compromise her country.

It must be someone else. But who?

# CHAPTER TWENTY-FOUR

LONDON, MAY 1972

It wasn't how Sadie had imagined it at all. She hadn't expected to do any talking. But somehow she found herself sitting on this stranger's sofa in her high-rise apartment and regaling Jean with the story of her life. All the time she was speaking, she was thinking how odd it was, but at the same time completely natural. Somehow, explaining what had led to her being there made it all clearer to Sadie herself; her complete satisfaction with the lovely life she'd had, the wonderful parents she'd been blessed with, the opportunities she'd been given.

And then the utter, horrendous shock of finding out the truth. Followed by the overpowering need to find out what had happened, to uncover her own history.

Jean listened quietly, only intervening every now and again to ask a question, elicit some further detail, about Sadie's school and her friends, her job and her life in London now she was a working girl.

At the end, Sadie stopped and spread out her hands in a gesture that said, *That's it. That's all about me.*

Jean nodded. 'I'm going to make tea,' she said, 'or coffee if you prefer.'

'And then...' prompted Sadie.

'Of course,' answered Jean, without having to hear the end of her sentence. 'And then I'll tell you everything I know, everything I remember.'

She bustled off into the kitchen, having ascertained that Sadie would like coffee rather than tea, milk and no sugar. Sadie looked around, taking in more of the room. On a side table was a display of photographs, presumably Jean's children and grandchildren. On the wall hung a reproduction of *The Hay Wain*, and there was a cosy rag rug on the floor. It was homely and inviting and, even though it wasn't the place where Sadie had been left, she felt that her birth mother had instinctively known, when Jean Jackson answered the door and agreed to look after her baby, that she would be in safe hands.

A short while later, Jean returned. She rearranged the coasters on a little side table and put the two mugs of coffee down on them. When they were both settled, Jean began to talk.

'It was the first of October,' she said, 'and the air had that autumnal smell to it. People think you don't notice things like that in London, amidst all the pollution, but I always do. I remember thinking, when I went to open the door, that it was a bit early for the kids to be knocking, wanting a penny for the guy for Bonfire Night. I couldn't think who it might be; I wasn't expecting anyone. It was a cold night, I can tell you that much, and there was no central heating in those old buildings. Well, you can imagine when I moved in here I couldn't believe my luck. My own bathroom just for me, hot running water, radiators! Luxury!' She smiled and seemed momentarily lost in the past.

'But you mustn't let me get sidetracked!' she exclaimed,

wagging her finger at Sadie in mock rebuke. 'Now, where was I?' She took a sip of her coffee and resumed her story.

'When I opened the door, there was a girl standing there, a slip of a thing. Only young she was, but then so was I, in those days, only in my late twenties. I would say she was a bit younger. At first I didn't notice, as it was getting dark. But after a moment, my eyes adjusted to the light and I saw that she had something in her arms. I strained and then I realised that she was carrying a baby.'

Sadie leant in a little as if scared she might miss a syllable of what Jean was saying.

'She was a beautiful girl and, as soon as I saw you, I noticed the resemblance. It was as if she'd come to my door again. You have the same shaped face as her, though your hair is darker and your complexion not as pale.'

Struggling to hold back tears, Sadie picked up her coffee mug and took a swig. The intensity in the air was palpable, electric.

'So this young girl clutching an infant, she stood there for a moment, saying nothing. I tried to work out what was going on. She seemed nervy, and her face was flushed; she might have been feverish, now I come to think about it. There was something desperate about her, as if she needed to get somewhere and didn't have much time.' Jean shook her head gently. 'I can still see her so clearly. There was something wrong, but I couldn't put my finger on what. All of this took a couple of seconds, you understand. She looked down at the bundle in her arms and I saw the love in her eyes, pure and simple. And then she muttered something about looking after the baby, thrust it into my arms and left.'

Jean faltered. Sadie saw that she was close to tears herself, her upper lip trembling, her eyes moistening.

'Keep going, please,' she whispered, and then wasn't sure if she'd actually said the words or just thought them.

'I couldn't run after her because I was holding the infant now, so I called for Alf to come and help – he'd only been demobbed a short time before. He didn't really like me doing things like answering the door – thought that was a man's job. I had to fight for my independence, Sadie. We all did. When he first got back he wouldn't let me change a lightbulb. "How do you think we managed when you was all away?" I asked him. It took a while to adjust, and that's no lie.

'But here I am, going off the point again. I was lost for words, and that doesn't happen to me often, I can tell you. My Alf came over and peered down at what I was holding. He nearly fainted when he realised. "A baby?" he shouted. "What are you doing with a baby?" I don't know if he thought it was mine, that I'd given birth to it in the few seconds I'd been on the doorstep.'

Despite the tension in the room, Sadie almost laughed at this idea. A sudden darkness fell upon them and then, only seconds later, lifted again.

'Aeroplane,' explained Jean. 'We're so high up, sometimes they block the sun momentarily.'

Sadie shuddered. Suddenly she wasn't so sure she'd like to live up here. She wondered if the tower wobbled in the wind. That would be terrifying.

'Anyway,' Jean resumed. 'I managed to calm him down and explain. I sat down and cradled the baby – I can still hardly believe it was you – in my arms. You were such a sweet little thing, quite newborn, not more than a day or two old. I thought that you'd wake up and want feeding, but you didn't stir, not for a good few hours. But long before that I'd begun to get worried. The woman – your mother – she'd said she'd only be a short while. She left you about seven in the evening and at midnight there was still no sign of her. We didn't know what to do. Alf said that we had to phone the authorities. We might get into trouble, else.'

Jean's face was taut with worry, as if she was still anxious. Sadie felt sorry for her. It was an impossible situation to be put in.

'I was sure, so very sure, that your mum meant to come back for you,' Jean continued. 'To this day, I think that. She loved you and she didn't want to abandon you, I know she didn't. Something must have...' Her words tailed off.

Sadie could tell what she was thinking. If something terrible had happened to her mother that night, if she had died – then Sadie had no hope of ever finding her or being reunited.

'So what did you do?' Sadie asked, gently. Jean was finding this hard, she could tell. Perhaps she wished she'd done more, though what she could have done differently Sadie didn't know.

'I kept saying we'd hold off a little longer. But Alf got more and more antsy and by two o'clock in the morning he put his foot down. The thing is, he knew how much I wanted a child. We'd been trying, every time he came home from leave. It was stupid I suppose, but I thought, if Alf... well, if he were to go, in the war and all, I wanted to have something to remember him by, his flesh and blood, our child. Morbid, I know. But anyway, I hadn't fallen pregnant yet. He knew what I was thinking. "You can't keep this baby, Jean," he told me. "She's not yours."

'I remember how I snapped back at him, "I know that, I'm not a fool." But secretly, I was already imagining what it would be like if you were mine, what little outfits I'd dress you in. I'm silly like that, always have been.'

Silently, Sadie shook her head. *Not silly*, she thought, but she couldn't get the words out. She touched her face and it was soaking wet. She hadn't realised she was crying. Jean was too, she saw now.

Jean gave a huge sigh as if her whole body were deflating. 'So in the early hours of the morning we called the ambulance and they came and took the baby – you – to hospital and in the morning the police came with an almoner and someone from the adoption agency. They asked me to write down what had happened. And that was it. That was the last I heard of you.'

Jean's tears were uncontrollable now, as were Sadie's. Through her sobs, Jean went stutteringly on. 'It was so h-hard to let you g-go. But some good did come of it, for me, anyway. They say holding a newborn is the best way to get pregnant. And the very next month, I fell. I had my Robert, then my Albert and then my Susan. So you brought me luck. I just w-wish your mother had c-come back for you. I've never forgotten about that night, or you. I always wished there'd been a way for me to keep in touch with you, to find out what happened. I'm so glad you came. So glad.'

Jean was so upset by this time that, despite her protestations that she was pleased to see her, Sadie almost felt bad for coming here and putting the other woman through this. Jean's obvious distress tugged at her heartstrings, and she thought for the umpteenth time what a difficult situation Jean had been put in. It was clear her mother had never intended to land her with such a terrible dilemma. And also clear what a kind, compassionate person Jean was. It was weird that Sadie was the one who'd been handed over to a stranger but it was Jean she felt sorry for. Sadie held Jean's hands and stroked the kind lady's fingers with her thumbs. Sniffing loudly, she managed to hold back her own tears for a moment.

'I-I didn't suffer,' she assured Jean, haltingly. 'I was f-fine. I've already told you how fine I was. It was a shock, finding out – but you weren't to blame. In fact, I don't think anyone's to blame. I just want to find out what happened. What happened to my mother, where she is now.' She screwed up her eyes and all of her courage.

'Even if she's dead. I want to know.'

# CHAPTER TWENTY-FIVE

NAPLES, MARCH 1944

The winter of 1943 to 1944 was long and hard, even in Italy. Betty and her friends worked relentlessly, buoyed up by the signs that the war was turning definitively in the Allies' favour. Even so, it was far from won. Further up the peninsula, the battle for Monte Cassino had been raging almost since the turn of the year. There was a constant need for more men, more equipment, reinforcements and rations; Deborah, in supplies, was run off her feet.

Day after day, Betty and Lily sat with their heavy headsets on, taking down messages in blocks of five letters. Sometimes, the transmissions would come so fast and hard they could hardly keep up. At other times, there would be a deafening silence on their frequency and they would long for something to transmit to relieve the long hours of boredom. As Betty and Lily listened diligently and attentively, Susan tapped away on her teleprinter, typing up the messages to be winged away to the ever-mysterious BP, where they would be decoded. There had been no further damage to equipment, and so far no one had been blamed for the sabotage. In the busyness of everyday life, the incident had faded from memory, to be replaced by ever-present concerns about what all the male soldiers were going through, the shortage of weaponry, the continued loss of life on the battlefields across the world.

Betty had less encoding work to do these days, simply because the American and British armies were moving further and further away and most of the work was handled by radio operatives in the field. But every now and again Lieutenant Corder would give her a top-secret communication to encode and she'd set to work with her crossword grid or the current book code, construct the message and use the grumbling Typex machine to send it.

One rainy Monday, Betty was surprised to be handed a sheaf of material for her attention.

'Get this done as soon as you can please, Sergeant Bean. Book code,' Lieutenant Corder instructed. 'It's important.'

That went without saying, but of course Betty didn't point this out. She knew that messages sent by both sides were often padded out by irrelevant material, to distract and divert the recipient, making them spend time trying to decipher words that meant nothing. Sometimes random rubbish was inserted, and at other times parts of nursery rhymes or recipes would be interspersed throughout the serious stuff. This seemed to be the case with what she'd just been given, but as far as possible Betty tried not to concentrate too hard on exactly what she was encoding. At the back of her mind was the thought that, if she hadn't taken too much notice of it and hadn't committed it to memory, she'd never be able to give it away if she were captured or tortured. Of course these things were unlikely to happen, but you never knew. Better safe than sorry.

Hunting around in the secure locked cabinet where the codebook was kept, she couldn't find it. It was always stored in one specific place and all of those who used it, who numbered only about half a dozen including Betty, knew to put it back in exactly the same spot after use. But now it was gone.

With increasing concern, Betty picked up piles of paper and hunted beneath and among them. No luck. She checked underneath the cabinet and behind it, to no avail. Frantically, she searched all the desks and tabletops in the vicinity but the codebook wasn't there, either.

For a moment, she stood in the room, her panicked breath coming fast and sharp. She couldn't send the messages in book code without the codebook, that much was obvious. She could use the low-grade cipher she was familiar with, but it wasn't as secure. And more to the point, it wasn't what Lieutenant Corder had asked for.

Casting her gaze anxiously from side to side, she hoped against hope that she'd see the book there, lying out where it shouldn't be, but nevertheless located. Nothing.

Suddenly, Susan was beside her. 'Are you all right, Betty?' she asked. 'You look a bit perturbed.'

Betty shook her head. 'No, no, it's fine,' she stuttered. 'I just... it's nothing.' She cast Susan a smile that she wanted to be calm and reassuring but was sure came across as anything but. 'Look, I need to go and see the lieutenant about something.'

Feeling sick with worry, she headed to Lieutenant Corder's office, knocked on the door and burst in, hardly waiting for him to admit her.

'Sergeant Bean,' he intoned, barely looking up from the paper strewn across his desk. 'What can I do for you today?'

Betty wrung her hands and desperately tried to summon the courage to make her confession.

'I... er, well...' she stuttered.

'Come on, spit it out,' barked the lieutenant. 'I haven't got all day.'

Of course he hadn't. Betty needed to get a grip.

'I'm afraid to tell you, Lieutenant Corder sir, that the codebook has gone missing.' Behind her back, Betty had her fingers crossed, praying that she wasn't going to get into trouble. 'I definitely put it back in the correct place myself, but I don't know who might have used it since then.'

There, it was out now. Betty waited with bated breath while the lieutenant absorbed the information she had given him. He had lifted his eyes and was staring at her, a cloud descending on his usually calm features. 'This is very irregular, Sergeant Bean,' he said, eventually. 'It makes me somewhat vexed.'

Betty nodded, suddenly incapable of speech. She wanted to say, 'It wasn't me' but that would sound childish and defensive. Better to stay silent than blurt out something stupid.

A clattering sound rang out as the lieutenant tossed his pen upon the table in front of him. He interlaced his fingers and put his hands behind his head, staring at the ceiling as if seeking inspiration.

'Leave it with me, Sergeant Bean,' he ordered, eventually. 'Go back to listening duty today. I'll update you in due course.'

Betty slunk back to her station, picked up her headset and tried to push away the loss of the book and concentrate on the task at hand. Later, when she, Deborah and Lily were at the NAAFI waiting for the film showing that was scheduled for that evening, it was still preying on Betty's mind, preventing her from joining in with her friends' playful banter.

'We're honoured to have your company,' Lily said to Deborah, teasingly. 'No date tonight? Don't tell us you're slowing down.'

Deborah grinned. 'What can I do?' she exclaimed in response to Lily's ribbing. 'They're all begging to go out with me; I can't turn them all down.'

'The problem is that you don't turn *any* of them down,' joked Lily. 'I'm surprised you don't get their names mixed up, call Jim John or Donald Doug. I know I would.'

Deborah chuckled, a deep guttural rumble like water going down a drain, which contained within it a healthy wickedness.

'You're only young once,' she retaliated. 'No one says on their deathbed, "I wish I'd had less fun and less boyfriends".'

'Fewer boyfriends,' corrected Lily, with a small smile. She sighed deeply. 'And yes, you're right,' she continued, digging Betty in the ribs with a sharp elbow. 'One must make the most of every moment. Who knows what's in store for any of us.' She made sure she had Betty's attention. 'Isn't that right, BB? Why are you so quiet tonight?'

Betty shrugged and bit her lip as a sudden urge to blurt it all out came over her. Not just the missing codebook, but the truth about Samuel and Gianni. Deborah and Lily talked so freely and light-heartedly about their loves and losses; Betty wished she could do the same. Outside, torrential spring rain was pouring down, seeming to fit in with the sudden sombre mood that had descended.

'Come on, Betty,' said Lily, gently, giving her a searching look. 'What's up? Spill the beans...' She gave an exaggerated grin and added, 'Geddit? Do you see what I did there?'

Betty smiled despite herself, but immediately the smile faded, to be replaced by a feeling of deep despair.

'Oh, it's nothing really,' she replied, attempting to brush it off. 'Just had a bit of bother at work today, something's gone missing and...' A vision of Samuel, drenched by a Far Eastern monsoon downpour, holding on for Betty's sake, flitted across her mind's eye and she stifled a sob.

Lily frowned. 'Shame,' she muttered, reaching out to pat Betty's hand. 'I'm sure whatever it is will turn up. Things usually do, in the end.'

*Maybe*, thought Betty. *And so will Samuel, when this war is over, and what will I do then?*

Deborah helped herself to one of Lily's cigarettes. 'Don't worry about it,' she advised. 'It'll be somewhere really obvious. I lost a crate of turnips the other day and then I got up and realised I was sitting on it.'

She hooted with laughter and Betty couldn't help but join in. Deborah's humour and irreverence was always catching. Betty couldn't solve the problem of Gianni and Samuel right now, but she could do her best to work out what had happened to the codebook. It hadn't grown legs and walked, that was for sure, so someone must have removed it, whether on purpose or by accident. Betty would keep her eyes peeled and all her senses on high alert from now on.

NEXT MORNING, she was asked to operate the Typex machine as another member of the team had come down with a nasty flu that was going round. Susan was manning the teleprinter as usual. For both of them it was absolutely essential that every letter or number was input correctly, as one mistake, one carelessly mistyped piece of code, could spell disaster. Frowning in concentration, Betty focused intently on her job.

Once she'd finished, she waited for the machine to spit out its confirmation slip. As she stood, her eyes wandered to Susan. She'd been looking peaky lately, pale and drawn, and occasionally she was tetchy with the others. Betty was a bit worried about her. Perhaps she was finding the work hard to cope with, the long hours and the shifts. Or maybe the pressure was getting to her. Betty must look out for her.

As she thought this, Betty glanced at the papers in Susan's hand, the strips of code noted down by the cipher operators at the listening stations, written down in blocks of five letters. Susan's job was to transcribe the letters into the teleprinter. Being blessed with excellent eyesight, Betty could just about see the strip Susan was currently working on from where she was standing.

XXYMT BDARQ ZNSFT...

Betty could also see Susan's other hand, pressing the teleprinter's keys. XXYMT BDERQ ZMZET...

*What?* Betty stared, straining her eyes, scarcely believing what she was seeing. Susan was keying in the code incorrectly. Was this further evidence that she was under the weather, struggling under the strain? Sending this mangled code could lead to terrible errors being made somewhere in the theatre of war. If Betty said anything, though, Susan would likely be furious with her for prying or interfering or doubting her competence.

For a split second, Betty considered this. And then she thrust her doubts aside. There was no choice to be made here. She had to act. Sending incorrect communications could cause a catastrophe.

'Susan,' she said, far more urgently and loudly than she'd intended. 'You're doing that wrong. You need to stop, now.'

# CHAPTER TWENTY-SIX

Sadie sat on the saggy sofa in her flat, the small package in her lap before her. Just when she'd thought that Jean Jackson had laid bare all she remembered about that night in 1945 when Sadie had been handed over to her, Jean had made her revelation. She had found something tucked inside Sadie's swaddling robes, something that she'd put on one side and, in the drama and confusion of the fateful night, clean forgotten about. By the time she'd remembered the object, it had been too late to pass it on to the police, and anyway Jean had known she needed to try to move on from the whole unsettling experience. Even if she had not felt this way, her husband Alf had forbidden her to talk about it any more. He'd said it was upsetting her too much and she needed to leave it be.

So Jean had put the object away and, as time passed, it had faded from memory. When she'd been packing her belongings to move to the new flat, she'd come across it again and had been about to throw it out, but some sixth sense had told her not to. So she'd kept it. Now that Sadie was here, she wanted to return it to her – it was hers, after all. But unfortunately, she was unable to recall where she'd put it.

Seeing the look of utter disappointment on Sadie's face, she'd promised she'd dig it out and send it on to her. And now here it presumably was, in a small parcel wrapped in brown paper and tied up with string, with an NW postmark. Sadie couldn't imagine what the item might be, what it was that Jean had discovered all those years ago and then had kept hold of until this moment.

Feeling hot and nauseous, Sadie cut the string and carefully unfolded the brown paper. Inside was a small object wrapped in pink tissue, and on top of it lay a letter.

*Dear Sadie,*

*Here's the little keepsake thingamajig I told you about. It didn't mean anything to me when I first found it, and it still doesn't now. But it might help you to find your parents. And if it does, it would make me very, very happy. Please keep in touch and let me know how you get on. And if you're ever in Camden Town, pop in for a coffee. Or a glass of that pop you like.*

*Love from Jean*

Sadie could see the wink that would accompany that last remark, and tears sprang to her eyes. *For God's sake*, she told herself. *You have turned into a sentimental wreck with all of this*. She picked up the pink-wrapped item and contemplated it for a moment, plucking up the courage to open it.

She remembered hearing once about the infants left at Thomas Coram's Foundling Hospital in the Victorian era, how the mothers attached little tokens to them, engraved metal pendants, scraps of fabric or pieces of cheap jewellery –

anything that might help them identify their baby in the future, if they were ever able to come back and claim them.

The sad truth was that almost none ever were reunited. Sadie didn't want to dwell on this fact right now. With shaking fingers, she pulled away the delicate layers of tissue.

Finally, the object was revealed.

A small wooden heart, skilfully carved by hand from some sort of pale, malleable wood. Attached to it by a string was a delicately sculpted key. Sadie wondered at the dexterity of whoever had done this, working the material so precisely, taking so much care over the task. She ran her fingers over it, wanting to feel its texture, the grain of the natural material. In so doing, she felt something on the back, an inscription of some sort. Turning the heart over and holding it up to the light, with mounting incredulity she read the words engraved there.

*From GU with love x*
*Eden Camp 1943*

A jolt of shock ran like a thunderbolt through Sadie.

Who was GU? Where, and what, was Eden Camp? And why was the date of 1943 significant? She had been born in 1945...

For a moment, Sadie despaired. This little keepsake had been made with love, and presumably tucked into her baby blankets by her mother for a reason. It had promised so much. Over the time she had spent waiting for Jean to find it, it had taken on totemic significance. Sadie had convinced herself that it was going to provide the answer, lead her straight to her mother and hopefully her father, too. But right now it seemed that all the little heart and key had thrown up were more questions, and further layers of mystery to unravel.

That evening, Sadie's boyfriend Simon returned from his work trip. He took her to dinner at Maggie Jones's cosy little restaurant tucked behind Kensington High Street. They ate duck pâté and chicken in tarragon sauce, and Sadie decided now was the moment to tell Simon what she had found out about herself. He knew nothing of her adoption and her subsequent search for information, and that felt wrong. Such a cataclysmic discovery should be shared with one's partner. She'd convinced herself that her failure to keep him informed was due to his absence, the cost of a long-distance phone call, the fact that news like this needed to be conveyed face to face, not over the airwaves.

But the truth was that she had a bad feeling about how he'd react.

At first, Simon's reaction to her story was astonishment, pure and simple. He didn't say much, just listened to the whole thing in near silence. Only when she got to the end and announced that she had already embarked on the journey that she hoped would lead her to the discovery of her parents did Simon speak up, and Sadie began to understand that her fears had been realised.

'I'll be honest with you, Sadie,' he said, frowning deeply. 'I'm not sure you're doing the right thing. In my personal opinion, it would be better if you left well alone. There's a reason your mother handed you over to this Mrs Jackson woman, and it might be an unsavoury one that you'd rather not delve into too deeply. And also—' Simon halted, his eyes darting around the restaurant's dimly lit interior as if searching for something. 'Look,' he began again eventually, as if he'd come to the conclusion there was no easy way to say what he had in mind. 'The way I see it is this. Being adopted – well, it's not something you want to broadcast. And really, there's no need for anyone else to know. Or any way they would ever know, if you don't tell them. So, if I were you, I'd keep quiet about the whole thing. You were happy with how things were before. Why jeopardise that with a search that will most likely be fruitless, or end up causing you more pain?'

Sadie gazed at him throughout this speech with mounting horror. What on earth was Simon's problem with her being adopted? How could he not see that the thirst for knowledge about her roots wasn't just going to go away, no matter how much he wanted it to?

And then it suddenly struck her. Simon was embarrassed about it. About the fact that she had been abandoned, that she didn't know who her real family were, what her heritage was. Simon's folk were landed gentry who, though untitled, belonged to the upper echelons of society. Sadie had always been aware of her social inferiority compared to Simon but, as he hadn't seemed to mind – well, not much, anyway – then neither did she. After all, the previous decade, the swinging sixties, had cast aside so many of those old class prejudices. Society was more egalitarian these days, wasn't it? Humble origins didn't stand in anyone's way – look at John Lennon, Michael Caine, David Bailey. They had all come from nothing and made it big. No one cared about people's backgrounds any more.

Or did they?

Sadie had the sudden, irrefutable understanding that for Simon it was still a big deal, a huge one. It had been all right when her parents had been honest, hard-working, salt-of-the-earth lower-middle-class types – this was acceptable in his circles. But to be a nobody, of no known ancestry, was utterly taboo. Sadie wondered if this was because of all the impregnated chambermaids and dairymaids and housemaids throughout history, and all the resulting children born out of wedlock, illegitimate non-heirs who had the power to bring disgrace to the families that disowned them.

'I'm sorry you don't agree with me,' she answered eventually, her voice tight and strained with suppressed anger. She was glad she hadn't mentioned the keepsake. It would have been unbearable to hear him disparage that precious item. It was all she had to link her to her parents and as such it already meant the world to her. 'And I'm sorry you can't support me in something that's so important. But if that's the way it is, so be it. Just be aware that I'm not going to give up just because you don't like it.'

Simon hesitated. Sadie could sense him considering how to respond. Eventually, he made his decision.

'Sadie,' he said gently, leaning forward and putting his arm round her shoulders. 'I love you so much, I adore you, and I can't bear to see you so cut up. I was going to—' He halted, passing her a napkin to wipe her tears and then sighing heavily before resuming. 'Well, that doesn't matter now, it's not the right time. But I think you should just leave it be.'

Incapable of further speech, Sadie nodded as if in agreement. But she didn't agree. She totally disagreed. Simon didn't seem to have made any real effort to understand what she was going through, or to offer her the support she desperately wanted.

After the meal, Simon drove Sadie home in his red TVR. She'd refused his offer to stay the night at his place. When he pulled up outside her front door, he turned to her with an air of weary disappointment.

'Sadie, I'm worried about where all this will end,' he said, slowly, as if she might not understand if he spoke too fast. 'You've found out you were adopted. But why does it matter? You had a perfectly good life before you found out this – this piece of information. Why don't you put the whole thing away and go back to being who you were before. Surely that would be easier, wouldn't it?'

His patronising tone, combined with the sheer illogicality of his argument, put Sadie's back right up. Enraged, she replied sharply. 'No, Simon, you've got that wrong. It's not that I *was* adopted. It's that I *am* adopted. It's not something that happened in the past and is over with now. It will always be the case. I am adopted. Present tense.'

Simon pursed his lips and looked steadfastly out of the front window. 'OK,' he replied, enunciating each letter with careful precision. 'If that's the way you want to look at it...'

'It is,' snapped back Sadie, opening the car door and clambering out. The seats were so low it was impossible to do this with any real dignity, but she did her best. She was through the front door and shutting it behind her before she heard the engine revving as Simon pulled away from the kerb. She had not waved goodbye.

The discovery of the adoption certificate meant that nothing in her life was the same any more. Including her feelings for Simon.

Her mother had been so anxious to see Sadie settled, constantly reminding her that she mustn't leave it too late to get married and have kids. Sadie had always listened indulgently to this advice and then completely ignored it. But now the truth hit her. She did want a husband, someone to love and cherish and be loved and cherished by. But that person wasn't Simon.

She saw everything with absolute clarity now. She just didn't love him.

# CHAPTER TWENTY-SEVEN

Betty had intervened just in time to stop the message being sent. Quietly, not wanting anyone else in the cipher room to overhear, Susan apologised and said she'd had a momentary lack of concentration. Betty wasn't so sure. For the rest of the shift, she watched Susan's every move with an eagle eye.

Later, in a secluded corner of the mess room, away from prying ears, Betty spoke to Susan about the incident. Betty was worried that this wasn't the first error that Susan had made, but Susan assured her that it had never happened before and wouldn't happen again.

'I don't know what came over me,' she confessed, her eyes moist with tears. 'Perhaps the work is getting to me, and I've been feeling so homesick... But this is the first time I've ever been any good at anything and I can't give it up.'

'I'm sorry you're feeling like that,' Betty replied. It was as she had thought; Susan was buckling under the strain of the responsibility they bore in the cipher room. 'You should have told us. We would have helped you. And if you need some sick leave, I'm sure Lieutenant Corder would agree. You're no use to anyone if you're not healthy and on tip-top form.'

Susan looked stricken. 'Please don't tell him,' she pleaded. 'He'll never let me work on the machines again. I'll have to go and wash dishes or something and I really don't want to do that. And don't tell Deborah or Lily, either. I don't want them thinking I'm an idiot.'

Betty considered this for a few moments. Her natural compassion prompted her reply. 'All right,' she said, slowly. 'I won't say anything. I know it was just a mistake, a momentary lapse of concentration. But just promise me you'll tell me if things start to get on top of you again. That's what friends are for, isn't it?' She looked into Susan's eyes and steadily held her gaze as she waited for her reply.

'Yes, of course,' said Susan eagerly, clearly grateful for the reprieve Betty had given her. She reached out her hand and took Betty's. Her palm was warm and moist. 'Thank you, Betty. You're a true pal.'

Betty smiled and nodded and followed Susan back to their table to join the others. She was still worried about her quiet, self-deprecating friend, and tried to think of what she could do to help her. The weather was getting better and all four of them were due a day off, as they had been working tirelessly since their arrival in Italy. If Susan was burnt out, perhaps they were all in danger of following suit.


OVER THE NEXT couple of days, Betty and Lily put their heads together and hatched a plan for an excursion. After all, a change was as good as a rest. It was only mid-March but spring seemed to have come early, bringing with it an end to the rain and the advent of some welcome sunshine; the perfect time to go exploring.

Ever since they had arrived in Italy, Betty had marvelled at the citrus trees in the streets or glimpsed through iron railings in private gardens. To see actual oranges, clementines, lemons and limes, those prized fruits that had become rarities in England since the war began, growing in such easy abundance was extraordinary.

'Girls,' she began excitedly, as they sat at breakfast one day towards the end of the month. 'Did you know this is prime time for the famous Sorrento lemons? Let's go, shall we, visit a lemon grove, watch the harvest, perhaps have a taste of some delicious limoncello?'

Her enthusiasm was obviously infectious; the others all quickly agreed.

'We can hitch a ride,' volunteered Lily. 'There are jeeps and trucks going up and down to Salerno all day long. And perhaps we could visit Pompeii, too.'

'I'm up for it,' agreed Deborah. She turned to her right. 'Susan? Are you coming?'

'Oh yes,' said Susan, in her tiny, meek voice. 'I wouldn't miss it for the world.'

On the allotted day that they had all managed to get off work, the four got ready in their best dress uniform and peaked caps, shoulder bags packed with water flasks and the knife, fork, spoon and tin mug kit that went everywhere with them. Deborah had been gifted a camera by one of her many paramours and, commandeering a passing orderly to help out, she insisted they all pose for a photograph sitting on the edge of the fountain in Villa Teresa's courtyard.

This done, they made their way out of the palace, past the sentinel parasol pines, down the steps and onto the street. It wasn't far to the main drag, where, as Lily had predicted, a constant stream of military vehicles whizzed past. Before too long, they had successfully flagged down a jeep and were ensconced in the back, clutching onto the benches as the driver roared down the coast road.

As they approached Sorrento, Betty had a sudden rush of memory, of staggering up the shore here after the shipwreck of the *Arcadia*. This time, though, the driver took a different route, not along the coast but high up above the sea. The women gasped and squealed as the jeep careered along single-lane tracks that gave onto precipitous drops to the rocks and the translucent blue water far below. Though they were mostly climbing, on occasion the road would descend for a short time as it wound its way round the contours of the hillside. On each of these descents, Betty was sure the driver had forgotten how to use the brakes as they hurtled downwards. But each time, disaster was averted and the jeep and its passengers survived to continue their rattling, teeth-jarring progress.

Eventually, the vehicle pulled into a lay-by and they climbed out. Thanking the driver, they followed a steep track that led up the hillside, following signs that simply read, LIMONI. Before long they had reached a narrow path cut into the rock where, seeming to defy the law of gravity, a long line of lemon trees clinging to a small sliver of earth announced the entrance to the grove. Betty marvelled to see that the trees bore fruit in varying stages of ripeness, from green to bright yellow, at the same time as they were blossoming. Someone had told her that Sorrento lemon trees fruited four times a year but she hadn't really believed it. Now, the living proof was right before her incredulous eyes.

A delicious citrus smell, so heady and intoxicating it almost made Betty feel giddy, emanated from the tiny blossom flowers, suffusing the sun-drenched air. As they walked, the scent grew stronger and stronger, and soon they were in the heart of the grove. Here, the trees were trained up and over wooden pergolas, creating tunnels of dappled shade. The size of the fruits was extraordinary; some were as big as melons. All around them was a hive of activity, women and elderly men picking and packing the precious harvest. They came across an old man, wizened and bent almost double with age, surveying the scene.

'Are these your trees?' asked Betty, in her best Italian.

'*Si*,' answered the man. 'All mine.'

'What's your name?' continued Betty.

'Salvatore,' he answered. And then, 'Come. Try some *limoni*.'

With that, he plucked two ripe lemons from the nearest tree, picked up a knife and, with its razor-sharp blade, sliced off chunks of the fruit. Demonstrating to the friends, he ate a slice, peel, pith and all, and then handed one to each of them.

Betty took a tentative nibble. Far from being sour and unpalatable, as she'd expected, it was delicious, zinging with freshness, tart, sharp and piquant.

'Wonderful,' she murmured appreciatively, her mouth salivating at the prospect of another bite.

'That tastes incredible,' exclaimed Deborah. 'I've never eaten a lemon before.'

'There's a first time for everything,' said Lily, laughing.

'Full of goodness,' enthused Salvatore, making a kissing motion with his free hand. 'Good for skin, teeth, hair.'

'Gosh,' responded Lily. She'd picked up quite a bit of the language by now and had understood before Betty had time to translate Salvatore's words. Deborah and Susan still hadn't got beyond '*grazie*'. 'We better all have another slice then. In this climate, my hair needs all the help it can get!'

They all laughed and eagerly took more lemon. All apart from Susan, that was, who Betty saw discreetly dropping her piece to the ground, obviously finding it not to her taste.

Salvatore led them onwards, pointing out the willow trees that provided the supple branches used to tie the lemons to the pergolas. Along the fringe of the grove, a row of beehives commanded a magnificent vista of the wide bay far below.

'They've got a room with a view,' remarked Betty, enviously.

'Who wouldn't be a bee and live here?' This enchanted place made her feel utterly transported, beyond the war, and Samuel, and missing home and family. And Gianni. In this magical grove, all seemed well with the world.

They reached the far corner of Salvatore's domain, where a path wound its way down the precipitous hillside. Women were effortlessly hoisting baskets loaded to the brim with lemons onto their heads and setting off on the winding journey down to the sea, where boats would carry the precious cargo to Naples for sale in the market.

Salvatore took more lemons, cut them in half, scooped out some of the flesh and filled them with water from a bubbling spring that emerged from the cliff.

'*Limonata!*' he said, handing the friends one each. 'Lemonade, the freshest you'll ever get.'

Betty drank hers greedily; the spring sunshine was hot and clambering up and down the terraces thirsty work. It was delicious.

As a parting gift, Salvatore piled their shoulder bags with dozens of the lumpy, bumpy fruits. Revived by the cold drinks, Betty, Lily, Deborah and Susan made their way back to the centre of the town. They found a café proclaiming that it served fresh fish and took a table overlooking the sea. The proprietor hurried out and hastily erected a sunshade to protect them from the midday sun, and then brought them plates of fresh swordfish and *patatine fritte.*

'Before I came here,' proclaimed Deborah, tucking into her meal with gusto, 'the only types of fish I'd ever tasted were cod and haddock. I'd barely heard of things like snapper, tuna, mullet...' She paused to swallow another mouthful. 'Chips, on the other hand,' she continued, waving one around on the end of her fork, 'I am very familiar with.'

Everyone laughed. Enjoying her own food, Betty thought it was about the best meal she'd ever eaten. She felt suddenly, overwhelmingly, lucky. Lucky to have had this opportunity to go overseas and to see and experience things she'd never even dreamt of before, to accomplish things that prior generations of British women would not have believed possible.

'This is the life, isn't it,' she mused, when she'd finished her plateful. 'Good food, good weather and, most importantly, good company.'

'Hear, hear,' Lily chipped in, raising her glass of water to the others. 'To Italy and to us!' The others all chinked glasses, while the waiter came to clear their plates and bring them the bitter black espresso that Betty had grown to love. At home, there had been nothing but ersatz Camp coffee made from chicory for ages, so to be able to taste the real thing again was another marvel.

'So, what's next?' asked Betty, when the meal was over. 'Pompeii? Shall we?'

Lily and Deborah agreed enthusiastically, but Betty noticed that Susan, who'd said hardly a word all day, gave no response. What was up with her? It troubled Betty's kind heart to see her friend so preoccupied. This day out was supposed to take their minds off their worries. But Susan seemed more subdued than ever.

# CHAPTER TWENTY-EIGHT

The foursome set off, another lift taking them right to the Porta Marina, the great stone gate that gave access to the excavated town of Pompeii. Betty could hardly believe that it was so intact after being buried under ash for nearly two millennia. Sadly, one of the buildings just inside the gates had been bombed the previous year and lay in ruins, modern warfare having destroyed what the pyroclastic flow had not.

Wandering through the paved streets that were lined with shops and houses, restaurants, stables and hotels, Betty looked with wonder at the inscriptions on building walls that still flaunted the names of favoured election candidates or advertised upcoming gladiator shows.

'It's so extraordinary to think that all of this was here,' she said to Lily, as they poked their noses into a baker's shop, 'and then it wasn't. Just like that. And then, at some future point, that the whole Roman civilisation ended and we slipped back into the Dark Ages.'

Lily nodded. 'Extraordinary indeed. There but for the grace of God go we, I suppose.'

With this sobering thought, they emerged from the

centuries-old building and into the light, where they hurried after Deborah and Susan.

'We could go to one of the vineyards now,' suggested Deborah, hopefully. 'You know they make the most amazing wine here – apparently the volcanic ash makes the ground really fertile or something.'

To Betty's mind, used as she was to the rich brown earth of Yorkshire, it didn't seem right that this black moonscape land was so fertile. But she knew what Deborah said was true.

'Fine by me,' she said. 'We can take the bus part of the way back to Naples and then walk.'

They set off towards the main road. As they walked, the conversation strayed back to work. After all, it was their main preoccupation, day after day.

'It's so strange that they never found out who damaged the headsets, isn't it,' mused Lily. 'You would have thought Lieutenant Corder would have got to the bottom of it. He's such a stickler.'

Betty nodded. 'I know. And then that lost codebook never materialised either.' Eventually, once the incident had faded into the background and the codebook had been supplanted by the new issue, she'd mentioned its loss to Lily and the others. They'd been as mystified as her. 'Plus,' she continued, 'I overheard Lieutenant Corder talking to another officer the other day and I got the impression something else had gone missing, some paperwork or such like.'

Deborah frowned. 'Gosh, that is mysterious. And worrying. We don't have dramas like that in supplies. Nothing gets in or out without being ticked off on our inventory. Not even a single carrot.'

Betty and Lily both laughed at the idea of root vegetables being so keenly guarded, but Susan did not so much as crack a smile. Betty had been surreptitiously observing her as they'd been chatting, wondering what her reaction would be to Lily's airing of the odd occurrences in the cipher room. The answer was that she had none. Susan's expression remained bland and unfathomable, her mouth and eyes set in a fixed position that gave no clue as to what she was thinking.

Lily lit a cigarette and drew on it, her forehead creased in contemplation. 'Joking aside,' she said, 'there's something about it all that doesn't sit right with me.'

Betty regarded her quizzically. She, too, had suspicions that there was more to the odd events than their superiors were letting on. But obviously none of the women could ask them directly; it was way above their station or pay grade.

'What do you think then, Lily?' Betty questioned. 'I've puzzled and puzzled over it, and I can't work it out at all.'

Lily shrugged. 'Oh, I don't know,' she replied, airily. 'Just that too many things seem to be happening for them all to be coincidences. But I really don't know any more than that.'

Further conversation on the matter was precluded by the arrival of the Naples bus. They all got on, and Betty asked the bus driver to drop them at the spot nearest to the vineyard they wanted to visit.

As they approached the place, Lily, Betty and Deborah gathered up their knapsacks and prepared to get off. Susan stayed put.

'I'm going straight back,' she said, abruptly. 'I've... got something to do.'

Betty wondered what was so urgent that Susan wanted to cut short this marvellous day out, freed temporarily from the pressures of work.

'What is it, Susan?' she asked.

At the same time, Lily chimed in. 'Surely mending your stockings or doing your laundry can wait, can't it?' Her tone was gently mocking and, though Betty knew she didn't mean to be cruel, she worried that Susan would misinterpret it.

'It would be a shame to miss out on the fun,' she urged

Susan.

But Susan just shook her head. By this time the bus had drawn to a halt, the driver waiting impatiently, fingers tapping the steering wheel, for the women to get off. Betty had no choice but to descend after Lily and Deborah.

'I wonder why she's in such a hurry to get back,' mused Lily, as they began striking out across the rough, stony ground.

Deborah made a moue of incomprehension. 'Up to her,' she answered, and turned her attention to the map. 'I think it's up here.' She pointed. 'I reckon it's about half an hour's walk.' She gesticulated vaguely up the mountain's slopes.

'Lead the way, then,' said Lily. 'We'll follow you.'

With a last glance at the bus as it receded rapidly into the distance, Betty turned to follow. She would remain vigilant where Susan was concerned; she was still worried about her and her state of mind.

After a hard hike over uneven ground, stumbling and tripping on rocks and hassocks of thick grass, they were nowhere near anything remotely resembling a vineyard. But they were a lot closer to Vesuvius, with its ever-smoking summit.

Deborah and Lily were busily arguing over the map when it suddenly struck Betty. The smoke. It wasn't the usual whitish-grey colour. This smoke was dark and almost black, and a lot thicker than normal. And, now she thought about it, every time the wind blew it brought with it a distinct sulphurous whiff, much stronger than usual. She fixed her eyes on the plume. She was imagining things, surely. There was nothing to worry about.

But, far from reassuring her, what she saw made goosebumps break out on her arms, despite the sunshine. An ashen grey cloud was billowing upwards from Vesuvius' summit, unmistakably denser and more voluminous than it had been even just seconds ago.

'I'm telling you it's this way,' insisted Lily.

'No it's not,' argued Deborah. 'You're looking at the map

upside down. North is that way!'

Their voices ricocheted around Betty's head. There was something terribly wrong and suddenly she couldn't move, was paralysed with fear. Vesuvius shouldn't look like that.

But no, she sternly told herself. Of course Vesuvius wasn't erupting. They'd know if that was about to happen, wouldn't they? The local people would know, Salvatore, the waitress in the café, they knew this mountain so well, its moods and tempers. They would have told them to stay clear, surely... And then it occurred to her how ironic it would be if they were caught in a volcanic eruption having just visited Pompeii—

Her thoughts were interrupted by a huge, ominous, hair-raising rumble that seemed to rise up from the depths of the ground beneath them.

Lily and Deborah fell instantly silent. All three looked at each other, eyes wide with fear. Betty recalled that moment on the *Arcadia*, after the torpedo hit, when they had clung together in the darkness, forced to contemplate the very real prospect of their own deaths. She had thought then that the threat posed by German U-boats was about as bad as it could get. But now they had a natural enemy to contend with.

Another hideous boom and reverberation, ten times louder than the loudest thunder Betty had ever heard, filled the air with sound. The earth beneath their feet trembled. The cloud spiralling above the mountain was mushroom-shaped now, getting bigger by the second. Betty felt drops on her upturned face and, for a second, relief surged through her. Rain would be a good thing, wouldn't it; it would dampen the fire rising to Vesuvius' surface and cool the lava it would soon start expelling.

And then Betty realised that it wasn't raindrops but cinders and ash, the debris being expelled from the mountain's grumbling innards.

Wild-eyed, she turned to Deborah and Lily. 'We need to get out of here,' she said, thin-lipped and terse. 'Quickly.'

# CHAPTER TWENTY-NINE

Sadie picked up her glass of orange juice and took a gulp, steeling herself for what she was about to do. Another day, another letter.

On the coffee table in front of her lay a crisp white envelope. Inside it, Sadie hoped, would be more pieces from the jigsaw of her life. At a loss as to any other way to find out more about the puzzling inscription on the memento Jean had sent her, she'd asked the doorman and general dogsbody at work, Stu, to help her. He'd been a tail-end Charlie in the war, the airman on board a bomber whose job was to sit in the glass bubble at the rear and defend the plane from enemy attack from the blind side. It was regarded as the loneliest and most dangerous job of any in the skies, and had left Stu with numerous physical scars and an absolute abhorrence of the cold. Despite this, he was always cheerful and accommodating, and proved no less so when Sadie enquired if he had ever heard of a place called Eden Camp.

Of course he had.

'It was a prisoner-of-war camp,' he told her, without hesitation. 'Up in Yorkshire, not far from where some cousins of mine live in Pickering.' He'd faltered then, and cast Sadie an anxious gaze. 'More than that I can't tell you, love,' he'd concluded.

It was enough. Thanking him profusely, Sadie had hurried to her desk, where she struggled to keep her mind on the invoices and purchase orders she was typing as she composed in her head a letter to the Ministry of Defence to request further information.

She'd put the letter in the post three weeks ago and hadn't expected to hear for ages. So to receive a reply so soon was both exciting and anxiety-provoking. Perhaps they'd been so quick because there was nothing to say?

Steeling herself for possible disappointment, she picked up the envelope and slid a fingernail along the flap. Her heart in her mouth, she pulled out the paper inside, unfolded it and began to read.

*Dear Miss Collins*

*Further to your letter, I am able to confirm that Eden Camp was a POW camp on the outskirts of Malton, North Yorkshire. Initially it held Italian POWs and, subsequently, German inmates. According to camp records, an Italian prisoner with the initials GU, full name Gianni Urso, was detained at Eden Camp until the Italian capitulation in 1943. After that time, Mr Urso was released. Unfortunately our records do not cover what happened to him subsequently. Eden Camp itself is in private ownership and no longer in use.*

Sadie picked up the wooden heart and key and rubbed it against her cheek. Had Gianni Urso made this little keepsake while a prisoner at the camp? It seemed so. The fact that it had been in her swaddling robes, tucked inside like a talisman to keep her safe, could surely mean only one thing.

This Gianni Urso was her father.

Who her mother was remained a complete mystery. But if Gianni was her dad, that meant she was at least half-Italian, a fact that was too unexpected and bewildering to fully take on board quite yet. It explained her dark hair and skin that tanned easily, she supposed, but lots of people who didn't have an ounce of foreign blood in them had those attributes.

Sadie trembled as she reread the letter again and again. It was at least a clue, something concrete to go on. All she had to do now was find Gianni Urso.

At that thought, she burst out laughing at her idiocy. How ludicrous! How on earth was she going to find one Italian in a nation of over 45 million people? She furrowed her brow, staring at the letter as if it held the answer buried within it, some cryptic message that, if only she could interpret it, would make everything clear.

But of course there was nothing.

Unfolding her legs, Sadie got up and walked over to the window. She leant on the sill and looked out at the street below, along which Londoners hurried, heading to the nearby station or the shops, intent on their purpose. But instead of the usual drab greys and blacks of their garb, the sun had brought out the bright colours. Women wore multicoloured dresses with wide sleeves and flowing skirts, and men sported shirts in red, pink or orange.

Sadie smiled at the sight. How could anyone prefer winter to summer? It was so much better when there was more colour in the world.

Then her smile abruptly faded. This wasn't helping her decide what to do. From her window she could see the domed roof of Paddington station. The obvious solution. She needed to get on a train and head north. She'd traced her roots to Mornington Crescent and now she would do the same in Yorkshire. It was more logistically challenging, and expensive – she'd have to spend the night up there, and then there was the train fare. But it had to be done. She'd got so far, there was no way she was going to quit now.

A FEW HOURS LATER, Sadie stepped down onto the platform of Malton station. The journey had given her plenty of time to prepare for what she needed to do in the town, but now she'd arrived she had a sudden attack of nerves. She'd had a cup of tea and an Eccles cake on the train, and wished she hadn't as it was uneasily swirling around inside her. The decision to come to Yorkshire had been taken in a matter of seconds. The journey had taken hours.

Hours during which she'd had nothing else to do but mull on what she was embarked upon. What if Kim was right and only unhappiness lay at the end of her search? Perhaps she wouldn't find her father or her mother, or perhaps, if she did, they wouldn't want to know her. At that thought, Sadie shuddered involuntarily. She was kidding herself if she believed she'd be fine with rejection. She wouldn't be fine. She'd be destroyed.

A sudden sense of panic gripped her. Maybe she shouldn't be doing this. She could cross over to the other platform, get the next train straight back to London. For a moment, Sadie dithered where she stood. She'd never felt so lonely, or so unsure.

And then the sun broke through a cloud and the light flooded onto the platform. It galvanised Sadie to action. She'd vowed not to give up and she couldn't go back on that. Steeling herself, she left the station and, outside on the street, looked around her and tried to decide what to do first. Perhaps she should find a room for the night and leave her bag there before she began her search. The prospect brought her out in a cold sweat. She'd never booked a hotel room by herself before. In fact, she'd only stayed in a hotel at all once or twice when on holiday on the south coast with her parents, and a couple of times with Simon. She found such places intimidating and she hated people waiting on her. She always wanted to get up and clear away the dinner plates herself, and she wouldn't dream of leaving the bed to be made by someone else.

But she was a grown adult now and there was nothing wrong with women travelling alone. It was the 1970s, for goodness' sake, not the 1950s. Lifting her head up high, Sadie marched out into the square. She stood for a moment, surveying the scene, and then proceeded along Railway Street. It was a beautiful day and, as she crossed the bridge over the River Derwent, she paused for a moment to watch the gently flowing water. Some children were sitting on the bank, dipping in their toes and shrieking in delight at the cold, and she thought how much she would have loved to do that when she was young.

On Yorkersgate, she saw the Derwent Hotel. It looked nice and, importantly, not too expensive, and it would certainly do for one night. Sadie realised as she walked towards the front door, above which swung the sign, that the place was also a pub. And where better to meet the locals and begin her enquiries than the bar?

She pushed open the hotel door and made her way to the reception. The woman on duty, whose name badge proclaimed her to be Mrs Carter, raised her eyebrows slightly as Sadie made her request for a one-night stay. Sadie could tell she was longing to know what had brought her to sleepy Malton.

'What will you be doing while you're here?' enquired Mrs Carter as they climbed the stairs, unable to quell her burning curiosity any longer.

'Oh, it's just that I'm looking for someone,' Sadie replied. 'An old family friend.' It was too personal, too extraordinary, to confess the real reason she wanted to find Gianni Urso. 'He was a prisoner-of-war, I believe, at Eden Camp, in 1943.'

They'd reached the room. Mrs Carter put the key in the lock and swung the door open. Inside, it was small and simply furnished but perfectly adequate for Sadie's needs.

'You'll want to talk to Bert Lewis, then,' Mrs Carter said, as she went to the window and flung it open. 'I'll let a bit of air in,' she added, breezily. 'Shame not to on such a lovely day. Now,' she continued, 'you've got your kettle here, tea and coffee, and the bathroom is just along the corridor, second on the left. Breakfast is served between eight and nine thirty. Let me know if there's anything you need.'

Sadie nodded, a tad impatiently. The minutiae of the hotel's facilities were not her focus right now.

'This Bert Lewis,' she asked, urgently. 'Why would he be good to talk to?'

Mrs Carter stopped fiddling with the arrangement of teabags on the tray by the kettle and stood up straight.

'Bert was the groundsman at the camp throughout the war. He knew almost everyone there, I shouldn't wonder he'd remember the name of this chap you're looking for. Of course the Italians were the first and then the Germans came but there was never any trouble with any of them, not so far as I know.'

'That's really interesting,' Sadie responded, trying to contain her excitement. 'And – where might I find Bert? Do you think he'd be happy to talk to me?'

Mrs Carter laughed. 'Bert'll talk to anyone who buys him a pint!' she exclaimed. 'He'll be propping up the bar later, like he is every Saturday night. Just pop down around six-ish and I'll point him out to you, introduce you if you like.' She paused and looked directly at Sadie, a smile spreading across her face. She seemed proud and pleased that she'd been able to help. 'And if you were thinking of visiting the camp, you can borrow my old bike. Much quicker than walking.'

# CHAPTER THIRTY

NAPLES, MARCH 1944

Betty, Deborah and Lily ran, as fast as their legs could carry them, back across the same rugged terrain they had so cheerfully traversed such a short time ago. All the weeks of PT and drill had made them fleet and fit. But the rumbling continued and the sky was thick with smoke and dust, volcanic ash and cinders, and all Betty could think was, *No matter how fast we are, we can't outrun a lava flow.*

The sulphurous stench Betty had detected earlier was now suffocating in its intensity. She had no idea if a full eruption had happened yet, still less what direction the lava would take when it did. The sooner they got off the mountain and back to the relative safety of Naples, the better.

The suddenness of the volcanic activity had taken them all by surprise. Now they had to flee for their lives to escape its venomous attack.

As she fled, Betty's hat was seized by the wind and flung away. She didn't stop to retrieve it. There was no time for that. Instead she raced on, her shoulder bag thumping awkwardly against her hip, her feet in their stiff lace-ups constantly slipping and sliding on the rough ground. Her hair, no longer held in place by the hat, blew across her face, intermittently blinding her.

The running seemed to go on forever. Betty's legs were heavy as lead, her lungs bursting, heart unable to beat any faster. She kept trying to pull her hair off her face, but it was either plastered to her skin by sweat or flying ever more uncontrollably around her head. She was ahead of Deborah but behind Lily, whose long legs allowed her to move with the speed of a gazelle.

Finally, miraculously, Betty spied the glint of a tarmac road ahead. At last! They were nearly there, somewhere they could hitch a ride or jump on a bus and get out of the volcano's range.

With a huge surge of effort, Betty forced her tired body to keep going. *Not far now*, she told herself, *you can do it*. A rock rose up in front of her and, just in time, she sidestepped it. And then she was falling, the ground coming up to meet her at remarkable speed, and she was down, flat out, every inch of her body crying out in pain.

She lay, unable to get up, winded. In her mind's eye, she saw an evil blanket of boiling lava creeping up behind her, felt its heat and destructive power as it moved inexorably closer.

*Move*, she told herself. *Pull yourself together*. She put her hands on the ground and pushed herself up. Suddenly Deborah was beside her, crouching down, peering anxiously at her, face white with concern.

'Betty, are you all right?' she asked. And then, before Betty could answer, added, 'Come on, let me help you up.'

Deborah put her hands under Betty's elbows and lifted her. All went well for a moment. And then Betty put her right foot on the ground and immediately shrieked with pain. Gritting her teeth, her eyes already full of tears, she held on to Deborah. Lily was back with them now, having realised they'd fallen behind.

'Betty, what's wrong?' she questioned urgently. 'Can you walk? If not, don't worry, we'll carry you...'

Betty shook her head. 'You can't do that,' she hissed, barely able to draw breath with the pain. 'Let me try again.' She looked down at her leg. Her foot was in the right place, not sticking out at some impossible, unnatural angle. Perhaps that meant it wasn't broken. Gingerly, she tried to rest some weight on it. Again, the same searing pain that made her feel sick and caused her to involuntarily cry out.

She looked at Deborah and Lily and shook her head. 'I can't do it,' she said. 'I can't walk.'

Another massive booming noise reverberated around them. Far from calming down, Vesuvius seemed to be getting angrier and angrier. It was clear this was no false alarm. Betty fixed her eyes on the mountain's peak. She was sure she could make out faint flickers of fire amidst the black pall that shrouded the summit. She shuddered and felt suddenly cold. The sun was now completely obscured by the spiralling cloud of smoke.

Lily took control. 'Come on, Deborah,' she instructed, briskly. 'You go that side and I'll take this. Hold your foot up, Betty, and lean on us.'

Like this, the trio made excruciatingly slow process over the last few hundred feet to the road. Once they got there, Betty collapsed down onto a rock. It was hardly comfortable but there was a limit to how long she could stand on one leg. Her ankle, swollen to twice its normal size, throbbed and ached.

It was a terrible end to the most marvellous day.

# CHAPTER THIRTY-ONE

In Naples, Betty was taken straight to the field hospital. By the time she was seen by the doctor, she was weak and exhausted from the unrelenting pain. His examination, the poking and prodding, hardly helped.

'I don't think it's broken,' he said, cheerfully, when he'd finished his inspection. 'Just a nasty twist. I'm going to get the nurses to give you an ice pack to reduce the swelling. Then we'll bandage it up, get some compression on it. You need to rest with your foot up on a pillow for a few days. You'll do that here in hospital, where we can keep an eye on you. Once the pain has reduced, you can start mobilising the ankle, but gentle exercise only until it's back to normal.'

He paused and peered sternly at Betty over the top of his glasses. 'I know what you young ATS ladies are like,' he went on. 'Wanting to get back to normal activity straight away. Well, you can't, do you hear me?' He smiled genially. 'Doctor knows best.'

Betty grimaced and nodded. He was a little patronising but, that notwithstanding, she had to take his advice. There would be no more excursions for a while.

'What about the volcano?' she blurted out. 'We were there, on the mountain, when it began. What will happen?'

The doctor frowned. 'We're being told it's serious. Naples is in no danger, but – well, there are villages that are under considerable threat.'

He sat down on his chair and began scribbling on a pad of paper. 'I've signed you off work for two weeks,' he said, handing Betty the chit. 'You look exhausted. And you are underweight. You need to beef yourself up a bit if you're going to be of use to the war effort. We can't have our most valuable people fainting all over the place.'

Betty bristled a little at the insinuation that she was like some Victorian lady having fits of the vapours. She was strong and her health was excellent! But the doctor was right, she *was* tired to her bones. She lay awake at night so often, worrying about everything, the war of course, and who was going to win – but also about Samuel, and Gianni. She'd told Gianni not to try to contact her, but, even if he had, she wasn't sure if her father would have passed on the letters. After all, he'd made clear his opinion on the matter before she left Yorkshire. As for Samuel, she had received just that one letter and nothing more. The truth was that she didn't know whether he was dead or alive.

Two things that should go together – love and duty – were in deadlock with each other, each constantly pulling her in opposite directions in a way that was exhausting and debilitating. A wave of fatigue washed over her. She imagined a bed in the hospital, the clean white sheets, a nurse caring for her, and suddenly a short stay here didn't seem so bad after all.

FOR THE FIRST TWENTY-FOUR HOURS, Betty slept, almost without waking. The next day, Lily came to visit.

'What's the news of the eruption?' Betty asked, her heart in her mouth.

Lily looked pained. 'It's continuing,' she said, simply. 'Ash and cinder are falling all the time, even here, and the streets are coated grey. In some of the villages right under the mountain, the lava dust is three feet thick and so heavy that roofs are caving in. Others, right in the path of the lava flow, have been obliterated. San Sebastiano, near where we were the other day, is destroyed.'

Betty could hardly believe it. The idea that in the twentieth century a natural phenomenon should have such a devastating effect seemed all wrong, as if modern man should have been able to tame Planet Earth by now.

'And the American airbase near Salerno was engulfed. Hundreds of B-52s swallowed up by molten lava – hardly what the Allies need right now.'

'How dreadful,' she breathed sadly. 'Has anyone died?'

'A few,' replied Lily. 'Local Italians, not army personnel. That's what the newsreels are reporting, anyway.'

'Poor souls.' Betty fell silent. More death and destruction when these people had already suffered so much of both. Bombing, volcanic eruptions, what did it matter the cause if you and your family were left living on the streets, your loved ones gone to eternal rest?

When Lily had left, she lay on her bed staring at the plain white ceiling. It was restful and calming after the frenetic-frescoed activity of the palace. The wind had been blowing south up until now, but that night it changed to a northerly. Betty woke the next day to the smell of sulphur and the taste of ash on her tongue. She was so grateful to be safe in this hospital, and hoped the Italians whose homes no longer existed would also find a place of sanctuary.

Lily had brought Betty some post from the palace and, when she could summon the energy, Betty propped herself upright on her pillows and opened them. The first was from Jane. She had had the baby at last, over two weeks late – a little boy called Archie. Overwhelmed with joy for her sister, Betty shed a few tears at the thought of being an auntie, and because it would be a long time until she would be able to meet her nephew.

The other one was from Samuel's mother, Julie. Betty opened it with trepidation. Julie never sent a letter that didn't mention the wedding she was anticipating when the war was over and both Betty and Samuel were back home in Malton. If it wasn't for rationing, Betty was sure she'd have bought her outfit already.

But today's missive didn't say anything about any of that. In fact, Julie had only one thing to tell Betty. She had heard on the relatives' grapevine that many of the men captured by the Japanese had succumbed to tropical fevers. No one knew how many were affected, or who had died, but it was perfectly possible that Samuel wouldn't make it, or that he would be permanently debilitated or disabled if he did. Julie knew this would be terrible for Betty to hear but she'd felt Betty should know.

After reading this, Betty lay back down on her bed, wanting to curl up in a ball but not able to do so with her injured leg. Instead she pulled the sheet over her face and tried to block out the world. Whatever her misgivings about getting married to Samuel, she still felt deeply for him and his suffering. She wanted him to be safe, and to be happy. It would be far easier to disentangle herself from their relationship if that were the case.

On the third day, Betty's friends came to visit en masse. She was glad to see their smiling faces after the news of yesterday – but surprised they had all been let in together.

'We had to do some sweet-talking, I can tell you,' Lily told her. 'But in the end the old dragon of a sister relented. I think everyone's a bit distracted at the moment.' She bent down and lowered her voice, though Betty wasn't sure why. There was only one other woman on the ward and she was far away down the other end. 'There's been a big offensive at Monte Cassino. The field hospital there can't cope with all the casualties, so those who can stand the journey will be brought here. The whole hospital will be full.'

Betty's eyes were wide with horror at the thought of the wounded men who would soon be arriving. What terrible injuries would they have sustained? She swung her legs over the side of her bed and struggled to her feet. Her ankle protested but did not collapse. The pain was bearable, too. Just about.

'Let's go then,' she said, abruptly. 'I don't want to get in the way of nurses and doctors who will have far better things to do than think about me and my stupid leg.'

She'd been given a crutch, which was leaning against the end of the bed. She grabbed it and felt immediately more stable and secure. They were halfway out of the building when a nurse came chasing after them.

'Wait!' she called. 'The doctor must give you some painkillers and check you over. He's not here at the moment, so you'll need to wait half an hour or so until he gets back.' She turned to Deborah, Lily and Susan. 'You girls will have to go,' she asserted, firmly. 'We need all the corridors clear.'

Betty turned to her friends. 'Don't worry about me,' she said. 'Thank you for coming, though. I'll be all right here until I've seen the doctor.'

Once they had left, Betty settled down on a chair tucked in a corner near the entrance. That way she would see the doctor when he returned from whatever errand he'd gone on. Around twenty minutes later, the first of the ambulances drew up, skidding to a halt on the driveway, which was thickly coated with volcanic ash. The doors slammed open and within seconds orderlies were carrying stretchers up the stone steps and into the hospital. Men with bandaged heads and limbs lay on them. Some of them were silent, others groaned and moaned. Betty had a sudden wish that she'd gone into nursing, not signals, so that she could be of some use now instead of sitting here doing nothing.

More and more ambulances arrived, and also jeeps, trucks and wagons. It was clear that any vehicle available was being used to transport the injured. The Battle of Monte Cassino had been through many phases over the last few months. Did this influx of wounded indicate that it had taken a decisive turn in the Allies' favour? Betty fervently hoped so.

She was still waiting, somewhat impatiently, for the doctor to arrive when it happened. A jeep drew away and, as soon as its spot by the front doors was vacated, another one took up its place. From the back doors spilled half a dozen men, uniforms bloodied and torn. They were clearly in need of urgent medical attention, but not so badly damaged as the first arrivals had been. Betty thanked God for that.

Not wanting to stare and seem rude, she averted her eyes. But something had caught her attention before she did so. Her heart seemed to stop beating and she felt sweat break out on her palms and forehead. It couldn't be. She must be hallucinating. It wasn't possible.

Very, very slowly, she turned back to look at the men hobbling through the hospital doors.

No, she wasn't imagining it. From her dark corner, into which the daylight did not penetrate, she had seen, quite clearly in the strong spring sunshine, a familiar figure, a well-known face. There, about to limp straight past her, was Gianni.

# CHAPTER THIRTY-TWO

MALTON, JULY 1972

Sadie wobbled slightly as she brought the bicycle to a halt. She'd taken up Mrs Carter's offer with some trepidation as she hadn't cycled in about fifteen years. But the adage that once you'd learnt to ride a bike you never forgot had proved true and she'd managed to arrive at Eden Camp in one piece.

Stashing the cycle behind a bush, she looked around at the barbed wire fences, behind which stood rows of huts that she presumed had been the prisoners' accommodation. As she wandered around the perimeter she found a place where the wire had been cut, making a hole just about big enough for her to fit through.

In a couple of moments she was inside the camp. As if afraid of being heard by the ghosts of its old inhabitants, she tiptoed towards the nearest hut. Pushing through the rampant under-growth, goosegrass and nettles and brambles, heedless of the scratches on her legs, she peered in through the grimy window that was hung about with dirty grey spiders' webs. There were bunk beds within, and a couple of chairs, and in the corner was a stove. Sadie shivered despite the heat of the day, imagining the cold of winter on the North York Moors. She could almost see the men, gathered together around the fire, swapping stories from home. It was almost impossible to comprehend that one of them might have been her father. It made her feel shaky and giddy.

Would this Gianni Urso have been a willing or reluctant combatant? It was impossible to know, unless she managed to find him and ask. And, assuming he was her father, what kind of a relationship had he had with whoever was her mother? Was she a local girl? Sadie shook her head as if trying to rid it of all the questions. It seemed that the more she found out, the more puzzles and enigmas were thrown up.

Letting go of the rotten windowsill, Sadie turned away, back to the potholed paths that led through the camp, where she ambled up and down, picturing the camp when it was full of men, talking in their own languages, Italian and then German, their busy chatter filling the air. The only workers here now were the ants, busily hurrying in all different directions, heedless of her presence.

After a while, Sadie was hit by a sudden fear of being caught here, trespassing, and of getting into trouble with the law. Hurriedly, she made her way back to the gap in the fence, forced herself through it and collected Mrs Carter's bike, which fortunately was still exactly where she had left it. Pedalling back into town, Sadie wondered if she should try to grab some food before tracking Bert down and regaling him with all her many questions. She didn't want a rumbling stomach to interfere with her mission. But, on the other hand, she felt far too nervous and keyed up to eat.

In the end, the matter was settled for her. No sooner had she returned the bicycle to its resting place than Mrs Carter was upon her, urging her to come on through to the public bar, where Bert was already ensconced on his favourite stool and ready to provide her with any information he could.

Flustered, Sadie followed Mrs Carter through the hotel's dim corridor to the bar. An old man wearing a flat cap sat on a high stool, a scruffy mongrel dog lying at his feet. As Mrs Carter made the introductions, Bert smiled toothlessly at Sadie. He held out his hand to her, a work-worn hand, skin permanently tanned a dark brown from years of toil on the land.

'Bert Lewis. Pleased to be of service, lass,' he said. 'Never any trouble to help out the young, 'specially not a lovely wee girl such as yourself.'

Sadie smiled. 'Thank you,' she replied. 'Um – can I get you a drink? Before we talk...'

Bert nodded and turned to the barman. 'Pint of ale please, John,' he said.

Once the drink was delivered, Bert took a gulp, then wiped his mouth with the back of his hand. He looked expectantly at Sadie, as if waiting for her to do something, perform a magic trick or tell a joke. Sadie felt strangely exposed and out of place, especially as she didn't have a drink of her own. She was about to order a Campari and soda but stopped just in time. She didn't want to come across as pretentious or some London type, all fancy tastes and airs and graces.

'Um, half a pint of – of the same as Mr Lewis is having,' she said to John, who was leaning over the pumps and smiling genially.

'Coming right up,' John replied. He filled the glass with amber liquid and placed it in front of her.

An expectant silence fell. Sadie realised it was up to her to break it. 'So, er, Mr Lewis,' she began, acutely aware of John hovering nearby, wiping the beer pumps with a cloth and then rearranging some of the glasses under the counter. 'I-I've heard that you worked at Eden Camp when it was a prisoner-of-war camp, and that you, er, you knew a lot of the men,' she continued, falteringly. 'I wondered, well, I'm trying to, I'm looking for someone called Gianni Urso. I don't suppose you remember him?'

Bert considered this for just a few seconds before replying. 'Gianni! Goodness me, blow me down, of course I knew Gianni. But he left, not like lots of the other Eyeties who still live around these parts to this day. No, he rejoined, went off to liberate his country from the Germans, or so I believe.'

Sadie stared at him in astonishment. It hadn't occurred to her that, once captured, the prisoners might then have been released and able to fight again, albeit on the other side from formerly. She wasn't sure how she felt about having a father who was a soldier. And then the absurdity of this thought hit her. She wasn't sure how she felt about knowing any of this stuff. She still hadn't begun to really come to terms with her adoption. Perhaps Simon was right and she was making everything worse for herself by trying to find her birth parents. And then another thought struck her, a terrible one. What if Gianni Urso had died in the fighting?

But she couldn't contemplate that. She *wouldn't* contemplate that.

'Do you know anyone who would know where he is now?' she persisted, anxiously. 'Anyone else I could ask?'

Bert took a long slug of his ale. 'I'm not sure. It's been a long time, hasn't it, love?' He paused, his brow wrinkled in thought. And then, 'Ah!' he exclaimed, suddenly. 'I do have something that might help you. A letter Gianni sent me once. It had an address on it, as far as I can re—'

'Can I have it?' Sadie interrupted, her words tripping over themselves in her hurry to get them out. 'I mean, it would be wonderful if I could see it,' she continued, in a more measured tone. 'Would you, er, would you be able to give it to me tonight? Or tomorrow morning? Because I'll have to be on the London train tomorrow afternoon.'

Bert nodded. He pushed his glass towards John the barman. 'You can be getting me another of those,' he instructed John, 'and while you're doing that, I'll pop home and have a look for something for this lass.'

Sadie was simultaneously overcome with gratitude and with joy. 'Are you sure it's no trouble?' she said, anxiously, not meaning it at all. However much trouble, she desperately needed Bert to do this.

'None whatsoever, love,' Bert replied. He was already off the bar stool and facing the exit. 'I'll be back soon.'

The time passed unimaginably slowly. But, after ten minutes that felt like ten hours, Bert returned, limping and shuffling into the public bar, followed by his faithful dog, who had gone with him. Sadie wondered how old Bert was. His gait aged him but his mind was clearly still sharp as a knife.

'Here you are. It's dated' – he peered at the letter, trying to make out the date – '1944,' he concluded. 'I lost a lot of things when my cottage flooded a few years back. This is the only one of Gianni's letters that survived. I don't know what happened to him after the war. We lost touch, you know how it is.' Bert gave a long sigh, as if the weight of all the years and all the people who had come and gone was suddenly too much for him. 'Anyway, this is the bit you need.'

He prodded at the bottom of the flimsy piece of paper before handing it to Sadie. The ink was faded, barely legible, and Sadie had to squint to make out the words.

*If you have time to write again, you can address the letter c/o the Villa Teresa, Naples, Italy – someone there will pass it on to me. I'll be here in the city until I've recovered from my injuries and I can go back to fight with my partisan unit in the north.*

Sadie gazed at the paper. A partisan? This was even more

totally unexpected than everything that had gone before. And Naples. So far away... What was she going to do now? How on earth could she go to Italy? How would she get there, how much would it cost and what about the language? She didn't speak a word of Italian.

Trying to hide her confusion, she thanked Bert profusely. A wave of tiredness brought on by the long journey, the unaccustomed bicycle ride and the eventful evening swept over her. Her mind was a whirl of conflicting emotions. She'd found out far more than she'd ever expected to in one visit to Malton. Yet the conclusion to her story lay as far out of reach as ever.

'I better get to bed,' she said. 'John will buy you as many drinks as you want and put them on my room tab.' She held out her hand to Bert's for a farewell shake.

'Let me know how you get on,' Bert urged her. 'You can leave a message here; it'll always get to me.'

'I will,' promised Sadie.

Though what she would have to tell him, and when, she had no idea.

# CHAPTER THIRTY-THREE

NAPLES, MARCH 1944

At first, the sight of the man she loved from the bottom of her heart was like a mirage. Betty stared, blinked, stared again. She stood up, stepping out of her dark corner and into the light. As she did so, Gianni faltered. He looked in Betty's direction. Their eyes locked and for a moment, both stood still, transfixed and disbelieving.

And then Betty rushed towards him, taking in as she did so his worn, battle-scarred face, his bloodied fatigues and his left arm hanging in a makeshift sling. Casting aside all thoughts of propriety and respectability as raw emotion ripped through her, she flung her arms round his neck. Looking up into his kind brown eyes, which now bore the weight of everything he had seen and done in the harsh battlefields of the north, she whispered his name. 'Gianni, Gianni. What happened to you? Where have you been? How on earth did you get here? What have you been doing? Are you all right?'

Gianni smiled down at her, the lopsided grin that turned her stomach inside out. 'Betty,' he murmured, ignoring all her questions. 'Is it really you? I don't believe it. Tell me it's really you.'

Betty gave a short laugh of pent-up emotion and anguish. 'Yes, it's me,' she replied, still clutching hold of him. 'It's definitely me. But we need to get you to see the doctor, do something about that arm of yours. Is there anywhere else that you're hurt?' she asked, dread filling her voice.

Gianni shook his head. 'I'm fine,' he asserted. 'There are men in a far worse state than me. I just need the bullet taken out of my shoulder and I'll be fine.'

Betty shuddered. Gianni had been shot! How? Was he in the army again? What on earth had been going on? And then at the same time, thank God, oh thank God, the bullet had missed his head, his heart. She lifted her face to his and he bent forward to kiss her, just briefly, in the midst of the bustle of the hospital, the influx of the wounded, the rushing to and fro of nurses and orderlies.

Betty kissed him back and then buried her face in his chest for one brief moment, before a clattering behind them announced stretcher-bearers trying to pass by.

Stepping out of the way, Betty took his right hand and squeezed it. 'Come on,' she said. 'Let's get you to the waiting room.'

It was a couple of hours before Gianni was allocated a bed. He did everything he could to resist staying at the hospital, but the doctor was unequivocal.

'We'll operate tomorrow,' he told Gianni, and then added, in no uncertain terms, 'and after that, you'll stay in for enough time to allow the wound to heal. Doctor's orders.'

Over the following days, Betty tried to visit. The matron of the ward was an absolute fiend and kept insisting that Gianni needed rest and could not see anyone. Finally, on day four, Betty's persistence prevailed and she was allowed in.

Rushing to Gianni's bedside, she resisted the urge to throw

her arms round him and hold him close. Apart from the lack of privacy, she was wary of touching his shoulder and jeopardising his recovery.

'How are you feeling?' she asked, as she sat down in the rickety chair beside his bed.

'Not too bad,' he replied, with a strained smile that belied his words. 'Getting better.'

Betty smiled wryly. Gianni would say that even if he was at death's door, she was sure, to stop her worrying. 'All right,' she responded. 'I'll believe you. But you need to tell me what happened. How did you get here? I thought you were still at Eden Camp, safe and sound.'

Gianni chuckled. 'I was. But after Italy capitulated and then declared war on the Germans, I knew I had to act. The Italian POWs were allowed to join the army, as long as they were commanded by British officers. But I didn't have time for all the paperwork and fuss. My cousin from Calabria was part of a partisan brigade up in the mountains in the north, destroying bridges, attacking German outposts, factories and weapons depots. I decided I would join him.'

Betty was speechless. The partisans were brave and heroic, and were greatly helping the Allies all across the country. They were causing so much trouble that the Germans now offered 1,200 lire as a reward for information leading to the capture of a partisan. Gianni had put himself in the utmost danger to fight with them.

'Our unit grew in number,' he continued, 'and eventually we split up and some of us moved south to join those fighting for Monte Cassino. We launched a big offensive and that's when the bullet got me.'

Gianni stopped, looking Betty directly in the eye. 'The last person I expected to bump into in Italy is you. I didn't know anything about you, where you'd gone or anything. Not long after you left, I went to your house and spoke to your father. He told me that you were promised to another and that I mustn't try to contact you as it could only lead to heartbreak.'

Betty squeezed Gianni's hand. Her father was only doing what he believed to be right, she couldn't blame him for that. He had thought it would be for the best, that Betty would forget about Gianni once they were parted. Little did he know that absence had only made her heart grow fonder.

'I'm sorry,' she said. 'And I should tell you that Samuel – the man my father mentioned – we think, or at least his mother does, that he's been ill. That he might not survive.' The last sentence flooded out of her. It was true, and it was dreadful. But it didn't change the fact that he was not the one Betty loved.

Gianni regarded her. His expression held a mixture of sympathy and something else, something Betty couldn't quite identify. Jealousy, perhaps? Anger?

A deep sense of dread filled her belly. She shifted uncomfortably in her chair. 'I... it's, you—' She halted, unsure how to continue. Gianni pursed his lips. Betty gripped the end of the white sheet that covered his bed and twisted it between her hands.

'You should have told me,' he said, eventually. 'Surely I deserved to know.'

Betty's shoulders slumped and bile rose in her throat. She had not been fair to Gianni. She had joined the ATS, thinking that would solve the problem. But running away never solved anything, she should have known that.

Wordlessly, she nodded.

They sat in silence for a while.

'I'm sorry,' breathed Betty, eventually. 'I never meant to deceive you. When I told you— when I said that I loved you, it was the truth. It still is. I've been torn in two since meeting you.'

The air between them hummed with unbearable tension.

Gianni leant back on his pillows and ran his good hand through his close-cropped hair. 'I don't blame you, Betty, for anything,' he said, softly. 'This is war. Nothing works the same way it does in peacetime, least of all affairs of the heart.' He sighed and then turned to look directly at her, his eyes full of the love that he had been holding in wait for her.

A flood of relief washed over Betty.

'I don't want to think of the past, or the future,' Gianni went on. 'Just the now.' He reached out and took her hand. 'Thank you for coming to see me. When I got out of the jeep and stumbled into the hospital only to see you in front of me – I thought I'd died on the journey and gone to heaven!' His voice trembled at the last words, and he flicked his gaze briefly to the ceiling, as if composing himself, before continuing. 'I'm not going to be here very long. I want to make the most of every second we can be together.'

Betty glanced quickly around her. There was no sign of Matron. Bending forward, she planted the lightest and gentlest of kisses on Gianni's poor, broken shoulder and then ran her thumb over his handsome, stubbly face.

'Thank you,' she said. 'Thank you for forgiving me.'

Gianni rolled his eyes and the mood lifted in an instant. 'Nothing to forgive,' he replied. 'Nothing whatsoever.'

'I think we need tea,' announced Betty, her voice a little squeaky with the release of tension. Such high emotion could only be satisfactorily assuaged by a brew; as a Yorkshire girl, that was incontrovertible.

By the time she returned with the cups, she'd plucked up her courage to ask the question that she wanted, and didn't want, to know the answer to.

'When do you think you'll be let out?' She wrapped her hands tightly around her cup to stop them shaking.

Gianni frowned. 'In a few more days, the doctor said earlier,' he replied. 'My shoulder is already much better. I just need a bit more time until I can pick up a weapon again, so I'll spend a few days in an army billet and then...' He made a whooshing sound with his mouth to indicate how quickly he'd be off to rejoin his unit. Betty understood that of course his priority would be to get back to the fighting. It was the same for all the men.

'Would it be all right if I gave your address to some people to write to?' he asked her. 'My family, and some of those from Malton I try to keep in touch with. The groundsman at the camp, Bert Lewis, for example. I don't know where I'll end up in Naples when I get out of here.'

'Of course,' agreed Betty. 'That's no problem.' She fumbled in her bag for a pen and piece of paper and carefully wrote down the address of the Villa Teresa. 'I'll keep an eye out for anything addressed to you.' Talking about practicalities was a relief after the profound conversation of earlier.

'Thank you.' Gianni looked at her appraisingly. 'But what about you? What happened to your ankle?' He pointed to her still-bandaged limb. 'I hope it's not too painful.'

Betty laughed self-deprecatingly. 'It was a small matter of having to flee from an erupting volcano,' she explained, making light of it. 'I caught my foot on something and fell flat on my face, twisting my ankle in the process.' She reached out to Gianni's shoulder, running a gentle hand over the dressing that covered it. 'A silly accident,' she went on. 'Not because I was being shot at.'

Gianni smiled in recognition of her acknowledgement of the danger he'd been in. 'Vesuvius can be an angry beast when it wants to be,' he said. 'You must have been very frightened.'

'Well.' Betty shrugged, affecting a nonchalance she certainly hadn't felt at the time. 'It was somewhat unexpected, I must say. Especially when you're not used to living with a fire-breathing monster on your doorstep!'

Gianni's eyes danced with amusement. 'Etna is the same. We give offerings to her patron saint, just as they do here. But – well, you saw for yourself how effective that is!'

They both laughed. She wondered if she should tell him about seeing Etna and Taormina from the *Arcadia*, how she had yearned for him at those moments. But, for some reason she couldn't have explained, she didn't.

'When will you be back at work?' asked Gianni, his voice full of concern once more.

'I was discharged fairly quickly,' answered Betty, 'but the dratted doctor told me to take two weeks off! I can't do that, though. I can't let the others cover all my shifts. A few more days and I'll be fine. I just need to be able to get up all the stairs to the cipher room.'

Gianni nodded. 'Perhaps we can have a few hours together before then?' he asked, the look of undisguised longing in his soft eyes melting Betty's heart. 'I'll send a note to the Villa Teresa, let you know where and when we could meet.' He opened his mouth as if about to say something else, but a nurse was suddenly beside them, bustling about, ordering Betty to leave as she had to change Gianni's dressings and check the wound.

As Betty trudged back to base, she wondered what she'd tell the others. She'd been so flustered after that first sighting of Gianni that she'd had to confess that, by enormous coincidence, as she was leaving the hospital she'd almost literally bumped into someone she knew from the Italian POW camp in Malton. Deborah and Susan had seemed to take this information at face value but not Lily.

'Who, exactly?' she had demanded, narrowing her eyes in suspicion.

'Well, just... an acquaintance,' Betty had replied, fumbling for the words that would satisfy Lily's curiosity but not give too much away. 'The person who, er, taught me Italian. It was such a surprise to see him! Totally out of the blue—' She stopped, abruptly, aware that she was burbling on while Lily regarded her with an unwavering stare. Beads of sweat broke out on Betty's forehead as she waited for any further questions.

'Right,' Lily had said, not looking entirely convinced. 'Well, it's nice you've had a chance to catch up,' she had concluded.

'Absolutely,' Betty had agreed. 'But I must get on now. Shoes to polish, letters to write...' She'd escaped to their dorm room to get on with her chores. Thank goodness Lily hadn't pushed the matter. Betty simply didn't know what she would say, how she would explain her feelings, feelings that had doubled in intensity since her unexpected reunion with Gianni.

This evening, she managed to slip into Villa Teresa unnoticed, and her absence didn't garner any inquisitive probings.

The next days passed torturously slowly. It was all Betty could do not to check her pigeonhole every five minutes for the promised message. She so desperately wanted to see Gianni again, it was the only thing she could think about. Concentrating on work was near impossible. It was only the memory of the mistake Susan had made when she was distracted that enabled Betty to maintain her own focus.

Eventually, after two days that had seemed like two weeks, a note arrived. Opening the envelope, Betty rapidly scanned what Gianni had written.

*Meet me outside Villa Teresa today at 5 p.m. With love and eager anticipation, Gianni.*

Betty's heart turned over. The day stretched out in front of her, interminable hours before she would see Gianni again. But she had plenty to do in that time. Wash her hair and iron her uniform for a start, though, even more importantly, she needed to find someone she could swap her shift with. She was supposed to start work at 4 p.m.

As hurriedly as she could with her bad ankle, Betty went to the mess, where breakfast was being served. Scouring the large room, she located a few of the other cipher operators and headed for them, asking them one by one if they would take her shift and she'd do theirs. Luckily, the fourth person she asked agreed.

By four thirty, Betty was ready. She'd brushed her hair and fixed her field cap on her head a hundred times, trying to ensure the best and most flattering angle. She'd pressed her khaki drill uniform to a tee and even applied a little lipstick, borrowed from Deborah. The only thing detracting from her appearance was the large bandage still strapped round her ankle. She could do without the crutch now, but her progress was still rather slow. Hopefully Gianni hadn't planned too much walking. Though with so much adrenaline pumping through her body as excitement and anticipation mingled, any pain would surely be numbed.

At ten to the hour she was sitting on a bench beneath the parasol pines, her insides fluttering insanely. As Gianni approached on the dot of five, she leapt up to greet him, then nearly fell over as her ankle almost gave way beneath her. Concerned, Gianni held out his good arm to her and she took it, using his support to help her down the stone steps. His other arm was in a sling but he assured her it no longer hurt.

'Look at the pair of us,' Betty said with a laugh, 'only three good legs and three good arms between us!'

Gianni chuckled. 'We'll be back in full health soon,' he said, confidently. 'But I don't want you to walk too far. I made an arrangement with someone...' He paused and looked around, scouring the neighbourhood for something. 'Oh yes – over there.'

Parked a little further along the street was an army ambulance.

'Shush,' whispered Gianni, turning to Betty with his finger on his lips. 'My friend offered to give us a lift – don't worry, the ambulance is empty. He's heading back to Caserta, so it's on his way.'

They jumped into the cab beside Gianni's friend and in no time were at Montesanto station, where Gianni escorted Betty onto the funicular that ran up to the top of the hill. She was entranced by this funny train that made light work of the steep incline.

'I've heard there's something similar in Whitby,' she said as they sat in the little carriage. 'But I've never been on it.'

Gianni smiled. 'There are several in Naples, and of course the cable car up Vesuvius. Just like we have in Sicily, on Mount Etna.' For a moment his cheerful expression faded, to be replaced by a wistfulness that revealed how much he pined for home. Betty's heart lurched. Being parted from her own family for so long was painful enough, and Gianni had not seen his folk in far longer. The impossibility of it all, of this great love she felt, threatened for a moment to drown her in a sudden tsunami of sorrow and forbidden dreams.

Forcing the thoughts away and plastering a smile upon her face, Betty concentrated on the view until they had reached the top. Once there, they walked for around five minutes before arriving at the enormous gates that led into the ancient Castel Sant'Elmo. Gianni led her through the castle, up to the roof where Naples lay spread out before them; the red-tiled houses and the azure sea, the distant curves of the coastline, its hills and rises smudged outlines in the late-afternoon light; the port; the promontory of Posillipo, and Vesuvius, quiet and placid again now after its recent activity. Gianni took Betty's hand and, as they stood against the parapet walls, the sun began to set, bathing everything in a honeyed, golden glow, making the city gleam and shimmer.

Betty was bedazzled by the glory of it all. 'It's so beautiful,' she breathed. 'I've never seen anything like this before.'

As she spoke, Gianni's hand tightened round hers in wordless recognition of this special moment. The view, magnificent though it was, seemed to fade into the distance momentarily as all Betty was conscious of was Gianni's proximity, the feel of his palm against hers, the faint but familiar scent of him.

In a final flourish, the sun's dying rays turned umber and ochre and then, almost imperceptibly, began to fade away, like a slowly extinguished flame. Gianni lit a cigarette and turned slightly away from Betty so as not to get the smoke in her eyes. She studied his profile, so familiar and yet so distant. Why couldn't life just be simple, she begged, of who she did not know.

'They say the castle is haunted,' Gianni said, with that lopsided grin Betty knew so well, 'so perhaps we better get out before nightfall.'

Betty laughed. 'I can't imagine a brave partisan would be afraid of ghosts,' she replied.

'That's true,' agreed Gianni. 'It's all just folklore anyway. It doesn't mean anything.' His eyes met hers and he held her gaze for a long minute that felt like an eternity. 'But this, Betty,' he continued, his voice low and soft. 'You and me. That means something, doesn't it?'

And then he was reaching out and drawing her close to him, and kissing her, and she kissed him back with all her heart because it did mean something, it meant everything. And they didn't have much time, just a day or so, before Gianni would be gone again, and they should make the most of every minute, surely they should.

Because who knew what was going to happen next?

# CHAPTER THIRTY-FOUR

ITALY, JULY 1972

Sadie emerged from Naples airport into the blazing heat of an Italian summer. Bewildered, she stood for a moment getting her bearings, her stomach flipping over with nervous anticipation. She could hardly believe she'd survived the flight, let alone that she was actually here, her feet on Italian soil. Looking around her, it all seemed impossibly foreign and alien, voluble conversations in excitable tones filling the air, Fiat 500s darting here and there, pulling in to the kerb and then shooting off again, passengers and luggage deposited or collected.

*What on earth am I doing here?* she thought to herself. *And what on earth am I going to do now I am here?* She had made one precipitous decision after another recently, but surely this decision to come to Italy was the most hare-brained of all. There was something deep inside her driving her on, a profound, indefinable need to find her birth family, to find that sense of connection that had been lacking all her life.

She raised her hand to make a visor against the sun and surveyed the many signs that dotted the area. All were incomprehensible. The travel agent had arranged a transfer to her accommodation for her, but had not told her where she was supposed to find the car and driver. Mystified, Sadie made her way towards the symbol for the taxi rank, hefting her suitcase with her. When someone tapped her on the shoulder, she almost jumped out of her skin.

'*Scusi, scusi,*' a man was saying as Sadie turned round. 'Signorina Collins?' He waggled a piece of cardboard in front of her face, which had her name written on it. This must be her driver. Thank goodness. Gratefully, she followed the man through the searing heat to a bright yellow car parked haphazardly under a sign that clearly indicated there was no parking allowed. Sadie grinned. Beneath her apprehension and fear, she already had a feeling she was going to like Italy.

As the driver sped off at what seemed like ninety miles an hour, Sadie contemplated how she'd got here. After her visit to Malton, she'd thought long and hard about what to do next. She simply couldn't work out how she could take the search to the continent of Europe. She'd never been further than Cornwall in her life.

But then, overnight, everything had changed. Simon had announced he was taking a job in Singapore and unceremoniously dumped her, her mother's house had got a buyer, meaning money wasn't such an issue any more, and at work, where they were going through a quiet patch, they were only too happy to let her take two or three months' unpaid leave.

And now here she was, in the bright, white heat of Italian summer, with no clue as to what she might discover on this trip, just the knowledge that she had to do it.

Once she had settled into her hotel room in the Spanish Quarter, Sadie ventured out into what seemed like an utterly alien world. She couldn't believe how hot it was, searingly hot, a heat unlike anything she'd ever experienced before. The travel agent, peering at her over the top of austere reading glasses, had warned Sadie that Naples in late July and into August would be 'like an oven', but Sadie hadn't listened. She'd been in no mood to wait. If she'd explained to the travel agent why she needed to go now, maybe the woman would have understood. But it was all far too complicated to go into. Let the agent think Sadie was crazy; it was easier that way.

Pulling her sunglasses over her eyes, she realised she'd also need to buy a hat. With that thought, she sallied forth – and was immediately almost mown down by a scooter rider mounting the kerb in order to get past a car that seemed to have randomly stopped in the middle of the road. Pressing her hand to her chest, Sadie checked around her for further speeding vehicles before daring to advance along the pavement. In her hand, she clutched a map of the town that she'd bought at the airport. She'd studied it in her hotel room and knew the first few turns she needed to take. But despite her best efforts, within a few minutes she had to accept she'd got hopelessly lost. Bewildered, she stood in the shade of one of the ancient buildings and observed the city in all its chaos and vitality.

The narrow alleys teemed with life, children running underfoot, stray dogs panting on street corners, fruit sellers advertising their wares in voices raised to be heard above the noise. It was an assault on the senses in every way and Sadie quailed in the face of this cacophony of noise and activity. She congratulated herself on having had the foresight to hire a local guide. She'd found Luca Ricci advertising his guiding and translation services in the guidebook to Naples that she'd taken out of the library, and had phoned him from a public phone box, not wanting to take the liberty of making an overseas call from the office. Even though his listing stated he spoke fluent English, Sadie had still been nervous in case he hadn't understood her request. But her worries had been unfounded. Luca did, indeed, speak English like a native, and was happy to offer up his services to Sadie during his university holidays. He'd started his

studies as a mature student, he explained, and still had another
year to go before he had earned his degree in travel and tourism.

Squinting to make out the small print of the map, Sadie
eventually got her bearings. Luca had asked her to meet him in
the Piazza del Plebiscito where he'd be holding a copy of *la
Repubblica*. When she arrived, she quickly spotted a young
man with cropped hair and round, gold-rimmed glasses, about
her own age, standing looking about him, complete with a
rolled-up newspaper in his hand.

Grasping the nettle, Sadie went over to him. 'Luca?' she
said as he looked up at her approach.

'Sadie?' he replied, with a warm smile. Despite the heat,
Luca appeared cool and collected, in chinos and an immaculate
white shirt that set off his smooth, tanned skin. Sadie was in the
process of holding out her hand for a shake, but Luca immediately greeted her the Italian way, with an air-kiss on both
cheeks. He smelt delicious, a combination of a delicate, citrusy
aftershave and laundry powder.

Sadie felt a hot flush engulf her. 'Umm, nice to meet you,'
she muttered, trying to hide her embarrassment. She hadn't
expected her hired guide to be so good-looking. Nor that they
would kiss immediately on meeting for the first time! But this
was the Continent, after all, where strange, very un-British
customs abounded.

Luca laughed easily. 'You are English!' he said, kindly, tactfully acknowledging her awkwardness. 'You'll get used to our
Italian ways in no time.'

Sadie smiled bashfully. She already felt more at ease.

'So,' continued Luca, 'where would you like to go first?
Whatever you want, that's what we'll do.'

Sadie silently thanked her lucky stars that providence had
delivered her such a helpful guide. All she had told Luca on the
phone was that she was trying to trace someone called Gianni
Urso, that the only information she had was the address of Villa

Teresa, the fact that he had been in Naples in 1944 and seemed to have had some connection that building, and that he had been a partisan. Thinking about it rationally, it was a wonder Luca had agreed to accompany her on such a wild goose chase. They had so little to go on.

'Villa Teresa,' she replied, instantly.

Luca frowned. '*Va bene.*' He met Sadie's anxious gaze with his soft brown eyes. 'Look, I'm not sure it's going to help us much. But of course we'll go there. It is important to you.'

Sadie felt a blush rising again. Luca seemed to innately understand that this mission mattered so much, though she hadn't explained to him how or why.

'It's only about ten minutes' walk,' Luca told her. 'Is that all right?'

'Of course,' Sadie answered. She wasn't going to admit defeat, even though she could already feel the sweat dripping down her back. They walked through the narrow, winding alleys of what was obviously a poor part of town before arriving in a more prosperous area, where the roads widened and the buildings lining them trebled in size. They rounded a corner and Sadie gasped in surprise. There, below them, lay the stunning expanse of the Bay of Naples, the bluest of seas dotted with craft of all types: ferries, yachts, container ships. To the left, she could make out the cone of Mount Vesuvius, towering over the city, dominating the skyline.

'It's so beautiful,' she breathed. 'I couldn't really understand why anyone would live so close to an active volcano – but now I get it. All of this' – she swept her arm out in an expansive gesture encompassing sea, sky and mountain – 'makes the danger seem worth it.'

Luca smiled. 'We get used to it. It's good to see it through a foreigner's eyes.'

After a couple more minutes' walking, Luca drew to a halt in front of a stone archway overgrown with ivy and a rampant

bougainvillea with scorching-pink flowers. Through the arch
Sadie saw a driveway leading to an ancient palazzo, the
entrance to which was guarded by two tall parasol pines.

'This is Villa Teresa,' said Luca. 'But' – he made a moue of
resigned disappointment – 'as you can see, it is more or less
derelict these days.'

'Oh no!' gasped Sadie. 'What happened? Why would
someone abandon such a place?'

Luca shrugged. 'After the war, when so many historic
houses were requisitioned, often the original owners didn't want
them back. They had no further use for them, and anyway they
didn't have the money to put them back into good repair.'

The two of them stood staring through the arch for a few
moments. 'But can we still go in?' asked Sadie. 'Just to
see... Well, to have a look around?'

Luca grinned. 'I don't see why not. There's no one to stop
us, is there?'

Their feet crunched on the weed-strewn gravel as they
advanced up the driveway towards the mighty front door that
was wind- and weather-battered, splintering and silvered with
age. Solid and forbidding, it didn't invite them in. But Luca gave
it a hearty shove and, to Sadie's amazement, with a creak and a
groan it shuddered open, protesting with all its might at being
disturbed.

'Wow,' said Sadie, inadequately. 'That easy!'

Luca flashed her a satisfied smirk. 'The magic touch,' he
replied, waving his hands around. He led the way cautiously
inside. 'Just watch your step,' he said. 'There might be loose
woodwork or masonry. Take care.'

Sadie followed him. They were in a cavernous hallway with
a wide corridor running off to the right and left. In front of them
was a magnificent cantilevered staircase and, behind that,
another enormous door. Luca headed towards this and, on
opening it, they found themselves looking out onto an internal

courtyard, paved with slabs worn shiny from years of use. In the centre was a long-disused fountain and in every crack and crevice weeds and grasses grew, wild and unpruned.

'I feel like I've stepped back in time,' murmured Sadie.

'The Villa was used as a billet and HQ for the British in the Second World War,' Luca informed her. 'As far as I can discover, the male soldiers were housed in one wing and the females in the other. The offices where they worked were in the middle. They ran their own operation here, but it all fed into the HQ for the whole of southern Italy, which was just up the road in Caserta.'

'But why would Gianni Urso have given this as a correspondence address?' mused Sadie, to herself as much as to Luca. 'If he was a partisan?'

Luca shook his head. 'That's what we have to find out.' He caught Sadie's look of concern. 'But don't worry, I have some ideas. First, though, let's go exploring.'

They went up to the first floor, where, in each palatial room, tall windows faced out towards the view, and the hot, white light of Italian summer flooded in. Sadie ran her hands down the damask curtains, releasing clouds of dust and bringing on a sneezing fit just like she'd had in her mother's attic. Luca offered her an immaculate white handkerchief and she took it, gratefully.

The walls were adorned with elaborate frescoes of cupids and angels, which must once have been magnificent but were now sadly faded and tarnished, colours dimmed and pieces missing where plaster had fallen and the paint peeled.

'I bet it was so grand, in its heyday,' said Sadie, a tone of sadness creeping into her voice. It was a shame to see something deteriorate in this way.

'I suppose so,' replied Luca. 'But Italy is full of old places like this, old paintings, old monuments. We have plenty of old. In my opinion, what we need is more new! New ideas, new buildings to replace the ones that are no use any more, new housing for the poor.'

Sadie frowned. She didn't feel qualified to respond to this. Instead she wondered if Gianni Urso had walked these same halls and corridors, all those years ago during the war. They carried on exploring the building, eventually coming to the rooms that must have been the offices. Furniture lay around, folding tables and uncomfortable-looking chairs, an old-fashioned typewriter with broken keys and ribbon and, on one desk shoved into a corner, a headset like those Sadie had seen in pictures of people doing war work.

'Gosh,' she exclaimed, gingerly picking the headset up. 'Can you imagine what these have heard? Secret messages from the enemy, communications of utmost urgency...' She slipped the headphones over her ears and furrowed her brow as if concentrating intently. 'Dot. Dot. Dot, dot, dash...'

Luca was looking at her, bemused.

'Morse code!' she explained, removing the headset and laughing. 'Isn't that what they did?'

They left the room together and made their way back to the entrance. 'You'd have to ask my mother about that,' Luca said. 'Signs and codes are not my area of expertise.'

He paused to let Sadie out through the huge wooden door first, catching as he did so her look of disbelief. 'What's the matter?' he asked as he followed her outside.

Beneath the two parasol pines that stood guard over the entrance, it was cool, the sun's heat blocked. A shiver rippled through Sadie.

'Your mother,' demanded Sadie. 'Why would your mother know?'

'She was here, in the war,' Luca answered. 'She was at Villa Teresa.'

# CHAPTER THIRTY-FIVE

NAPLES, MARCH 1944

Saying goodbye to Gianni was even worse this time than before. Betty had to use every ounce of her resolve not to cry as they parted. She didn't want Gianni to worry about her. He was committed to doing what he could to oust the Germans from his country for good and the last thing he needed was to feel responsible for her or her feelings. So she held back the tears and put on a brave face.

'I'm going to miss you, Betty Bean,' Gianni said, as they stood outside his army billet. He was hitching a ride back to his brigade with an army convoy. It was a little unorthodox, but this wasn't the time for rules and regulations. The battle for Monte Cassino was almost won, and Rome was within the Allies' sight. Once they had seized back the capital city from the Axis forces, the symbolism of the victory would carry them onwards on waves of glory until the job was done.

'Me too,' replied Betty. She was concentrating so hard on preventing her voice from breaking that she couldn't say anything more than that. Memories of that first goodbye, in Yorkshire, swirled through her mind. Gianni had said they would meet again and, against all the odds, they had. Betty could hardly bear to contemplate that this time, their parting really might be forever. A silence fell again that for a moment felt like an invisible barrier keeping them apart.

And then Gianni took Betty in his arms and hugged her close, burying his face in her hair. She could feel the beating of his heart through his army fatigues, so vital and life-giving, so easily destroyed by a bullet or a shell.

'Please be careful,' she begged him, even while knowing what a meaningless exhortation it was. Of course Gianni wouldn't be careful. He'd throw himself into the thick of the fighting just as he had before. 'And come back safe,' she added.

*Come back to what?* echoed in her head. She couldn't invite him to come back to her.

Gianni released his hold, stepped back, held her by her shoulders and looked straight into her eyes. Betty's heart missed a beat. 'I'll do my best,' he said, solemnly. 'And you – keep working hard, doing your valuable work. It's what you do back here that enables us to do what we do. We all need each other.'

And then an army truck swept up and ground to a halt, the driver tooting the horn impatiently.

'It's time for me to go.' There were other men making their way towards the vehicle, casting interested glances in Gianni and Betty's direction.

Kissing in public was something nice girls didn't do, Betty knew. But what did being nice or well-brought up matter, if she might never see Gianni again? Gianni took the initiative. He reached out his hand, tilted her chin up towards him and bent down to kiss her, an even longer, more passionate kiss than ever before.

And then a shout rang out, instructing Gianni to get into the truck.

He wrenched himself away from her and Betty watched, tears pricking her eyes, as he climbed aboard. Once she'd waved him away, she waited until the vehicle had disappeared from sight and the cloud of dust and fumes it had left in its wake disappeared. Then she walked disconsolately back to the Villa Teresa, the taste of his lips still on hers. Her heart was in pieces, her emotions in turmoil. How could this love, that felt so right, be so impossible?

At the palace, the familiar parasol pines cast deep shadows over the front lawns. Instead of going inside, Betty made a sudden decision to walk on, down to the waterfront promenade and then back up into the city, through the crowded, chaotic jumble of streets that comprised the Spanish Quarter. She was too restless to go inside and too disconsolate to join the others. Lily would be bound to ask more probing questions and Betty simply didn't have the answers. The agony in her heart seemed to radiate through her body, worse in a way than when her mother had died. Then, she had known it was final, and she'd had to be strong for her father, who'd been lost in bottomless grief for many weeks. But there was no one here to be strong for her, and she felt her own strength fading with every mile of distance between her and Gianni.

She trudged for a long time, but eventually she realised she must go back. Her ankle throbbed and she could not stay out here all night. Trying to cheer herself up, she thought that perhaps she and the others would go to the NAAFI that evening, see what was going on there. It might be good to get out, stop her brooding. As she limped back down the steep streets, skirting around the potholes and the holes in the roads where the manhole covers had been stolen for their metal, she was lost in thought, ruminating on everything she had to contend with.

She stopped to cross a road, waiting for an army convoy to rattle past. There had been a noticeable increase in troop movements around Naples lately, and an influx of more soldiers arriving on giant ships just like the *Arcadia*, from the UK but also from America and South Africa. Rumours were flying about what all this activity meant – a major offensive, an attack on the capital – but no one was really sure. Betty had also heard from Jane that, for those based back in the UK, all leave had been cancelled and Jane didn't know when she would see her husband Andrew again.

Betty followed the convoy with curious eyes. Whatever was going on, the likes of her would never know about it. It would be top secret, as such things always were. When the last vehicle had roared away, to her surprise a familiar figure was revealed. Betty peered at her and, sure that it was indeed Susan, she waved and called, but the din from the departing trucks and jeeps rattling over the uneven surfaces swallowed up her voice so Susan did not hear her. As Betty watched, she disappeared up one of the many semi-derelict alleyways. Thinking that Susan must be heading back to Villa Theresa via a short cut she knew, Betty followed after her, planning to catch her up and walk with her the rest of the way.

Betty had certainly been preoccupied with Gianni and her own ankle injury over the last week, but it had not escaped her notice that Susan had been even quieter than normal. Betty worried that her homesickness and low mood had got worse, not better. And the return of hotter, stickier weather as the months passed would not help, for Susan didn't like the heat at all. Now that Gianni had gone, Betty must redouble her efforts to chivvy her along. A little walk together would be the perfect opportunity to touch base with her, find out how she was doing and what, if anything, Betty could do to help.

She hurried after Susan but Susan was striding out, moving very fast. With her still-tender ankle, Betty couldn't quite catch her up. Susan was following a very strange route through the labyrinthine passages and alleyways, with no clear direction, and Betty wondered what on earth she was doing. She couldn't just be enjoying a stroll through the lively city – she was walking far too fast and purposefully for that. She hadn't learnt more than a word or two of Italian. As such, she'd always professed herself reluctant to venture too far from the safety of the palace on her own.

Pondering the reason for Susan's strange actions, Betty temporarily lost concentration – and Susan. When she realised Susan had gone out of her view, she stopped short, searching the street ahead, annoyed with herself. Then, just as she was about to give up, she suddenly spotted Susan again, standing in the doorway of one of the run-down and dilapidated houses. Surprised, Betty continued towards her. Who could Susan know who she would be visiting in this part of town? It wasn't where any of the servicemen or women lived. Here resided only Italians.

Betty continued onwards. Susan had her back to her and seemed to be talking to someone inside the building, out of Betty's sight. Some sixth sense told Betty to hold back, not to barge right on in as she was usually wont to do. Slipping into the deep shade afforded by the tall buildings and the narrow street, she cautiously crept a little closer. She could hear Susan speaking, but could not yet make out what she was saying. Sidling even nearer, Betty kept her ears pricked. Two tiny children scampered by, dark eyes flashing bright in the dusk. Betty held her breath, hoping they would not draw attention to her presence by stopping to beg from her. She always gave the young ones something if she could; many of them plainly had so little. But the pair hurtled onwards.

A door, long since pulled from its hinges by a bomb blast, leant against a wall, providing Betty with some additional shelter. She flattened herself against the building, peering over the top of the door. At that moment, Susan stepped out of the doorway and into the alley, and her interlocutor followed her just enough to come into Betty's view. He was dark-haired and olive-skinned, and there was something shady about his manner and bearing, giving Betty the instant impression that he was untrustworthy. She could not really hear what they were saying, but she caught brief snatches that told her they were talking in Italian. Betty was shocked to find that Susan had been lying all along; she was clearly speaking with a fluency that hadn't been recently acquired.

'*Arrivederci*,' she heard Susan say, and then something in a low mumble that she couldn't catch.

Abruptly, Susan turned on her heels to retrace her steps to the entrance of the alleyway. Scarcely daring to breathe, Betty adopted a semi-crouch behind the door, praying that Susan wouldn't spot her.

As Susan passed Betty's hiding place, she paused and Betty's heart stopped. But after a moment or two, Susan walked on, and Betty began to relax. Once she was sure Susan had got far enough ahead of her, she slowly extracted herself from behind the door and, smiling at two elderly ladies who were staring at her in utter bemusement, made her way out of the alleyway and onto the main drag. She purposely did not search for Susan, but instead took one of the various ways she knew to get back to the Villa Theresa. If she bumped into Susan she would just tell her the truth: that she had gone for a stroll to clear her head.

As Betty hobbled along on her still-sore ankle, she considered what she should do. There was something about the scene she had witnessed that made her feel deeply uneasy. She had no proof of any wrongdoing and talking to someone was hardly a crime, but still, it didn't sit right.

By the time the familiar facade of the villa hove into view, the parasol pines guarding the entrance, Betty had made her decision.

Ten minutes later, she was outside Lieutenant Corder's office, rapping on the door.

'Come in,' he barked from within.

Gingerly, Betty stepped inside.

'Ah,' said the lieutenant. 'Sergeant Bean. How may I assist you?'

Betty bit her lip nervously. He was uncharacteristically affable today, nothing like his usually rather austere self. He must have had some good news, she thought. And now she was about to shatter his benign mood.

'I saw something today that I thought was suspicious,' she began, tentatively at first, but gradually warming to her subject. 'It was – well, I don't really know what to make of it.'

Lieutenant Corder raised his eyebrows. There was a slight superciliousness in his expression, as if he was prepared to be underwhelmed.

'What I mean is,' Betty continued, struggling for coherence, 'that I saw Sergeant Davies in the town, talking with someone in Italian, although she's always maintained that she doesn't know any of the language. And, well, I thought it's a bit... he might be a spy... or she might be... and then there were the vandalised headphones, and that codebook, you remember, the one that went missing without explanation...' Her voice trailed off. As she was burbling on, she had realised how flimsy her story was, totally lacking in substance, and how idiotic she sounded. Lieutenant Corder would think she was mad.

Glancing up at him to gauge his reaction, she saw that she was completely correct in her assumption. Lieutenant Corder was regarding her as if she were a simpleton. Should she add to her accusation, mention the mistyped message she'd seen Susan almost send? The pilfered Morse code strips? But if she did, wouldn't he wonder why she hadn't spoken up before? As she tried frantically to decide, Lieutenant Corder steepled his fingers and pursed his lips. He held the silence for what seemed like an ocean of time before responding.

'Thank you, Sergeant Bean, for bringing me this piece of... intelligence. Now, what I suggest you do is put all fanciful notions of spies out of your mind, return to duty, and worry no more about it.' He paused and flashed her a glacial smile.

'Understood?'

# CHAPTER THIRTY-SIX

NAPLES, APRIL 1944

Smarting from her encounter with Lieutenant Corder, but still curious about what Susan had been doing in the city that day, Betty tried to focus on work. But if those distractions weren't enough to affect her concentration, there was also the constant tugging at her heartstrings caused by missing Gianni so terribly.

A few days after she had confronted the lieutenant with her concerns, he called all those working in the cipher room together again. Betty had thought that Susan was on the same shift as her, but she wasn't there in the little group huddled around the huge desk that dominated Corder's office. Betty wondered why Susan was absent; she hadn't said anything that morning about feeling unwell or having swapped her hours.

'We have uncovered the person we believe to be responsible for the sabotage and missing items,' Lieutenant Corder told the assembled company. 'And I'm sorry to tell you that the culprit is someone we had placed our trust in, mistakenly as it has turned out.'

There was a pregnant pause, in which you could have heard

a pin drop. Betty imagined everyone searching through their mind for the guilty party. Was this the reason for Susan's absence? Because she was languishing in a cell somewhere—

'It is,' continued Lieutenant Corder, his voice breaking through Betty's ruminations, 'Signor Conti.'

There was a collective sharp intake of breath. Cheerful Signor Conti, the voluble Neapolitan who was responsible for maintenance of the signalling and radio equipment, and general caretaking tasks, was a criminal? He had always seemed so genial, so obliging and loyal. Betty didn't understand.

'We have reason to believe he was behind all the misdemeanours,' the lieutenant informed them. 'And some other – er, irregularities. Our understanding is that he has a grudge against the British, and particularly the American troops, who blanketbombed the city earlier in the war. He has, of course, been sacked, and now that he is gone we can all hope that there are no further disturbances to our work.'

After the briefing, Betty returned to her station and picked up her headset. It felt particularly heavy today, weighted with the knowledge of Signor Conti's wrongdoing. She wished she could discuss it with Gianni, get his take on the matter.

Turning the tuning knob on the radio, she found her allotted frequency, picked up her thick black pencil and placed a stack of paper strips in front of her. She couldn't let her mind continue to wander; she had work to do.

The signaller she was listening to today wasn't hard to distinguish from all the others on the same or nearby frequencies. He had a unique style, hammering out the dots and dashes of Morse code as if they were bullets fired at the enemy. The aggression seemed to transfer itself into Betty's veins, making her feel agitated and on edge. She imagined Gianni facing those bullets, his already damaged body being subjected to hostile fire as he fought for his country, stalwart and loyal to the bitter end. He could die, up there in the north, and that thought was quite literally unbearable. Betty winced as if she'd been dealt a body blow. Would she even know if Gianni was killed? Who would tell her? She almost choked on the bile that rose in her throat at that thought. The rest of her shift passed in a blur.

When work finished for the day, Betty left the cipher room with Morse code ringing in her ears. She was exhausted with so much emotion; the pining for Gianni and fear about what he was going through, the unknown plight of Samuel, the desperate homesickness she was experiencing more and more often these days. Being in Naples was an adventure and a mission, and in general she loved it here, but sometimes she longed for her dull, quiet former life, for her father and sister Jane, for her new nephew, for sleepy Malton and the predictability of her job at the telephone exchange. A life where there were few dilemmas to face or decisions to make, and where no one's survival depended on her.

In their dorm room, Lily was getting ready for a date. She had recently achieved her stated aim of finding a handsome GI and was now often to be found trying out new hairstyles or filing her nails to perfection, scrubbing her face with oatmeal or moisturising it with the local olive oil. Betty didn't blame her; far from it. She envied her the simplicity of her relationship.

'What do you think?' Lily asked Betty as soon as she walked in the door.

Betty surveyed her friend. Lily had read in the *Bystander* magazine that American men didn't like overly made-up women, so she'd ditched the red lipstick and frantically sought out the shade deemed most suitable, which was burnt sugar, perfect for both lips and nails.

It was hard for Betty to know what to say because Lily always looked gorgeous.

'I think it looks very nice,' she said, diplomatically. 'But the truth is that you don't really need anything, Lily. You are so glamorous and attractive as you are. And Jim is clearly besotted.

I don't think he'd mind if you turned up with your hair in rollers! He'd see straight past to the beauty that lies within.'

Lily laughed, a hearty chortle. 'Oh gosh, that's very kind of you to say. But I can read the subtext, which is that I'm obsessing over something very trivial at a time of great danger. So I promise to stop.' She glanced at herself in the mirror, pulling her lips into an exaggerated pout. 'Once you've actually told me what you really think,' she added.

Betty smiled. 'I like it. No, I love it. And Jim will like it too, because he likes you. Now, I'm going to lie down for a few minutes. I'm shattered.'

Lily tore herself away from the mirror to cast Betty a concerned glance. 'Are you OK, Bean?' she asked. 'It's not like you to take to your bed.'

Betty mustered a laugh. 'I'm just taking the weight off my feet for a bit. My ankle, you know...' She gestured towards the offending limb, which genuinely still ached from time to time. It was actually all right at the moment, but it provided a good excuse behind which she could hide what was really affecting her: the aching of her heart.

'As long as you're sure,' Lily said, frowning a little as if she wasn't wholly convinced. Shooting one more quizzical look in Betty's direction, she turned back to her preparations. 'Now, where are those tweezers? I lent them to Susan, I'm sure I did...' Lily began opening drawers in the small units beside each set of bunk beds. Two of them had to share one unit, but they each had designated drawers of their own. Lily, however, disregarded this in her quest for the tweezers and threw open one after the other, scrabbling around inside.

'What are you doing?'

The loudness and anger in the voice made both Lily and Betty jump out of their skins. Betty leapt to her feet and both simultaneously turned their heads towards the speaker.

Susan.

Sounding more authoritative than she ever had before, and crosser, she had appeared from nowhere, coming through the door completely silently, but now as she marched across the marble floor her angry footsteps resounded across the room. Above, the nymphs and cherubs in the frescoes looked down as they always did, impassively.

Lily, who had frozen with a hand just inside one of Susan's drawers, stared at her, dumbfounded. Having got to her side, Susan reached out and slammed the drawer shut, almost trapping Lily's fingers inside.

'Please don't touch my things,' she said, in a voice as cold as ice. 'They're private.'

Lily and Betty regarded Susan in stunned silence. They had never seen her behave like this. It wasn't just how furious she was, but the sudden assertiveness in her manner and tone. Gone was the timid girl who wouldn't say boo to a goose and in her place had materialised a veritable sergeant-major of a woman.

'S-s-sorry,' spluttered Lily, almost too taken aback to articulate her apology. 'I wasn't prying, I was just looking for my tweezers, can't find them anywhere and wondered if you—'

'I gave them back to you.' Susan's voice was clipped and terse. 'You put them in your washbag, as I recall.'

'Ohhh!' cried Lily, overly enthusiastically, a cheery smile plastered onto her face as if that would dispel the terrible atmosphere. 'Of course you did! Silly me, I totally forgot.' There was a pause and then she repeated, 'I really am sorry, Susan. I didn't mean to cause offence.'

'None taken,' said Susan, relenting a little. 'I'm sorry – I've been a little touchy lately. Not sleeping well, you know how it is.'

Lily, who always slept like a log, didn't, but Betty did. With so much going around her mind, her nights were often disturbed too. She hadn't noticed Susan tossing and turning but she shared her set of bunk beds with Lily, so perhaps that was why. She wondered what on earth Susan could have in her bedside drawers that she so clearly did not want anyone to find.

At this point, Deborah breezed in, fresh from taking tea in the NAAFI with an English lieutenant named Frank. Or at least Betty thought that was who she'd said she was going to see; Deborah had so many dates with so many men it was hard to keep up sometimes.

'How are you all?' asked Deborah, cheerily, oblivious to the tension in the air. 'I'm dead beat. Early shift and then had to meet Lieutenant Lovestruck to give him the brush-off. I tell you what girls, there's definitely something afoot, something bigger than ever before. We've been inundated with supply requests and everyone's getting a little twitchy. Have you guys heard anything juicy?'

Lily and Betty shook their heads and Deborah turned to Susan and fixed her with an expectant gaze. For a second, Susan looked flustered. But almost immediately she regained her composure. 'No,' she replied simply. 'Nothing. I think you're exaggerating, Deborah. I haven't heard a whiff of any rumours.'

Deborah, who'd begun to brush her hair, continued making vigorous strokes through her luxuriant chestnut locks. Eventually, she responded. 'All right then. Must be me reading too much into everything.'

She put the brush into a drawer, thankfully her own and not one of Susan's. 'Anyway, on to far more interesting matters. There's a film on this evening, girls, if you're interested. Can't remember the name but it's about Nelson and Lady Hamilton. Anyone up for it? I said I'd meet Simon the sailor man there, but he won't mind if you tag along.'

Betty smiled at the nicknames Deborah used. She always had them for her men; Arthur the artilleryman, Gus the gunner and Major Monty were just some of them. If they didn't have an alliterative name, she made one up for them, like Lieutenant Lovestruck. She was so irreverent, but the men seemed to like it; at least they always came back for more. Betty couldn't imagine being as bold and brave and self-assured as Deborah when it came to relations with the opposite sex.

That evening, she took up the invitation to join Deborah and Simon at the NAAFI. Simon was in a strange mood, Betty thought. He said he and his unit were moving on the day after next but they had not been told where they were going, just that they'd be at sea for some days.

'I think we might be heading back round to the Channel,' Simon mused. 'There's something being planned, that's for sure. We're taking a few platoons with us. The rest – well, there's talk that the big prize will be in our hands soon.'

Betty pressed him on this. 'What do you mean, the big prize?'

But Simon just pulled on his eye in a gesture that indicated he could not say more.

Betty tried to concentrate on the film. When it had been released, many people had been shocked to see an adulterous relationship portrayed as a romance rather than a sin. But the stunning Vivien Leigh and the handsome Laurence Olivier, themselves newly-weds during the time they were filming, swept Betty away with the dreamy loveliness of it all. She thought she'd sleep well that night, but in bed her ankle ached, and she couldn't stop thinking about the film's most evocative moments. To see famous actors playing famous people on screen, and doing things most people considered reprehensible, such as having affairs, but doing it so beautifully it made you want to cry, surely showed that there were as many different love stories as there were people on this planet.

# CHAPTER THIRTY-SEVEN

NAPLES, MAY–JUNE 1944

Over the next few days and weeks, Betty upped her covert surveillance of Susan, but at no point did she see her do anything the slightest bit suspicious. And then everyone's attention was distracted by a decisive victory. On the eighteenth of May, the news that everyone had been waiting for finally came through. After five long months, the Battle of Monte Cassino was over, the Winter Line broken. And four days after that, more jubilation erupted as Rome was taken back. Yet more good news came on the sixth of June, with the announcement that the D-Day landings had begun in France. From that moment on, the course of the war began to turn, slowly but irrevocably, in favour of the Allies.

'Isn't it wonderful,' Betty said to Susan one afternoon as they left the cipher room together. 'Rome liberated and now the troops advancing across France.' As she spoke, she studied Susan's expression carefully. Susan had been so low lately; perhaps the good news of the war's progress would alleviate her concerns.

But instead of relief or optimism, what Betty saw cross Susan's face was completely different. For a moment, Betty couldn't name the emotion she saw.

And then it came to her, hitting her like a thunderbolt.

Regret. Disappointment. A touch of anger or annoyance. That was what Betty had spotted. The realisation made her breath catch in her throat.

Why?

Betty's thoughts whirled. She had observed Susan conversing with that man in the centre of Naples. She'd caught her transmitting an incorrect message. Seen her removing the code strips from the cipher office. Suddenly, Betty's suspicions crystallised into one, overwhelming understanding.

Thinking fast, she spoke again, keeping her tone as casual as she could. 'Then again, so many men are dying, trying to retake France,' she mused, as if this was something she had given a lot of consideration to. 'Sometimes I wonder if it's worth it. Perhaps we should just let Hitler do what he wants, and save any more bloodshed.' Fingers tightly crossed behind her back, she hoped she would be forgiven for giving voice to such a heresy. It was necessary, though; Betty was desperate to inveigle her way into Susan's confidence. Showing her she shared the same mindset – even if, of course, it was totally untrue – was the only way she could think of to do this.

Susan halted abruptly on the marble stairway, holding on to the mahogany banister rail that was polished so bright you could see your face in it, and turned to Betty.

'Betty!' she exclaimed, sounding utterly horrified. 'How can you say such a thing? You should be careful. If anyone hears you, they might think you're a Hitler sympathiser, one of those dreadful Oswald Mosley people, a Blackshirt...' Her voice trailed off, as if she were too appalled to continue. And with that she marched off down the stairs, leaving Betty staring after her, open-mouthed.

Her own stupidity hit her in the gut. She had no real evidence that Susan wasn't exactly who she said she was. Her doubts and suspicions probably were, as Lieutenant Corder had alluded to, ridiculous flights of fantasy.

And yet... despite Susan's protestations, something just didn't sit right with Betty.

She had more time to dwell on the whole matter as June sweltered on, for Naples became noticeably quieter after the D-Day landings. As well as worrying about Susan, not a day went by when Betty didn't fear for Gianni's life. The reports were that the fighting up north was fiercer and more violent by the day. When an army knows it's on the way down, it wants to take everyone with it – and that was the situation for the Axis forces in Italy right now.

At the same time, there had still been no word from Samuel, and even Julie's letters had dried up. The absence of information about her son seemed to have left his mother temporarily wordless.

With all of this weighing on her mind, for the first time since she had joined the ATS the hours spent at work began to drag for Betty. Though they still had things to do, the periods of inactivity were much more frequent than before and Betty often sat with her headset on, longing for someone to transmit something, *anything*, to alleviate the boredom – and the negative thoughts swirling around her mind.


ONE NIGHT, unable to sleep, Betty decided to get up and write some letters. She was behind in her correspondence, owing both her father and Jane replies, and she thought she might as well do that rather than lying in her bed, tormented and wide awake. Sitting up, she could see directly into Susan's bunk, which she was surprised to notice was empty. As she stared, a noise at the door put all her senses on edge. Instantaneously she lay back down, a sudden instinct telling her to pretend to be asleep. Perhaps it was an intruder, someone who knew where a roomful of defenceless women slept and wanted to prey on them.

Curling up on her side, she opened her eyes to slits, just enough to see out of but still look as if she were slumbering. The faint sound of bare feet on the marble floor rose to her ears. Whoever it was had taken care to make as little noise as possible, taking off their shoes and presumably moving on tiptoe. Betty's body went tense, fear radiating through her shoulders and down her spine, paralysing her. This was no opportunist, this was someone who knew what they were doing.

Another thrill of utter terror gripped her. Perhaps whoever it was had already taken Susan. That was why her bed was empty. Perhaps they were coming back for more victims—

A clang and a muffled 'ouch' made her heart nearly stop. Whoever it was had, in the gloom, stubbed their toe on the metal bed frame. She opened her eyes a tiny bit more, wanting and not wanting to see who was there. If she screamed, really really loudly, she'd raise the alarm and the others would be able to get away. No intruder, however strong, could overcome twenty women all at the same time.

But she didn't have to scream. The person in the room rounded the end of the bunk bed, took off her jacket and, extremely slowly and extremely cautiously, so as not to cause the bed to rock or move at all, got into it.

It was no marauding killer. It was Susan.

# CHAPTER THIRTY-EIGHT

Luca's revelation bowled Sadie over. It took her a good few moments to get over this bolt from the blue. She had known that Gianni Urso was somehow associated with Villa Teresa from his letter to Bert but had had no clear idea how to pursue this lead. That had all changed now, though. Surely they were on to something concrete here. Sadie felt the familiar rush of adrenaline, combined with the undercurrent of nausea, that every step closer to her origins aroused in her.

Eventually, she recovered enough to question Luca further. 'Did your mother know Gianni Urso?' she ventured, both wanting and not wanting to know the answer. It could be the beginning of the next stage of the quest – or a dead end. 'Did you ask her?'

Luca grimaced. 'Of course I did.'

Sadie sensed a 'but' coming. She wanted to grab hold of Luca and shake the information out of him. Or perhaps she just wanted to touch him, to be held by his strong arms. That feeling of loneliness she'd felt in Malton had not reoccurred here in

Italy, even though she was so much further from home now. There was something about having her feet on Italian soil that made her feel grounded, connected. And Luca, though she'd only just met him, was already part of that.

'What did she say?' she demanded, unable to temper her desperation to know.

Shaking his head, Luca gave a sigh before replying. 'She'd never heard of him.'

Sadie's whole body seemed to crumple with disappointment. So she had been right about the 'but'. In her confusion and distress, she tried to reason with herself. Luca's mother knowing Gianni would have been an inconceivable stroke of luck. It obviously wasn't going to be that easy. Nothing ever was.

'OK,' she responded. 'That's a shame.' She turned her head away, looking up at the impossibly blue sky as she tried to rapidly blink the tears away. Attempting, but failing, to hide her frustration, she took a few steps back down the gravel driveway, then paused to kick at a clump of weeds. She had to find out *something* about Gianni Urso while she was here.

'Thanks for enquiring, anyway,' she said, after a while. They were walking in step now, their feet crunching against the stones, a pigeon cooing from the branches of a cypress tree.

'Of course.' An expression of pain crossed Luca's face. 'Look, it'll all work out, don't worry,' he assured her. 'But I think we've done all we can today and it's getting late – six o'clock already. I'll take you back to your hotel so that you can have a rest and freshen up. And then, if you don't have any other plans for dinner, why don't you let me take you to a little place I know? It serves authentic Neapolitan food and wine and has a great atmosphere.'

Sadie met his gaze and saw the kindness in his eyes, and that the invitation was genuine, not given out of politeness or duty. Luca raised his eyebrows questioningly as she tried to formulate her answer.

'Umm, er, that would be lovely,' she stuttered, overcome with bashfulness.

Luca paused almost imperceptibly, and then a smile spread across his face. 'Great,' he said. 'That's – really great.'

The moment hung between them, pregnant with expectation.

And then they stepped out onto the street, and the evening rush hour was in full force, cars, motorbikes and trucks thundering past, no account whatsoever taken of any speed limits, potholes or indeed nearby pedestrians.

Luca not only escorted her to her hotel but also came to collect her again at eight o'clock. He led her through a maze of streets and alleys, Sadie staying close to his shoulder, aware that if she lost sight of him she'd probably be missing here for the rest of her life. The city was busy by day but by night it seemed to come alive anew, a completely different set of people crowding every thoroughfare, mostly young and dressed to the nines in the latest fashions, darkly beautiful women and dashing, moustachioed men.

'Be careful,' warned Luca, as they stepped onto a particularly busy avenue. 'There are a lot of pickpockets in Naples. Hold tight to your bag. And to me!' He flashed her one of his disarming smiles as he said the last words, and as he did so something passed between them. Sadie felt herself blushing, though on the other hand it was still baking hot, so it was probably just the heat that was making her cheeks feel as if they were on fire.

The throng thickened and Luca reached out his hand to take hers. His palm was cool and dry despite the temperature still being in the high twenties. Tentatively, Sadie extended her arm so that he could firm up his grasp. His fingers tightened round hers and, despite the whirl and bustle all around them, it was as if for a moment it was just the two of them in Naples on a sun-baked summer evening.

Eventually they arrived at a tiny trattoria nestling amidst a row of artisan workplaces; a hardware shop, a ship's chandlers and, alarmingly, what appeared to be a coffin workshop. As she stepped inside the restaurant, a warm fug of alluring aromas assailed Sadie's nostrils. An eclectic mix of objects hung from the ceiling – dried herbs, huge wooden spoons big enough for a giant's porridge pot, brass pans – and each table was adorned with a white tablecloth edged with handmade lace.

The proprietor, who greeted Luca like his long-lost son, took them to a cosy corner table and then immediately returned carrying a bottle with a cork like those on champagne bottles. With a flourish, the proprietor popped the cork and poured them both a glass. Luca thanked him, then lifted his glass, bubbles fizzing invitingly, and tilted it towards Sadie's.

'*Salute*,' he said, watching as Sadie took a delicate sip. 'Do you like it?' he asked, anxiously.

'Oh yes,' Sadie replied, taking another sip and trying to sound much more sophisticated than she actually was. 'It's delicious.' Her act took a hit as the fizz made her burp.

'Sorry.' She giggled. 'Is it champagne?'

'Certainly not!' exclaimed Luca, with an expression that was half affronted and half amused. 'It's prosecco, our own Italian version of sparkling wine.'

Sadie had never heard of the stuff. But she'd be seeking it out in future. It was lovely. 'Oh dear.' She giggled again, feeling a little tipsy already. 'My mistake. And, I mean, I don't know anything about wine but I really like it.'

Luca smiled. 'I'm glad,' he said, meeting Sadie's eyes and holding her gaze for a lingering moment. 'And now, let's consider what we should eat.'

The waiter came over and an intense conversation in voluble Italian ensued, with much pointing and gesticulating.

While they talked, Sadie's mind drifted. If her father was Italian, had her mother ever been to this country? To Naples? Eaten a meal like this in a place like this? Would she have liked the food? Whatever was being concocted in the kitchen, the aromas were amazing. British cooking didn't smell a bit like this.

An overwhelming feeling of sorrow and panic subsumed Sadie for a moment. If she ever did meet her parents, there would be so much to find out about them, a lifetime of knowledge to catch up on. What if there wasn't time? What if it was already too late?

She was prevented from dwelling more on these thoughts as the food started to arrive, dish after dish of Italian delicacies that Sadie had never experienced before in her life, more food than she could imagine but she kept eating it, even after she was full, because it all tasted so good. The proprietor whisked away their empty prosecco glasses and brought wine, plonking a bottle on the table. Sadie read the label. Chianti. Well, she recognised that. But in the gingham-tableclothed Italian restaurants Simon had taken her to in London, it came in a little wicker basket.

At the memory of Simon, she felt suddenly bereft. She hadn't been in love with him. Not at all. But being dumped was painful nevertheless and she missed the companionship he had offered. She missed Kim, too, and her mum. The pain she felt at her adoption being kept secret didn't diminish her love for Evelyn.

'What's the matter?' asked Luca, gently. 'There's something on your mind, I can tell.' He paused and drank some wine, then tentatively reached out to where her hand lay on the table. Resting his palm upon it, he looked into her eyes and continued, 'Why don't you tell me why you've really come to Italy and who Gianni Urso really is?' He gave her fingers a tiny, reassuring squeeze. 'I know there's more to it than you're letting on.'

And because he was so kind and she was feeling so forlorn, Sadie spilled it all out, the whole story; her mother's death, finding she was adopted, then that she'd been abandoned, tracking Jean Jackson down, being given the keepsake, getting the name Gianni Urso, going to Yorkshire, breaking up with her boyfriend and then coming here, desperate to find out anything she could about her parents.

Throughout the telling, Luca listened intently, prompting every now and again with a question – When was this? What happened next? – until Sadie finally got to the end.

'I'm sorry you've had such a difficult time,' he said sympathetically. 'I can't pretend to know exactly what you've been through, but I understand how difficult it must have been. And still is.'

He paused, and sighed as if the weight of Sadie's worries were his own too. A huge rush of compassion and gratitude surged through her. How different his reaction was to what Simon's had been.

'I'll do anything I can to help you,' Luca concluded, solemnly.

Sadie reached into her shoulder bag and pulled out the handkerchief he'd given her earlier. She passed it over to him. 'It's still quite clean,' she said, apologetically. Luca's eyes were glistening with tears and she thought he might need it. He dabbed his eyes and then returned it to her and Sadie did the same, as she was crying too.

A loaded silence descended for a moment and then was dispelled by the proprietor bringing two tiny glasses containing a thick yellow liquid. 'Limoncello,' he announced. 'You must try!'

Sadie eyed the glass dubiously. 'I'm not sure I should,' she murmured. 'I've had rather more alcohol than I'm used to already.'

'It's good for you,' responded the proprietor. 'A digestif. Like medicine.'

'Oh well, if it's for medicinal purposes I suppose it's all

right.' Sadie giggled. The tense atmosphere had evaporated in an instant, her troubles and worries receding to somewhere deep within her soul. None of it could be sorted right now. She wanted to enjoy the moment, here in Naples in an amazing restaurant with a handsome companion. Just let everything be that simple for a while.

She took a sip of the limoncello and almost choked, it was so strong. But it was also ice-cold, intensely lemony and fresh, so she drank some more. When in Rome – or Naples – and all that.

Luca swirled the liquid around in his glass before also drinking. 'Look,' he said, thoughtfully. 'I did ask my mum about Gianni, as I said, and she denied all knowledge. But the truth is that her memory is shot to pieces. She had meningitis a year or so ago and it really affected her, made her very forgetful and quite deaf. I'm thinking... maybe if she met you, she might remember something. You might look like your real mum or dad and seeing you might jog her memory. So why don't you come to my house tomorrow and we'll see what she can recall.'

Immediately, Sadie nodded and enthusiastically agreed. 'That would be great. Definitely, let's do it.' It might be clutching at straws but she had vowed to leave no stone unturned and to take her search to the ends of the earth, if necessary, she thought to herself in a jumble of somewhat drunken mixed metaphors.

When they arrived back at her hotel, Sadie could hardly recall how she'd got there. That didn't bode well for her hangover.

'Good night,' she said as they stood in the entrance foyer. 'I'll see you tomorrow.'

Luca nodded, his gaze grazing her face and lingering there for a moment longer than necessary. He smiled, and stepped towards her. Sadie felt breathless, an air of expectancy descending around her. He leant in, one hand placed gently on her shoulder, and repeated the air-kisses of greeting in farewell. The gorgeous smell of him washed over Sadie and for a second she felt faint, dizzy.

Then Luca stepped back and turned to go.

'By the way,' Sadie said when she'd regained the power of speech, suddenly remembering something she'd meant to ask earlier. 'What's your mother's name?'

Luca looked back over his shoulder. 'Deborah,' he replied, with his lovely smile. 'Deborah Castle was her maiden name.'

# CHAPTER THIRTY-NINE

Next morning, exhausted from having been awake all night, Betty could not get Susan's night-time antics out of her mind. Why had she got up? Where had she been? If it had been Deborah, or even Lily, Betty would have immediately suspected a boyfriend. But Susan had never had any male friends or admirers in all the time they'd been here, and anyway she had always seemed far too timid to break the curfew. It could have been for a trip to the lav... but Susan had been fully clothed and you wouldn't get dressed just to go and spend a penny. And anyway, there were two doors in their dorm, one that led to the bathrooms and one to the staircase and front door, and it was this latter one that Susan had used.

It was all adding up to load suspicion onto Susan's antics; her sending of inaccurate messages, her taking of the cipher strips, her sensitivity about Lily looking in her drawers, not to mention Betty's sighting of her conversing in Italian with a shady-looking character. Plus there was that time when Vesuvius erupted and Susan had gone home alone early. Why had she ducked out of their excursion, when they'd all been having such fun? What had she had to do in Naples that was so pressing it couldn't wait?

Betty considered going to Lieutenant Corder again. But she had been so roundly rebuffed the first time, she wasn't in any hurry to be made to feel two feet small again. The only thing for it was to bide her time; surely at some point Susan would make a wrong move? And at that moment, Betty could take the appropriate action.

It was all about playing a waiting game. And Betty could wait, as long as was necessary.

In the event, weeks passed and nothing happened.

And then, one night, everything changed. Betty's eyes snapped open, disturbed by something. She strained her ears, but for a few seconds silence reigned. And then she heard it. A shuffling noise from the opposite bunk, which told her that her instincts were correct. Susan, still in bed, was surreptitiously pulling on her clothes. She was clearly intending to go somewhere.

Immediately, Betty knew that there was only one thing to do. Follow her.

Susan climbed down from her bunk, picked up her shoes and tiptoed across the room. As soon as she had gone through the door, Betty was out of her own bunk. Her mind was racing with thoughts of how she could avoid detection should Susan see her. And then it came to her. Deborah had gathered together the typical costume of an Italian agricultural worker, ready for a fancy dress party that the NAAFI was holding later in the month. Betty would wear it now. Hastily pulling it out of their shared wardrobe, she flung the oversized garments on over her pyjamas any old how. Ramming the pork pie hat onto her head, she hastened after Susan.

The front door was bolted from the inside. From a vantage point hidden behind a pillar, Betty watched as Susan pulled back the thick iron bars, opened the door and slipped outside. Trying to keep a safe distance, but also not to let her out of her sight, Betty followed. It was the middle of the night but the moon was almost full, bathing everything in a pale and ghostly light. The leaves of the stately parasol pines rippled in the slight breeze and Betty shivered. Though the days were getting hotter, the nights could still be cool, especially when the sky was very clear.

Susan went first to a dense patch of shrubs and plants and, crouching down, pulled out from among the undergrowth a small knapsack. Betty observed her actions, dumbstruck. Susan had obviously spent some time planning what she was about to do, if she'd hidden things in advance.

The knapsack seemed to be heavy, judging by the way Susan hoisted it onto her shoulders. This done, she proceeded towards an old coach house, in front of which was a bicycle rack with bikes that any of the personnel could use. Susan grabbed a bike, pushed it to the villa's cobbled driveway and leapt onto the saddle.

Panicking, Betty shrank back into the shadow of a huge fern until Susan had passed her. Then she, too, took a bicycle and began pedalling furiously in Susan's wake. She hoped beyond hope that Susan would not look behind her, as it would be impossible for Betty to hide. Her disguise was decent but she wasn't convinced it would fool Susan up close. It might be all right from a distance, and if the moonlight faded, but otherwise there was no chance she'd get away with it.

There was not much Betty could do other than hope for the best. She needed to focus on keeping up with Susan, who was cycling at some considerable speed. Susan rode purposefully on and on, constantly uphill, through bombed-out streets Betty had never encountered before. It became obvious that she was heading for the outskirts of the city, but, as the buildings thinned out and they left the urban sprawl behind, Betty was no clearer about where Susan would end up or what she was planning to do when she got there.

But Betty did know that, out here in the countryside, it was dangerous at night. They had always been warned of this, told about the ruffians and outlaws who abounded in these environs. Despite the heat generated by the strenuous cycle, Betty shivered again, not sure what she was most afraid of now; Susan or a *bandito*.

Eventually, at the summit of a hill, Susan jumped off her bike and leant it against a tree. Betty, her heart pounding from both the difficult ride and the mixture of fear and apprehension that was coursing through her, threw herself off her own bicycle and into a ditch, terrified that Susan would see her. But Susan didn't seem to have any suspicion that she had been followed, and did not so much as cast a glance behind her.

Instead, she strode towards an open area well beyond the trees and hedges that fringed the road. Crawling through the dew-soaked grass, Betty crept after her, using the undergrowth as cover. Susan cast her eyes skywards as if searching for something. Then, bending down, she took a box out of her knapsack. At first Betty wasn't sure what it was. A miniature radio set? She knew those were being produced for field operatives and that new technology was enabling them to be made smaller and smaller. But the object in Susan's hands was the wrong shape for that – and anyway, would Susan be able to work such a thing? Betty was sure she wouldn't but, then again, she'd recently found out all sorts of things about Susan that she'd not known about – her ability to speak Italian, for a start. Anything was possible.

Betty strained her eyes to see more clearly. The moon was partially shrouded by clouds now and it was difficult to make anything out in the sickly light. But then it all came clear. Susan put the object on the ground and flicked a switch. Suddenly, illumination streamed out. Hastily, Susan shut it down. Now Betty knew what she had. An Aldis lamp, the type used for ground-to-air signalling. The cipher operators had learnt a little about such devices. They could transmit at a speed of eight to ten words a minute in the hands of a skilled operator.

But Susan wasn't a skilled operator. How could she be? She didn't even know Morse.

Confusion flooded through Betty, followed by a terrible feeling of dread. She watched, spellbound with fear, as Susan began to use the lamp, manipulating the shutters via the trigger switch, beams of light intermittently flooding upwards to the pallid night sky and then shutting off.

It very quickly became abundantly evident that Susan *did* know Morse. Her protestations that she was not intelligent enough to learn it had been false – just like all the other things Betty had been finding were not true. Nothing about her could be trusted.

Betty tried to concentrate on the Morse that Susan was transmitting. She memorised each piece of code, in blocks of five letters, as she had been taught, as she had been diligently doing for months on end now. At first, though she could recognise the letters, she could not understand the words they were making. Perhaps Susan was using a cipher? But then, as the signals continued, Betty began to wonder if it was German, a language she frustratingly didn't speak herself.

Even so, it still didn't explain who, or what, Susan was signalling to.

Suddenly, the answer to this question appeared. High in the sky, quite distant at first, Betty heard a noise. The sound of an aircraft. Narrowing her eyes and searching the heavens, she tried to locate the plane. At first, she could make nothing out. The noise grew louder until it must be almost overhead, and only then did Betty see it. A German Messerschmitt, flying without lights. Betty's heart stopped momentarily and then began to thump at double pace. Cold sweat broke out on her brow.

It was obvious now what Susan was up to. Sending messages to the enemy.

# CHAPTER FORTY

Menacingly, the aircraft circled overhead, the buzz of its engines like a noisy and particularly repellent bluebottle. Betty was frozen to the spot by a paralysing mix of terror, shock and indecision. Forcing herself to calm down, to think rationally, she weighed up her options. That she must do something was obvious. But what would be the best course of action to take? She could confront Susan, wrestle her to the ground, wrest the lamp from her, break the bulb so that it would no longer function. But what if the pilot saw this, or realised something had gone wrong? The plane was low enough for a gunner to shoot her down, or they could even drop a bomb on her and Susan. It seemed ridiculous, outlandish, impossible. But Betty was quickly discovering that nothing was out of the question where Susan was concerned. She could even be armed. That thought sent another dreadful jolt of fear racing down Betty's spine.

The main thing was that the information Susan was transmitting could almost certainly jeopardise whatever action was taking place in the north, and perhaps also that under way further afield, in France and Belgium. Without a shadow of a doubt it would put lives in danger, the lives of men fighting to secure freedom for Europe and indeed the world. This could not be countenanced; it would be a tragedy.

*Pull yourself together*, she told herself sternly. Clenching her fists, she mentally prepared herself. She could not risk challenging Susan and unleashing the wrath of the plane's occupants. Instead, she would sneak away, do her best to avoid being spotted. Jump on the bicycle and pedal hell for leather back into Naples. The HQ of all Allied operations in Italy was situated in Caserta, slightly to the north of the city, but that was too far and Betty wasn't entirely sure of the way. She would stick with what she knew, go to Naples, to the highest officers there. They could disseminate the information Betty had discovered to all who needed to know it.

Once she had made her plan, she felt her frayed nerves settle somewhat. It was always better to have a focus. Slowly and carefully, her heart in her mouth, Betty began to creep back, commando-style, towards the road and the ditch where she had dumped her bicycle. All she had to do was to get back there without being seen.

Every inch she covered seemed to take a lifetime. Her arms protested at every sharp stone they landed on as she dragged her body along the ground. But she was making progress, that was all that mattered. With no lights, hopefully the pilot would not see her. After all, he would presumably be focusing on the signals rather than looking for covert spies hidden in the grass.

After what felt like a millennium, Betty was within sight of the ditch. She could see the handlebars of the bike poking above the dense undergrowth. She'd made it. Thank God. For the last foot or so, she would have to stand up, to get around the hedge and the ditch and onto the road. She did not dare to look behind her, to see if there was any sign of Susan having noticed her.

The flashes of light she could see out of the corner of her eye indicated that Susan was still signalling.

Taking a deep breath and praying for good luck, she stood.

As fast as she could, she raced for the bicycle, wrenched it upright and got on. She bumped the front wheel off the verge and onto the road and pushed off. Only then did she look up, to see Susan haring across the grass, lamp abandoned. In moments, Susan had mounted her own bicycle and was coming straight for Betty. Meanwhile, up above the plane circled and swooped, its engines roaring. Suddenly, the sharp, staccato sound of machine-gun fire rang out and bullets strafed the hillside, sending mud and small stones flying into the air to spatter back down onto the track.

Betty's heart nearly stopped in fear and panic. She was being pursued on the ground and in the air. But she mustn't give up now. If she were to die here, no one would ever know what she had witnessed. Finding strength within herself that she hadn't known she had, she pedalled harder, hurtling round the hairpin bends, bumping over potholes and rocks, heedless of the danger, just desperate to get away.

But the road was poorly made, not tarmac but stone and, rounding a corner, Betty's front tyre skidded. In a split second she was off, flying through the air over the handlebars. She landed with a sickening thud, but she had no time to wonder if she was injured or not, just had to scramble to her feet and run. Her weak ankle protested at every step, but she kept going, fired up by the importance of her mission, and her terror. She ran into the fields beside the track, knowing that the grass was too tall and thick there for Susan's bike to handle. Betty did not dare look over her shoulder to see how close Susan was; she did not want Susan to see her face. Hopefully the farm worker's clothing had fooled her so far, and Betty did not want to jeopardise that.

Haring onwards as fast as she could, Betty felt her breath

become laboured, her lungs straining, her legs aching, her heart about to explode. She could just make out the sound of Susan's footsteps behind her, thudding on the soft ground.

*Keep going*, she urged herself. Both she and Susan had become fit with the endless hours of drill and PT, but Betty was sure she had the edge and could outrun the other woman. She ran and ran, down the steep hills, tripping and stumbling, her ankle crying out in pain. Willing it to stay strong, she pressed on, no idea how far behind her Susan was.

Up ahead, an early-rising farmer pulled an ancient truck into the opening of a field. He jumped down, leaving the engine running, and went to open the gate. Betty expected him to come straight back but he didn't. Instead he seemed to be having trouble undoing the bolt. She saw her chance.

She leapt up into the truck's cab and within seconds was on the move, finding first gear and pressing on the accelerator, the angry cries of the farmer rising above the noise of the engine.

*I'll bring it back*, she silently promised him, hoping he would forgive her. Glancing in the mirror, she saw Susan, some way behind her now, stopping and bending double in an effort to get her breath back. When she stood back up again, Betty made out something in her hand that glinted in the moonlight. A knife. So Susan had come armed. Betty shuddered. She'd had a lucky escape.

As she drove the truck towards Naples as fast as its straining engine would go, the first telltale signs of dawn began to show on the horizon, the gradual lightening of the sky, the pale rose blush that replaced the pallid moonlight. Despite this brightening, it was still hard to navigate the rutted and potholed road, or to see the edges of the ditches on either side, which, if she drove into one, would trap the truck for good. She couldn't switch the headlights on for fear of the plane, but she had driven her father's old vehicle so often that she was a deft and fearless driver. Now she had to call on all of those skills to get back to Naples safely.

Plucking up courage to look in the mirror once more, she could not see any sign of Susan, though the many trees cast deep shadows over the road that could easily conceal a human. All Betty could do was to press on, and hope this ancient truck didn't give up the ghost on her.

Just as she was beginning to relax a little and believe that, through the truck's top speed was barely more than a snail's pace, it would still outrun Susan, she heard another noise above the sound of the engine. Foreboding subsumed her.

The plane.

It was directly overhead now and, just as Betty caught it in her gaze, almost as if the whites of her eyes had given her away, a flurry of bullets whistled through the air towards her, so close she could feel their heat and power. Betty put her head down and floored the accelerator, but the truck hardly gained speed and the bullets kept coming, shattering against the truck's rusty metal body and ricocheting off into the undergrowth. Would it be better to abandon the vehicle and go on foot? It would be much harder for the plane to spot her then. But she was surely pretty close to the town now and the buildings would provide cover. Betty decided to keep going.

Another volley of gunfire and, instantaneously, Betty felt a stab of pain in her ear. Putting her hand up to it, she felt it grow quickly wet. Almost too scared to look, she withdrew her hand and glanced at it.

Blood. Even in the darkness, she could see its viscous red. There was a lot of it. Had the shot ripped her ear off? She could still hear, but whether out of both ears or just one was impossible to tell. Shaking with fear, Betty wiped her hand on the rough fabric of the farm worker's trousers and put it back on the steering wheel. She could feel the blood dripping down onto the shirt. Deborah wouldn't be able to wear this to the party now. Betty almost laughed at herself, worrying about such a thing.

The plane passed back over again so low that Betty glimpsed the gunner, his expression of grim determination. He wasn't giving up any time soon. Another hail of bullets. This was a nightmare from which Betty felt she would never wake. Trembling, she could hardly keep hold of the wheel, her palms were so slick with sweat and blood.

She reached the outskirts of the city, the first low-built, humble peasant dwellings, some looking reasonably intact, with red-tiled roofs and glazed windows, others in ruins, with caved-in ceilings and frames without doors, empty orifices staring blankly outwards. Betty had no idea exactly where she was; all she could do was head downhill, towards the sea and the port, from where she would be able to orientate herself. If she could get there.

The angry screaming of aircraft engines drowned out all other sounds, even the guttural rumbling of the truck's labouring engine. The plane came past again, even lower, so low Betty thought it would shear off the tops of the houses. A booming sound, followed by an explosion.

The sensation of falling. And then of nothing.

# CHAPTER FORTY-ONE

Luca's family home was on the fourth floor of a building in a working-class suburb in the west of the city.

'My mum got caught up in the 1944 eruption of Vesuvius,' he explained to Sadie as they made their way up the stairs to his flat. 'So she didn't want to live anywhere near the mountain.'

'I'm not surprised,' sympathised Sadie, panting slightly as she tried to keep pace with Luca. There were a lot of steps.

At a half-landing, Luca stopped, waiting for her to catch up. 'Sadie, I want you to know that I told my mother a bit of what you shared with me last night. I thought that, if she knew that you were adopted and you're searching for your parents, it might help her to remember something. She said that so many women who got pregnant out of wedlock had to give up their babies back in those days, and she always felt so sorry for them, because losing any of us would have been unbearable. I hope you don't mind.'

Sadie shook her head. 'No, that's fine. Whatever it takes. Whatever you think is best.'

Deborah was waiting for them at the door as they arrived. She was tall and striking, with dark chestnut hair, and was wearing a floaty kaftan-style dress that looked blissfully cool. In her arms, she held a little dog that yapped excitedly as Luca and Sadie approached.

'Shush, Buddy,' Deborah said, 'it's just Luca and his friend.'

Sadie was flattered that she'd used that word, though she wasn't sure what else she might have said. Client? Customer? The truth was that she already did feel that Luca was a friend. They'd met only one day ago but it was as if they'd known each other for ages. Luca had let her pay him for the first day they had spent together, but refused to take any more of her money. 'I'm doing it because I want to,' he'd said. 'And I don't want paying.'

'Come in, love,' Deborah was saying. She still had a strong London accent, despite having lived for so many years in Italy.

Sadie and Luca followed her down a corridor and into a living room with a small balcony that looked out over an urban garden, a little square of dusty grass and stunted trees that were drooping in the heat. A table was laid with a jug of iced water, a dish of pastries that vaguely resembled cream horns and three plates.

'I'll make coffee,' said Luca, disappearing to the room next door. Sadie heard whistling and whooshing noises filtering through the open doorway, and soon he had returned carrying a tray bearing three tiny cups of espresso.

Once the coffees and cakes had been distributed, Luca brought up the subject of their visit.

'Sadie has come from England to try to find this person called Gianni Urso,' he said to his mother, speaking loudly and clearly. 'Remember I asked you if you knew him a week or so ago. I know you said you didn't – but has anything come back to you since then?'

Deborah frowned, concentrating hard. 'Well, now I come to

think about it, perhaps I have heard that name before. But I really can't remember exactly where or when.' She shook her head sorrowfully. 'I've racked my brain – well, what I've got left of a brain since that illness I had – and I know there's something there but I can't quite grab hold of it. This happens all the time these days. It so frustrating. All the memories are there, but just out of reach.'

Luca reached out and squeezed his mother's hand. 'It's all right,' he reassured her. Sadie's brow wrinkled in sympathy. How awful to be robbed of your past like this.

'Can't remember my own children's names sometimes,' Deborah went on. 'I have four, you know. Luca's my eldest. The youngest is still at school, only fifteen. He's gone to stay with cousins in Puglia for the summer. Keeps him out of trouble.'

Sadie smiled. 'I would have loved to have cousins to play with and spend holidays with,' she said. 'I didn't have anyone.'

Deborah shook her head. 'Well, that's too bad.'

Luca went to the bookcase in the corner of the room and pulled out a large, black volume. He brought it over to the table.

'I wondered if looking at your photographs would remind you of anything,' he suggested. 'And even if not, Sadie might like to see what Naples looked like in the war.'

Deborah nodded. 'That's a good idea.' She turned to Sadie. 'Always full of good ideas, my Luca. And he's the only one I've managed to get speaking English. The others don't like to. Prefer Italian. Well, I suppose it's only natural, seeing as they live here.'

Luca coughed. 'Sadie doesn't want to know all that, Mum.' He turned the pages of the album until he reached the middle and then stopped. He moved places to sit beside Sadie and his mother on the sofa. Sadie peered intently at the grainy black-and-white photos, willing some sixth sense to tell her when someone significant appeared. But of course there was nothing. Just groups of smiling people in khaki uniforms, with old-fashioned hairdos and make-up-free faces. A few shots showed glimpses of Naples itself and Sadie was shocked to see them. The city was in pieces, bombed-out buildings sitting amidst piles of rubble and debris, barefoot urchins wearing ragged clothes or sometimes nothing at all. The extent of the damage and the poverty was sobering.

A few pages in, Sadie stopped and pointed to an image that depicted four women sitting together on the rim of a fountain.

'That's Villa Teresa,' she exclaimed, excitedly. 'The court-yard! I'm sure it is, isn't it Luca?'

Luca peered closer. 'Looks like it,' he agreed.

Sadie lifted the album closer to her eyes to read the caption. 'It says, Me, Lily, Susan and' – she squinted, tilting the page to better catch the light – 'and Betty, Villa Teresa, 1945.' She looked at Luca, and then at Deborah. 'Who are these people? Do you remember them?'

Deborah thought for a moment and then nodded. 'They were my friends from the ATS. Betty and Lily, they were much cleverer than me, they were cipher operators. Susan worked in teleprinting and I was in supplies.' She sighed and stared out of the window, where the sky was azure blue, not a cloud in sight. 'Oh, those were the days! Such fun we had, I do remember that. I was given the camera by one of...' Deborah faltered, shooting a quick glance at Luca. Sadie wondered what she had been about to say, but thought better of. 'An acquaintance from the US gave me the camera, as I recall. I asked someone to take a picture of the four of us, the morning we went to Sorrento and Vesuvius erupted.' She paused for another moment, immersed in the mists of time, and then resumed.

'After the war ended, I lost touch with Betty. She went back to England to care for her widower father and I never heard from her again, nor Susan for that matter. Lily – well, Lily, she's a right one! Married and divorced three times and doesn't see any reason to stop there. I still see her, sometimes. She likes to come to the Amalfi coast, for the holidays, you know. She's here most years, in the summer, August usually. She can afford all the posh hotels. Made of money, she is. But nice, all the same.'

Sadie listened to all of this spellbound. It was as if the picture, or the names, had opened a gate into Deborah's closed-off memory and it had all come spilling out, unstoppable. What a brilliant idea of Luca's to get the album out.

'And just to ask again about Gianni Urso,' she said, gently but insistently. 'You definitely don't remember him? Nothing at all? He was a prisoner-of-war in Yorkshire but he came back to Italy to fight with the partisans and he definitely had a connection to Villa Teresa. Could you ever have met him? Would he have known any of your friends?'

Deborah stared at the picture of her young self, running her finger over her face and then the accompanying caption.

'I think it was Betty,' she said, slowly and deliberately, as if wary of making a mistake. 'Betty Bean. She knew him. She never went on dates with any of the soldiers or sailors, not like me and Lily. But he turned up in the hospital one day, out of the blue, and she was at his bedside every spare moment she had. I think she was in love with him, though she never admitted it. I think something happened between them at some point. Not something she regretted. But something. She was different afterwards.'

Sadie held her breath. *Don't stop*, she willed Deborah. She didn't dare say anything for fear of interrupting the other woman's train of thought, but she wished Deborah could be a bit clearer. *Something* wasn't overly precise.

Suddenly, Deborah flicked her gaze sharply to Sadie. 'When were you born?' she demanded.

Sadie's heart was in her mouth. 'The very end of September, I think,' she whispered. Her birthday had always been celebrated on the first of October, but she now knew that was just the date when she was handed to Mrs Jackson. Jean had said she was one or two days old when that happened. So really she must have been born on the twenty-ninth or thirtieth of September. Nine months after the beginning of the year.

'That figures,' mused Deborah. 'Betty was a good girl, better than me, that's for sure...' Her voice trailed off, as she drifted back to the past. 'But on the other hand, those were desperate times, passionate ones, too. Lots of people did things they wouldn't have done if there hadn't been a war on.'

Sadie's mouth dropped open. She felt sick and dizzy, suffocated, almost like when she'd found her adoption certificate.

'Wh-what are you saying?' she stuttered. Her hands were clamped to the photo album and she'd broken out in a cold sweat. She could see the damp fingerprints she was leaving on the black leather cover and the cardboard pages, and hastily put the book down so as not to spoil it. 'Do you think – could Betty be my mum?'

A stunned silence descended on the little group, broken only by a sudden uproar of barking from Buddy. He came flying down the hallway, slithering to a stop in front of them.

'Buddy!' remonstrated Deborah. 'Whatever is the matter!'

Sadie bent forward and stroked the little dog's head. It enabled her to hide her face while she fought back the tears.

Deborah reached for the album and took out the picture. She held it up beside Sadie. 'You look a bit like her,' she said, eventually. 'Not the eyes, and your colouring is darker. But then look at that chin. Very similar.'

Sadie stared at the photo. There was a resemblance. Possibly. Her mind whirled with where they could go from here. Everything was happening too fast: coming to Italy, visiting Villa Teresa, meeting Deborah – all things that were so significant but none of which actually brought her to her parents. She scrutinised the photo again, trying to find the likeness. But this time she couldn't see it. It didn't help that the photo was faded and a little out of focus. She rubbed her hands over her eyes as if she needed to clear her vision and then turned her attention back to Deborah, who was speaking again.

'But no, I doubt Betty was your mother. I mean, it's unlikely, isn't it.' She didn't wait for a response to this remark as another thought seemed to strike her. 'But something else did happen, here in Naples,' Deborah murmured, as if lost in that distant past.

*Not another something*, Sadie almost cried out.

'Something that was in the newspaper, *Il Mattino*, just before she left for England. I've got a feeling she—'

Abruptly, Deborah fell silent. She had gone pale and Sadie caught a flash of something on her face, doubt or fear. A chill descended on the room, as if the 'feeling' was not a good one. Sadie waited with bated breath for what Deborah might say next.

But Deborah just shook her head. 'No,' she said, definitively. 'That's it. That's all I can remember. The rest is gone.'

She picked up the photo album and snapped it shut. Sadie got the sense that there was more, but that Deborah didn't want to share.

She clenched her fists. So near and yet so far. So many questions, and not many answers. She looked at Luca imploringly. This couldn't be the end of it.

Immediately understanding, he got up and quickly cleared the tea things away.

'We better get going, Mum,' he said. 'Leave you in peace.'

Sadie smiled gratefully at him. It had been lovely to meet Deborah. But now she needed to get out of the flat and discuss it all with Luca. She was sure he'd have an idea of what to do now.

He hadn't let her down so far. But whether he could unravel all these 'somethings' was another matter altogether.

# CHAPTER FORTY-TWO

NAPLES, JUNE 1944

The blast flung Betty from the truck.

She lay in a crumpled heap on the stony track, temporarily stunned by the shock of the impact. The noise of the explosion echoed between the half-ruined buildings, and she heard the sound of falling masonry, a slow cascade speeding up as it gathered momentum. More destruction for the people of Naples to cope with. But she couldn't worry about that now. She needed to get to the army offices. Susan might not be far behind.

Hauling herself to her feet, she brushed her hair out of her eyes and took a quick look around her. A few people had emerged from the nearby dwellings and were surveying the rubble, and the overturned truck, expressions of bewilderment on their faces. They had thought the aerial bombardment was over, that the Luftwaffe had moved on to other targets these days.

Betty glanced up at the sky. Had the plane finally gone now? She hoped so. She'd lost the pork pie hat when she had fallen, but there was no time to collect it. She had bigger worries right now than going out bareheaded. With a gait that was half run, half limp, she made her way through the streets as the light of dawn slowly grew, bathing everything in a rose-tinted glow. It was a beautiful morning, which made it harder for Betty to understand what had happened in the preceding few hours. When she had met Susan on the deck of the *Arcadia* all that time ago, there was no way she would ever have guessed what Susan would be capable of. She was quite literally the last person who seemed to have it in her to be a traitor. But presumably that was what Susan had banked on. That she was so unnoticeable, so self-effacing and easy to ignore, that no one would suspect her of anything.

Well, Betty had her number now, as indeed she had done for some time. It was just a question of getting the information to the right people.

When she got to the army offices she almost fell through the doors, her exhaustion and desperate thirst making her lightheaded and woozy. A confused orderly guarding the entrance clearly thought that he was dealing with a mad person. Betty had to beg him to take her seriously, though she was in such a state by this time that she could hardly formulate the words.

'Traitor... plane... Morse code signals,' she gasped, struggling to get back her breath after climbing the steep stone stairs. 'Don't know what they mean. Need to tell someone. Please help!'

The final plea seemed to soften the man's heart. Even if this woman dressed as a farm worker was deranged, it was pretty clear she wasn't dangerous. And her bloodstained face and clothing indicated that she'd been in some kind of tussle. He led her inside and sat her down, ordering someone to fetch her a glass of water. By the time Betty had gulped it down, she felt better and was able to give a more coherent account of what had happened.

The orderly, his expression suddenly taking on an expression of alarm, took her through to the office of Colonel Green, who was the highest army official based in Naples. Betty went through her story, starting right at the beginning with seeing Susan take papers out of the cipher room, the damaged headsets that had been blamed on Signor Conti but which Betty was sure had actually been Susan's work, Susan's meeting with a mysterious Italian, her lying about her ability to use Morse code and speak Italian. Now that she was putting it all together, the evidence against Susan seemed overwhelming, but it was impossible to judge what the colonel was making of it as his expression remained impassive throughout.

'I've memorised the Morse code letters,' concluded Betty. 'Those that I saw, anyway. I can write them down if you'll give me a piece of paper. I don't know if they're encrypted or in another language.'

Colonel Green considered this for a moment. His huge leather-covered desk was loaded with the paraphernalia of war: a telephone, reading lamp, and piles and piles of paperwork. He scrabbled around for a moment before locating a pad of paper and a pencil, which he passed to Betty. 'Please go ahead,' he said.

Frowning, both with concentration on her task and puzzlement at the colonel's enigmatic behaviour, Betty noted down the sequences of letters that she could remember. When she had finished, Colonel Green took the paper from her, glancing at it quickly and then placing it carefully on a spare bit of desk to his right.

Betty sat, waiting for the colonel to say something. He remained silent.

'So – you'll send people out to find Sergeant Davies, won't you?' Betty asked. 'She'll be arrested, court-martialled...' She dried up, quashed by Colonel Green's lack of response.

He stood up, strolled to the window and lingered there,

surveying the view of the Bay of Naples, shimmering under the now strong sunshine. Betty sat in silence, wondering if she had crossed some invisible line she wasn't aware of. Why wasn't the colonel saying anything?

'Naples in summertime,' he reflected, suddenly breaking the silence. 'So beautiful. There's something about the quality of the light here, don't you think, Sergeant Bean? It has an airiness to it, a delicacy, at least until the heat really builds. Then, as we both know, it can be brutal.'

Betty nodded, bemused and somewhat frustrated by the colonel's unexpected waxing lyrical about the weather. She wanted to know what was going to be done about Susan, not listen to his meteorological musings.

Eventually he walked, very slowly and deliberately, back to his chair, where he sat down and interlaced his fingers.

'In answer to your question,' he began, his tone heavy and grave, 'no. We will not send out a search party for Sergeant Davies.'

'But why not?' exclaimed Betty. 'She's dangerous, soldiers could be harmed because of the intelligence she's passing on, people could be in great danger.' She was angry and exasperated that the colonel didn't seem to understand the importance of taking action.

Slowly, Colonel Green unlocked his fingers and placed his palms on the desk. 'Do not alarm yourself,' he said. 'I am not saying that Sergeant Davies' actions will go unpunished. That is not my plan at all.'

Betty was on tenterhooks. Why didn't he just get on with it and tell her what he was on about?

'Sergeant Bean,' the colonel intoned, sensing her urgency but not responding to it by speaking faster, 'I am not going to do anything about Sergeant Davies. You, however, are.'

Open-mouthed, Betty stared at the colonel, not sure she was hearing correctly. 'Me?' she questioned, stupefied.

'Oh yes,' Colonel Green replied. 'I have a job for you to do. A very important job, one that is vital for ensuring the outcome to this war that we have all been working so hard to achieve. Do you accept the challenge, Sergeant Bean? Yes or no?'

# CHAPTER FORTY-THREE

Betty's head was reeling as she left Colonel Green's office. She had hoped to hand over to her superiors all the information about Susan that she had gleaned and be done with the whole business, no longer her responsibility. The last thing she had expected was to be drawn into a plan of espionage and surveillance.

But that was what had happened.

Now Betty had agreed to that plan and was honour-bound to see it through. Colonel Green had impressed on her the importance of her mission, and the fact that she was the only person who could do it.

'We need to find out everything,' he had told her. 'Who is Sergeant Davies working with, who is the recipient of the intelligence she passes on, what is their ultimate aim? If we apprehend Sergeant Davies now, we will have her – but her alone. There is no guarantee that we will be able to make her talk.'

Betty frowned at this statement. She didn't like to think of how it was possible to make someone talk – it sounded rather ominous. If anyone had asked her before all of this which of the four of them was most likely to crack under interrogation, she would have said Susan. But last night, out on that hillside in the darkness, she had seen Susan's stony determination and iron will, and now she hated to think how an interrogator would go about getting anything useful out of her.

'We will, of course, ensure that we only give Sergeant Davies work to do in the cipher room that is of no consequence to the war. But as we have seen, she has co-conspirators, collaborators – call them what you will – on the outside. It will be better – much better,' the colonel had continued, 'if you, her tried and trusted friend, become one of her accomplices. And then, when we have got to the bottom of her little plot, we can gather them all up. Every single one of the traitorous gang.'

Betty had stared at the colonel, wide-eyed with horror and disbelief. 'Right,' she said, gulping down her instinctive reaction, which was to cry out, 'No, I can't do this.'

'How you broach with Sergeant Davies that you would like to work with her I leave up to you.' Colonel Green smiled. 'You are obviously a very resourceful young lady,' he complimented her, 'you've shown that by your actions leading up to, and including, last night. So I have no doubt that you will come up with something plausible and appropriate.'

He flashed her another of his glacial smiles. 'And it goes without saying that this is entirely confidential. Not a word to anyone, Sergeant Bean.'

The colonel's words rang in Betty's ears as she made her way back to Villa Teresa. She was exhausted and still dressed in the farm labourer's clothes. She hoped she could slip into the dorm room unnoticed while everyone was either at breakfast or already on shift. She'd have a wash and change into her uniform and then, as he'd ordered her, she'd get both the wound on her ear and her ankle checked out before returning to work.

Fortunately, the first part of the plan was accomplished

successfully, though when she looked in the bathroom mirror she hardly recognised herself. Her hair was a tangled mess, her face blotched with mud and grass stains and a liberal smattering of blood. Gingerly inspecting her ear, she found that the bullet must have grazed the lobe, causing a lot of blood but no real injury. It suddenly struck her with full force that she could have died. She leant forward, resting her forehead against the cool glass, and breathed deeply, in and out, until the panic at the thought of her own near demise began to diminish.

After she'd washed and tidied herself up a bit, Betty headed to the medical room. On her way there, she bumped into Lily and Deborah returning from the mess.

'Betty!' exclaimed Deborah. 'You look terrible. What's up? Are you ill? There's a few people who've come down with a nasty cold – I hope you haven't caught it.'

Betty shook her head. 'No, I'm feeling fine, never better,' she lied. 'Just the old ankle.' She gestured towards her leg. 'It's never been quite right since that fall on Vesuvius and it's playing me up a bit. Painful, you know.' She grimaced as if to show how much it hurt. 'I'm not on shift until this afternoon, so I'll put it up for a while and I'm sure it'll soon improve.'

Lily frowned, clearly unconvinced. 'What's that on your neck?' she asked, leaning forward, peering closely. 'It looks like —' She stood up and met Betty's gaze. 'Blood. It looks like blood. What on earth happened?'

Betty shifted uncomfortably. 'I, er, I went for a walk,' she stuttered. 'Get some fresh air, you know. I caught myself on a thorn bush, so stupid of me. Wasn't looking where I was going.'

Lily's brow was more creased than ever by now. Betty crossed her fingers behind her back and hoped that she wouldn't ask her any more awkward questions that necessitated lies as answers. She hated not telling the truth; it was entirely against her nature.

With a soft tut and a resigned shake of her head, Lily

stepped away, towards their dorm room. 'Well, take care of yourself,' she said. 'And don't go having arguments with any more aggressive plants!'

'I won't,' replied Betty, as breezily as she could. 'And I'll see you both later.'

With that, she turned on her heel and hurried off to the medical room. Once she'd had the flesh wound on her ear properly cleaned, and her ankle strapped, the doctor wrote her a note excusing her from duty that day. Normally Betty would have protested and said she was absolutely fine, but she really did feel exhausted. And some time off would allow her to address the huge problem that was lodged at the forefront of her mind. How on earth was she going to convince Susan to take her into her confidence and share her nefarious secrets? And what if she managed it, but Susan discovered that she was spying on her? The very thought terrified the living daylights out of Betty.

She remembered how Susan had brushed her off when she'd tried to flush out her true feelings about the Nazis. It was clear that a strategy that obvious was not going to work. Betty was going to have to try a whole lot harder if she were to fulfil the mission Colonel Green had entrusted her with.

But as Betty lay on her bunk with her bad ankle propped up on a box at the end of the bed, she thought of all of the soldiers, battling for Europe, a struggle that was already into its fifth year. Most of all she thought of Gianni, up in the north, engaged in brutal assaults and energy-sapping offensives against the remaining German forces. The partisans were quick and mobile, able to melt into the hills and go underground, popping up to make impromptu strikes on the enemy when least expected. But this put them in constant danger, never able to relax, always looking over their shoulders. This was how Gianni lived, day to day, not planning for the future, because there might not be a future.

Betty would not dream of comparing her own situation with Gianni's; he was clearly facing much more peril than she was, Susan notwithstanding. But nevertheless, she passionately wished that she could tell him about the mission she had been given, ask his advice, share with him her fear of failure. Lying there, gazing up at the frescoed ceiling, Betty's longing for Gianni suffused her veins and tightened in a band round her heart. But it also steeled her soul to action.

She had to do all she could to help the war effort, however terrifying, difficult and daunting the task. It was her duty, simple as that.

# CHAPTER FORTY-FOUR

NAPLES, JULY 1972

Back outside, the sun was high in the sky and the streets were quiet, windows and shutters closed as people settled down for their siesta.

'Why would Betty Bean have been in an Italian newspaper? We've got to find out more about her,' said Sadie, urgently. 'What about the phone book? I could call my flatmate, get her to phone directory enquiries, see if her name is listed in Malton, where Eden Camp is. Because that's the only way it makes sense, isn't it? If they met there, Gianni Urso gave her the keepsake, and then they met again in Italy?'

'Yes, I think you're right.' Luca nodded. 'And the phone book is a good idea. But we can do that later. Right now, I've got a better one. Come with me.'

Immediately, he was heading off up the street, Sadie swept along in his wake. They got on a bus, and then a tram, which hurtled them through the streets at a considerable speed. Eventually, they were in front of a large building with the name IL MATTINO blazoned across the front.

'The newspaper my mum mentioned,' Luca said, breath-lessly. They'd been practically running all the way from the station. 'My friend works here. The archive is in the basement, all the copies ever printed. He'll let us in. And then we just have to look through them. Betty would most likely have left some time in the spring of 1945, before VE Day probably.'

'That's still a lot of papers,' Sadie replied. 'It'll take ages. Will that be all right, do you think?' It suddenly seemed vitally important that they were able to follow this lead right here, right now. The name Betty Bean was still reverberating around Sadie's head. Though she had embarked on this quest with the sole aim of finding her parents, and had thought of little else since finding her adoption certificate, now there was actually the possibility that she might be closing in on her mother it felt overwhelming. Clenching her fists, she tried desperately to quell her fear and doubts.

Luca shrugged. 'Course. This is Italy. If you have the right connections, anything's possible.' He turned to Sadie and smiled, and in that instant her mood lifted. She wasn't alone in this. She had Luca by her side, leading her, in fact. It wasn't all down to her.

*Thank goodness you do, then*, she thought, as they marched into the imposing building.

Down in the basement it was blissfully cool. Sadie shivered at the change in temperature. It was two in the afternoon. Most of the newspaper staff had gone home; they'd come back later to prepare the morning's edition. Luca's friend said they could stay as long as they liked – they wouldn't be disturbed and the secu-rity guard would let them out when they wanted to leave.

It seemed too good to be true. Sadie could hardly believe that, by the time night fell, she might have solved the mystery of who her mother was and where to find her. Suppressing an involuntary shudder of anticipation, she followed Luca through the archive room, watching as he checked the dates on the great wheeled rows of shelving until they found 1945.

Luca pulled out the huge, bound volumes one by one and handed them to Sadie to pile onto a trolley. She focused on the task, trying not to let her mind run away with her. *Just do what needs to be done*, she told herself. *Be methodical. Concentrate. Don't get your hopes up. It might all come to nothing.*

Hours later, they were still searching. Sadie was working forward from January and Luca backward from May. All Sadie could do was scan the text for the name Betty Bean, as obviously she couldn't make head nor tail of the Italian. They searched and searched until their eyes were aching and their backs breaking from lugging the great heavy piles of bound newspapers from the shelves to the table. It was utterly silent in the cavernous room, the only sounds those of their own breathing and the rustle of turning pages.

Until suddenly, Luca shouted, 'Look!'

Sadie jumped out of her skin and looked over to him. At the excitement in his voice, a rush of dizziness seized her. She gripped the reading table to steady herself, closing her eyes momentarily, hoping that Luca wouldn't notice. He didn't; his eyes were glued to the page, scanning rapidly up and down the columns. He opened his mouth to speak, then closed it again.

And then everything changed.

'Oh,' he said, in a completely different tone. He paused, coughed to clear his throat. 'No, sorry, false alarm, I was wrong. It's nothing.'

Sadie stared at him, confused. He had seemed so certain that he'd found something.

Sensing her quizzical gaze upon him, Luca shrugged apologetically. 'I'm sorry,' he muttered. 'My eyes are playing tricks on me.' He lifted up his metal-framed glasses and rubbed his eyes, then exhaled forcefully. 'Too much tension. Too much hope.'

Guilt seared through Sadie. She didn't want Luca to feel bad – he was doing so much to help her, more than she could ever have imagined or expected. She moved closer to him, peering over his shoulder at the newspaper he was reading, searching for whatever it was that had falsely caught Luca's attention.

But before she could take a proper look, he had firmly closed the paper and was picking it up, ready to put it back on the trolley.

'I think we're done now, aren't we?' he suggested. 'My mum must have been mistaken. Or perhaps it was in a different paper, not *Il Mattino*.'

Sadie's heart sank and despondency set in. Which paper? A national one, headquartered in Rome or Milan? There was no chance of searching all of them. She'd been right to tell herself not to get her hopes up, but utterly wrong if she'd thought that it was possible not to do that. Of course it wasn't. She'd been drenched in hope, saturated with it.

And now, nothing.

Trying to hide her disappointment from Luca, she forced a smile. 'Not to worry,' she said, cheerily. 'Thank your friend for me, won't you? I probably won't see him again and I want him to know how—'

'Certainly.' Luca's voice cut across hers. 'I will definitely do that.'

There was a momentary silence. Sadie sensed something behind it, something unsaid, though she didn't know what it could be. Trying to shake off the uneasy feeling, she checked her watch. She was amazed to see it was nearly 7 p.m.

Once they were outside on the street, busy with shoppers and diners now the siesta had ended, Sadie rubbed her hand across her forehead.

'Are you all right?' asked Luca. 'You look a little pale.'

Sadie shook her head. 'I'm fine,' she answered distractedly. 'It's just – it all feels so enormous. I came to Italy so sure of what I was setting out to achieve. But now all that certainty has gone and I'm not sure what I'm doing here.' Tears pricked behind her eyelids and she was too tired and too wrung out to blink them back. One squeezed out and trickled slowly down her cheek.

Luca looked at her, distraught. 'You probably need something to eat. My mum always says no one can think straight on an empty stomach.'

Sadie smiled wanly. 'No,' she answered. 'I think I'd like to go back to the hotel and crash out. I can get something from room service.' She wasn't so preoccupied that her inner self didn't snort ironically at the ease with which she referenced room service, something she had never, ever even considered using before.

But a lot of things were different on this journey.

Luca walked her back to the hotel and they parted on the front steps, having made an arrangement to meet again in the morning. As he walked away, Sadie stood watching him. She had a sudden urge to run after him, to throw her arms round him, beg him to stay with her. But of course she couldn't do that. They were friends, Luca was helping with her search, that was all.

And yet there was no doubt that, deep within Sadie, feelings for Luca were stirring that she had never felt before. Simon had never had such an effect on her, nor had any of the boyfriends who had preceded him. It was as if, here in Italy, every step she took closer to her roots was also taking her closer to Luca.

Sadie was gripped by another panicked sensation. What if Luca didn't feel the same way as she did? But then this fear was banished as another, worse one crystallised. He'd been very quiet after that strange moment in the archive when it had seemed as if he had found something and then said that he hadn't. Perhaps he *had* read something of interest, but didn't want to share it with her? If so, what could it have been?

Sadie was suddenly certain. Luca was hiding something from her. But exactly what was a total mystery.

# CHAPTER FORTY-FIVE

NAPLES, OCTOBER 1944

Betty turned the problem of how to gain Susan's confidence over and over in her head until it drove her mad. She struggled to stay focused on her work, but in all honesty that wasn't too much of a problem any more. There was very little activity on any of the airwaves she and her fellow cipher operators were monitoring. Things had changed immeasurably since they had first arrived in Naples, when their radios would fizz and hiss with constant transmissions.

Betty knew that Colonel Green had arranged with Lieutenant Corder that Susan should be given duplicates of every cipher strip, and that the messages she sent to BP would be disregarded. Those sent by another operative – a trustworthy one – would be used instead. So there was no danger of Susan disrupting the war effort from inside Y-Signals HQ. But of course, there were numerous other ways she could cause harm. Betty had been put on an identical shift pattern to Susan so she could surreptitiously observe everything the other woman was up to, including following her when she went into town. For weeks, all Susan did was visit the shops, or go to a café for one of the delicious cappuccino coffees that they had all become addicted to. There was no chance of ever getting a drink like this back home, so it had to be appreciated and enjoyed whenever possible.

Then, after several months of nothing happening, one day Susan's foray into town took a different direction – towards the docks. Amidst the cries of the dockers and the grinding of the cranes, Betty watched as Susan slipped into a small office with a bent and battered sign advertising it as premises belonging to a fruit exporting company. Plucking up all her courage, Betty slunk forward, ignoring the curious glances of a lorryload of road-builders on their way to their next assignment.

Flattening herself against the stone wall, she strained to get a glimpse of what was going on inside. She could just make out the back of Susan's head as she stood, deep in conversation with a bearded man, both of them staring intently at a map spread out on the table before them. Try as she might, Betty could not discern what part of Italy they were scrutinising, but wherever it was had them talking animatedly and intermittently prodding at various places on the map. As well as her limited field of vision, Betty had the closed windows to contend with; she could pick up the faint overtones of voices but was unable to hear any details of their discussion.

After a few minutes, Betty began to worry that Susan would soon come out and find her there. She ducked below window level, crept along the side of the building and the one next to it and, once she had cleared the corner, she ran, along the docks and on to the furthest access road, far from where they had entered. Only when she was sure that Susan had not seen her and was not following her did she slow down.

It was more interesting than anything else she'd seen Susan do since the night of the plane attack – but it was hardly helpful. Betty hadn't been able to hear what Susan and her interlocutor had been talking about. All she could do was report back what she had observed to Colonel Green in their weekly debriefing. But this in itself was unsatisfactory. Colonel Green wanted her to gain Susan's confidence and be taken into the inner circle of her traitorous cabal.

Unless and until Betty had done this, she would have failed.

Galvanised by the fear of failure, Betty made her decision. She wrote Susan a note, asking to meet her in secret and suggesting that, if she did so, Susan would hear something to her advantage. It was a little basic, falling far short of anything the brilliant Sherlock Holmes would have come up with, but it was the best Betty could think of.

The next morning, Betty hid the note among a bundle of cipher strips, which she placed purposefully in Susan's in-tray.

As she sat at her wireless with her headset clamped over her ears, she observed Susan on the other side of the large room, standing over her teleprinter. She scrutinised her to see if there was any sign that she'd seen Betty's note, but there was no indication. Susan really was a strange fish – her acting abilities were second to none. Betty took a deep breath to try to calm her racing heart. There was nothing she could do but wait and see if Susan took the bait.

That evening there was a dance at the NAAFI that she, Lily and Deborah had all decided to go to. Susan had already said she wouldn't be going. Previously, Betty had thought Susan was just shy, but that was obviously not the case. Nowadays, Betty was more inclined to believe that she wanted the time alone and undisturbed for her nefarious activities. On the other hand, could it also show that Susan had a conscience? That she didn't want to party and frolic with people she was busy betraying? It was impossible to tell.

Checking her pigeonhole on her way back from the NAAFI that evening, Betty found three letters inside. One was from Julie, Samuel's mother, another from Gianni, and the third was addressed in handwriting Betty did not recognise. Retreating to the privacy of the bathroom to open it, she ripped the envelope's seal with trembling fingers. Pulling out the paper inside, she hastily scanned the words. As she did so, her heart began to pound. The letter was not signed but Betty knew instantly it was from Susan. She must have left her name off it to avoid detection should the missive be intercepted. Its message was brief but to the point.

*Meet me at the old castle, 6 p.m. Friday. Tell no one. Come alone.*

Betty's palms were slick with sweat as she attempted to push the paper clumsily back into the envelope. Breathing heavily, she shoved it deep into her pocket, then immediately took it out again, ripping it into tiny shreds and flushing it down the lavatory. She must destroy the evidence – after all, that would be what Susan expected of her, wouldn't it? What any self-respecting betrayer of king and country would do? Hard as it was, Betty needed to think with the mind of a traitor now.

It wasn't until she was back in their dorm room, watched over by the frescoed cupids, that Betty remembered the other two letters. Studying them both, she weighed up which to open first. Julie's, which surely could contain only bad news, or Gianni's, which might be equally difficult to read, calling to mind as it was sure to do the constant danger he was in?

In the end, it was Julie's she started with, only to be confronted by stark news. Like Betty, Julie had not heard from Samuel for many, many months. And then one night she had woken suddenly from feverish dreams with a sense of such utter doom that she was sure it could mean only one thing. That Samuel was dead. It had not been confirmed by the military authorities, but a mother's instinct told her so.

Betty felt bile rise in her throat as she read this. She did not want Samuel to die. It was so long since she had seen him that she had forgotten almost everything about him, but she knew that he was a good person, a brave soldier, and that he, like all of those slain by this war, did not deserve to have his life ended so young.

After long minutes lost to contemplation of Samuel's fate, she turned her attention to Gianni's letter. Since the summer, constant attacks launched by partisans hiding in the forests and hills of the Apennines and the Alps had led to many acts of revenge by the German army. At the beginning of the month, hundreds of civilians, men, women and children, had been massacred near Marzabotto in retaliation. There was no let-up in the fighting – or the danger. Betty shuddered at the thought of what Gianni was facing. She wished she could be with him, helping him through the ordeal, holding his hand, hugging him tight, urging him on to battle – and being there to welcome him when he returned.

Opening the envelope and casting her eyes to the page, Betty read Gianni's words, drinking them in as she imagined him sitting there beside her, smiling at her with his lopsided grin, watching her read with love and loyalty in his soft brown eyes. Of course he couldn't tell her sensitive information about the campaigns he was involved in, but instead he always wrote about life, about the Alpine flowers that flourished in the mountains, so different to what he was used in his native Sicily, about a child who had performed a folk dance to entertain the crowds at a country fiesta. And then, at the end of the letter, something totally, wonderfully, unexpected.

*Do you remember how I taught you to ask for a ticket to Rome, per favore, all that time ago in Yorkshire? I have been granted leave over Christmas so can you use those words now and meet me there, in the Eternal City, so that we can celebrate the festivities together?*

At first Betty could hardly believe what she was seeing. Her heart pounded in her chest as she read and reread the words. She imagined herself and Gianni, together for day after day, able to talk and hug and kiss as much as they wanted, free from censorious eyes or gossiping tongues. How she would relish any and every such moment she could spend with him. The very thought of his presence made her blood run hot and her fingertips tingle in anticipation of his touch.

Of course she would accept his invitation. She was owed leave herself; she would ask the commander of Y-Signals straight away. She would go to Rome. She would spend the holiday with Gianni.

But first she had to brave the clandestine meeting with Susan.

# CHAPTER FORTY-SIX

NAPLES, OCTOBER 1944

As Betty waited for Friday to come, her longing for Gianni almost outweighed the anxiety and trepidation she felt for the mission she was on. She wondered if Susan had become suspicious of the changes that had been made to their rotas so that the pair of them were always on shift together. Susan hadn't seemed to consider the possibility that Betty might not be free at 6 p.m. on Friday. Had she guessed what was going on? Was the meeting a trap?

Betty was sick with nerves and, by the time the day came, she could eat neither lunch nor tea. Her stomach gurgled and groaned but every time she thought about consuming anything solid she knew she'd immediately be sick if she so much as attempted to. She rehearsed endlessly in her head what she would say if Susan questioned her commitment to the cause. 'I've always admired Hitler and the fascist cause', or 'A strong leader such as the Führer is exactly what Europe needs'. In the grounds of Villa Teresa, far from prying eyes and listening ears, she practised saying the words out loud, trying to sound convincing. But would Susan really believe her?

Finally, it was the hour for Betty to leave Villa Teresa and head to the rendezvous point. As she approached the medieval Castel dell'Ovo on its promontory surrounded on three sides by sea, dusk was falling. She crossed the long causeway, her army shoes rapping against the cobbles, sounding impossibly loud in the evening hush. A massive seagull swooped low before her, almost colliding with her, setting her heart thumping and her pulse racing. The nearer she got, the taller, more forbidding and intimidating the castle's sheer stone walls appeared.

*What am I doing here?* she thought to herself, panic rising in her throat. *I'm not cut out for this. I'm not a hero.* The thoughts echoed around her mind until she forced them away. This was no time to give in to fear and dread. She needed to be strong, brave like Gianni was every day.

The castle, as far as Betty knew, was a barracks now and it occurred to her that this was a strange choice of meeting place when you had evil on your mind. But on the other hand, perhaps hiding in plain sight was a clever option? Either way, looking around her Betty could see absolutely no one around. The huge castle doors were locked and bolted; no one was getting through those.

She paused to take stock. Susan had not given any precise indication of exactly where she would be. Betty hoped she wouldn't have to wait long; the wind was getting up, and she was cold, despite the protection of her army greatcoat. Shivering, she contemplated the expanse of sea that lay all around, no longer calm and unruffled but, stirred by the wind, jumping and rolling with white-topped waves.

She slunk into the shadows cast by the edifice's monumental walls and hovered there, her eyes flicking from side to side, scanning her surroundings. The gathering gloom made it hard to see more than a few feet ahead, and the wind, increasing in strength by the minute, began to seize up fistfuls of seawater and fling them over the causeway, darkening the stone and sprinkling Betty's coat with shimmering droplets.

Betty checked her watch. It was six fifteen. Was she in the wrong place? Was Susan keeping her waiting to test her resolve? How long should she stay here before giving up?

She was just deciding that she'd give it until six thirty when a movement in the shadows caught her eye. Straining to see, she made out a figure looming towards her. Fists clenched, ready to run if necessary, Betty stepped forward.

'Susan?'

'Betty?'

They both spoke at the same time and Betty felt relief that it was Susan and not some unknown assailant – and then, immediately after that, panic again because now it was really happening. Now was the time when she would have to lie like she had never lied in her life before, nor ever wanted to again. She wasn't entirely convinced that she could do it – or that, even if she could, she could do it convincingly. But she'd give it her best shot.

Susan indicated to Betty to follow her. She led her to the left side of the castle entrance, where one wall jutted out ahead of another, providing a small, concealed nook. Betty didn't like the feeling of being cornered there, but at least she was out of the gale and the angry spray.

'We don't have much time,' Susan said, breathily and urgently. 'The soldiers in the barracks change shifts at seven. It's best if we're not still here then.'

At this, Betty nodded fervently. She definitely didn't want to be here for another three-quarters of an hour.

'Why do you want to join me in my aim of destabilising the interim government of this country, ousting the Allies and reinstating Mussolini?' Susan's question was all-encompassing and direct.

For a moment, Betty's mind went blank. All the answers she'd so assiduously prepared deserted her. She gulped, clenched her fists, implored herself to keep calm.

'I-I've been studying, reading the newspapers and the history books,' she eventually managed to stutter. 'It's taken time, but I now believe that fascism is the answer to the world's problems and I regret everything I've done to help the war effort. I wish to redress the balance and make amends for my mistakes. I believe the Führer is exactly the leader the world needs.'

*Oh God*, a silent voice was muttering inside her head as she spoke. *I can't believe I'm doing this. Colonel Green better be right that this is the best course of action. And he better be grateful, too.*

Susan gave a cursory nod. 'All right, very good,' she said.

Betty almost burst into tears with relief at being believed. And then something leapt, unbidden, to her mind. Maybe Susan wasn't fooled at all. Maybe she was just pretending... Maybe Betty had fallen straight into some kind of trap Susan had laid for her.

But it was too late to backtrack, or back out. Susan was speaking again.

'I need you to do something,' she said, 'your first mission. One of our accomplices works at the docks. He's a brilliant code-breaker. He gained access to a British Army codebook some time ago.'

Betty's heart leapt at this statement. So that was what had happened to the missing codebook all those months ago, for surely this must be the same one. Susan had stolen it. But the code was changed and updated every month, so she wasn't sure what use it could still be to him now.

'Using this book, he has been able to predict and decipher the subsequent codes that have been issued. However, he is no

longer able to do this. The codes have become more sophisticated.'

Susan stopped, looking straight into Betty's eyes and fixing
her with a glacial stare. 'You are to remove the current codebook
from the cipher room and deliver it to him. I'll tell you the
address – you must not write it down. You have to memorise it.'
Susan rapped her ankles together as if on drill – the drill she
could never do properly on the parade ground but now seemed
to have perfected. Involuntarily, Betty found herself raising her
arm in a salute. She got halfway there and then dropped it
again.

Susan observed this with a wry look, as if she found Betty's
ingrained obedience amusing.

'I will,' Betty assured her. 'Remember it, I mean. And
deliver the book.' Even as she said the words, she knew this was
a test. Of her loyalty. Of her trustworthiness. What if she
should fail? What fate would befall her, what punishment
would Susan and her cronies mete out? Dry-mouthed and
panicky, Betty tried to push such thoughts away. Right now,
they weren't helpful.

She listened while Susan told her the address and made her
repeat it back. She didn't even need to know it; she knew
exactly where the office was, having followed Susan there so
recently.

'Now we must go,' instructed Susan, once she was happy
with Betty's memory. 'You leave first. I'll follow at a short
interval.'

Betty could hardly get her legs to work quick enough.
Emerging from the shelter of the castle walls, the full force of
the wind hit her, taking her breath away, making her struggle for
air. Putting her head down, she forged ahead into its vortex. The
waves were gigantic now, rolling shorewards with single-minded
intent, crashing against the causeway walls and exploding over

the sides. Shuddering at each one that hit, showering her with icy drops, Betty narrowed her eyes and battled on. The cobbles had become treacherously slippery and at one point her legs almost went out from under her. She managed to right herself but nevertheless the near-fall had pulled at her ankle and the familiar pain recurred. *Dratted thing,* she hissed under her breath, *and dratted Vesuvius that caused the weakness.*

Even as she battled on, she thought of Gianni, what he would say if he knew what she had got herself mixed up in. Would he approve, or would he think she had lost her mind to let herself get involved in such an outlandish plot? Betty didn't know, but just the picture of him that her mind's eye conjured up calmed her frayed nerves.

She wondered how far behind her Susan was. As well as the battering of the storm, there was something unnerving about having her back to her former friend. It would be so easy for Susan to creep up behind her, bash her on the head, tip her over the retaining wall and into the broiling sea...

But no. Betty must not let her always too-vivid imagination run away with her.

She reached the end of the causeway and began to breathe more easily. The wind was calmer here where it was less exposed. Surrounding the castle was a marina, along the dock of which stood fish restaurants and tavernas, frequented by locals and army personnel alike. Lights shone out from inside their steamed-up windows and Betty felt the comfort of familiarity, the promise of the company of other people, normal people, meaning she was no longer alone with an enemy of the state, no longer—

The hand on her shoulder made her jump out of her skin. Her heart skipped several beats and she crumpled in two, barely able to stand.

'Sergeant Bean?' questioned the voice. 'Are you all right? I'm sorry if I startled you.'

Struggling to steady her heart rate and pull herself upright, Betty tried to recompose her features from utter shock and fear into something approaching normal. Facing her assailant, she saw a face she recognised but at first couldn't place.

And then she got it. It was one of Deborah's ex-boyfriends, the one she'd nicknamed Lieutenant Lovestruck. In the midst of her terror, Betty almost giggled as she recalled the nickname.The rapid change of emotions was making her a bit hysterical.

'Lieutenant...' Betty couldn't recall his actual name. 'Lieutenant!' she repeated, adding an exclamation mark in place of a surname. 'How nice to see you.'

It really wasn't that nice, to be standing making small talk in the middle of a raging tempest when she was soaking wet, weak from all the tension and longing to get back to bed, but not even what she'd just been through was enough to shake the expectations of convention.

Lieutenant Lovestruck smiled curiously at her, as if she were a particularly interesting specimen in a lab. 'What are you doing out here on a night like this?' he enquired, not unreasonably.

Betty struggled to come up with something plausible. 'I wanted some fresh air,' she said, thinking fast. 'I didn't realise the weather was going to turn. Bit silly, I know, but I do get cabin fever sometimes, us girls so cramped together. It's nice to get out for a bit.'

'Right.' Lieutenant Lovestruck didn't sound entirely convinced but it was the best Betty could do.

'Anyway, I got rather wet and it's a bit cold standing here, so if you don't mind I'll be on my way,' she said.

'You don't want a brandy to warm you up? I'm heading for that little place on the corner, meeting some of the fellas there. It's always nice to have some female company.' Lieutenant Lovestruck seemed genuinely to mean this.

'Oh no,' replied Betty, hastily. 'It's very kind of you but I don't really drink and anyway, as I said, I'm rather chilly. Thank you again. Have a nice evening.'

And with that, she turned on her heel and made off in the direction of Villa Teresa. When she dared to turn round, the lieutenant had disappeared, presumably by now safely ensconced in the taverna.

Thank goodness for that. Betty had got through the first assignment. But how would she fare in the next?

# CHAPTER FORTY-SEVEN

NAPLES, JULY 1972

Next day, when he came to meet Sadie, Luca was in ebullient mood.

'I've got some news,' he announced, excitedly.

'Oh?' Sadie tried to sound enthusiastic, though in reality she was feeling utterly down in the dumps. She understood now how naive she'd been about what the search for her birth parents would entail. That it would be a rollercoaster ride was to be expected – but now she felt she was hurtling along on the ghost train and wasn't sure she'd ever get out. Kim and Simon had both warned her, and reminding herself of this did not improve her mood one bit; she had been determined to prove them wrong. And then there was the episode the day before in the archive. She'd been sure Luca had read something he wasn't sharing with her.

'You know the friend my mum mentioned?' Luca asked. 'Lily? My mum called her up after your visit – she felt so bad that she couldn't remember more, and was aware that you'd left disappointed—'

'Oh no!' interjected Sadie, appalled that she'd unwittingly given Deborah that impression. 'I wasn't disappointed at all.'

Luca smiled down at her as they walked along the busy pavement. 'Well, I think you were a bit. And she just wants to do what she can to help. So anyway, she spoke to Lily and, as luck would have it, Lily is heading to the Amalfi coast next week. She hadn't planned to stop in Naples this year but as soon as my mum told her about you she immediately said she'd change her itinerary.' Luca stopped still, to the annoyance of several other pedestrians, who tutted loudly as they skirted around him and Sadie. He grabbed hold of Sadie's hands. 'We're going to join her at the Britannique Hotel for dinner on Saturday evening. So hopefully we'll find out some more then.'

Sadie did her best to look as delighted as she knew Luca wanted her to be. But she didn't fool him.

'What's the matter? You don't want to meet Lily?' he asked, peering at her anxiously as if trying to work out what he'd got wrong.

Sadie looked away. 'Of course I do. If she has anything she can add to the little I already know, that would be amazing. She might be able to shed some light on Gianni Urso, where or how I might find him. But...' She hesitated, not sure whether or not it was wise to continue. Should she broach her suspicion that he was keeping something from her?

Luca was eyeing her with a puzzled look. 'Come on, Sadie,' he urged. 'What's up? I can tell there's something.'

With a sigh, Sadie took the plunge. 'It's about yesterday,' she blurted out. 'In the archive. I get the feeling that you – that maybe you did find something but you just didn't want to tell me.'

As she spoke she was intently scrutinising Luca's face, which seemed to her more handsome by the day. A hint of something indefinable flitted across it. Was it fear? But what did Luca have to be frightened of? Doubt? But why? And then it was gone, and Luca was smiling in his easy-going way, his clear, honest brown eyes warm with reassurance.

'There was nothing, truly,' he said. 'If I behaved oddly – well, it's just because I know how much this means to you and I was sorry we didn't find what we were searching for.'

Sadie hesitated for a moment. There was no reason for Luca to lie to her. No reason at all.

'OK, no problem then,' she responded. 'I'm sorry for interrogating you. It's all so wonderful, being here and everything, and at the same time so – well, painful, I suppose. Being keyed up all the time about finding something and then also apprehensive that it's not going to work out.'

Luca touched her elbow gently. 'What's not going to work out?' he asked, quietly.

'You know,' said Sadie, a little wildly now, 'any of it. I'm not going to find my parents and, even if I did, they might be dead or not want to know me...' Her voice trailed off, leaving the last words unspoken. *And whatever's going on between the two of us, perhaps I'm imagining it, perhaps it'll all come to nothing – even though, for the first time in my life, here in Italy, in your company, I feel that I belong.*

Luca frowned. 'I get that,' he said. 'But you've come so far now and I, for one, am not going to let you throw in the towel.' He reached out and rested his hands on Sadie's shoulders. 'Look at me,' he continued, more authoritatively than he had ever spoken to her before. 'Look me right in the eyes.'

Sadie complied. For one unbearable moment, she thought, *This is it. He's going to kiss me...* Her knees trembled in anticipation and her heart turned over.

'Repeat after me,' Luca said. 'I will not give up.'

Hesitating, Sadie opened and shut her mouth a couple of times, then gave herself a little internal shake before managing to do as he asked. She needed to rid her head of nonsensical thoughts, she told herself sternly. All this emotion was making her fanciful.

Releasing her from his grasp, Luca pointed ahead of them, down a wide street lined with shops and crowded with people. 'I promised Mum I'd pick up some things she needs from the market,' he told Sadie. 'I hope you don't mind doing the chores with me, but you might find the *mercato* interesting. Tourists usually do.' He gave her a cheeky wink, his earlier good spirits seemingly restored. 'Not that you're really a tourist any more. You're practically a local now.'

Sadie beamed, her own mood lifting along with his. This was a compliment indeed. 'Now all I've got to do is learn some Italian,' she joked. 'Beyond *si, non, grazie* and prosecco.'

Luca laughed and then gestured to her to be careful as they crossed the road.

The market announced itself by the clamour of voluble Italian, spoken at breakneck speed and high volume, and the smell, an aroma like nothing Sadie had ever experienced before, of fish and pungent herbs, of ripe peaches and juicy melons. Organised chaos was the best description Sadie could come up with for the atmosphere. She followed as Luca weaved a path through stalls piled high with seafood: great heaps of silver sardines, piles of prawns, glistening sea bass and sea bream and a tuna, huge and glassy-eyed, ready to be sliced into steaks. Shuddering, Sadie watched as a man skilfully and speedily gutted a snapper, throwing the entrails into a bucket. She had never seen so much fish in her life. Did everything really get bought and eaten? It was all a far cry from the small display in the fishmongers in Broadstairs.

Luca stopped by a display of what, at first glance, looked to Sadie like pale starfish. Then, scrutinising it more closely, she realised it was octopus, the stars actually each creature's many tentacles, coiling outwards from soft bellies. Once realisation hit, instinctively she recoiled, feeling a little freaked out by the rubbery suckers and glossy skin. Oblivious to her squeamishness, Luca had already embarked on a lengthy altercation with the stallholder, which became more and more emphatic with every word. Sadie watched, fascinated.

All of a sudden the deal was completed and, with smiles all round, the octopus was weighed out, placed in a bag and handed to Luca, who stowed it away in his mother's shopper, departing the stall with a breezy *adieu*.

'That was impressive,' Sadie said, with a laugh, as they walked away. 'I thought World War Three was about to break out, the way the two of you were going.'

Luca smiled and shrugged. 'That's shopping the Italian way. You have to haggle or they'll take you for a mug, and it's part of the enjoyment, anyway. You toss the price back and forth for a bit until both parties are happy and then – hey presto! Everyone's a winner.'

Sadie grimaced. 'That's not how things work back home! And even here – I just wouldn't have the nerve. But I love watching you do it.'

Luca blew on his fingernails and brushed them lightly against his shirt front in a gesture acknowledging his prowess as a street bargainer. They both laughed.

'So what's Deborah going to make with the octopus?' asked Sadie, genuinely curious. She couldn't for the life of her think what one would do with such a bizarre-looking creature, or what it would taste like, and wasn't entirely sure she wanted to find out. But she was trying to be open-minded about new foodstuffs while she was here.

'*Polpo alla Luciana*,' explained Luca. 'It's a Neapolitan speciality. But don't ask me exactly how you cook it because I have no idea. Mum got my grandma to give her lessons when she got married to my dad just after the war, but it's all done verbally, nothing written down.'

Sadie considered this for a moment. They were in the fruit

and veg section now, surrounded by gaggles of housewives all haggling vociferously over the price of courgettes and cucumbers. Driving a hard bargain certainly did seem to be the Italian way.

'I'm surprised your mother didn't go home once the war was over,' she commented to Luca, as he stopped beside one particular stall, where huge, glossy red tomatoes were bursting their skins with ripeness, and orange and yellow peppers gleamed brighter than the sun, and waved a greeting to the proprietor.

Luca shook his head. 'She didn't want to. Her parents had died in the Blitz and, once she met my father, staying was the only option anyway. In fact, I think she'd made that decision even before she met Dad,' he joked. 'Perhaps he just conveniently happened along at the right moment.'

Sadie smiled. 'I'm sure it was a true love story,' she remonstrated. 'I'm happy for her it worked out. It doesn't sound as if she had much left in England.'

'Living in Naples has never been easy,' Luca countered. 'You see the poverty, the corruption, the hardship. It's all around.' He made a wide sweeping gesture to encapsulate the market and the wider city. The abundance of the fresh produce on display right here slightly belied his assertion, but Sadie understood what he meant. At the same time, she also understood the appeal of staying here. All this brightness, all these colours, so much life. London seemed grey, dull and a tad sleazy in comparison.

It occurred to her that, even in the short time she'd been in Italy, her memories of home had faded. She had hardly thought of London, of the flat in Paddington or the office in Dean Street, for ages. When she'd got the job a year ago at Roger Cheryl's film facilities company, it had been the realisation of a dream. To be in Soho, the throbbing heart of the film business; media moguls passing along the narrow cobbled streets; callow youths pushing their wheelbarrows piled high with silver cans containing the rushes of cutting-edge movies; strippers, wearing more make-up than clothes, flitting along the streets from one strip club to another, the 'boys' who they employed to retrieve their lingerie racing along behind them... it had all seemed so wildly glamorous.

Now she wasn't quite sure what the allure had been.

She glanced at Luca. He was examining a crate of large, purple vegetables, displaying a label saying MELANZANA. Melon? No, it certainly wasn't that. Sadie fumbled for the Italian–English pocket dictionary she had brought with her and, turning away from Luca, discreetly looked it up. She didn't want him to think her a complete ignoramus.

Aubergine, the dictionary told her. She shrugged, confounded. What were aubergines when they were at home? Luca piled three or four of the vegetables into his bag and Sadie made a mental note to look carefully on the menu wherever she ate out in the days ahead so that she could make sure she chose something containing this mysterious ingredient.

They wandered on, to an area that specialised in grocery shop products. To Sadie's amazement, olive oil was for sale in huge bottles, vats, jugs and cans. She paused to pick one up.

'In England, you buy this in tiny quantities in the pharmacy, for medicinal purposes only,' she told Luca. 'And I've got to confess,' she added, her earlier bashfulness over her ignorance of aubergines having evaporated, 'I'm not entirely sure what it's used for, what exactly it's supposed to treat.'

Luca stopped still where he stood and stared at her, something very akin to horror in his eyes. 'What do you mean?' he expostulated. 'What do you cook with, if not olive oil? How do you dress a salad?'

Sadie's mind went blank. Cooking was done with lard or butter. But what did a salad in Blighty wear? And then it came to her. Salad cream, obviously, that slightly sharp, vinegary sauce that Sadie had always actively disliked. She couldn't tell

Luca this. Somehow she doubted that salad cream had ever made an appearance on a self-respecting Italian's table.

'I like the design on the label,' she said, neatly sidestepping the question. The picture was of a grove of trees with silvery leaves, and superimposed on top of it a small, black fruit like a grape. 'I guess this is what it's made from?'

Now Luca looked more flabbergasted than ever. 'You've never seen an olive,' he gasped, incredulously.

Sadie shook her head with elaborate sorrow. 'Nope. Nor eaten one, as far as I know.'

Luca put his head in his hands in an overplayed display of faux despair. 'We need to fix this right now,' he announced. 'Come.' He reached out his hand and took Sadie's. A bolt of electricity shot through her. But there was no lingering this time. Briskly, Luca led her through the still-heaving market to a place where takeaway food was sold. There he bustled around, buying bits and pieces at various stalls and, when he had assembled a picnic, took Sadie to a small, elaborately paved square, where they sat down on a bench overlooking the sea.

'Here,' he said, thrusting a cone fashioned from newspaper at her. 'Try this.'

Tentatively, Sadie dug in and took out something small and battered that vaguely resembled a potato chip. 'What is it?' she asked, before braving a taste. This street food was even more exotic than anything she'd so far encountered in a Neapolitan restaurant.

'*Alici* and *calamari*,' replied Luca, already tucking into his cone. 'Anchovies and – well, calamari. I don't think there is an English word.'

Sadie took her first mouthful. Beneath the crunch of the batter it was soft and melt-in-the-mouth tender. She reached in and pulled out what was clearly a small fish. When she bit into it, the saltiness exploded into her mouth. 'Gosh, that's strong,' she said. 'But delicious.' She recalled the Gentleman's Relish her father used to sometimes eat, a paste made from anchovies. Sadie had always thought the smell and taste revolting; far too strong, overpowering almost. But this little fried fish was delicious.

'And now,' said Luca, once their cones were finished, 'you must try your first olive. Drum roll please.'

Laughing, Sadie rapped her fingers on the bench in a ratta-tat-tat. Luca passed her a little jar full of shiny black and green fruits, sprinkled with herbs and doused in oil.

'These are pitted,' he said, 'so no need to worry about the stone.'

Enthusiastically, Sadie took one. So far, so good – Luca's choices had been excellent and she was looking forward to this. Popping the olive into her mouth, she waited for a moment.

And then was standing up, choking and spluttering, thinking she was going to die but at the same time trying to be discreet about spitting out the revolting object. When she had finally got rid of it, and had a long swig of water to clear the abominable taste, she sat down on the bench again, breathing heavily.

'That was revolting,' she exclaimed. 'Absolutely vile. Like eating a mouthful of seawater. Yuck.' She shuddered, then turned to catch sight of Luca, who at first looked appalled and then began to laugh loudly.

'I'm sorry,' he spluttered, once he'd regained the power of speech. 'Your face! You look like I tried to poison you. I've never seen anyone react like that to an olive!'

Sadie thumped him playfully on the arm. 'Thanks for your support,' she responded, with mock indignation.

Luca continued chortling away. 'So funny,' he repeated. 'Wait until I tell Mum. She'll think it's hilarious.'

Sadie folded her arms and pursed her lips, fixing him with a stare. 'It's all right. I don't mind being the butt of the joke.' And then she too burst out laughing, and they laughed and laughed until Luca announced it was time to go.

'Here,' he said, holding out his hand to help her up from the bench.

Sadie took it, for the second time that day. And this time Luca didn't take it away and they strolled, hand in hand, back to her hotel. Outside, Sadie yawned. 'I'm getting used to this siesta business,' she said.

Luca's fingers squeezed hers. 'See,' he said. 'I told you that you were almost Italian now.'

His gaze lingered on hers for a moment, until he dropped her hand and waved goodbye. Climbing the steps to the hotel foyer, Sadie still felt the imprint of his palm on hers.

Later, after the siesta, Sadie called Kim and asked her to phone directory enquiries and see if there were any Beans in Malton. Then she hung around by the hotel phone booth for a few minutes before redialling Kim's work phone number.

'Nothing,' Kim reported back. 'No Beans in Malton.'

'Right,' said Sadie, her spirits plummeting once more. 'OK. Can you do something else for me? I want to contact the Ministry of Defence again, see if they have any war records for Betty Bean, but I don't know how long a letter might take to get from Naples to London. If I dictate it to you, would you write it out and send it for me?'

There was a slight delay on the line, so it was a second or two before Kim answered. 'Of course I will. I've got a pen and paper; ready and waiting.'

Once Sadie had finished, she and Kim said goodbye, Kim promising to check the post every day for a reply.

'Take care, Sadie,' Kim said, just as Sadie was about to hang up. 'Come home soon.'

Sadie replaced the receiver but remained in the booth. Kim's last words had struck her to the core. The things she missed about England had somehow, during her sojourn in Italy, reduced to just one – Kim herself.

Another guest rapped irritatedly at the booth door, wondering why Sadie was hogging the phone. Stepping out into the hotel foyer, Sadie headed pensively for the exit. If Gianni Urso were really her father she was at least half-Italian anyway, she mused as she walked. Perhaps, just like Luca's mum Deborah, she would stay.

After all, what did she have to go home for?

# CHAPTER FORTY-EIGHT

Betty reported back to Colonel Green that it was Susan who had stolen the codebook and that she, Betty, now had to steal another one. Colonel Green listened to this with grave attention.

'So you must do as she asks,' he told Betty. 'I will handle it at this end. Please give me a full description of the person you deliver to.'

In the cipher room the next day, Betty ambled up to the cupboard where the codebook was kept with all the cool equanimity she could muster. Inside, she was a quivering wreck, her hands shaking, beads of nervous sweat breaking out on her forehead. She could hardly get the key into the lock, she was trembling so badly. But eventually she managed it and, retrieving the book, she tucked it inside her uniform jacket and left the room.

Had anyone noticed what she had done? She had not dared to look around; if she'd caught anyone's eye, her demeanour would have immediately given her away.

Down at the docks it was a beautiful December morning,

nothing like the night of the storm, the sun shining on a flat calm sea that glimmered in the light. The city of Naples, rising up the many hillsides, looked charming and colourful, a place of hope and optimism again after all the destruction. It seemed far too nice and cheerful a day for what Betty was doing, even though she knew that precautions had been put in place to make sure that no actual harm would be caused by the purloining of the codebook.

At the dingy office where she had watched Susan and the bearded man poring over a map, Betty knocked timidly on the door. Almost immediately, it was flung open and there the man stood, much taller and more imposing than Betty had realised. His mop of black hair, thick eyebrows and even thicker moustache were so prominent that the rest of his features were barely noticeable, but Betty could just make out the snarl set into his thin lips. The thick smell of tobacco smoke flooded out of the door with him, mixing with the salt-and-seaweed scent of the sea. Trembling at the knees, Betty thrust the package towards him.

'Here is the book you ordered,' she rattled out, her voice an odd monotone of apprehension and the fear that she'd get the spiel wrong. 'I hope it is to your satisfaction thank you and good-bye.' Punctuation had deserted her entirely and she was sure she was about to be sick. She needed to get away from there as soon as possible. She'd turned and was about to flee when a stentorian voice commanded her to stop.

'There's no need to go so quickly,' the man barked at her.

Betty's stomach turned over and bile rose in her throat. Why did he want her to stay? She was nothing to him, just a messenger, a pawn in whatever Susan's grand game-plan was.

'Come inside, take a grappa with me, why don't you? A pretty girl like you will cheer me up no end.'

Clenching her fists, her nails biting into her palms, Betty stood motionless, too stunned to speak. The last thing on earth she wanted to do was go inside that stinky hut with this odious man. But if she refused, would that blow her cover? Would the game be up?

Slowly, she raised her gaze from the dirty grey paving slabs to the man's face. His eyes, already dark and seemingly bottomless, had clouded over, as if in anticipation of her refusal. Something snapped inside Betty. She would go so far with this treachery and no further.

Calmly and directly, she addressed the man. 'Thank you for the invitation,' she said, with all the politeness she could muster. 'But I have to go. Goodbye.'

Refusing to give way to her intense desire to run, and forcing her legs to keep her upright, she turned and walked away. She longed for a dockworker to appear before her, hurrying on his way to work, but there was absolutely nobody around. Nevertheless, she did not falter. She could feel the man's eyes boring into her and at every moment she expected to hear his heavy tread behind her, his hand stretching out to grab her...

Finally, she reached the corner, and rounded it. And as soon as she knew she was out of sight, she ran, even faster than she had the night of the encounter with Susan, even faster than when they'd been up in the hills with an enemy aeroplane firing at her. Something told Betty that, in escaping the bearded man, she'd escaped a fate worse than death.

After the horror of the docks, Betty hoped against hope that Susan would lie low for a while. All she wanted to do was to get to Rome to be with Gianni for a few precious days. She'd given her all to the war effort, especially during these last few weeks pretending to connive with Susan, and she was mentally and emotionally exhausted. Now she craved Gianni's calm presence, his solidity. She needed him in the same way that she needed air to breathe and food to eat.

. . .

FINDING herself alone with Susan in the dorm room the next day, Betty ventured to ask about her plans. She'd never have taken such a risk if there wasn't so much at stake.

'Do you know when you'll next have a job for me to do?' she asked, having first checked that the door was shut and there was no chance of anyone passing by outside hearing her.

Susan flashed her a look of animosity. Betty quailed and clenched her fists against the force of Susan's disapproval.

'We shouldn't talk here,' she hissed, her voice bristling with fury.

For a moment, Betty felt like crying. And then she steeled herself. Susan had no right to lord it over her or make her feel inferior.

'I'd like to know,' Betty continued, as calmly as she could manage.

Susan's mouth was set in a hard, tight line but Betty saw her waver. Eventually, she said, 'Nothing until next year now. We have been instructed to lie low for a while.'

Trying not to let the relief show on her face, Betty nodded briefly. 'Thank you. Please keep me informed.' And with that she left the room, mustering all the willpower she had to walk at a steady pace rather than doing what she wanted to do, which was run away as fast as her legs could carry her.

It took a while for Susan's words to sink in, and for the realisation to dawn on Betty. She could go to Rome to be with Gianni. It was more than a dream come true. It was a fantasy come to life, a never-imagined opportunity to spend time with her soulmate.

She told Lily and Deborah that she was going away for a few days, but didn't mention Gianni. Instead, she said that she'd been invited to visit by one of the Y-Signals women who'd been transferred to Rome after the city's liberation and now worked for the Allied Commission there.

'What's her name then, this person you're visiting?' Usually it was Lily who asked the awkward questions, but this time it was Deborah who seemed suspicious.

Betty's mind went blank. What an idiot! She'd been so preoccupied with Susan that she hadn't thought through this particular subterfuge.

'Um, Ethel,' she floundered, 'you remember her, the one with the really curly hair whose hat kept falling off.' Ethel had indeed been transferred, but whether it was to Rome or somewhere else, Betty couldn't remember. She hoped none of the others could, either. She hated fibbing – and, as was patently obvious, she was no good at it. But it was too difficult to explain Gianni, and anyway, what was there to explain? They would have a few days in each other's company and then they would part again and... Betty didn't want to contemplate what came next.

Lily took a drag on her cigarette. 'She was frightfully dull, if I remember correctly,' she said, airily. 'Make sure you take a good book and your knitting. You'll need something to entertain you.'

Betty opened her mouth to respond and then shut it again. What was there to say?

'Wouldn't it be amazing if you bumped into someone else you knew there,' Lily continued. 'Like you did in the hospital that one time?'

Betty broke out in a cold sweat. Had Lily worked out that Gianni was more than just the casual acquaintance Betty had made him out to be? At the same time, her heart twisted with regret and longing. Regret that she couldn't just tell Lily and Deborah, her staunch friends, the truth, and longing for Gianni himself and for their relationship not to have to be kept secret.

'I don't know what you're talking about,' replied Betty, trying to make her voice light and jocular.

She turned away, back to making her bed. But not before she'd spotted the over-exaggerated wink Lily gave Deborah.

As Christmas approached, those in charge of the NAAFI tried to raise everyone's mood with festive decorations, made with great resourcefulness and ingenuity with whatever materials and provisions could be procured. Performances at the Garrison theatre were designed to lift spirits, and the arrival of Alfred Lunt and his wife Lynn Fontanne to star in Noël Coward's play *Design for Living* caused great excitement. Betty tried to enjoy herself but found that, embroiled in so much subterfuge and treachery, and on such tenterhooks for her trip, it was hard to do so.

When the day finally came to set off for Rome, she determined to put everything out of her mind and make the most of a once-in-a-lifetime opportunity – to see the city and all its famous sites, and to spend time with Gianni.

Captain Treacy had arranged for Betty to stay at the Imperial Hotel on Via Veneto, where all the ATS women in the city were billeted and where Betty would be, as she put it, 'safe'.

As she had imparted this information to Betty, she had peered at her over the top of her reading glasses. Betty had a feeling she was implying something about safety that didn't relate to the danger posed by guns, bombs and bullets but more to the protection of one's honour and virtue. They had had several lectures over their time in the ATS about the dangers of venereal disease and the damage to reputations that could be done by 'fraternising'.

Nodding furiously, Betty had thanked her for her consideration and willed the conversation to come to an end. Dismissed a few moments later, she had scurried along the corridor back to the dorm, the all-knowing cupids and angels seeming to smirk down at her as she went.

Betty got to Rome by hitching a ride on the post van. It left early on a winter-cold morning and travelled through countryside that seemed almost unaffected by war. Only the occasional abandoned vehicle, or bomb-blasted tree or building, bore testament to the conflict. They passed through placid olive groves, silver leaves gleaming with a light dusting of hoar frost, and through tranquil villages where ancient stone houses lined the road. To their right, at all times, Betty could see the blurred outlines of the Apennines, the mountain range forming the spine of Italy, rising up into the clouds. As dawn broke, the sunrise streaked the sky with shades of pink, purple and orange.

After a long drive on ill-kept, bumpy roads, they finally arrived in Rome. Of course Betty had seen pictures of the city before, but nothing had prepared her for the real thing. Driving through the ancient streets, round every corner seemed to lie something from legend or history: a baroque church, an aristocrat's palace, a medieval square.

The sun was up by now, and though it was winter it still had warmth and light, which it shed on the honey-coloured buildings, bathing the streets in a buttery glow. She and Gianni had arranged to meet at 3 p.m., as neither of them had been absolutely certain about what time they would arrive in the city. It was a beautiful day and after being cooped up in the van, being jolted to and fro, Betty was desperate to stretch her legs. She wandered up the Via Veneto, past her lodgings, with no real idea where she was going but just soaking up the atmosphere. It was so different from Naples, not least because Rome had not been bombed at all. Betty had almost forgotten what intact streets looked like.

As she strolled, she glanced constantly at her watch. Even though she knew she had hours to spare, she was still terrified of losing track of time and not being at the meeting spot when Gianni got there. She willed the hands of the clock to move faster, to get Gianni to her more quickly.

The streets were busy with locals but also with troops and forces personnel from Britain, America, Canada, New Zealand, France, Morocco, South Africa and Poland, and a cacophony of languages resounded between the ancient buildings. Walking urgently, Betty pushed through the crowds, eventually arriving at Porta Pinciana, the fifth-century gate that provided a passageway through the ancient city walls. Passing beneath its majestic arch, she found herself in the grounds of the Villa Borghese, a park with fountains, follies and bandstands. On a lake she saw a multitude of wooden rowing boats pulled up on the shore, waiting for summer to come again, and the weather to be right for messing about on the water.

Eventually, tired and hungry, Betty retraced her steps, found her lodgings and, having deposited her small bag in her dorm room, made her way back outside to the street, where she found a little café that was serving lunch: pasta with ragù sauce. It was delicious; rich and meaty, and Betty wondered how she would ever get used to the bland food of home again, the boiled potatoes and fatty, greasy lamb chops, after having sampled Italian specialities.

Finally, it was time to meet Gianni. As Betty set off for the appointed place, her heart fluttered in her chest, she was nervous about seeing him. They had not laid eyes on each other since the spring. Gianni had been involved in non-stop fighting ever since. Who knew how these experiences might have changed him? People talked of men destroyed by shell shock or numbed of all feeling. Would he be the same Gianni that she knew and loved, or would he be someone different, a new Gianni who she would have to get to know all over again?

Rounding a corner, she narrowed her eyes and searched the area for Gianni's familiar form. At first, she couldn't see him. And then, out of the corner of her eye, she saw someone approaching. It was him.

As soon as he laid eyes on her he began to run. He limped a little and one arm hung a little heavily by his side, but he moved with speed and vigour. Scarcely able to believe it was really him, Betty stood, transfixed, her heart leaping in her chest, butterflies turning her stomach upside down. He reached her side, swept her up in his arms and hugged her tight, lifting her clean off her feet.

Putting her down, he gazed into her eyes, then raised her chin to kiss her. In that moment, all Betty's inhibitions about kissing in public vanished like the vapour from her breath in the freezing air, and she returned the kiss with fervour.

When finally they broke apart, the sound of clapping rose up around them, echoing off the ancient buildings. Bewildered, Betty looked over her shoulder, to see a group of Canadian soldiers applauding her and Gianni. Normally she would have been mortified to attract such attention but today, giddy with joy, dizzy with love, she just smiled and then turned back to Gianni as he linked his arm in hers and began to lead her away.

Looking down at her with his familiar, lopsided grin, he said, simply, 'I can't believe you're really here. It's so good to see you.'

# CHAPTER FORTY-NINE

ROME, DECEMBER 1944

Gianni was as handsome as ever in Betty's eyes, but it was clear that the fighting was taking its toll. Betty shuddered inwardly at the thought of what he had been through since she last saw him. But, though he was thinner, older, wearier, he was cheerful as ever, and solicitous as always.

'You must be tired,' he said, regarding her anxiously. 'You had such an early start.'

'I'm fine,' Betty assured him. 'Absolutely fine. I'm so excited to be in Rome. I want to see everything!'

Gianni laughed. 'Me too. I know I'm Italian – or Sicilian – but I've never been to Rome before, either. I'd only set foot on the mainland twice before this war. It's giving all of us experiences we never thought we'd have.' He paused for a moment. 'Some of them better than others, obviously. The battles I have seen—' He halted, his voice breaking, and looked off into the far distance, to the shadowy outline of one of Rome's seven hills. 'We have had to endure things I never imagined.'

There was a pause. Betty didn't know what to say. Any

blandishments would seem inadequate. She took Gianni's
hand, stroking her thumb across his rough palm. What did she
know about the realities of conflict? Like all women in the
services, she had worked her socks off to do her bit. But she
would never know what it was like on the frontline.

'Anyway,' continued Gianni, suddenly restored to his
usual equilibrium. 'Let's go. There's something just round the
corner I've wanted all my life to see. And now we'll do it
together.'

Taking her by the hand, he led her a little way and then
stopped, putting one hand over her eyes.

'All you have to do is trust me now,' he said. 'And no
peeking.'

Tentatively, Betty nodded, and then allowed him to guide
her another few hundred feet or so.

'Now!' exclaimed Gianni, once they'd drawn to a halt.

Betty opened her eyes, to be confronted with the most spectacular sight she'd ever seen. A huge structure of travertine
stone, with statues and carvings of the Greek god Oceanus
flanked by seahorses and mermen, in front of which was a pool
of limpid water, cool blue in the fading light.

'It's stunning,' she whispered. As she feasted her eyes upon
it, passers-by were continually coming between her and the
view. 'How can they all walk past it with barely a sideways
glance?' she questioned Gianni.

'They're used to it, I suppose,' he replied, with a chuckle.

They went closer and dipped their hands in the freezing
water. Resting on the bottom were a few coins, silver and gold,
their outlines distorted by the surface ripples.

'It's supposed to be good luck to throw in a coin,' Gianni
told her. 'So I think we should.'

They stood next to each other with their backs to the fountain and each threw a coin over their shoulder into the water.

'The authorities fish the money out every night,' Gianni told her, 'if the children haven't made off with it all first! But it's a bit cold for diving in at the moment, I suppose.'

'Well, I love swimming,' said Betty, laughing, 'and this would be the grandest pool ever. But as you say – better in the summertime.'

Gianni reached out and put his arm round her shoulders, drawing her close to him. 'It's chilly here,' he said, 'but freezing up in the north, in the mountains. It's a good thing I spent a winter in Yorkshire before becoming a partisan or I'd never have survived the cold.'

Betty nestled her head against his chest, the fabric of his greatcoat scratchy and rough against her cheek. It smelt of woodsmoke and earth, and Betty imagined Gianni bedding down in it, pulling it over him as protection from the bitter weather as he sheltered in some shepherd's hut or abandoned barn. It seemed so unbelievable that he could step straight out of that world, constantly on edge, plotting and planning attacks night and day, launching forays against the enemy forces, his life always hanging by a thread, and then that he could come here, to Rome, and stroll around admiring ancient fountains without looking over his shoulder or watching his back, as if it were just a normal day.

The pair stood for a little while longer, appreciating all the fountain's many intricate details, before leaving to walk some more through the city's streets. Now that she was with Gianni, Betty barely noticed her surroundings. She had eyes only for him and ears only for his voice, as he told her stories of what he and his brigade had been doing that chilled the blood in her veins. They talked and talked, and the hours of the short afternoon soon passed by.

That evening, they dined on the traditional Roman dish of *coda alla vaccinara*, oxtail stew, in a diminutive trattoria where Gianni ordered a whole bottle of wine just for the two of them. Betty felt a little tipsy after drinking a whole glass of it; she barely ever drank. After dinner, they walked in the Pincio Gardens, a part of the park Betty hadn't visited earlier. The warming effects of the wine meant that she hardly felt the chill, and anyway Gianni's hand holding hers seemed to give her any extra heat that she needed. Gianni told her a funny story about one of the British soldiers he'd ended up defending a position with, who'd arranged a date with a beautiful Italian woman from the local village. He'd been quite surprised when she agreed to meet him, as he'd heard that these young women weren't given a great deal of freedom. However, his surprise turned to alarm when she arrived at the designated meeting place with not just one, but two, chaperones for the evening: her mother and grandmother.

'He said it was – how do you say – a bit of a passion killer,' said Gianni, grinning. 'He clearly didn't understand Italian traditional family values!'

Betty laughed, too. Her protective father Harold would probably have done the same if he'd thought he could get away with it, she thought, and felt a pang of homesickness.

After the meal, Gianni walked Betty back to her digs before going to where he was staying, in an apartment belonging to the family of one of his fellow partisans.

The next day was Christmas Eve. All the foreign forces in the city, as well as Italians, were invited to attend midnight mass at St Peter's Basilica. Of course they couldn't all fit inside, so Gianni insisted that they get there early. Vatican City was breathtaking in its loveliness. As they were there, they took the opportunity to see the Sistine Chapel with Michelangelo's famous ceiling frescoes. Emerging from the building, they found the whole area bedecked with Christmas lights and decorations. It was all so lovely Betty almost wept.

The church that evening was packed to the rafters. American soldiers unable to find seats climbed on top of a confessional booth, so eager were they not to miss it. Pope Pius conducted the service; it was the first time since Charlemagne's coronation in 800 CE that a pope had done so. Betty had the feeling of witnessing history as the ancient words and rituals flowed around her and organ music swelled and filled the holy place.

On Christmas Day, Gianni gave Betty a gift, a jewellery box he'd carved by hand from olive wood.

'I'm sorry it's such a small thing,' he apologised as she opened it. 'And that I don't have any jewels to give you to put in it yet. But I made it with love and I hope you like it.'

Betty squeezed back the tears that were filling her eyes. 'I love it. It's beautiful and I don't care about jewels.'

She gave him two pairs of socks she'd knitted from the finest merino wool she could find. 'To keep your poor feet warm through this winter weather.'

'Thank you,' he cried, pressing the fabric against his face to feel its warmth and softness. 'You don't know how badly I need these!'

Over the next few days, they ranged far and wide over the city, seeing everything there was to see, from ancient Roman ruins to gardens and palaces. They climbed the seven hills and visited the garden of the Knights of St John of Jerusalem, where Betty looked through the keyhole and saw the dome of the Vatican perfectly framed within it.

On New Year's Eve, they went out for a walk. The streets were quiet, everyone inside busily cooking or preparing for the evening's entertainment. Betty thought Gianni seemed preoccupied, but the day was so beautiful, the sun winter-bright, that she didn't say anything. They ambled down to the Trevi Fountai again, where Betty had been so spellbound on that first day in the city.

'Betty,' said Gianni, suddenly, his voice low and urgent. 'I've got to go today, earlier than we planned. I'm really sorry. But my unit is moving on and every single one of us is needed. I thought we would have this evening, see in the New Year together, but it is not to be.'

Betty's heart lurched in her chest. This was terrible news. She too had hoped to spend another precious twenty-four hours with Gianni. She wanted to blurt out to him, 'No, don't go, stay with me,' but of course she didn't. It would be completely wrong to try to hold him back. And yet at the same time she longed to grab onto his arm, cling to him and never let him out of her grasp.

Though her chest felt hollowed out, her heart shrivelled up and barely beating, Betty steeled herself. She put on a bright, brave smile. 'I understand,' she said. 'Don't worry.'

Gianni looked as if he were about to cry. Betty could hardly bear his pain, any more than she could bear her own.

'Come back to my lodgings with me while I pack,' Gianni asked her. 'So that we can be together every possible moment.'

Betty nodded in agreement and they set off. A bitter wind had begun to blow and they walked briskly in its face. At the billet, Betty made tea as Gianni bustled around gathering up his few possessions.

He turned to her, a pair of socks in his hand. 'These are the most valuable thing I have,' he said light-heartedly. Betty could tell he was making a big effort to put on a brave face. 'The other pair are already on my feet, so they'll be safe. Unless I lose a leg,' he joked, with the black humour that infected everyone from time to time.

Betty mustered a wan smile in response. She watched as he stowed his few paltry belongings in his battered kitbag. Suddenly all her earlier resolve, not to make a fuss, not to say anything that might make Gianni feel guilty, deserted her.

'I don't want you to go,' she blurted out, all of a sudden. 'Don't leave. Stay here with me – just one more night.' She tried but failed to keep the desperation out of her voice. She wanted to say, *just one more week. Month. Lifetime.* But she managed to stop herself. It would have been impossible to put into words the way every pore in her body ached at that moment, how her insides churned, how longing had invaded every cell. She knew she couldn't, shouldn't, wouldn't, keep him away from the role he had chosen to play in the partisans. But she wished with every ounce of her being that this was not the case.

Gianni stopped his packing and reached for her. With her in his arms, he whispered in her ear, 'I don't want to go either. If I could stay, I would. If it were possible, I'd stay forever.'

Later she walked with him to the station, where he was getting a train as far north as he could before rejoining his brigade. They kissed on the platform and Betty thought she could not bear to let him go.

A rumbling noise announced the train's arrival. Instinctively, Betty looked down the track, and saw it lumbering towards them, just a minute or so away now, headlamps beaming through the winter twilight.

'Betty,' said Gianni, cupping her chin in his hand and looking directly into her eyes. 'I don't know what's going to happen back there, up in the north. It's more dangerous than ever these days. So...' he paused as the train pulled into the station, brakes whistling as it slowed to a halt. 'So if I don't return, I want you to know how much I love you—' He broke off again, then blinked rapidly a few times before resuming. 'I said it first in Yorkshire, and I still mean it, more now than ever. I really, really love you.'

Betty's heart broke in two. The train blew its horn and the stationmaster hove into view, exhorting those travelling to board, shutting doors with an emphatic slam.

'I love you too,' she replied, in anguished tones, her voice barely above a whisper, as if that would stop all those who knew she was supposed to love another from hearing. 'I love you.'

The stationmaster blew his whistle. 'Hurry up,' he exhorted Gianni, and a couple of other lingering passengers.

Gianni leant forward and kissed Betty again. When he let her go, he climbed into the train with dragging heels. Standing and waving, Betty couldn't mistake it. The look of longing in his eyes that mirrored that in her own.

The engine leapt into action and the train began to leave. Leaning out of the window, Gianni waved and waved, and Betty waved back until he had diminished into a tiny speck in the distance and then was gone.

Utterly disconsolate, she trudged the city streets. For the first time since leaving Naples, she really felt the bitter cold. It seemed to have gnawed its way right inside her, chilling her from the inside out now there was just the vacuum of life without Gianni ahead of her. Betty couldn't bear to go to the hostel or to the NAAFI, where everyone would be jolly and looking forward to celebrating. She passed the Church of Tutti Santi to see a couple emerging, the bride in a delicate white lace dress that Betty was sure must be an heirloom borrowed for the occasion from an Italian friend, the groom resplendent in British Army dress uniform. After being showered in rose-petal confetti, the pair drove off in a cavalcade flanked by army dispatch riders on motorcycles, while a small crowd of guests and miscellaneous onlookers clapped and cheered.

She and Gianni had not discussed the future because, in wartime, no one could be sure that they had one, especially someone fighting in a partisan brigade. And for Betty, with all her concerns and dilemmas about who she most owed her allegiance to – Gianni or Samuel – it was too difficult. Best just to leave well alone, live in the moment.

But even so, Betty couldn't help but think of her and Gianni, similarly attired, in some other church, in Sicily maybe, where she could live with him and enjoy fresh lemons all year round, like in Sorrento. The last days had been perfect, Gianni so attentive and adoring, his obvious feelings for her reciprocated in full.

Too perfect.

Angrily, Betty shook her head. There was no sense in daydreaming about what could not be. Perhaps, when this war was over and peace restored, and if Samuel were really dead, it might be possible for her and Gianni to make a life together.

But that was for the future, not for now.

# CHAPTER FIFTY

The quay was packed with jostling families wielding huge picnic baskets and trying to keep hold of umpteen unruly children when Luca and Sadie arrived there early the next morning. The sun was still low in the sky, the blue streaked by striated clouds tinged with vibrant pink and orange. There was a sense of expectancy in the air, of holidays and fun.

When Luca had suggested taking a day off from the search, Sadie had been reluctant at first. But having been persuaded, now she was here, boarding the ferry via a rickety gangplank, relief flooded through her. Hopefully the sea air would clear her head and banish the rollercoaster of emotion she had been experiencing over the last few days. She had already decided that she'd made a mountain out of a molehill in terms of her concerns about what Luca may, or may not, have seen in the archive.

'Phew,' she said, flopping onto one of the few seating spaces still available. 'It's so busy!'

Luca shrugged. 'August in Italy. Everyone goes on holiday

in August.' He sat down beside her as the boat's engines started up with a low rumble.

'So where are we off to?' Sadie asked, intrigued. In all the pandemonium, she hadn't noticed any signs in the harbour or the boat itself.

'We are going,' began Luca, before pausing for dramatic effect, 'to paradise, otherwise known as the island of Capri!'

Sadie grabbed hold of her sunhat as the boat picked up speed and a gust of wind snatched at it. 'Well!' She laughed. 'I've never been to paradise before, so it sounds good to me!'

As the boat churned through the azure water, Luca pointed out the sights to Sadie. She marvelled at Sorrento, rising up on steep cliffs that seemed to emerge straight from the water, the gorge that split the town in two, the pretty, multicoloured houses joyous in the strong spring sunshine.

Soon after passing Sorrento, they were out of the shelter of the bay and forging across open water, a trail of frothy white waves in their wake. Something caught Sadie's eye and, as she stared, a pod of dolphins broke the surface, leaping in perfect formation, their every movement defined by exquisite grace.

At the sight, exuberant cries of '*delfini!*' rose up from the children on board, and half the passengers swarmed to the side to view the spectacle, rocking the boat rather alarmingly. The dolphins seemed to be racing them, disappearing beneath the surface for long moments and then emerging, their streamlined forms keeping easy pace with the engine power.

'They're so pretty,' breathed Sadie, entranced. 'Wait until I tell my flatmate Kim I've seen real, live dolphins.'

'I paid extra to get them to show up,' Luca teased. 'They don't come out for just anyone, you know.'

Sadie laughed. 'Well, thank you for taking the trouble,' she said, demurely. 'I appreciate it.'

After the excitement of the dolphins, Sadie and Luca settled back down onto their seats, squashed between two

Italian families in loud, celebratory mood. The sun was rising rapidly in the sky but a brisk breeze kept it from feeling too hot. Sadie found herself entering a trance-like state, lulled by the movement of the boat, the fresh air and the prospect of the day to come. She pictured herself and Luca, walking hand in hand, two energetic little children in tow, beside themselves with anticipation at the swimming and boating they were going to do. Sadie's mother, Evelyn, looked on with pride, delighted that Sadie had finally heeded her advice, settled down and started a family.

Abruptly, Sadie sat up and rubbed her eyes. She must have dropped off to sleep. Looking around her, wondering where the children had got to, she suddenly came to her senses. Of course there were none; what was she thinking? She cast an embarrassed glance at Luca, almost fearing that, with his uncanny ability to know what was going through her head, he could also see her dreams. But he was absorbed in a book and didn't seem to have noticed her dozing.

They landed at Capri town's *marina grande*, where they had a quick breakfast of bitter black espressos and *cornetti*, and then Luca led Sadie to a little building that looked like a train station. She was surprised to think there was a railway somewhere so small. But when they boarded one of the tiny four-wheeled carriages, she realised that it was actually a funicular that whisked passengers up to the hilltop town that was the island's main settlement. There, they wandered along narrow, winding alleyways lined by houses whose pergolas overflowed with colourful blooms, and stopped to drink another espresso in Piazza Umberto, the town square. They visited the thirteenth-century church of Sant' Anna. In the cool, dark interior the original painted frescoes, smudged and blurred by time, portrayed the ever-familiar Bible scenes.

Sadie could have stayed in the town all day but Luca had other plans. He took her to a winding footpath that led down a precipitous hillside to a sandy bay. A jagged rock right by the water's edge had formed into a natural arch and, in the distance, the huge forms of more rocks rose out of the sea.

They were both thirsty after the walk and Luca took a picnic blanket out of his knapsack and laid it on the sand and then pulled out a bottle of water and one of wine, as well as a host of Italian snacks and a couple of tin mugs. Among the picnic fare was a jar of olives.

Sadie grimaced at the sight of them.

'Don't worry,' said Luca, laughing. 'Those are all for me.'

Sadie shook her head and chuckled. 'I still can't believe you actually like them.'

Luca grinned, opened the jar and popped one in his mouth. 'Delicious,' he replied, touching his fingers to his mouth in a gesture of appreciation. 'But maybe they're an acquired taste. Though, now that you are becoming an Italian, one that you should probably work on.'

Sadie grimaced. 'Maybe. But not right now. I don't know how olive oil can taste so nice and the actual olives it's made from so disgusting.'

They both laughed as Luca filled their mugs, first with water and then with wine. After they'd eaten and drunk they sat for a while, watching children skipping and playing in the sea.

Eventually, Luca checked his watch, and then jumped up. 'Come on,' he said. 'Next stop.'

Sadie followed him to a wooden pier that jutted out over the water. A line of brightly coloured wooden rowing boats tugged at their mooring ropes. An old man, his deeply wrinkled face burnt dark brown by the summer sun, sat in a deckchair with an umbrella strapped to the back. Luca said a few words to him, handed over a handful of notes and then unleashed one of the boats.

'Jump in,' he instructed Sadie. 'And sit at the prow.'

Luca got in after her and took the middle seat, placing an oar in each rowlock.

'Where now?' asked Sadie, excitedly. She realised she hadn't thought about her real mother and father for at least the last ten minutes. Luca's medicine of a day out seemed to be working.

'The Faraglioni rocks,' he explained. 'In the olden days, they used to burn fires on top so the rocks acted as lighthouses. And they're the only place in the world where the blue lizard lives. If we're lucky, we might see one.'

Luca rowed with swift, strong strokes and the boat leapt forward, bringing the looming formations closer by the minute. Sadie looked ahead with eager anticipation. Everything about the day was perfect so far. She thought about Broadstairs, which was beautiful in its way. But the light here in Italy was so much brighter, more hopeful somehow. For the umpteenth time, she wondered how she would ever be able to go back.

Luca brought the boat right up to the largest rock, which towered over them, its sheer sides reaching to the sky. Sadie laid her hands on its craggy surface, which glowed with heat from the sun. She ran her fingertips along one of the many cracks and crevices the rock was pitted with, thinking about all the years the structure had stood here for, battered by the elements, tormented by winter storms and summer heat.

'Look!' cried Luca, animatedly. 'A lizard. There!'

Sadie looked where he was pointing and just caught a glimpse of a small, sinewy creature, which was indeed bright blue, disappearing into a sheltering fissure.

Once the lizard had gone, Luca rowed on. Sadie saw that the sea had worn an arch into one of the stacks, and Luca was heading straight for it. As they neared the opening, he let the oars rest for a minute. 'They say,' he said, a teasing note in his voice, 'that, if you kiss your lover as you pass through the archway, you'll have thirty years' happiness and good luck.'

Sadie was glad of her wide-brimmed hat as she felt herself blush, that infuriating habit of hers that she wished she would grow out of. Teenagers blushed! Twenty-seven-year-old women of the world like her should be able to preserve an enigmatic aloofness at all times.

Luca was grinning at her expectantly. Sadie trailed her hand in the water, hoping that the coolness would spread to her face.

'Pity neither of us has a lover with us then, isn't it?' she replied, only just managing to maintain the lightness of tone she was aiming for.

A silence descended between them. The boat rocked as tiny waves caused by a larger ship further out to sea sent water lapping at its sides. Sadie wondered if Luca was thinking what she was thinking. That she wouldn't mind if he kissed her. She really wouldn't mind one little bit.

And then a motor cruiser full of laughing, shrieking holiday-makers zoomed up alongside them, powerful engines rending the air with their roaring, and the moment was lost. Luca rowed through the arch and out the other side and then began to make his way back to the beach.

'Can I have a go at rowing?' asked Sadie. 'I've never done it before.'

'Sure.' Luca shifted position so that Sadie could take over. He watched as she clumsily took hold of the oars and tried to emulate the motion he had made. The flat blades slapped ineffectually at the water, covering them both with spray and achieving precisely nothing.

Luca couldn't help but snigger.

'Oh dear,' wailed Sadie. 'It's a lot harder than it looks.'

Luca came to sit beside her and put his hands upon hers. They were warm, strong and capable. Sadie felt herself gripping the oars tighter in an effort to stifle the desire that was stirring within her.

Gently but firmly, Luca guided her so that the oars were dipping below the surface and then sweeping back so that their power gave the boat forward momentum. They began to inch towards the shore.

'Now you try by yourself,' Luca said, once Sadie seemed to have got the rhythm.

Biting her lip and frowning with concentration, she managed to propel their craft almost to the pier. Once they were nearly upon it, Luca took over to bring them alongside.

'Well done,' he congratulated her. 'You were great once you got the hang of it.'

Sadie let her arms hang by her side and rolled her eyes at him. 'It's exhausting! I'll leave it all to you next time.'

They both laughed. *Will there be a next time?* thought Sadie. It was impossible to know.

Back on the beach, they stripped to their swimming costumes and splashed into the water. They swam and basked for hours. Finally, as the sun was beginning to set, they trudged back up the steep incline of the footpath on one side of the island and came down in the funicular on the other, then caught the boat back to Naples. They arrived in the city as the light was fading, enjoyably tired from the sea air and exercise.

As they said their farewells, Luca kissed Sadie on both cheeks as normal, but rather than stepping away he remained close to her, his hands placed gently on her shoulders. The sultry air around them seemed to hum with anticipation, the city noise to fade into the background. Sadie felt a little light-headed, from the long day, the sun and the wine, and for a second she was back on the ferry, swaying with its rhythmic motion.

Luca leant towards her and for one breathless second the world stood still. And then he was kissing her and Sadie was kissing him back, and the kiss seemed to last forever.

When they did eventually break apart, Luca took her hands and looked into her eyes with his soft, brown gaze.

'I've had a brilliant day,' he said. 'Thank you.'

Sadie, too overcome to say much, merely nodded and mumbled, 'Me too.'

As she climbed into bed that night, her cheeks glowing from the sun, her lips still tingling from the touch of his. In that moment, it hit her with full force. Whatever the situation with the hunt for her birth parents, she was falling in love with Luca.

And falling hard.

# CHAPTER FIFTY-ONE

NAPLES, APRIL 1945

Back in Naples, the emotion Betty felt most frequently during the long, dark months of January, February and March was boredom. There was so little to do at work and some members of Y-Signals had already been repatriated to Britain, their services no longer needed, their home lives calling them back. The knowledge that it would all come to an end was more and more certain, and Betty couldn't help but view this with mixed emotions. Going home would mean being reunited with her family – but saying goodbye to Gianni forever. There just didn't seem to be any other choice. She had always been family-orientated, and the untimely death of her mother had only exacerbated those feelings, which centred around love but included obligation. There was no way she could abandon her father, sister and sweetheart, relocate to another part of Europe... It was inconceivable.

It was an impossible situation and no amount of worrying at it was going to solve it. Trying to put everything to one side, Betty refocused her efforts on Susan.

For ages, nothing happened. Betty slept badly, paranoid about not waking up if Susan were to go out on her night-time antics again. The stress and strain made her feel constantly bilious and she lost her appetite almost completely. During her shifts, the lack of activity on the radio waves, combined with her sleeplessness, made her eyelids close and several times she jerked awake with no idea whether she had dozed for one minute or ten. Lieutenant Corder reprimanded her in front of everyone, which nearly made her cry. He knew how much strain she was under and yet gave her no leeway. Underneath, Betty knew this was the right and necessary way for him to behave – eyebrows would be raised if the other cipher operators saw Betty getting away with things that they wouldn't, and of course it was essential that Susan didn't guess what was going on.

Lily took her to one side and asked her if everything was all right. 'You just haven't seemed yourself lately,' she said, her brow creased with worry and concern.

In a panic, Betty flailed around for an answer. 'Oh no, I mean yes,' she stumbled. 'I'm all right, just feeling very tired for some reason.' She paused, trying to calm the panic that was swirling inside her. For a moment she wanted desperately to tell Lily everything, not just about Susan but about the awful dilemma of her love for Gianni and her commitment to Samuel. But she couldn't confess to any of it. Not one word. As a person who was generally painfully honest, this was a heavy burden for Betty to bear.

In her pocket, her hand felt for the wooden heart and she closed her fingers round it, taking courage from its solid presence. She'd been storing it in the olive-wood box that Gianni had given her at Christmas, but had been feeling so low recently that she'd taken to carrying it everywhere with her. It felt like all she had to hang on to.

'I, er, I need to get on,' she said to Lily. 'Thanks for your concern, but I'm honestly fine.'

With that, she turned on her heel and retreated to the bathroom, where hopefully no one would follow her. In the cubicle, she pulled out Gianni's latest letter. He had written from a small village north of Bologna where he and his fellow partisans were lying low, waiting for their next strike. Soon they would be ready for what Gianni referred to as 'the final push', moving back down to the *pianura*, the wide plains by the River Po. Meanwhile, they were holed up in local villagers' houses and barns; most were more than happy to put them up and therefore help them in their brave missions. It put everyone at huge risk – but it had to be done, in order to win this war.

Betty unfolded the wafer-thin sheet of paper covered with Gianni's untidy scrawl and read it for the hundredth time. His final words made her heart throb with longing.

> *Every day I think of Rome and our days there together. They were the best of my whole life and I will never forget them. I'm not scared of what might happen to me any more because I've already been to heaven, with you.*
>
> *Please destroy this letter as soon as you have read it in case it should fall into the wrong hands.*
>
> *With all my love,*
>
> *Gianni*

Betty lifted the paper to her lips and kissed it, before tearing it into tiny pieces and flushing it down the pan.

LATER THAT DAY, she clutched the heart again as she made her way to the back stairway that she and Lily had seen Susan using all that time ago. More people had discovered it since then, and occasionally used it, but only at the beginning and end of shift changes. The rest of the time it was deserted – and this was where Susan had asked Betty to meet her.

Pushing back the curtain that guarded the top of the staircase, Betty had her heart in her mouth. She was rapidly losing the stomach for this role that had been thrust upon her, but she couldn't let Susan see that. In the darkness, she could see very little, but it was clear that Susan wasn't there yet. Betty leant against the stone wall, hoping its coolness would calm her racing pulse.

After a few moments, Susan appeared, looking furtively behind her as she stepped into the dingy space behind the curtain.

'There's going to be a reprisal,' she whispered, standing so close to Betty that Betty could feel the other woman's breath on her neck. 'A big one. The Axis forces will conduct an aerial bombardment of a village where we know partisans are hiding. You need to take this message into town and give it to the person I'll direct you to. I can't go as I think I may have been spotted.'

Betty baulked at this. To deliver a message that could result in many deaths, not just of partisans but also of civilians, who would inevitably be caught up in the bombing, was bad enough. But Susan suspecting she was under surveillance was also of critical importance. If her handlers knew this too, they would surely decommission her; it would be too dangerous to continue to use her. Someone else, someone that the army leaders didn't know about, would continue her traitorous and murderous campaign. And that would mean that Betty had failed.

Trying to keep control of her emotions and show nothing in her facial expression, Betty nodded. Susan passed her a slim envelope. 'This is the message,' she said. 'It needs to be delivered tomorrow morning at six a.m.'

With trembling fingers, Betty took hold of the missive. 'I understand,' she murmured, hardly able to speak.

'You go down this way and I'll go back to the main stairway,' Susan continued, briskly. 'Make sure no one sees you.'

Betty nodded but Susan had already disappeared beyond the curtain. As soon as Betty was sure she had moved far enough away not to hear, she let out a great, shuddering gust of air. This was too much. She couldn't deliver this message. What if the Allies were not able to stop the bombing? So many RAF and American bombers were supporting the advance on Berlin – what if there were no aircraft available to shoot down the German planes in Italy? Many lives were at risk.

And only Betty had the power to stop it.

For the second time that day, she went to the bathroom, the only place she could be sure she would not be disturbed. Sitting on the water closet with the lid down, she buried her head in her hands. She was sure she wasn't supposed to actually read the messages she delivered but she didn't care any more. She had the dreadful feeling that this was her last chance to make an impact, that something terrible might occur if she got this wrong.

Carefully peeling back the envelope's seal, she took out the paper inside and read it. As she registered what it said, nausea rose within her and she was suddenly violently sick. Afterwards, she sat very still for long moments, shivering and shaking, waiting for the giddiness to subside.

When it finally did, she tried to stand up but found she had no strength in her legs, and immediately sank back down again. What she had seen in the words of Susan's letter had chilled her to the bone.

The village where the reprisal strike was to take place was the one where Gianni and his band were sheltering.

# CHAPTER FIFTY-TWO

That night there was a dance at the NAAFI. Everyone was going; Lily, Deborah, and the rest of the ATS women at the Villa Teresa. Even Susan had decided to attend, which surprised everyone except Betty. She was sure that Susan was trying as hard as possible to fit in, to seem 'normal' and just like all the others, due to her fear that her cover had been blown.

Betty maintained that she would be there right up to the last minute. But just as they were all preparing to leave, she put her hand to her forehead and grimaced.

'Hey, BB!' exclaimed Lily. 'You still don't look great – a bit green around the gills, I'd say. Are you sure you're eating properly?'

Betty shook her head. 'I've just got a headache,' she said. 'I'll take some aspirin and I'm sure I'll feel better. If I do, I'll meet you there later. You go on though, don't let me hold you up.'

Casting a worried glance over her shoulder as she left, Lily followed the others to the Villa Teresa's front door. Betty waited until they had disappeared from sight and then, biting her lip and clenching her fists, set off for the administrative office, which was on the floor below the cipher room. They did not work shifts in this department, just a normal nine-to-five day, so Betty hoped it would be empty. If not, she had prepared an excuse that she needed to type a letter to her father as his eyesight was failing and he could read typescript better than handwriting.

Cautiously opening the door, she peered inside. It seemed her hopes were to be realised; there was no one there. Nevertheless, she crept across the threshold, not wanting to alert anyone who might be in the vicinity to her presence.

Betty selected a typewriter in the middle of the room, deciding that, if anyone were to come in, it would be much less suspicious if she didn't look as if she were trying to conceal herself. Settling down in front of it, she took a piece of paper and fed it between the rollers. She had memorised the initial message so that she didn't need to bring it with her, and had thought long and hard about how to change it so that it would seem plausible – and stop the bombardment. She knew her instructions were just to do as Susan asked her and report back. But this was too big for that. There was no way she could turn a blind eye to the real and direct threat to Gianni and all the other partisans. Up to now, her missions had had no obvious victims, so hadn't felt too terrible. This was different. Scores of brave partisans were at risk and there was no way on earth that Betty could do nothing.

She had to act.

In the end, she'd decided to keep it simple. She would reiterate the original communication almost exactly. Except that, where it said 'the bombing will take place on 22nd April 1945', Betty simply inserted a 'not'. She pondered whether she should add another line, emphasising that it would not take place at all, on any date, but thought that might be going too far. Instructions were generally followed to the letter, so this should work.

Just as she'd finished typing and was about to take the paper out of the typewriter, she heard a noise from out in the hallway. Footsteps coming along the marble corridor, getting louder and louder. And then stopping right outside the door.

Betty's hands froze. The paper, stark white with its sparse writing, shone out accusingly in front of her, glaringly obvious to anyone who might enter. She did her best to look innocent, with the result that she was sure she would come across as guilty as hell. But there was nothing to be done. Someone was coming in and she would have to deal with it.

The door creaked open. Betty reached forward and removed the message from the typewriter, placing it face down on the desk beside her. Busily, she took another fresh piece of paper and threaded it into the machine, humming to herself in an attempt to appear wholly nonchalant.

'Betty! What are you doing here so late?'

Betty's heart sank even lower than it had already been. The person disturbing her peace was a cipher called Millicent, who Betty knew was a huge gossip and always stuck her nose into everything. There was no way she was going to go away quietly without thoroughly quizzing Betty about what she was up to.

Relieved that she had her story ready, she trotted it out now, breezily telling Millicent about her father's struggles with his eyesight and the need for typewritten letters, hoping that God would forgive her for her lies.

Millicent furrowed her brow in sympathy. 'I'm sorry to hear that,' she said. 'My grandad's hearing is going so I know what it's like. It's no fun getting old, is it? That's what my grandma always says and I reckon she's right.'

Betty nodded, though she never really thought of her father as old, but it was true that he and her mother hadn't had their family as young as some, as they had wanted to save up and buy a house before they had children.

'But what's this one?' Millicent went on, pointing at the

completed message lying on the wooden tabletop. The indentations of the typewriter's keys could be seen through the thin paper, and the black outlines of the words, in two brief lines only. 'It's not very long! Not much to say there, then.'

She must have caught sight of Betty's stricken expression because suddenly her tone altered, softening and slowing. 'Oh dear, is that one not to your dad?' she asked, anxiously. 'Is it a Dear John letter? I had to write one of those recently, just realised I didn't love him any more. Sid, he was, still is, I suppose. I'd known him since I was a kid. If it hadn't been for this war I'm sure I'd have stuck with him. But coming here, meeting other people – well, you know how it is...' Millicent tailed off, seeming to realise that Betty wasn't really responding.

Betty could feel herself breaking out in a cold sweat. The combination of the fear of discovery, together with the way in which Millicent's experience with her childhood sweetheart mirrored her own, was making her feel faint.

'Shall I have a look at it?' suggested Millicent. 'See if I think you've hit the right note? It's so hard to get it right, isn't it, you don't want to say too much but you don't want to say too little, either.' As she spoke, she reached out her hand towards the piece of paper. Her fingers were almost upon it when Betty suddenly snatched it up and crumpled it into a ball.

'No,' she almost shouted. 'Don't touch it!'

Millicent stared at her as if Betty had lost her mind. 'Sorry,' she replied, haughtily. 'Didn't mean to offend, I'm sure.'

'No, no, I'm sorry,' mumbled Betty, aware that she'd been rude but wanting the whole encounter over and done with. 'But if you don't mind, I need to get this letter written...'

Millicent sniffed disapprovingly. 'I'm not sure we're really allowed in the office when there's no superior officer on duty,' she said, obviously pleased to be taking the moral high ground. 'But I'll go and leave you to it. Bye.'

And with that she was gone, her heels tapping away down the marble corridor.

Betty looked at the scrumpled ball in her hand. She'd smooth it out and it would have to do. There was no way she was hanging around here to do it again.

NEXT MORNING, Betty was awake long before dawn had broken. Slipping out of her bunk and dressing as quietly as she could, she still disturbed Deborah, who turned over in her bed and opened one eye.

'You're up early,' she mumbled, still half asleep.

'Yes,' replied Betty, tersely. She was too strung up to watch her tone. 'I need some fresh air. Feeling a little peaky.' With that, she crept out of the dorm, leaving Deborah to turn over and go back to sleep again.

The city streets were beginning to waken as she made her way to the designated meeting place. At first she had thought it was the address that she had seen Susan go to that afternoon over a year ago, but it turned out not to be. How many collaborators were there in Naples? Betty still couldn't really understand it.

Arriving at the house, tucked halfway down a narrow alleyway draped with rows of washing hanging out to dry, she rapped softly on the door. She waited, hopping from one foot to the other, desperate for this mission to be over as soon as possible. Eventually, a man opened it and stared at her with a hostile gaze.

'Sunrise is at seven a.m. today,' she said, as he regarded her questioningly.

'And it will set at seven fifty-two,' he replied.

This was exactly the correct response. Suppressing a huge sigh of relief, Betty handed over the letter. As soon as he had taken it out of her hand, she left. It took all of her self-control to stop herself from running, but she mustn't give away her fear.

Reaching the end of the alley, she waited until there was no traffic on the main road. Army vehicles rattled noisily over the cobbles, followed by an old man leading an ancient donkey pulling an even more ancient cart piled high with lemons. The citrus fragrance filled the air, overpowering the lingering smell of diesel engines. It was harvest time again. For a brief moment, Betty was back in the Sorrento grove, tasting fresh lemonade, still flush with the novelty of everything she was experiencing in Italy. She thought of that day now as a time when she had been so carefree, before her plight, caught between Gianni and Samuel, had intensified to its later degree. Before she had unwillingly become a spy.

Suddenly desperate to get back to the safety and sanctuary of Villa Teresa, she stepped out onto the pavement. And stopped.

There, in front of her, were four soldiers in American army uniforms. And just behind them was a young man in a tattered suit, wielding a reporter's notebook and calling something to her that she couldn't hear. Betty took a step forward, then faltered. The soldiers had not budged and were completely blocking her way. And the reporter was closer now, within earshot, and he was shouting, 'What do you say to the charge of espionage, Sergeant Bean?'

Betty's heart lurched and sweat broke out on her forehead. How on earth did he know about her? Who had contacted the press? As these thoughts were tumbling through her agitated mind, she became aware of the four soldiers moving closer until in a trice they were upon her.

Without saying anything, they grabbed her firmly by the arms and bundled her into the back of their jeep, slamming the door behind her.

# CHAPTER FIFTY-THREE

NAPLES, AUGUST 1972

Finally, Saturday came and the much-anticipated meeting with Lily – who may, or may not, be able to give Sadie the information she yearned for.

As Luca was coming from home with Deborah, Sadie made her way there alone, twisting and turning through streets lined with baroque buildings in various stages of elegant disrepair, from whose elaborate wrought-iron balconies bright blooms of geraniums erupted in a fizz of colour. Every time she ventured out into the city she felt she saw a different side to it; gaudy, bawdy, run-down, exuberant, hard-edged – Naples had so many moods and dispositions, it was bewildering and exhilarating.

Her own moods and dispositions were another matter entirely. She could hardly contain herself at the thought of meeting Lily, of what Lily might be able to divulge. This search had been taking two steps forward and one backwards since she'd been here and she was desperate for a breakthrough, for the one fact, the small nugget, that might break the deadlock.

Could Lily provide it?

In the opulent dining room of the Britannique Hotel, Sadie sat at the table, chewing at the inside of her cheek and nervously pulling the sleeves of her cardigan over her hands. Luca had arrived with Deborah and now the three of them were waiting for Lily.

'She's usually late,' Deborah said. 'In the war, she was always the last one onto the parade ground, only making it on time by the skin of her teeth.' She chuckled at the recollection. Luca shot Sadie a look and gave the briefest of nods, signalling that Deborah's memory was having a good day today. 'Having said that, I was the one who was always in trouble.'

Luca laughed. 'Hard to believe, Mum,' he joked.

The waiter came over and they sent him away until Lily's arrival. Then all of a sudden she was there, an elegant, pencil-slim figure in beautifully cut, high-waisted trousers and a silk blouse, her blond hair styled to perfection. Sadie cast an admiring glance at Lily's gorgeous wedge-heeled shoes and her leather shoulder bag – was it Balmain? – which oozed quality. She really was ridiculously glamorous and clearly very wealthy. But it was instantly obvious that she was also lovely. She exuded a warmth and geniality that made Sadie feel immediately at ease.

They all stood up to say hello. Lily greeted Deborah and Luca, and then turned to Sadie. Putting her hands on Sadie's shoulders, Lily leant back and scrutinised her, tilting her head to one side and then the other as if taking in every detail. 'You must be Sadie,' she said, eventually. 'And you are every bit as beautiful as Deborah said you were. Just gorgeous. It's a pleasure to meet you, darling.'

She air-kissed Sadie's cheeks before releasing her.

'Good to meet you, too,' replied Sadie, feeling suddenly a little intimidated by this woman who seemed so cosmopolitan and self-assured. 'Thank you so much for giving up your precious time to come and meet us.'

Taking her seat, Lily waved Sadie's gratitude away with a careless flick of her wrist. 'Don't even mention it. I would have been cross if Deborah hadn't called me and told me about you.' She picked up a menu and ran her eyes down it absent-mindedly before placing it back down on the table. 'I think we deserve to spoil ourselves tonight, don't we?' she announced. 'So dinner is on me and I'm ordering champagne.'

Without waiting for their acquiescence, Lily had hailed the waiter and asked him to bring a bottle of Moët. Sadie gulped.

'It's very generous of you,' she interjected. 'But there's no need for you to pay.'

'Nonsense,' expostulated Lily. 'My ex-husband turned out to be a bit of a rogue, as the judge reflected when assessing my divorce settlement. I've got to spend it somehow – you can't take it with you, you know.'

Sadie suppressed a giggle. Lily was hilarious.

Once they'd all put in their orders, Lily turned to Sadie. 'So I gather that you are looking for your birth parents, and that you have reason to believe Gianni Urso might be your father?'

For a moment, Sadie was a little taken aback by Lily's forthright broaching of the subject so soon. But then almost immediately she was grateful. She was not in the mood for beating about the bush or dealing in euphemisms. She wanted to know what Lily knew. Simple as that.

'The only thing I have to go on is this,' she replied, reaching into her bag and taking out the carved heart and key, and the scrap of paper with the Villa Teresa address she'd got from Bert. She laid the items on the table and Lily picked them up, one at a time, examining them closely as she listened intently to what Sadie was saying. 'So I started looking for Gianni Urso and that led me to Naples and hiring Luca as my guide, which in turn led to Deborah – and now you.' She paused, wondering if Deborah should be telling this part of the story. She flicked her eyes to Luca and he gave her an almost imperceptible nod, indicating that she should continue.

'Deborah mentioned the name Betty Bean...' Sadie hesitated again, not sure how to put it. 'She thought she and Gianni might have been in a relationship.' The last word exploded out of her mouth louder and more emphatically than she intended. 'But she couldn't remember much more than that.' Sadie glanced apologetically at Deborah as she said this, but Deborah didn't seem to mind.

Lily nodded slowly and lifted her gaze from the keepsake to meet Sadie's eyes. 'I hope this is what you want to hear from me,' she said slowly, as if carefully choosing her words. 'I can't imagine being in your situation but I'm sure it must be very difficult. Painful, even. So I don't say this lightly. But I think Deborah could well be right. This Gianni Urso definitely knew Betty, I believe from when he was a prisoner-of-war back in Blighty. He spent some time in the army hospital in Naples while we were in the ATS, and it makes sense that, through her, he might have used Villa Teresa as a correspondence address during that time.'

Sadie's head reeled. Lily was substantiating what Deborah had suggested. There were so many questions, she didn't know where to start. 'Why was Gianni in hospital?'

Lily picked up her napkin, gave it a well-practised flick to open it up, and placed it on her knees.

'He had been badly injured, as I recall,' she replied. 'Poor chap.'

'Injured!' Sadie didn't know why she was so surprised to hear this. You'd be a lucky person not to get hurt when fighting in a war.

Lily grimaced. 'Oh yes, he got shot in the shoulder, I think. But he recovered. Betty was... well, she re-met him in the hospital, she hurt her ankle when we were fleeing Vesuvius...'

She must have caught Sadie's uncomprehending look. 'It's a

long story, for another day. But Betty said she'd happened across this old friend who she'd known in Yorkshire' – Sadie didn't miss that she pronounced the word 'friend' as if it were in inverted commas – 'and I think it rekindled something.'

Sadie groaned inwardly. Not another *something*.

'And why...' She paused, took a deep breath and began again. 'What makes you so sure Betty is my mum?'

'Because she and Gianni were in love,' answered Lily, simply. 'She never told us as much, but she didn't need to. It was plain for all to see. She was totally and utterly, head-over-heels in love with him. And he was with her, I'm sure.'

Sadie's heart lurched. That was good, wasn't it? To be conceived out of love? But then what could possibly have gone so wrong that led to her being abandoned?

Lily sighed before continuing. 'But Betty went back to England just before the end of the war, a little before the rest of us. I didn't know she was pregnant, but then she left under—' She stopped abruptly.

Sadie realised she had been holding her breath. 'Under what?' she asked, sharply. Under cover? Under a cloud?

As she spoke, a movement made by Luca caught her eye. She flicked her gaze to him and saw that he was rubbing his forehead and looking distraught. She glanced back to Lily, who'd turned pale under her flawless make-up, her creamy complexion visibly blanched white.

'Lily,' said Sadie, almost whispering, the tension in the air palpable. 'What is it?' What happened?'

Lily, so self-confident, so self-assured, visibly squirmed. 'I don't know how to say this,' she said. 'Betty... there was a problem. She was—' Lily stopped and threw her hands in the air, dislodging her napkin. It parachuted to the floor and lay there momentarily before an eagle-eyed waiter swooped down, scooped it up and replaced it with a clean one. Silence reigned until he had left.

'Look, Sadie, this isn't going to be easy for you to hear,' Lily finally began. 'But Betty Bean was arrested as a traitor. She was released, on compassionate grounds, I think, as her father was very unwell. She went home. I don't know what really happened. I really don't.'

Sadie felt as if she'd been punched in the solar plexus. The nausea of earlier returned with a vengeance. She put her hand over her mouth, hoping she wasn't actually going to be sick, in the dining room of this posh hotel. She looked around the table. Deborah squirmed awkwardly in her chair as Sadie's gaze fell upon her. And Sadie's eyes met Luca's. And in that instant, it was obvious.

Luca knew.

Sadie thought back to that afternoon in the newspaper archive. He *had* read something about Betty Bean. Something that he didn't want to tell her. Every time he'd been quiet since, every time he'd fallen silent or looked preoccupied, it was because of what he had found out, and not told her. A fresh wave of nausea washed over her as the bitter stab of Luca's betrayal hit home.

Her eyes roved from Luca to Lily and back again. 'One of you needs to tell me what you know,' she said, sharply, forcing herself not to cry. 'You owe me that, at least. You owe me the truth.'

# CHAPTER FIFTY-FOUR

NAPLES, APRIL 1945

After two days in a cell, when Betty stepped outside for the first time the bright spring sunshine made her eyes throb as her pupils contracted. She blinked and looked around her, bewildered for a moment by the freedom that had come as suddenly as her unexpected incarceration. For the forty-eight hours she had been held at Caserta HQ she had tried to get those questioning her to believe her story that she was not actually a spy, but was merely fulfilling a mission given to her by Colonel Green of the British Army.

She recalled her interrogator's smirk as she had launched into her explanation for the umpteenth time. 'I'm Sergeant Bean of Y-Signals,' she'd insisted, imperiously. 'You have to let me go.'

'Yes, yes,' he'd said, almost laughing at this point. 'And I'm Roosevelt, risen from the dead.'

Betty thought about slapping his mocking face. But that was hardly going to help. She wanted to cry, but didn't think that would do much good, either. He didn't seem the sympathetic type. In the end, after the first twenty-four hours, her tormentor had been suddenly called away on urgent business and she'd been left to languish, her food pushed through the hatch in the door three times a day and nothing whatsoever to do for all the rest of the long, long hours. She wondered what was happening at Villa Teresa. When would the alarm be raised as to her disappearance? Would Millicent come forward to reveal that she'd seen Betty in the admin office?

When she'd finally been let out, it had been an orderly who'd come to the cell. Betty had asked him what was happening but he didn't have a clue.

'Instructions to release you without further delay, Sergeant,' he told her. And that was that.

Trudging home through the familiar city, Betty wondered how she could dare to show her face. How much gossip would there be? What would everyone be saying about her?

But as she walked, she sensed something in the air, something exciting, intangible but definitely there. Everyone on the streets was smiling, and the reason seemed to be more than just that the sun was shining and spring was well under way.

At a newspaper stall, she paused to read the headline.

L'ITALIA E' LIBERA
L'ITALIA RISORGERA

She translated the words quickly in her head.

ITALY IS FREE
ITALY RISES AGAIN

What had happened while she had been incarcerated? She had no money to buy a paper, so instead she asked the stall-holder to explain.

'Why, the partisans have declared a day of general insurrection,' he explained. 'Bologna and Genova have been retaken. Torino and Milano will be next. The war is nearly over.'

'Gosh.' Betty's response was wholly inadequate but she was lost for words. It was hard to believe the end was in sight. But now it did indeed seem to be true.

Trance-like, she stumbled back to Villa Teresa. When the familiar parasol pines hove into view, she'd never been so happy to see them. She dragged her heavy, tired limbs up the steps and through the majestic doorway, where she paused a moment, suddenly nervous about carrying on.

Captain Treacy, who'd been on the *Arcadia* all the way from Glasgow, and who had tortured the ATS women with drill and PT for all the months of their sojourn in Naples, came round the corner.

'Sergeant Bean.' Her stentorian voice rang out, echoing around the stone walls and high ceilings. 'I have urgent news for you.'

Betty halted, thinking *Here we go.* Now she was going to be reprimanded or scolded or locked up again, when all she had been doing was following orders. Why would no one believe her?

But Captain Treacy's expression was one of kindness, and her tone of voice was compassionate, not angry. She bustled Betty into her office and shut the door.

'Sit down, please,' she instructed, gesturing at a chair that sat on one side of her desk. 'We have received a cable,' she went on, once Betty was seated. 'I'm sorry to tell you that your father is dangerously ill with pneumonia. You are to return to the UK at once. There is a ship sailing today at four p.m. and you are to be on it.'

Betty opened her mouth to protest, to say that she couldn't possibly go home, she was needed here... And then she thought of her father, desperately unwell, asking for her. Of course she had to go. Plus she wasn't needed here any more, was she? The war was all but over, the Allies and the partisans storming through the north, ridding the country of the hated Nazis. There was nothing to do now but clear up the mess, and there were plenty of people to do that. But what had happened to Susan?

In a daze, Betty headed to the dorm room and packed up her few possessions. Even if she'd been demobbed, she'd have to wear her uniform on board ship; she didn't have any other clothes. She went to the bathroom to bathe and change into a fresh shirt and underwear, and then she sat on her bunk beneath the frescoed ceiling, unable to believe it was really all over. How could she go back to sleepy Malton after everything she'd experienced in her eighteen months abroad? She was a different person now but she knew already that Malton would be just the same as ever. And as for leaving Gianni... A torrent of despair swept over her at the thought.

Looking up, it seemed the painted cupids were crying with her, as sorry to see her go as she was to be leaving. She had no idea of the status of her special, undercover mission, why she'd been imprisoned and then released so suddenly. It was all a confusing mystery. But what did it matter, if she was leaving anyway?

Eventually, when she had managed to summon up the energy, she made her way to Colonel Green's office to see if she could gain some clarity. But the door was shut, an officious-looking orderly guarding it.

'No disturbances, Colonel's orders,' he told Betty. 'There's a war to be won. He don't have time for trivialities.'

Betty smarted a bit at his choice of words but she knew the man was only doing his job. And she was trivial, in the great scheme of things. That was how she felt, anyway. She'd taken on the surveillance role because she'd been given no choice in the matter. Once thrust into the role, she'd made the best of it and had perhaps even hoped that she, Betty Bean of Malton, would be instrumental in changing the course of the war, in getting traitors brought to book. But the great firework of the secret mission had ended up a damp squib.

*You stopped the bombing of the village,* she tried to tell herself, in an attempt to shore herself up and prevent a weeping fit.

*Maybe,* her mean, judgemental self retorted. *On the other hand, maybe you didn't make any difference at all.*

With that sad thought, Betty went to the mess for lunch. None of her friends were there and she avoided Millicent like the plague. Had it been her who'd reported her to the Americans? Betty wouldn't put it past her.

But what did it matter now? Betty's war, with all its fear and excitement and purpose and adrenaline, was over. Nothing this good, or bad, would ever happen to her again.

At 4 p.m., Betty slunk out of the Villa Teresa alone. In her hand was the last letter she'd ever take from her pigeon-hole inside the huge wooden door. She bade farewell to the magnificent building and her familiar friends, the parasol pines, and made her way to the docks. She wanted to be early. If she missed this passage, there wouldn't be another one for a week.

Once on board, she put her bag in her tiny cabin and made her way to the deck. She looked out at the beautiful, chaotic, colourful city of Naples, spread out over its hills like a careless giant had dropped it there and not bothered to clear up after himself. The sky was a deep Mediterranean blue, the sea a mix of turquoise blending to cerulean blending to navy. Palm trees swayed their fronds in the breeze and the haunting cries of seabirds rose above the clatter and clamour of the busy quay-side. When she had first seen this beautiful view, it had taken her breath away. Now it did so again. But this time, because of how much she was going to miss it.

As the ship made its preparations to leave, Betty became

aware of two people, remonstrating with a sailor holding a rope, waving their arms and gesticulating wildly.

Lily and Deborah.

They were trying to get aboard, wanting to come and say goodbye. But the sailor shook his head, threw the coiled rope onto a bollard and gestured to the two women to step back as the gangplank began to rise.

Betty hesitated. Her friends did not know what she had been involved in and in that knowledge vacuum there were probably all sorts of rumours going around, which no one would be able to counter, least of all Betty herself. Should she slink away and hope that they hadn't seen her? And then it was too late because Deborah had caught sight of her and was nudging Lily, pointing upwards and then breaking off to do more waving and blowing of air-kisses.

Narrowing her eyes, Betty fixed her gaze on the two of them, far below on the quayside. Tentatively at first, and then more enthusiastically, she began to wave back.

Lily was saying something, mouthing out a question, but Betty could not hear. Straining to see, she made out the words through lip-reading.

'What happened?' Lily was entreating. 'Where have you been?'

Tears flooded Betty's eyes. She shouldn't have to leave like this, with doubt and misunderstandings left behind. But it was too late to do anything about it.

The ship's horn sounded once, and then again, the blaring noise resounding around the deck. Betty was subsumed with dreadful sadness at parting from her friends, and at leaving behind this city and country, where she had lived the most amazing, terrible, beautiful months of her life.

Lily was still shouting, but there was less chance of Betty hearing than ever, what with the rumbling of the engines, the rattling of chains and cries of the sailors on board. The ship began to build up speed and Lily and Deborah to recede from view. Behind their tiny figures, Naples was a smudge of ochre and yellow and terracotta, fading into the afternoon light.

For a moment, Betty was sure she could smell the scent of lemon blossom, carried on the breeze from the steep seaside terraces of Sorrento, and then that, too, disappeared.

Eventually, Betty opened the letter that she'd collected on her way out of Villa Teresa. It was from Gianni.

*Dearest Betty,*

*I hope that you are well and enjoying the start of spring in Naples. The warmer weather has been a huge relief to us in the north. It was so cold up here all winter, snow on the ground and a freezing wind. Just like Yorkshire, although possibly even worse. Your socks made all the difference so thank you again. I'm not sure how often I'll need them in Sicily, but I'll treasure them forever.*

*You might wonder why I mention my homeland. The reason is because I'm going there, soon. The partisan groups are disarming and disbanding; our job is done. My family need me at home. All the old men have died now, and many of the young, too. So I must return.*

*The war will be over in a matter of days, I think. And then we can start again. I miss you with all my heart and entreat you to come with me to my beautiful island. You told me how much you love lemons. Sorrento lemons are good but Sicilian lemons are the best, big and juicy and fragrant. In Sicily, you could have fresh lemons every day of your life. Will you think about it, Betty? For me? For us? I hope and trust that you will.*

*Until then, with all my love, goodbye. Yours ever,*

*Gianni*

Instantaneously, tears leapt to Betty's eyes. She didn't quite understand what the words meant. 'Until then'. Until when? She went back out on deck, where the breeze dried her tears.

'*My family need me at home.*' Those six words said it all. Betty knew enough of Italy by now to understand that family ties overrode all others. If she and Gianni were married, of course it would be different. She would be his first priority. But they weren't. And she was tied to her own family commitments, anyway. She couldn't abandon her father in his hour of need. If, despite his mother's premonitions, Samuel were still alive, she couldn't leave him, either. He would have suffered unimaginable horrors in the Far East; his mother had constantly told Betty that only the steadfast knowledge that Betty would be waiting would have kept him going, if indeed he had survived this long. She could not betray Samuel, nor their respective families. There was no conceivable way she could let everyone down by reneging on her promise. So Gianni was going south and she was going north. She'd thought when she left Yorkshire a year and a half ago that that would be the end of her and Gianni. They had had two more glorious, unexpected encounters.

But now it really was over.

# CHAPTER FIFTY-FIVE

NAPLES, AUGUST 1972

Lily fumbled in her bag and pulled out a newspaper cutting, brown with age and curling at the edges. She passed it to Sadie, who took it with trembling hands.

'It's from *Il Mattino*,' explained Lily. 'I've kept it all these years, tucked away in my pocketbook. I don't really know why. Perhaps I always hoped I'd solve the mystery one day.'

Sadie ran her eyes down the text. She couldn't read the Italian – but she quickly spotted the name Betty Bean. Wonderingly, she stared at it. She recalled how strangely Luca had acted when they were in the archives, how he'd shouted out as if he'd found something and then immediately fallen silent, closed the newspaper and announced that it was time to go, that they'd done all they could. Sadie had known there was something strange going on.

Lifting her eyes from the cutting, she fixed them on him. 'It's the same piece that you read, isn't it?' she demanded.

With a guilty look, Luca nodded. Awkwardness emanated out from him. Fleetingly, Sadie thought of their kiss, the somersaults in her stomach, her fluttering heart. But he'd lied to her. Or if not exactly lied, at least been economical with the truth. She couldn't trust him after this, could not forgive him. Anger flared through her. She pushed the cutting across the table towards him.

'So,' she questioned, 'what does it say? Read it out to me, please.'

The hubbub of chatter that filled the dining room receded into the background. All Sadie could hear was the silence at their table as she waited for Luca to read the cutting, and the pounding of the blood in her head.

'*A British woman working for the ATS, stationed in Naples at Villa Teresa, was today arrested under threat of court martial by the American forces based at Caserta.*'

Luca's voice was monotone and dry. He paused, glancing uncertainly up at Sadie, as if to request her permission to continue.

'Well, go on,' she said, unable to keep the impatience out of her tone.

'*Sergeant Betty Bean,*' Luca resumed, '*of Y-Signals, is alleged to have been passing secrets to the enemy. Her co-conspirator, Sergeant Susan Davies, is at large somewhere in the community and could be dangerous.*

'*Anybody with any information should contact the military or the police immediately.* Il Mattino *attempted to obtain further details but was unsuccessful due to the top-secret classification of this case.*'

Horror cut Sadie in two. So her mother really had been a traitor? She'd come all this way, worked so hard, to find the woman who gave birth to her, only to find out that she had betrayed her country. That she'd left – been discharged from – the army in disgrace.

'I-I don't believe it,' she stuttered.

Lily reached out and took her hand. Sadie had almost

forgotten she was there, or Deborah. Her entire focus had been on Luca, and the newspaper cutting.

'I don't either,' said Lily, stalwartly. 'I never have.' She topped up their glasses with champagne. 'Betty was the most honest, straight and true person I've ever met,' she asserted. 'She disappeared one day. We – that's Deborah and I – hadn't a clue where she was. And the next we heard, she was at the port, on a homeward-bound ship. We ran down there at top speed to try to speak to her. But we were too late; she had already set sail. We never found out the whole story.' She reached for a glass and took a swig of the golden sparkling liquid. 'But there's no way Betty Bean was a traitor. I'm adamant about that.'

A silence fell at that remark, as if they were all absorbing what Lily had said.

Sadie's insides were churning. She took a sip of her champagne. She should probably stop drinking, have a Coca-Cola instead, but what the hell. For a moment she bitterly regretted her vow that she would find her birth parents. She could have done what Simon suggested, and forgotten all about it. Then she would have been saved this agony. Kim had warned her to be careful what she wished for, and she had ignored her. Now she was paying the price in emotional torture.

'W-where is she?' She managed to get the words out, eventually, at a volume no higher than a whisper. 'Where can I find her? I need to know.'

Lily shook her head. Her gold cigarette case lay on the table, and she picked it up, took one out and lit it. Sadie almost considered asking for one herself, even though she'd never smoked. She needed something to calm her nerves. And quell the rage she was still feeling towards Luca. He'd let her spend days thinking he hadn't found anything – and it wasn't true.

Taking a drag on her cigarette, Lily released a cloud of smoke into the air. 'That I cannot tell you,' she answered, sounding unbelievably sad all of a sudden. 'All my efforts to contact Betty back in England were in vain. After she left Naples, I never heard from her again.'

Sadie let her head drop into her hands. This was crazy, insane. How come no one knew anything about Betty Bean's whereabouts? How could she be so near to her potential birth mother, and yet so far? It was like a cruel joke, as if some master of the universe was laughing at her in her distress. Her emotions were all over the place, a mixture of fury, disbelief, confusion and dread.

Nothing made any sense, least of all the revelations about Betty.

And then it struck Sadie, like a bolt from the blue. If Betty was her mother, and Betty was a traitor, did she even want to track her down? Did she want to know her?

The meal finished, Sadie hardly conscious of what she was eating. Deborah, Luca and Lily tried to keep up a semblance of conviviality, but after the reading of the cutting the mood around the table had soured, becoming depressed and disconsolate.

At last, it was time to leave. As well as settling the bill, Lily had insisted on stumping up for their transportation home. One taxi swept Luca and Deborah away, leaving Lily and Sadie on the hotel steps waiting for theirs. Sadie was glad she didn't have to share with Luca. She could hardly look at him, after what this evening had revealed.

Once she and Lily were in the taxi, sweeping through the dark city streets, Lily turned to address her.

'My poor lamb,' she said, 'you look absolutely sideswiped by this evening.' She reached out to give Sadie's hand a little pat. 'I've got a suggestion,' she continued. 'I'm off to Amalfi in the morning. Why don't you come with me for a few days, as my guest? Take your mind off it all. I can tell you the story of how I washed ashore there with the fishermen, back in '43. And you can tell me all about yourself. I love the young! So full of energy and vitality. You'll take me back to my own youth.'

Numbed though she was, Sadie didn't even need to think about her answer. Of course it was a yes. She'd already started worrying about how she'd avoid Luca if she stayed in Naples. At this moment, she never wanted to speak to him again. Taking up Lily's offer at least meant she didn't have to come up with a solution for forty-eight hours or so.

'I'd love to,' she said. She meant to say more but suddenly couldn't, knowing she wouldn't be able to stop her voice from breaking. For a few moments, she fought back the tears that were threatening, gripping her bag strap tightly. Feeling Lily's eyes upon her, she mustered a smile. 'Amalfi sounds wonderful.' And then she had to stop again, overwhelmed with the memories of the perfect day she and Luca had spent on Capri. At one point, she had thought that maybe she and Luca could explore the rest of the coast together...

Lily chattered away as Sadie stared out of the window at the night-black city and tried to focus on what she was saying.

'My driver will pick you up at eleven o'clock,' she told Sadie. 'We'll be at the hotel in good time for lunch.'

That night, in her hotel bed, Sadie could not sleep. Everything was a mess. She hadn't found her parents, not her mother Betty, who most probably had committed treason in the war, rather than being some sort of hero, nor her father Gianni, and didn't know if she ever would. And she had been stupid enough to begin to fall in love with someone who, in all honesty, she hardly knew. So it was her own fault if she now felt crushed and devastated; she shouldn't have put so much trust in Luca.

BY THE NEXT morning she was exhausted, flattened. The car, when it arrived, was baking hot and the heat, combined with her sleepless night, lulled Sadie to sleep. She woke as they drew to a halt, opening her eyes to a magical sight: an expanse of blue sea, interspersed with long jetties alongside which boats bobbed and swayed, and backed by jagged cliffs dotted with clusters of white, pink and blue houses. It was utterly enchanting.

'Here's the hotel, darling,' said Lily, as the driver opened the car doors and helped them both out. Sadie looked around her. All she could see was the entrance to a tunnel and a small glass door nestled alongside it, seeming to lead into the earth itself.

Lily caught her expression and laughed. 'Come on, follow me,' she urged. 'The porter will follow with our luggage.'

Sadie did as bidden and, once inside, Lily led them to a lift in which they ascended for several minutes. When they stepped out at the upper level, Sadie was once again left speechless. The hotel was entirely built along the side of a cliff, curving as the rock curved, seeming to defy gravity. Far down below lay the beach they had parked beside; up here, the outlook was entirely made up of blues and greens. The blue of the sea and sky, and the green of the luscious vegetation that clung to the cliff face, growing out of every cavity, nook and cranny. A bougainvillea-covered terrace provided a walkway from one end of the hotel to the other, and they were taken along this to their rooms, beside which was an outdoor sitting room situated within the ancient colonnades of the thirteenth-century convent that had originally inhabited the site.

'Wow,' breathed Sadie. Even mired in her misery, she could not fail to appreciate the hotel's splendour. 'I'm pinching myself to check that I'm awake. This is stupendous.'

Lily smiled. She fumbled with the clasp of her handbag, a different one from the night before that looked equally expensive, and thrust a tip at the valet who'd brought up their bags. 'I knew you'd like it,' she said. 'It's a short walk into town or we can just laze by the pool. If we don't deserve a bit of rest and relaxation, I don't know who does.'

Sadie wasn't entirely sure what Lily had done that was so

strenuous she needed a break in a super-luxury hotel, or herself for that matter, but she wasn't about to argue. When she stepped inside the door to her room, the sight of the linen-white bed was like a marvel. Whether she had reason or not, she was definitely worn out, emotionally exhausted, done in.

For the rest of that day, they did exactly what Lily had proposed: took it easy. Sadie had a long siesta in a lounger by the pool and still went to bed at nine. The next day passed in much the same way, though by the evening Sadie was feeling more energetic. Lily wanted to take her to the restaurant that had the best view of the sunset. Sitting at their table under a pergola festooned with bright pink bougainvillea, she ordered *spremuta di limone* for them both, and showed Sadie how to mix the lemon juice with sugar and water to make it to her taste.

'We visited a lemon grove in Sorrento once,' mused Lily as she laconically stirred her glass. 'Those lemons were incredible. And before that, on the *Arcadia*, when we docked in Sicily they brought local Taormina lemons on board, crates of them, and oranges too. The juice was nectar from the gods to us, the war had deprived us of such things for so long.'

'Taormina,' repeated Sadie, savouring the strange word on her tongue. 'It sounds so foreign and exotic.'

'It's a gorgeous place,' agreed Lily. 'I've been there several times since the war ended. It was strange, that day, though. At first, Betty shared our excitement, but then she seemed to have a bit of a funny turn.'

'What?' asked Sadie, puzzled. 'Why?'

Lily sighed and shrugged. 'I've no idea. I'm probably imagining it, anyway. We were getting closer to Naples and what awaited us there, so we were all keyed up, tense as bowstrings. I'm sure it didn't mean anything.' She drew on her cigarette and released the smoke in the form of a perfect circle. 'Betty loved lemons the most of any of us,' she concluded.

Sadie felt the familiar ache of her heart at the mention of the woman who was probably her mother.

'I love lemons, too,' she said. Perhaps she had inherited this trait from Betty. She shook her head, trying to dispel the fanciful notion. 'But then again, who doesn't?' she added, countering herself. She needed to stop being so suggestible, stop reading too much into things. Especially when it seemed that only disappointment lay ahead of her.

The pair were silent for a moment, both lost in thought.

'Lily,' ventured Sadie eventually, as the sunset painted the sky rose pink and orange. 'Do you think I'm wasting my time? Will I ever find my birth parents?'

Lily sighed and stubbed out her cigarette with elegant fingers. Her nails were flawlessly painted in a shade of vibrant red that Sadie knew was all the rage this season. She had never been a follower of fashion, but seeing Lily so effortlessly on trend was making her feel that maybe she should be. 'I don't know, darling,' Lily replied, speaking slowly and thoughtfully. 'But I can say one thing for certain. You'd never forgive yourself if you didn't try.'

Sadie bit her lip and willed herself not to cry. She was crying – or trying not to – all the time these days.

'Yeah,' she whispered faintly. 'You're right. I would never forgive myself.'

# CHAPTER FIFTY-SIX

YORKSHIRE, APRIL 1945

Stepping off the train onto the platform at Malton station, Betty tugged her coat more tightly around her. It had been chilly in Naples in winter, and freezing in Rome. But even in April this English cold was something different, immediately getting into her bones.

Looking around her, nothing seemed to have changed. The advertising hoardings were the same, for Bovril and Cadbury's, just a little more faded. The people too, were the same, just a little more faded, faces pale and grey, clothing patched and worn.

Jane had come to stay with their father when he'd been discharged from hospital, and she met Betty at the station. In the pram sat Archie. Betty flung her arms round her sister and then her nephew, who accepted her embrace without protest. He regarded her with solemn eyes as she gushed about how handsome and strong he looked.

'He's gorgeous, Jane,' she enthused, again and again.

'Shush,' Jane frowned. 'It'll go to his head and spoil him.'

Betty ignored her. The Italians showered praise on children left, right and centre and they didn't seem to end up any more spoilt than an English child.

She and Jane walked back to the cottage side by side. An army truck rattled by, loaded with men.

'Going back to Eden Camp,' said Jane. 'It's all Germans there now. I think the regime isn't quite as relaxed as it was with the Italians.'

'I heard as much,' replied Betty. She sighed. 'Everything changes, doesn't it? Sometimes for good, sometimes for bad.'

'Why so serious all of a sudden?' teased Jane. 'You must be glad to be back on home soil, aren't you? All that foreign food and wearing uniform...' She glanced at Betty's khaki drill. 'You'll be glad to be wearing civvies, I'm sure.'

Betty smiled. She understood that her sister didn't understand. She'd only left Malton to move to Scarborough, and had never had a job, marrying almost straight out of school. She had no concept of how much the vast majority of the ATS women, and the WRNS, and the WAAFs, had loved their time in the forces, being useful, necessary, wanted. Betty wondered how any of them were just going to sink back into their old lives of domesticity, days filled with nothing but housework, cooking, childcare. Women were already having to give up their exciting, demanding, responsible jobs on the land, in factories, in shops, so that men returning from the fighting could have them. It seemed so unfair. All those many incredible contributions thrown away, all that skill going to waste.

Betty had no great desire to return to the telephone exchange. She'd rather do something that used her brain, that challenged her, as being a cipher operator had. But even if she had been desperate to get back to her old job, she couldn't. She must take over from her sister in looking after their father so that Jane could return to her husband.

At home, Harold was sitting up in his favourite armchair,

drawn up to the kitchen fire. Betty had to hide her shock at seeing him. He was a shadow of his former self, seeming to have shrunk to half his size. His hair, what was left of it, was wispy and unkempt and his breathing was laboured.

'Dad!' she cried, dropping to her knees in front of him. 'How are you? I came as soon as I could.'

Harold smiled at her with tired eyes. 'I know, Betty love. Thank you for coming. It's good to see you.'

Jane made a pot of tea and poured them all a cup. Archie was sitting on the floor, playing with some wooden building blocks. Betty sat beside him and helped him to make towers and knock them down. Jane had saved up butter and jam rations so that she could make a cake, a Victoria sponge, and they all had a slice.

Betty had an overwhelming feeling that her life had gone backwards. It was almost as if the last year and a half hadn't happened. Jane's cake was delicious and moist but it cloyed in Betty's mouth and she could hardly swallow it down. It reminded her of every dull, rainy Sunday of her teenage years, of every visit to Samuel's house, and of her mother's funeral. On that latter occasion, some well-meaning person had insisted Betty eat a slice of cake 'to keep her strength up', and the sweetness of it had been sickening, sticking in her gullet, choking her. Now she felt the same.

The future looked bleak and grey, and, even though Betty was back in the bosom of her family, overwhelmingly lonely.

Once they'd finished tea, it was time for Jane to get the train back to Scarborough. Betty walked with her to the station, retracing their steps from earlier. She pushed Archie's pram, imagining having her own baby to dote upon and love with all her heart as her sister did her son. Kissing them both farewell, her spirits sank even lower. Jane was so solid and sure. She did not doubt or question her role as mother and caregiver, did not harbour any expectations for career success, or indeed any career at all, and in general saw life through a much simpler prism than Betty did.

Waving them off, Betty felt that there had been far too many goodbyes recently.

She took the long route home, prolonging the journey, and on the way gave herself a strict talking-to. Her father was relying on her and she needed to pull herself together and cheer up. No convalescing invalid wanted a misery-guts around them, making them feel even lower than they already did.

By the time she was back at the cottage, she'd managed to plaster a smile across her face. Now that Jane and Archie had left, Harold was able to grill Betty about all the details of her time in Naples. They sat in the kitchen in front of the fire and Betty talked and talked, telling her father about the friends she'd made, the work she'd done, and describing the city, the volcano and the coastline in as much detail as she could. She didn't tell him about Susan, or spying, or being arrested. It was too complicated, and she didn't understand it well enough herself to explain it to anyone else.

After a couple of hours of almost non-stop talking, Betty told her father about the lemons of Sorrento, about how the blossom filled the air with scent, about how the lemon groves were impervious to war and devastation but just kept on providing their fruit, again and again.

'You made the most of your time away,' her father responded, with a breathy chuckle. His lungs were still bad, not yet clear of the pneumonia that had struck him so hard. 'So many adventures! My goodness, what your mother would have said about it all I can't imagine.'

Betty smiled, almost choking up at the memory of her mum, and father and daughter sat in silence for a while, remembering.

# CHAPTER FIFTY-SEVEN

The next couple of weeks passed slowly as April turned to May. The weather improved, the days got longer, and Betty continued in her efforts to be as cheerful as possible, even though she was lonely, bored and, above all, heartbroken.

She received a letter from Val telling her that she was engaged to be married – and that her military service in Portsmouth was ending and she was coming home. Betty went to the station to meet her. As soon as she was off the train, the pair flung themselves at each other, hugging and hugging for long minutes.

'Betty Bean!' cried Val. 'I've missed you so much. Look at you! You don't look any different, except maybe a bit older and wiser. And a bit chubbier. I guess I can put that down to all that fabulous Italian food.'

Betty dug her elbow into her friend. 'Cheeky!' she responded, laughingly. The clothes she'd left behind in her wardrobe were a little tight these days, but Betty was good with a needle and had managed to let them out. 'And what about you? All grown up and about to be a wife.'

Val blushed. 'I know. I'm so excited. We could have got

married down south, and I would have done if it hadn't been that we all knew the war was ending. Once that was certain, we decided to wait so that we could do it properly, with family and everything.' She paused and sighed. 'I can't believe I'm not going to be Val Edwards any more, but Val Whitaker. It sounds nice, doesn't it? Val Whitaker.' She repeated the name as if savouring its taste and feel.

Betty nodded. 'Wonderful.' Then she added, 'I'm jealous,' but she didn't know why. The whole marriage thing was too complicated to think of.

Val looked at her suspiciously. 'Right,' she said, briskly. 'You and I are going to get a cup of tea somewhere and you're going to tell me everything. I've read your letters, but I know you too well, Betty Bean. There are things you're not letting on, aren't there? Hmm? Am I right or am I right?'

Tears rose in Betty's eyes, unbidden. She'd deliberately been vague with Val about her feelings for Samuel – or lack of them – and her love for Gianni. It had felt easier for no one to know. But now she saw that she could not conceal the truth from her best friend.

They found a quiet table in the café in the market square, where the normally brusque and forthright Val, gently and sensitively, teased the real story from Betty. It was cathartic to spill it all out. But at the end of the telling, there was no easy solution.

'And you still don't know for sure whether Samuel is dead or alive?' asked Val.

Betty shook her head miserably.

'If he is, then of course I have to be here for him,' she said.

'Why?' questioned Val, bluntly. 'Can't you just tell him you've moved on, things have changed? Enough couples have split and found new partners amidst all this mayhem.'

'No.' Betty's answer was unequivocal. 'I promised, didn't I?

That I'd wait for him, that we'd be married when he came back. I can't go back on my promise.'

Val looked dubious. 'What about Gianni?' She frowned as she spoke. 'Can you just let go of him?'

Tears sprang to Betty's eyes and she choked back a sob that rose in her throat. 'He's in Sicily, isn't he, so far away. I don't want to give up on him. But I have to, and that's all there is to it.'

The expression on Val's face was as stricken as Betty's own. 'I didn't know exactly how hard you'd fallen for him,' she admitted. 'This Gianni chap.' She picked up her teacup and stared into it as if it might hold the answer. 'I thought you'd forget about him when you left for the ATS.'

Quietly, Betty's shoulders heaved with stifled sobs.

'I see why you can't go to Sicily, what with your mum having passed and your dad relying on you so much,' ventured Val, speaking very slowly, as if she was working it all out in her own head. 'And Samuel... well, I get it. Plus Sicily – I'm not even sure exactly where that is. But too far. Much too far.' She paused and sighed heavily. 'And he probably can't come back here for all the same reasons, and anyway, what would be the point? To have a duel with Samuel?' Val shuddered, reached for the teapot and poured more tea into first Betty's cup and then her own.

'It's a right royal mess and no mistake,' she concluded, with another huge sigh.

Betty smiled wanly through her tears. At least she could always rely on Val to tell it like it was, call a spade a spade. No meaningless platitudes from her, which was all for the better because Betty didn't think she would have been able to cope with anyone telling her everything would be all right, when it so clearly wouldn't be.

.  .  .

Two DAYS LATER, a letter dropped through the letter box of the cottage at the end of the lane in Malton. Snatching it up from the doormat, Betty felt all the air empty out of her lungs. Clutching onto the hat stand to avoid collapsing, she stared at the flimsy envelope, scarcely able to believe her eyes. There was her address, scrawling across the paper, written in a familiar hand.

Samuel's.

Did this mean he was alive after all? Betty tore at the flap, nearly ripping the whole thing, and pulled out the paper inside. She studied the date, thinking that maybe the letter was old, that it had been written ages ago but only just got through the system. But no. The letter was dated 10 April 1945.

Barely breathing, Betty sank down on the bottom stair and read.

*My dearest darling Betty,*

*This is the first letter I have written in a while. I'm sorry for leaving you in the dark for so long but, if I am to be truthful, I have not been in the right spirit for writing. I cannot even begin to tell you what we have endured over here.*

The next few lines were blotted out by the thick black pen of the censor. Betty's eyes skipped down to where the letter resumed.

*One thing has kept me going through it all, the thing that fills my dreams and every waking moment – and that thing is the thought of you, and that if I ever do get home you will be waiting for me.*

*Please be there for me, Betty. I need you more now than I can ever say. I'm sure you have written but no letters are*

*getting through to us at the moment. It doesn't matter. Just*
*know that I love you more and more each day.*

*Forever yours,*

*Samuel*

With each line she read, Betty's heart turned over anew.
The black blots were glaring evidence of horrors that could not
be recounted. Her imagination ran wild, thinking of what
Samuel had had to endure, was still enduring. It made her feel
physically sick.

And then to hear Samuel's words of love and adoration and,
more than that, to understand how much he needed her, how
much he would always need her – it filled her heart with pity
and guilt. How could she ever have even considered reneging
on her promise?

It was not to be countenanced, would be the deed of an evil,
duplicitous renegade, and Betty Bean was not such a person nor
ever would be.

She put the letter back into the envelope and tucked it into
her apron pocket, then went into the kitchen to make her father
his breakfast. He was getting stronger by the day but, now that
she was here and had the time to dedicate herself to his care, she
had insisted he get as much rest as possible, which included
morning tea and toast in bed.

'It's like my birthday every day!' he joked when she brought
in the tray.

With a supreme effort, Betty forced herself to be cheerful.
'Not really.' She laughed. 'You've never, ever had breakfast in
bed on your birthday, as far as I'm aware. Or any other day, for
that matter.'

Harold chuckled merrily as Betty hurriedly left the room
and headed for her bedroom, blinking back tears. Samuel was

alive. One day, he would come home. It should be the happiest day of her life. That it wasn't was her own shame, no one else's.

The love she and Gianni had shared had been a wonderful thing but it had never been meant to last. For a fleeting second, Betty allowed herself a few seconds indulging might-have-beens: her and Gianni pledging themselves to each other, having a child, or children, two would be a good number... And then she shoved such images from her mind.

She picked up the photo that stood on the nightstand. It was of herself and Samuel, with Betty's mother on one side, Samuel's on the other and Harold behind them all, grinning over Betty's head with an overwhelming look of pride.

These were the people that mattered, her family and community, those friends and relatives she had been surrounded by, and loved by, for all of her life. These were also the people, the living and the dead, who she would be irrevocably letting down if she did anything but fulfil her promise to Samuel.

Putting the photo gently back down, Betty straightened her shoulders, brushed her hair and went downstairs to clear up after breakfast.


THE DAY after she received Samuel's letter, the war in Europe ended, just as he had predicted.

The eighth of May brought celebrations for VE Day, the likes of which Malton had never seen before. All around the market square red, white and blue bunting fluttered cheerily in the breeze. The whole town turned out for the parade and the dancing. Even Harold mustered the energy to join in for a few hours. Once he had gone back home, Val and Betty were left to party the night away. The land girls and the munitions workers, the WAAFs and WRNS and ATS, thronged the streets and public bars, together with recently released soldiers, sailors and airmen, everyone crazy with excitement and relief that the longest conflict in modern history was finally over.

Except that it wasn't. In the Far East, thousands of men still lingered in Japanese prisoner-of-war camps and no one knew when they would be set free. It was impossible to imagine how ill-treated they had been. What a contrast to Eden Camp, thought Betty, with the guards lending the POWs their clothes so that they could go out for the evening with their sweethearts.

Towards the end of the night, the singing began. Betty sang the national anthem, and 'The White Cliffs of Dover', and 'Sentimental Journey', along with everybody else. But when it came to 'We'll Meet Again', she fell silent. Gianni had said those words to her when she was leaving Malton all those months ago, and they had met again, completely out of the blue, in Italy. But with the arrival of Samuel's letter had come the realisation that there would be no more meetings.

She and Gianni would never see each other again.

# CHAPTER FIFTY-EIGHT

The trip to Amalfi was over all too quickly. Lily was meeting an old family friend and Sadie didn't want to intrude. She took the bus back to Naples, holding tight to her seat as it careered along roads that were vertiginously steep and far too narrow for all the traffic, especially as not a single car, motorbike, van or truck seemed to possess the slightest inclination to give way to others.

She'd kept her room at the hotel for the two nights she'd been away and it was nice to be back in its familiar surroundings. And also impossibly lonely. She had come here with such high hopes and expectations. But really, what had she achieved? She had names but no addresses, possibility without certainty.

It was utterly demoralising.

And she had to work out what to do about Luca. Over the time away, her anger had diluted somewhat, her heart softening. But not enough for her to seek him out and make things up. Not at all. Instead, she wanted to pay him for all the hours he had spent helping her with her search, leave everything fair and square. She had let a business relationship stray into the personal and that was always a bad idea. Putting it back on its original footing as a financial transaction would clear up any doubt and uncertainty and enable her to leave Naples with a clear conscience.

Because that was what she had decided to do. There was no point in staying here now that she had reached a dead end. She was spending money she should really be saving for the future and, as much as the idea of quitting this unique, chaotic city broke her heart, there was no other option.

Listlessly, she pulled on her shoes, picked up her hat and headed for the door. She would go to the travel agent and book her flight home, tomorrow or the next day if possible.

In a daze, she stepped out into the white light of a Neapolitan summer afternoon. It would be good to leave this blistering sun behind, she told herself sternly, even though she loved the heat, the brightness, the cloudless skies.

'Sadie!'

The cry of her name made her jump out of her skin. Holding her hand to her thumping heart, she looked around her.

And there he was, his round, gold-rimmed glasses glinting, his neat hair uncharacteristically tousled. He looked tired. He also looked completely gorgeous.

'Sadie!' Luca repeated. 'I... where have you been? You disappeared off the face of the earth, I've been so worried about you. Are you all right?'

Sadie was still staring at him, open-mouthed, disorientated. She had known she'd need to see Luca again, to pay him if nothing else, but hadn't thought through what she would say when that meeting occurred. Now, caught off guard, how should she react? She had not anticipated how just the sight of him would so thoroughly knock her sideways.

'Yes,' she answered, weakly. And then, 'no,' she added,

barely audibly. And then, 'I don't know,' which last was accompanied by a flood of uncontrollable tears.

Luca stepped towards her, his face full of loving concern. He put his arms round her. She didn't protest. In fact, she moved closer into his embrace, an urgent need for his solidity and comfort overwhelming her. In the street, surrounded by bustling pedestrians, Luca held her in his strong embrace until the crying stopped. Then he lifted her chin and kissed her and she had the sudden, certain feeling that everything was going to be all right after all.

They went to a coffee shop and fell over each other trying to apologise.

'I've been an idiot,' said Sadie, fortified by a strong espresso. 'I'm so sorry. I don't know why I reacted so badly. I was so furious with you for not telling me the truth.'

'I know it's not a good enough excuse, but I was only trying to protect you,' Luca replied, sorrowfully. 'When I read that article, saw what it said about Betty – I thought it was best if you didn't know. I was wrong, I understand that now. I'm so, so sorry. When I couldn't find you, when they said you'd left the hotel, I was beside myself. Thank God you're back. Thank God.' He gripped her hands and held them tight. 'Don't do that again, all right?' he ordered, sternly. 'Next time I'll have an actual heart attack, not just an imaginary one.'

Sadie uttered a little laugh through her tears. More crying. But this time, from relief rather than misery.

'There are a hundred reasons why I was so desperate for you to come back,' continued Luca. 'The main one – well, we can talk about that later. But in the meantime, I've got something to show you.' He pulled a piece of paper from his pocket. 'I went back to the newspaper archive. I spent all day there yesterday. And I found this.'

He passed the slip of paper across to Sadie. She picked it up and unfolded it. In English, copied out in neat, slanted hand-writing, was the following:

> *A major combined force of partisans and Allied troops have eroded the last foothold of the Axis forces in the Po valley... Several partisan brigades were involved and unfortunately casualties are reported to have been high... immense bravery under fire... Commendations for military honours... among those singled out are Francesco Bianchi of Torino, Roberto Romano of Verona and Gianni Urso from Taormina, Sicily.*

Sadie read every word carefully, and then once again. She looked up at Luca, incredulous. 'Gianni Urso,' she said, wonderingly. 'Do you think it might be my Gianni? The one who made the keepsake that my mother left with me?'

Silently, Luca nodded, then said, 'Yes, I think it might be him.'

Blinking, Sadie tried to take it in. 'Lily said something about Taormina,' she recalled, recalling their sunset drink of lemon juice. 'She said Betty had a reaction to seeing the town's name on some crates delivered to their transport ship.' She looked down at the paper and then up at Luca. 'Perhaps it was because Taormina reminded her of Gianni. She would have known where he was from.'

'Maybe,' agreed Luca. 'So anyway,' he continued, somewhat warily, as if unsure of Sadie's reaction, 'I thought perhaps we should go there. To Sicily. To Taormina. See what we can find. What do you think?'

Sadie ran her hands through her hair. After being about to go home, her tail between her legs, now this sudden volte-face. It was a lot to take in. But it didn't take long to decide.

'Yes, definitely,' she said. 'Let's do it. After all, we've got nothing to lose, have we?'

They left the café and went to the travel agent, but not to buy a ticket home to London.

'Two tickets for the Palermo ferry,' Luca requested, handing over a wad of lire. 'A twin cabin on tonight's sailing, please.'


THERE WASN'T long for Sadie to get packed up, hand in her hotel room key and meet Luca at the port. He'd gone home to collect his own things, a much further distance, but he was still there first.

Aboard the ferry, a cooling wind sent Sadie's hair flying across her face. She pulled it back with her hand and watched as the sky darkened and the city's lights came on. She was off again, on another stage of her journey, one that might prove definitive. Filled with trepidation, her stomach danced and churned. So much upheaval, so much tension. But at least she had Luca with her, by her side, their silly quarrel behind them now.

She reached out to him, taking his hand. Following her cue, he moved closer, putting an arm round her shoulders and drawing her close. As the twinkling lights of Naples receded into the distance, they kissed.

For one blissful moment, Sadie forgot about everything but this moment and this man, and was content.

# CHAPTER FIFTY-NINE

YORKSHIRE, SEPTEMBER 1945

The boy whistled as he cycled down the lane. Betty heard him
from the kitchen where she was standing at the sink, her hands
deep in washing-up water. When he knocked at the door, she
was already halfway there, as if she had known he was coming
to the Bean household.

Wiping her hands on her apron, she opened the door.

'Morning,' the boy chirruped cheerfully. 'Telegram for Miss
Bean.'

Betty took the envelope he held out to her. The yellowish
card inside held a simple message.

BACK SOON. MEET CLOCK 29.09.45. SAMUEL

Three months after the wild celebrations for VE Day, the
Americans had dropped their nuclear bombs on Japan and, a
week later, Japan had surrendered. Betty had been waiting to
hear from Samuel. His last letter had made clear what bad
shape he and the other prisoners were in and so there had been

every possibility that he might have died in the extra months that the war dragged on in the Far East. But now here it was. The telegram that proved for certain that Samuel had survived and would soon be on home soil.

Tucking the telegram behind the carriage clock on the mantelpiece, Betty smoothed down her hair and tried to compose herself. Her hands were shaking and she felt cold, goosebumps breaking out on her arms even though the weather was still mild.

Her father was back at work driving the truck, delivering fruit and veg around Yorkshire, but he'd shortened his rounds and, though he still started at 5 a.m., he was usually finished by midday. Betty went to tell him that she was going to London to meet Samuel. She'd be taking the next train out of Malton and would find a cheap hotel in the capital for a couple of nights. She wanted to go early, make sure she was there in plenty of time.

'That's grand, Betty love,' Harold replied, with a huge smile. 'You'll be right pleased to see him, I bet.'

Betty nodded, not trusting herself to speak. As she turned to go and get ready, pack an overnight bag, he called her back.

'Betty,' he said, frowning now, his tone suddenly serious. 'Just don't expect too much, all right? He's been away a long while, had a tough time. It won't be young love from the word go.'

Taken aback, Betty wasn't sure how to respond. Of course she understood how much Samuel had suffered – or at least she thought she did. She was trying to.

'Yes, Dad,' she replied eventually. And then, 'Will you be all right while I'm gone?'

'Course, love,' Harold replied. 'Take as long as you need. Have a night out in London, if Samuel's up to it. Don't hurry back.'

At the station, Betty's stomach leapt and jittered with

nerves. She felt nauseated and headachy, wishing she could go back to bed rather than sit on a packed train all the way to London. But she was too keyed up to even snooze, too on edge.

As the train barrelled along, Betty stared out of the window at the countryside speeding past. The harvest had been gathered in, and the fields stood empty, shorn of their wheat, barley or rye.

The lemons of Sicily and Sorrento had never seemed so far away.


BETTY WAS two days late getting to the meeting point. It wasn't because she hadn't known where to go. As soon as she'd received the telegram, she'd understood. During the six years of the war, the clock at Paddington station had seen a million greetings and farewells; passionate, tragic, optimistic, fateful.

Now it would see another one.

Betty's delay was due to her falling ill with a fever. Knowing that she couldn't let Samuel down, on the first of October she forced herself to get up. When she arrived at the station she stumbled along the platform, searching for directions from the tube to the main concourse. She felt hot and febrile, her eyes dry and sore, as if she'd been in the desert. Running her hand over her brow, she was shocked to find that she was burning up. The fever was far from over. All she wanted to do was lie down somewhere, in the dark, and be left alone. But she had to find Samuel.

The clock was world famous; it had been in a thousand films and newsreels. Betty gritted her teeth, clenched her sweat-damp hands into fists and forced herself onwards. She almost cried out with relief when the familiar object came into her vision.

She recognised the clock, but at first she did not recognise Samuel. There was a man standing beneath the clock, but he was skeletally thin, gaunt and stooped, and looked about forty-five, when Samuel was only twenty-five. As she walked, Betty glanced from right to left to see if Samuel was approaching from a different direction.

And then she got a bit nearer and realised, with a sickening jolt of shock, that the ill- and exhausted-looking man was Samuel. There had been reports in the newspapers lately of the terrible conditions the Japanese prisoners had endured, the torture, starvation, forced labour and disease, but even so Betty had been unable to envisage Samuel so weak and damaged. But now here he was in front of her, the living proof.

She stepped forward, almost unable to look at him. With a huge effort, she forced herself to meet his gaze.

'Betty!' His cry of greeting was full of desperate love. She ran towards him and they hugged. Betty was scared to hold him too tight in case he broke. He was so thin, frail almost.

'I knew you'd come, I knew it. I've been here every day, waiting for you.' Samuel's face was buried in her neck. Betty had the feeling he didn't want to lift his head up in case she saw that he was crying. But she could feel the dampness of his tears moistening her hair.

'Of course,' she murmured, gently smoothing his head with her hand. 'Of course I came.'

Finally, they drew apart. In her fevered state, it was a while before Betty realised that he hadn't kissed her. Or even tried to.

'Betty, you don't look well,' Samuel said, scrutinising her face. 'And you're burning hot. I think we should get you to somewhere you can sit down.'

It struck Betty how incongruous it was for him to be saying this. He was the one who looked terrible; emaciated, worn out, old before his time.

'I'm all right,' she mumbled, shutting her eyes to block out the noise, all the people, the train announcements, the artificial lighting that was making her head throb. She'd feel better soon, she was sure. It was the shock, of seeing Samuel like this, and after all this time... and then her thoughts went blank as her legs disappeared from under her and she collapsed onto the cold station floor.

OPENING HER EYES, Betty stared around her. Where was she? The white curtains around the bed, the hum of noise in the background, the sound of brisk footsteps.

Hospital? Was she in hospital? But why? Where?

The voice got louder and a hand reached in and pulled back the curtains. A nurse in pristine uniform appeared and behind her was Samuel, carrying two cups of tea. When he saw she was awake, he raced towards her, slopping the brown liquid over the side of the cups and onto the floor.

'Betty, thank God you're awake.'

Betty wasn't sure she was awake. Everything felt distant and muted, as if she was in some parallel universe. She wasn't sure about anything. She didn't know what had happened. How had she got here? The last thing she could remember was being at Paddington, not feeling too great, and then fainting. Hah. She'd been cross when the commander in Naples had implied that, being a young lady, she had a tendency to faint.

She shut her eyes again. It was all too confusing. She must have drifted off. When she woke, she was aware of Samuel sitting on the bed beside her, holding her hand and rubbing it. This was ironic. He was the one who had been ill, so sick from his years imprisoned in terrible conditions. Now it was her who was the invalid. How had that happened?

'Just ten minutes, Mr Wainwright,' said the nurse. 'You mustn't tire her out.'

Samuel said something so quietly in reply that Betty didn't catch it.

'How are you feeling?' Samuel asked her once the nurse had

left. 'I've been so worried.' He paused, taking a deep breath, before continuing. 'You've been unconscious for nearly three weeks. I've been beside myself with worry. Your father and sister were going to come down but I managed to put them off – I didn't think you needed anyone else fussing over you. Not that you knew what was going on.'

'I'm sorry,' murmured Betty, inadequately.

'Don't be sorry,' answered Samuel, gently. He stroked her hand with his thumb. 'We just want you to get better.'

'Yes,' said Betty. 'Yes, I will. Get better. Very soon.'

Five days later, Betty was pronounced fit to leave the hospital and travel back to Yorkshire.

Just over two months after that, on the twenty-ninth of December 1945, exactly a year after Betty had watched the wedding at the Church of Tutti Santi in Rome, she and Samuel were married at St Michael's in Market Place, Malton. Unlike the Roman wedding, there were no army dispatch riders, but Harold hired a Rolls-Royce to convey his daughter to the church. The reception was held at a local hotel and, afterwards, Samuel and Betty travelled to the Lake District for a short honeymoon.

# CHAPTER SIXTY

SICILY, AUGUST 1972

The bus wound its way up the steep hillside, twisting and turning round the hairpin bends, accelerating alarmingly on any straight stretch of road, however short, and braking hard when faced with another turn or an oncoming vehicle. Sadie, feeling a little queasy, fixed her eyes on the distant summit of Mount Etna, from which emerged a pale grey plume of smoke that hung lazily in the clear air. She couldn't understand how Luca could be so impervious to the lurching and leaping.

They were part of a long line of traffic heading for Taormina, which Sadie's guidebook informed her was 'one of Italy's best-known tourist centres'. But unlike all the other visitors, she and Luca were not here for a tour of the volcano or a beach holiday on Isola Bella.

They had come to find her father.

With every kilometre travelled southwards, Sadie's apprehension and excitement had risen, until now she was a nervous wreck. Since the moment they had docked at Palermo, she had wanted to go up to every man she saw of the right sort of age and demand of them, 'Are you Gianni Urso?'

But of course she couldn't do that.

In the small *pensione* in which they had booked a room, the first thing they did was to ask the receptionist for the phone book. After a few moments fumbling under the desk, she produced a slim volume with the words *Direttore telefonico* on the front and plonked it on the counter. Snatching it up, Sadie uttered a thank-you and took the book to a table in the corner, Luca standing over her shoulder. Opening the stiff cover, she began to urgently leaf through the pages. There were countless surnames beginning with the letters B, C, G, L, M, R... but only a very few with the letter U.

And one of those was an Urso. With an address.

Urso, G, 119 v. Nave, Taormina.

'There it is!' she almost screamed, jabbing her finger at the text. Luca bent down closer to read the small print.

'It looks like it,' he agreed. 'Wow!' His normal caution thrown to the wind, he grabbed Sadie by the hands. 'I didn't think it would be this easy.'

Sadie reflected momentarily that the journey so far had felt anything but easy, but finding the address was definitely a huge step forward. She hardly dared to hope as she breathlessly copied the address onto a piece of paper. She pulled the town map she'd bought earlier out of her bag, but she was so agitated that the text leapt and jumped before her eyes.

Frustrated, she thrust the map at Luca. 'I can't read it,' she said, breathlessly. 'You'll have to do it.'

Calmly, Luca did as asked. In no time at all, he had located Via Nave. Ship Street. The town was fairly small, bordered on one side by the sea and on the other by Etna's steep foothills. It wouldn't take long to walk there.

At the door of the hotel, Sadie hesitated. 'Back in a mo,' she gulped, and rushed back inside to the bathroom. She needed a moment to gather herself. Steadying her hands on the sink, she took several deep breaths to calm her thumping heart. Maybe this was it, maybe she was about to meet her birth father. It seemed completely unbelievable and at the same time absolutely right, like one of those dreams that seem logical when you are having them but that when you wake up you realise are completely insane.

When she reappeared, Luca was leaning against the door jamb, a worried expression on his face.

'Are you all right?' he asked, gently reaching out to touch her shoulder.

Wordlessly, Sadie nodded. 'There's no time like the present,' she muttered, her voice taut enough to snap. She stepped out onto the pavement and, as she passed Luca, he whispered, 'I'm right there with you, remember?'

In the midst of her anxiety and trepidation, Luca's kindness and thoughtfulness steeled her heart. In that moment, she knew she had been crazy to ever think she could have done this alone. She couldn't. Absolutely no way.

Pushing her hat firmly onto her head and slipping her sunglasses over her eyes, Sadie struck out with determination along the narrow street, past stone walls dripping with vibrant masses of hot pink bougainvillea blooms. Cats stretched and yawned in the shadows and tiny lizards darted up stone walls and disappeared into crevices.

She and Luca were soon at Ship Street, a charming little road along one side of which stood a series of stone houses painted in various hues of cinnamon, apricot and honey. On the other side there were no dwellings because there was nothing to build them on, just a perpendicular cliff that plunged down to the sea far below. Holding on to the rather flimsy-looking railing, Sadie peered tentatively over and down to the beach, where tiny ant-like people were lying on loungers or swimming in the sea, going about their business, impervious to what was happening high above them.

'Nineteen,' Sadie said as she and Luca studied the houses, none of which seemed to have numbers clearly on display. They walked up and down a few times until eventually Luca spotted a mailbox, overgrown with rampant ivy, which bore the number sixteen. From this, they worked out which house must be the one they were looking for.

At the gate, Sadie paused for a moment to study the property. It was two storeys, with a wide frontage and a door in the middle, just like a child would draw. The front garden was luxuriant, with well-tended plants and shrubs, waves of purple lavender contrasting with the silver-grey leaves of olive trees in pots. It was very pretty and it was obvious that whoever lived here took pride in their patch.

With trembling fingers, Sadie lifted the catch on the gate and pushed it open. The journey from gate to door could have taken five seconds, five minutes or five hours, she couldn't tell. Time warped and buckled around her during that walk. Nothing seemed real any more; the sun too yellow, the sky too blue, the grass too green, like she'd arrived in Oz or Wonderland.

Just as she reached the front door, as if by magic it opened. Sadie gasped, taken by surprise. A man stepped out. Behind him, the interior of the house appeared cool and dark, in stark contrast to the heat outside. The sun had climbed higher in the sky and, even with her straw hat, Sadie could feel its rays on her head. Perhaps it was that which was making her light-headed. Or perhaps it was the person standing in front of her.

Because as soon as she laid eyes on the man, Sadie recognised him. His hair was not dark, like hers, but slightly greying. But in other respects, he looked just like her. Or she looked just like him; the same wide, dark eyes and narrow nose, the same broad mouth.

'*Posso aiutarla?*' he asked, his tone pleasant and calm.

Sadie froze. She sensed Luca beside her, cautious of butting in but ready to intervene if translation were needed. And then she remembered that, if this really was Gianni Urso, the man who'd been a POW in North Yorkshire, then he must speak at least some English.

'I'm looking for Gianni Urso,' she said. 'Um, I – is that you?'

The man's eyes narrowed in curiosity. He surveyed Sadie closely. Then, hesitantly, in slightly stilted English, he replied, 'Yes. I am he. Why do you want him?'

What Sadie had planned suddenly seemed far too bold. But right here, right now, in the heat of the moment, she couldn't think of an alternative. So she did it anyway. She reached out and handed the man something.

Brow furrowed, he took the object and examined it closely. As he did so, Sadie saw his expression change, from puzzlement to gradual recollection. He raised his astonished gaze to meet hers and seemed to double-take, as if he had suddenly noticed the family resemblance between himself and this girl who had turned up out of the blue.

'Wh-where did you get this?' he asked. 'Who gave it to you?'

Sadie shifted her weight uneasily from one foot to the other. 'It must have belonged to my mother,' she explained, as best she could when there was so little certainty to her situation. 'I was... adopted,' she went on, 'and a few months ago, when I found out, I decided to try to find my birth parents. This keepsake is the only thing connecting me to them. It's a long story, but eventually it led me here.' She paused, gauging Gianni's face to see if he seemed to be following this lengthy explanation in English. Satisfied that he did, and that the incomprehension on his face was due to the story itself rather than language difficulties, she continued. 'I think you might be my father.'

A silence descended on the pretty Mediterranean garden

and the three people standing there. The pigeons stopped cooing and the bees were quiet.

'*Gianni, cosa fai?*' a woman's voice called from within the dim interior of the house, followed by the sound of footsteps approaching the door, breaking the quietude.

Sadie stepped backward, nervous at the prospect of meeting someone else, someone who might be a relative, if she were right in her suppositions. And exactly at that moment, Gianni's legs buckled underneath him and he fell, landing heavily on the stone path and lying there, motionless.

# CHAPTER SIXTY-ONE

Sadie gazed around her, overcome by the occasion. She was seated at the head of a long table in the back garden of the house on the edge of the cliff in Taormina. Luca sat beside her, his arm slung casually over the back of her chair, and gathered around in the rest of the seats were a host of voluble Sicilians, chattering and laughing and joking at top volume. The wine was flowing freely and the table was loaded with bowls and plates filled with delicious local appetisers; *arancini, involtini di pesce spada, panelle* and *caponata,* along with loaves of crisp fresh bread and jugs of wine and water.

Over the preceding few days, Sadie had had a crash course in Sicilian hospitality, which centred around huge meals; antipasti, plates of meat, bowls of pasta and then desserts, all of them sweet and toothsome. Sadie had honestly never seen so much food served up at one sitting, but all of it seemed to get eaten. She was sure she'd be going back to England two stone heavier after overindulging in all this good food.

A sharp ringing sound filled the air, quelling the conversation. Sadie looked up to see Gianni, at the other end of the table, calling the party to order. His niece Maria and nephew Matteo hurriedly began shushing the younger children while everyone else focused on Gianni. Sadie was still getting used to this huge extended family and attendant hangers-on; it was unlike anything she'd ever experienced before.

Gianni cleared his throat, and Sadie felt Luca's hand under the table reach for hers and hold it tight. He had been a rock these last few days. Thankfully, the fall had caused Gianni no lasting harm. Gianni's mother, who'd come to the door that day just in time to see him keel over like a downed tree in the forest, had immediately called for an ambulance, thinking her son had had a heart attack. But when the paramedics had arrived, they had found Gianni sitting up and quite well, just completely overcome with emotion at coming face to face with a daughter he didn't know he had.

That evening Gianni and Sadie had sat in this very garden, talking all through the night. Luca had stayed away, saying it was important for father and daughter to spend time alone together. Once Gianni had started speaking English again, it had all come flooding back to him and he was able to converse fluently and easily. Sadie had explained everything to him; her shock discovery of her adoption, her determination to find out about her roots and the quest that had brought her to Sicily.

In turn, Gianni had told her about himself, his capture in North Africa, which had led to him being sent to Eden Camp, where he had befriended a local girl called Betty Bean.

'We fell in love, in that cold Yorkshire climate, over pots of tea and currant buns as we taught each other our languages,' Gianni explained, his eyes taking on a faraway look, as if imagining another time and another place, another him perhaps, one who was young, fiery and passionate.

'So – what happened?' Sadie asked, leaning forward

eagerly, desperate to hear what Gianni had to say. 'Why didn't you stay together?'

Gianni took a deep breath and Sadie saw that he was fighting back tears. 'She joined up, became part of the ATS and was posted abroad.'

At this, a thousand more questions leapt into Sadie's mind, and she had to make a great effort to keep quiet and not blurt them all out. She couldn't rush Gianni; the story had to be told at his pace.

'Betty was sent to Naples,' Gianni continued, 'and, by some alignment of the stars, we met again there.' He laughed, a wistful expression descending upon his still handsome face. 'She was something special, your mother.' And then he corrected himself. '*Is*, I mean. I think she's still alive. I'm sure she is.'

A tight knot formed in Sadie's stomach at these words. As Gianni spoke, Betty Bean was starting to become real to Sadie, a person with a history and a personality who Sadie longed to know more of.

'H-how do you know that?' she stuttered. 'What makes you so sure?'

Gianni shifted awkwardly in his chair. 'I have one Italian friend from the camp who stayed in Yorkshire after the war. He promised me he'd keep his eye out. Let me know if he heard that anything had happened to her.' He sighed. 'He never has. So...'

The conclusion was left unsaid, but Sadie understood. A weight lifted from her heart at the thought that her mother was almost definitely not dead.

'What was she like? Tell me about her,' Sadie demanded, falling over herself to get the words out.

'What can I say?' Gianni responded. 'She was beautiful, kind, courageous and loyal. And brave, and intelligent...'

Sadie listened, stunned. This was the exact opposite of

what she had read in the newspaper report. 'But... I... so she wasn't a traitor?'

Gianni stared at Sadie, brow tightly furrowed, frowning. 'No, of course she wasn't. Why would you think that?'

Sadie shook her head. 'Just something that was reported in *Il Mattino*. But maybe they got it wrong.' After all, Gianni was only reiterating what Lily had said.

Gianni made a moue of disapproval. 'Journalists. What do they know?' he harrumphed. 'Whatever you read, I don't believe it.'

Sadie absorbed this categorical statement for a moment. 'So,' she continued, eventually. 'What about me? How did I come about?'

Gianni sighed. 'After the Italian capitulation, I joined the partisans. I wanted to rid my country of those vile Nazis, once and for all.' He gulped, coughed, took a long draught of red wine. He wiped his eyes with his handkerchief before continuing. Sadie was on tenterhooks, breathless, waiting to hear the next part of the story.

Her story.

'We were able to get leave and have one wonderful New Year together in Rome before we parted again. I knew it could never be. My mother' – he gesticulated towards the house, where his mum was asleep in bed – 'needed me here, as did my sisters, my cousins. I had to return. In Sicily family is everything, you know. Betty couldn't come with me. She had to keep her word to her childhood sweetheart.'

With those words, Gianni fell silent. The night air was alive with the fluttering wings of moths and the bats that circled overhead. Sadie had never been anywhere so peaceful but the quietude of the night was at odds with her swirling emotions. All this information, coming so thick and fast, was bewildering and overwhelming. Sadie desperately wanted to know who was this sweetheart her mother had been promised to. And why she couldn't break that promise. She wrung her hands together under the table. *Don't stop now*, she silently begged her new-found father. *Keep going. I need to know it all.*

'So that is ironic, is it not?' Gianni continued, eventually. 'Family is all, and yet I was to become a father and I would not know.' He shook his head ruefully. 'I told you that your mother was loyal. I suppose she wasn't able to tell her childhood sweetheart. But I don't believe she willingly gave you up. She would have loved you, more than the world. I know she would. Something must have happened, something bad.'

Sadie picked up a napkin from the table and gripped it. 'What could have happened that was so bad she gave me to a stranger?'

Gianni shook his head sorrowfully, and reached across the table to take Sadie's hand. 'I don't know,' he said.

'I'd like to meet her,' Sadie mused. 'I need to meet her. Will you help me?'

Gianni smiled, his eyes crinkling at the edges. 'Of course I'll help you,' he replied. 'That friend – I'll get in touch...' He trailed off, as if overwhelmed by what was happening. 'Though I can't permit you to rush back home to England too soon,' he added, making an effort to sound light-hearted. 'I want to spend some time with you first, get used to having a daughter.'

Sadie smiled too. It wasn't that she'd ever felt unloved; she knew that her adoptive parents had adored her. She wished they had told her the truth but didn't resent them for not doing so. The grief she had felt at her mother's death was ongoing and much of it was about the feeling of being all alone in the world. In Sicily, Sadie couldn't imagine that ever happening. There were so many people; uncles, aunts, cousins, nieces, nephews, second cousins, in-laws... as many relatives as grains of rice in a sack.

It was a wonderful feeling, and she felt it again now as she surveyed the company around the table, the many faces filled with joy and happiness, love and camaraderie. How lucky was she to have found this Sicilian family now, just when she needed it so badly? It would never replace the mum and dad who'd brought her up, but it would be an addition that, now she'd got more used to the idea of being adopted, she was lucky to have.

She glanced around the table. They were all still waiting for Gianni to speak, but he seemed to be having some difficulty. He was sipping water, his throat clearly too dry to address the assembled company. Sadie's gaze grazed against Luca's and he gave a brief, reassuring smile.

Gianni coughed, drank more water, coughed again.

'My dearest family and friends,' he said, in Italian and then in English. 'We are here today for a celebration. The most incredible celebration of my life. You all know by now about the amazing thing that happened to me two days ago. I met, for the first time, my daughter, a daughter I didn't know I had. You have all welcomed her and taken her to your hearts and for that I thank you. But most of all, I must thank my daughter, my Sadie, for finding me. From now on she will forever be my *principessa*, like all Sicilian daughters are to their fathers.' He stopped and wiped tears from his eyes. No one seemed surprised that he was crying; several of the other guests were, too. Sadie had already noticed how much freer with their emotions Italian men were compared to English ones. There was none of the British stiff upper lip here – and society was all the better for it, she was sure.

'I want everyone to raise a toast to Sadie.'

Glasses were lifted, and a few cheers rang out.

'*Alla salute!*' cried Gianni, finally returned to full voice, tears momentarily quelled.

'*Alla salute, alla salute!*' came the echoing response. Glasses were chinked, hugs and kisses exchanged, and the little children ran around like mad things, revelling in the party atmosphere.

Sadie wondered if she should say anything. But what was there to say? She turned to Gianni.

'Thank you,' she said. '*Grazie. Grazie mille.*' And then she burst out crying.

# CHAPTER SIXTY-TWO

Sadie gazed out of the car window, wondering where they were going. Gianni had said that he wanted her to see the family vineyard in the foothills of Mount Etna, where he had a surprise for her. He had gone off somewhere in his battered old vehicle, while Maria and Matteo had been given the job of conveying Sadie and Luca there in Matteo's similarly ancient jalopy.

At first they chatted about this and that, both Maria and Matteo keen to improve their English. But ten minutes into the journey, lulled by the heat and torpid air, they had all fallen silent. Sadie gazed out of the window at fields of sunflowers turning their bright faces to the sun. In so many ways she had arrived in an alien world, like a sailor washed ashore on some previously unimagined new land. But then she had been embraced with such immediate warmth from Gianni and the extended family that she already felt quite at home.

As they got nearer to their destination, they passed by vine-

yard after vineyard, row upon row of vines snaking across wide
fields, rising and falling with the undulations of the land and, in
the distance, always the peak of Mount Etna, smoking. Gianni
had told her that it was quite common for Sicilians to have a
small amount of land where they grew vines. They would use
the grapes to make wine for their own personal consumption;
the idea of having to go to a shop and buy a bottle was anathema
to many Sicilians.

Eventually, Matteo slowed down and indicated left. They
turned off the tarmac road onto a rough track that wound uphill
for five minutes or so, surrounded by the now ubiquitous vines,
and then Matteo pulled the car to a halt in front of a building
made of creamy stone and hung with a vigorous wisteria that
clambered right up to the roof. In front of the house was a
charming terrace fringed by billows of purple lavender. To the
right side of the terrace was a pergola shaded with a luscious
vine that dripped with grapes; underneath it was a table and
chairs sitting ready for the guests to arrive.

'Gosh, it's so lovely,' breathed Sadie once they were all out
of the car. Everywhere she went in Sicily she was dazzled by
how gorgeous it all was. 'I didn't realise there'd be a house here
as well.'

Maria laughed. 'Well, it's pretty basic,' she said. 'But they
have to feed the pickers when they're working, and there is
always a big party out here when the crop has all been gathered
in. It's such fun.'

'I bet,' agreed Sadie. 'Sounds wonderful.' She could imagine
it; a harvest moon hanging low in a navy sky, the table loaded
with delicious Sicilian fare, the wine flowing freely, the hubbub
of friendly chatter and laughter.

'Now, you go and sit down in the shade,' instructed Maria.
'I'm going to bring you something to drink and then the three of
us are going to go and do a few jobs in the fields. Luca has said

he doesn't mind helping and we could do with a bit of muscle,' she went on, teasing her brother. 'We'll be back soon.'

'I can help, too,' countered Sadie. 'I'd love to.'

Maria shook her head. 'No, it's too hot for you. And Gianni will be here soon, so you must wait for him.'

Sadie shrugged. 'If you say so,' she responded, knowing when she was beaten. There was no arguing with these Sicilians, she'd discovered. Maria fetched a jug of water in which slices of refreshing cucumber floated, together with a bottle of white wine in a bucket of ice and glasses. She poured Sadie some of the water and then left.

Underneath the pergola, Sadie shut her eyes and listened to the silence, broken only by the sound of insects and the infrequent call of a bird. Only when she heard the noise of an approaching car, tyres crunching on the loose stone, did she open her eyes again. It was Gianni's car. Sadie sat up straighter in her chair and watched as Gianni got out of the vehicle and then went round to open the passenger door.

A woman emerged, a scarf over her head for the dust, a leather handbag clutched in her hand. She wore a distinctly un-Sicilian beige two-piece suit and court shoes. As Sadie watched her and Gianni approach the pergola, she thought how pretty the woman was, but how anxious she looked. Another member of the vast Urso extended family, she could only think.

With great courtesy, Gianni escorted the woman over to the shade of the pergola. There was something odd in the way she held herself, as if she were both reluctant and overeager to get there. Sadie got up as they neared the table, politely ready to welcome the guest. Maybe it was testament, she reflected, to how comfortable she already felt in the folds of the Urso family that she no longer saw herself as the visitor.

'Hello,' she said to the woman, and to her father. She looked at them both expectantly, waiting to be introduced.

'Sadie,' said the woman, faintly. 'I – what a pretty name. It suits you so well. It's... I...' But whatever she was going to say was lost as her words tailed off.

Gianni gestured to Sadie and the woman to sit down, but he remained standing. 'This might come as a shock to you, Sadie,' he said. 'Just as it was to me when you arrived at my door. But I knew how desperately you wanted to meet your mother. And I also knew how desperately she would want to see you. I managed to contact her, and over the past couple of weeks I was able to persuade her to come to Sicily. And here she is.'

Sadie stared at the woman. Her complexion was delicate and pale, her eyes fringed by fine lines. Sadie searched for it, but she couldn't see the resemblance that Deborah had pointed out. And yet she immediately felt something deeper, an invisible bond directly connecting her to this person. Her mother.

She could hear the blood rushing through her ears and the pounding of her own heart. Her palms were hot and clammy as she gripped the cool water glass in front of her.

'Is it really you?' she whispered. 'I don't know what to say...'

There was a moment when no one did anything. The heat pulsated around them like an invisible force field. And then a breeze sprang up, lightening the atmosphere, lifting the tension. Simultaneously, Betty and Sadie walked towards each other, Sadie almost tripping up on a chair leg, blind to anything other than her mother standing before her. They flung their arms round each other and hugged for a long, long time.

When they finally sat back down, Sadie glanced towards Gianni. In the emotion of the meeting, she had momentarily forgotten about him. He was seated at the head of the table, looking winded. Sadie suddenly understood what a huge moment this was for him, too, how much emotion he must be dealing with. Her mother was the person he had admitted was the love of his life, who he'd stayed away from for years out of respect for her prior commitment, and who he had selflessly sought out in order to help Sadie fulfil her dream. No wonder he was exhausted at the culmination of it all. Seeing her concerned expression, he sat up straight and smiled. He reached for a bottle of wine, and poured them all a glass.

'Let's drink to our reunion,' he proposed. 'And to all of our future happiness.'

# CHAPTER SIXTY-THREE

SICILY, AUGUST 1972

Gradually, over the next few hours, the story of what had happened to Betty and Sadie emerged. She and Samuel had had two children of their own, a boy and a girl, called Richard and Sally, both now in their twenties and married. Samuel had died some years ago, never having fully recovered from the illness and injury he suffered as a prisoner-of-war, and one by one her children had emigrated, Richard to Canada and Sally to Australia, leaving Betty all alone in Yorkshire. Throughout all the years, Betty had never stopped thinking about her first child, her little daughter, and blaming herself for what had happened to her. It was clear that the loss of her baby had affected Betty deeply.

'I tried to find you so many times,' she told Sadie that day, under the grape-hung pergola. 'I searched everywhere, high and low. As soon as I could, I went back to the house where I'd left you, but I never saw the woman again. Instead, her husband came to the door. He told me to go away and never come back.

He said he'd call the police and have me sectioned or arrested if I ever went there again.'

Sadie listened, horrified. 'I don't think Mrs Jackson knew that,' she said. 'She didn't mention it to me. I don't think her husband told her.'

Betty shook her head. Tears were rolling down her face. 'No, I'm sure he didn't. I think he was scared of her getting involved. He was very cross with me, which is understandable. But he made no effort to comprehend how desperate I was, what a terrible situation I was in.'

Sadie played with her wine glass, watching the golden liquid move as one body as she swirled it round and round. 'So – why did you leave me with Mrs Jackson? And—' Her voice broke, despite how hard she was trying not to cry. 'Why didn't you come back that evening?' Her plea was plaintive as a child's and in that moment she imagined herself that tiny infant, mewling for her mother, needing a mother's love and succour.

Betty wrung her handkerchief in her hands, twisting and twisting it. Her face was contorted as if she were in physical pain.

'It's so hard to explain,' she breathed, 'and I know it will be impossible for you to understand. Things are different now. Society is different. But back then—' She stopped, sighed, pressed the handkerchief against her eyes and then released it. 'I think Gianni has explained to you that I was promised to my sweetheart Samuel. Right at the beginning of the war we'd vowed to each other we'd marry when it was all over. He was sent straight to the Far East and I didn't see him for nearly six years. That's a long time in anyone's life, Sadie, but especially when you are young. I was sixteen when I made the promise and twenty-two when he came back. Think how much you changed between those years.

'When I joined the ATS, I genuinely intended to completely cut myself off from Gianni. I didn't write to him and

I'd told him not to try to contact me. That's the way it would have remained if not for a remarkable turn of fate. Gianni was injured fighting with the Italian partisans and I had a little accident and we ended up in the same hospital together.'

She turned to look pleadingly at Gianni. He gave her an almost imperceptible nod and, at the same time, reached out his hand to hers and gave her fingers a quick squeeze. Fortified by his action, Betty resumed.

'W-we rekindled our relationship,' she continued, falteringly, 'but it was still – well, I was very strict. It wasn't physical, if you know what I mean. Gianni went off to fight again and once more I told myself I'd never see him again. But then he asked me to meet him for Christmas and New Year in Rome and—' Betty broke off again, overwhelmed with the memories. Gianni shifted his chair closer to hers and, this time, put an arm round her shoulders.

'Something happened that shouldn't have happened,' Betty continued, eventually. 'But the war was ending and then my father became ill and I had to go home to him. When I got back to Yorkshire, after everything that had happened, I wasn't the same person any more. Soon after, Samuel returned from the East, and it was apparent that neither was he. But he was relying on me, after all the terrible, terrible things he'd been through, to put him back together again, and I couldn't let him down. If I had walked away from him, I would have been hated, reviled, for turning my back on my promise, for letting down a returned soldier, a war hero. It was never a possibility. And I did have love in my heart for him, I really did. J-just not the same kind of love I felt for Gianni.'

Betty's face was wet with tears, her hair plastered to her cheeks and forehead. She still looked beautiful, though, thought Sadie, as she reached out her hand to take Betty's.

'It sounds like an impossible dilemma,' she agreed.

'I wrote to Gianni and, once again, told him not to contact

me again. I knew I was pregnant but I refused to acknowledge it, to myself or anyone else. Some women don't show much with their first and I was able to conceal my bump quite easily. If anyone noticed I looked a little plumper, they put it down to me not being in the ATS any more, no more drill and PT for hours a week, or to all the good Italian food. I don't know what I thought was going to happen when the baby came. I honestly don't. I was in total denial, until the last moment, when I was on a train to London to meet Samuel. I went into labour and had the baby in the Temperance Hospital on Liverpool Road. They wanted me to stay in but I had to go; I was already two days late to meet Samuel. I discharged myself and walked across London. I was out of my mind with terror about what I would tell him about the baby and what would happen, but what I didn't realise at the time was that I had contracted an infection and I was also out of my mind with fever and illness.'

Betty's voice rose on the last word, and Sadie felt how important it was for her mother to know she understood. She squeezed Betty's hand to show her this.

'I thought, if I can just get someone to mind the baby for an hour or two, I can go to Paddington, see Samuel and then explain to him,' Betty said. 'I would tell him that he could break off the engagement if he wanted to; I didn't expect him to bring up another man's child. I had no intention of giving up my baby. As soon as I set eyes on you, I loved you, and I knew I'd do anything to keep you safe. If Samuel didn't want us both, then he would have neither of us.' Betty drank some water and gazed at the glass, lost in that faraway world of pain and fear. 'But I'm doing Samuel a disservice by saying that. He wasn't a cruel man. He might well have accepted the baby, when he saw how much it meant to me.

'In any case, it all went terribly wrong. Almost as soon as Samuel and I were reunited under the clock at Paddington station, I collapsed and was rushed to hospital. The infection had taken over my body and I was left fighting for my life. It was nearly three weeks before I came out of the coma, and Samuel took us back to Yorkshire as soon as I was discharged from the hospital. I couldn't get to you, he never left my side in all that time.'

Betty stopped and Sadie could hear her gasping for breath as if she was running a marathon. It was clearly awful for her to recall. Sadie hoped it was also cathartic, to spill it all out after all these years buried deep within her.

'Before I was discharged, the nurse confided in me. She said, we know you've had a miscarriage, Miss Bean. We – me and the other nurses – we pleaded with the doctor not to tell your fiancé. The doctor's a bit old-fashioned, a bit – disapproving, see. But me and the other girls – well, we're women of the world. These things can happen, especially in a war. We thought, the baby's gone so there's no need for your fella to know. Just go home, get married and have another one. That'll be for the best.'

Sadie listened, appalled. The nurse was trying to be kind, but how terrible her words must have sounded to Betty. She glanced at her. Betty's eyes glistened with fresh tears.

'They thought my baby had died. But you hadn't. Sadie, I need you to know, I moved heaven and earth to get you back. I ran away from home. I got a train to London without telling a soul where I was going. I went to Jean Jackson's house, as I already said, with no luck. And I went round all the hospitals but found nothing. Eventually, despite Mr Jackson's warning, there was no other option but to go back to the house where I'd left you. Again, I waited outside the door until I saw her go in, but, when I knocked, no one answered. Perhaps her husband had told her not to, because of my first visit. When I saw him coming home from work, I ran up to him and I begged and pleaded him to tell me what they had done with my baby. He relented then. He told me the baby had been handed to an adoption agency and he gave me the name. As soon as it was morning, I went straight there.'

Betty gave a great, heaving sob before resuming her story. 'But they said it was too late. The baby had already been adopted. All the legalities had been done and there was nothing I could do to get her back. I'd willingly given her away and that meant I had no rights to her. And anyway, they said to me, what future would an illegitimate baby have? It was for the best that she would be brought up by a properly married couple. They told me that the adoptive parents were lovely and desperate for a child and that you'd have a good life with them, better than I could give you.

'I tried to take comfort from that.'

Sadie felt dazed by what her mother was saying, as if someone had punched her nose or she'd had a blow to the head. When she shut her eyes, stars danced behind the lids. 'They were lovely,' she said, simply. 'If it helps you to know that. I did have a good life. I didn't know any different until Mum died. I had no idea I could have had a whole different upbringing. It's hard to – I mean, of course I should have been with you but—'

'I'm glad,' Betty interrupted, as if what Sadie was saying was too painful to hear. 'Really glad. Thank you for telling me that. As for me – well, I returned to Yorkshire and, right after Samuel and I got married, I got ill again. For weeks and months I could hardly get out of bed. No one knew what was wrong with me but of course I did. Now we would know that I had post-natal depression, compounded by the terrible mistake I'd made. Back then, everyone assumed it was something to do with the war, with being in the ATS. Nervous exhaustion, they said, or some other rubbish. But I'll tell you now, Sadie, nearly every woman I've ever met loved the war work they did. Saying it made women ill just gave the men an excuse to put us all back in our boxes, make sure we toed the line as housewives again, just like we had before 1939.'

Sadie smiled faintly at this. Her mother's role in the war was part of the reason why women in the 1970s had so much more freedom than they'd ever had before.

'I had my other children,' continued Betty, a desperate sadness in her tone. 'My Sally and my Richard. And they were wonderful. But they didn't make up for losing you. I missed you every day. I thought about you constantly, wondering what you looked like, where you lived. Hoping you were happy. Did you like to read? To sing? Or maybe you preferred playing outside and getting your hands dirty, or swimming. I loved swimming when I was a child and I would have made sure I taught you. I was utterly desperate to know you.'

Sadie took a sip of her wine. Her head throbbed with all she was learning. It was an almost unbelievable story, one she could never in a million years have imagined. She thought about the half-siblings she'd never met.

'Do you have any pictures of your... of Richard? And Sally?' she asked, faltering over the words, wondering if she had the right to call them by their names, feeling suddenly like an imposter in their lives, a cuckoo in the nest.

But Betty showed no such reticence. Fumbling in her hand-bag, she produced a photo, and passed it to Sadie. In it, Betty stood flanked by her son and her daughter. They were all smiling but Sadie was sure there was a wistfulness in Betty's expression. The picture wasn't framed that well and there was a wider gap on the right than on the left. As if another child should be standing there, grinning for the camera.

Once Sadie had studied it for a while, Gianni reached out his hand and took it and also examined it closely. Sadie watched Betty watching him, waiting for his reaction. He smiled, and Betty smiled too. Sadie wondered if Gianni's love for Betty had prevented him from getting married and having a family, or if he were jealous of Betty's husband, to have had what he so badly desired. If so, he'd had a long time to get used to it.

'Every now and again,' Betty murmured, as she placed the photograph carefully back inside her handbag, 'I would remember that little carved heart and key that Gianni had made for me, and that I had tucked inside your blankets as a kind of talisman, a token, and think, *Maybe she'll find me. Maybe that will give her the clue she needs.*'

Sadie felt in her pocket and pulled out the keepsake. Gianni must have told Betty, when he contacted her and arranged for her to come to Sicily, that this had provided the key information Sadie had needed to track him down. She laid it on the table. At the sight of it, Betty's sobs redoubled, quietly and urgently. Sadie felt bad for a moment, but then she realised Betty needed to cry out all the hurt and pain of all the years. It was best to do so.

Sadie should cry too, but she felt surprisingly dry-eyed. It was all too much, too hard to absorb in one go. And she still had to ask the big question.

Was her mother a traitor?

With every moment Sadie spent in Betty's company it seemed more and more unlikely, but she had to know the truth. There was nothing to do but to broach the subject, get it out there and over and done with. Sadie coughed and ran her hand across her brow. It was hotter than ever this afternoon.

'Luca and I found a report in the newspaper,' she said. She hadn't even told Betty she'd met Deborah and Lily yet. That could wait for later. 'And it said you did something bad. In the war. Something... traitorous.'

Betty stared at Sadie in horror. 'How did you find that out?' she cried.

For a terrible moment, Sadie thought this might mean it was true. But then Betty was talking again and soon she had explained about Susan and the mission she had been given, the fact that the British hadn't told the Americans what Betty was doing and how it had all got out of hand. They were watching the house Betty had to deliver the message to. They knew the man there was part of an underground network working against the Allies and they were waiting for his source to reveal themselves. It was simply a silly mistake, a misunderstanding due to lack of communication.

'But I did achieve one thing,' Betty concluded. She twisted her handkerchief between her restless fingers. 'There was going to be a bombing, of a village suspected of harbouring partisans. I mangled the message so that it didn't happen.'

Gianni had looked at her sharply at the mention of the word 'partisan'.

'It was the place where you were staying, Gianni,' Betty continued, her voice taut with tension.

Gianni shook his head as if stunned by Betty's revelation. 'I can hardly believe it,' he murmured.

Betty grimaced. 'It was my final act of the war, I suppose,' she said. 'I was arrested straight afterwards. It was cleared up before I set sail for England but at that point I hardly cared. I needed to get home to my father.'

She glanced back at Gianni, who had been so patient throughout this meeting of mother and daughter, and was still clearly reeling from the news that Betty's actions, which had carried so much risk for her, had probably saved his life. 'After I had the baby – you,' she went on, 'and it all went so terribly wrong, I cut off all contact with anyone from the past. Samuel got a job in York so we moved down there and I tried to start again...' Once more, Betty's words tailed off, and Sadie heard in them all the anguish and despair she had experienced over so many years. It occurred to Sadie that she was the lucky one. She had been blissfully unaware that anything was wrong with her life until a few months ago.

Betty had had half a lifetime for regrets.

Luca, Maria and Matteo now returned from what Sadie now knew had been a fictitious errand in order to leave the way clear for the reunion. They all sat down round the table, Luca next to Sadie. His presence there was comforting. It felt right. It was suddenly apparent to Sadie that there was no way she was going to let happen to her and Luca what had happened to her mother and father. Nothing and nobody was going to tear them apart.

Having the three other young people there broke the tension in the atmosphere, and alleviated the sadness that had wrapped itself around the pergola.

As she looked around her, Sadie knew her own tears would come, at some point. But for now, she could only sit there, under the vine-draped pergola, in a beautiful Sicilian vineyard, with her mother and her father close to her, and Luca, and think that some stories really do have happy endings.

# EPILOGUE

## SICILY, 1982

The beach at Isola Bella was usually crowded, packed full of tourists from all over the world who came in their droves to experience Sicily. But now it was October, and the holidaymakers had mostly gone home, leaving the residents of Taormina to breathe a sigh of relief and retake possession of their iconic town in the shadow of Mount Etna.

A small girl, with melting almond eyes and dark hair pulled back into a messy ponytail, ran up to her grandparents, who were sitting on a pair of sunloungers keeping an eagle eye on the three youngsters in their charge. '*Nonna, nonno,* can I have an ice-cream? Lorenzo wants one too, and Leonardo. *Per favore...*' Her little face creased up as she exaggerated her pleading tone.

The grandfather leant forward and ruffled her hair, then playfully tweaked her button nose. 'Lucia, you know we can never say no to you,' he joked. He rummaged in his pocket for some money, pulled out a handful of coins and dropped them in her outstretched palm. 'You take your brothers and go and get them. The vendor will be going home soon so, if you're lucky, he'll give you extra-big scoops.'

Lucia beamed and rubbed her belly with a small, tanned hand. 'Thank you,' she cried, setting off at pace to collect her siblings. '*Grazie...*'

'I hope her mother won't be cross with us,' said the grandmother, 'for spoiling their *cena*.'

The grandfather laughed. 'It's traditional in Sicily to have an afternoon snack, as you know, a little *merenda*. And anyway, they've been swimming all afternoon, they'll still be hungry this evening.'

The grandmother nodded. 'You're right. It's just what we were always told, when I was young. I might have left Yorkshire, but has Yorkshire left me?'

The pair caught each other's eyes and laughed, then reached across and held hands. They were still doing so when the children's mother and father appeared, some twenty minutes later. The ice-creams had long been dispatched, leaving just the telltale traces of strawberry and chocolate around three little mouths.

'You're like young lovers still, you two,' joked the father.

'Well, we missed a lot of time,' responded the grandfather, his kind eyes twinkling. 'We have to make up for it before it's too late.'

The mother, who'd been busy wiping off the ice-cream stains, stopped what she was doing and turned round. 'You're both going to live into your nineties, like Sicilians do!' she said, chuckling. 'But now we must be getting back. These three need a good wash before dinner.'

The little group collected up the paraphernalia of a day by the seaside – buckets and spades, towels and discarded items of clothing – and gradually made their way up the beach. On the cable car back to the town that clung to the clifftops above, Sadie looked out at the view in pure contentment. Her youngest son, Lorenzo, was sitting on her lap and had finally stopped squirming, and she buried her nose in his hair and breathed in the sun-kissed scent of him.

It had taken time, a lot of time, for Sadie, Betty and Gianni to be a family. It had been helped by Gianni and Betty rekindling their great love affair, and Sadie and Luca beginning theirs. The arrival of the grandchildren had cemented their new-found bonds.

Luca, sitting opposite, smiled at her and winked, a silent gesture that said that he, too, knew how good life was and how lucky they were. As they made their way up through the streets of Taormina, homeward bound, Gianni and Betty were still holding hands. The children, tired now, dragged their feet, so Luca swung little Lorenzo up onto his shoulders.

Above them, always, lay the peak of Mount Etna, its plume of smoke purplish now in the dusk.

Later that evening, the little ones in bed and sleeping soundly, and the adults sitting in the garden drinking wine from the vineyard, Sadie proposed a toast.

'To Sicily, to all of us, and to love,' she said.

'To Sicily, to all of us, and to love,' came the echoing responses.

# A LETTER FROM ROSE

Dear reader,

I want to say a huge thank you for choosing to read *A Letter from Italy*. If you enjoyed it, and want to keep up to date with all my latest releases, just sign up at the following link. Your email address will never be shared and you can unsubscribe at any time.

*www.bookouture.com/rose-alexander*

Many years ago, during my first career as a TV director, I worked on a series for Channel 4 called *Great Estates* and spent many weeks living in Yorkshire and filming at Castle Howard. While there, people told us about Eden Camp, and how well the Italian POWs got along with the locals, how the guards would lend the inmates their clothes so that they could go out on dates in civvies and how many of the Italians stayed on after they were released, a fact that can be seen in some of the surnames in the area. This story fascinated me at the time and became the inspiration for my latest book. The women of Y-Signals did extremely important work throughout the war and, although Betty and her chums are entirely fictional characters, I like to think that there were many real ATS women as brave, kind, hard-working, skilful and generous as them.

If you liked *A Letter from Italy*, and I hope you did, I would be so grateful if you could spare the time to write a review. I'd love to hear what you think and it really helps new readers to find my books for the first time.

I love hearing from my readers – you can get in touch through social media or my website.

Thanks,

Rose Alexander

www.rosealexander.co.uk

 x.com/RoseA_writer

# ACKNOWLEDGEMENTS

My thanks, as always, go to my agent Megan Carroll at Watson, Little, who has presided over my writing career since the beginning and been a huge help and benefit to me. Similarly, thanks to the team at Bookouture, especially my editor Kelsie Marsden, publicist Sarah Hardy and all the other brilliant people who put so much hard work into making every book the best that it can be. They say you shouldn't judge a book by its cover but I don't think that's true – certainly the beautiful covers of *The Lost Diary* and *A Letter from Italy* are better than I could ever have hoped for.

Thanks also to my family for putting up with me sitting at my desk in my bedroom for hours on end, trying to get the next book finished – or started, for that matter! And finally, thank you to all the many readers who read my work and leave such lovely reviews.

# PUBLISHING TEAM

**Turning a manuscript into a book requires the efforts of many people. The publishing team at Bookouture would like to acknowledge everyone who contributed to this publication.**

### Audio
Alba Proko
Sinead O'Connor
Melissa Tran

### Commercial
Lauren Morrissette
Jil Thielen
Imogen Allport

### Cover design
Debbie Clement

### Data and analysis
Mark Alder
Mohamed Bussuri

### Editorial
Kelsie Marsden
Jen Shannon